Praise for Chris Fabry

"A thoroughly enjoyable read. . . . Chris Fabry is a masterful storyteller."

CBA RETAILERS+RESOURCES

"In this edge-of-your-seat romantic suspense, all of the characters ring true. . . ."

BOOKLIST, **STARRED REVIEW**

"In this suspense-filled drama, Fabry covers hot topics. . . . Readers will be immersed in the lives of Maria and J. D."

ROMANTIC TIMES

"[*Borders of the Heart* is] character driven with strong characters facing moral dilemmas."

LIBRARY JOURNAL

"Ups the ante for fans of Fabry's high-charged, emotionally driven fiction by adding a strong suspense thread."

TITLETRAKK.COM

Not in the Heart

"A story of hope, redemption, and sacrifice. . . . It's hard to imagine inspirational fiction done better than this."

WORLD **MAGAZINE**

"Christy Award–winning Fabry has written a nail-biter with plenty of twists and turns. Fans of Jodi Picoult might want to try this title."

LIBRARY JOURNAL

"A fine piece of storytelling. . . . Down to its final pages, *Not in the Heart* is a gripping read. While the mystery at its core is compelling, it's Wiley's inner conflict that's truly engrossing."

"This absorbing novel should further boost Fabry's reputation as one of the most talented authors in Christian fiction."

"The best book I have read in a long time. The plot is unique and creative . . . [and] manages to keep the reader hanging until the last page."

Almost Heaven

"[A] mesmerizing tale . . . [*Almost Heaven*] will surprise readers in the best possible way; plot twists unfold and unexpected character transformations occur throughout this tender story."

"Fabry has a true gift for prose, and [*Almost Heaven*] is amazing. . . . You'll most definitely want to move this to the top of your 'to buy' list."

"Fabry is a talented writer with a lilting flow to his words."

June Bug

"[*June Bug*] is a stunning success, and readers will find themselves responding with enthusiastic inner applause."

"An involving novel with enough plot twists and dramatic tension to keep readers turning the pages."
BOOKLIST

"I haven't read anything so riveting and unforgettable since *Redeeming Love* by Francine Rivers. . . . A remarkable love story, filled with sacrifice, hope, and forgiveness!"
NOVEL REVIEWS

"Precise details of places and experiences immediately set you in the story, and the complex, likable characters give *June Bug* the enduring quality of a classic."
TITLETRAKK.COM

Dogwood

"[*Dogwood*] is difficult to put down, what with Fabry's surprising plot resolution and themes of forgiveness, sacrificial love, and suffering."
PUBLISHERS WEEKLY

"Ultimately a story of love and forgiveness, [*Dogwood*] should appeal to a wide audience."
CBA RETAILERS+RESOURCES

"Solidly literary fiction with deep, flawed characters and beautiful prose, *Dogwood* also contains a mystery within the story that adds tension and a deepening plot."
NOVEL REVIEWS

Every Waking Moment

EVERY *Waking* MOMENT

A NOVEL

CHRIS FABRY

TYNDALE HOUSE PUBLISHERS, INC.
CAROL STREAM, ILLINOIS

Visit Tyndale online at www.tyndale.com.

Visit Chris Fabry's website at www.chrisfabry.com.

TYNDALE and Tyndale's quill logo are registered trademarks of Tyndale House Publishers, Inc.

Every Waking Moment

Designed by Beth Sparkman

Edited by Sarah Mason

Published in association with Creative Trust Literary Group, 5141 Virginia Way, Suite 320, Brentwood, Tennessee 37027, www.creativetrust.com.

All Scripture quotations, unless otherwise indicated, are taken from the Holy Bible, *New International Version,*® *NIV.*® Copyright © 1973, 1978, 1984, 2011 by Biblica, Inc.™ Used by permission of Zondervan. All rights reserved worldwide. www.zondervan.com.

Ephesians 1:18, quoted in chapter 18, and Scripture quoted in chapter 43 are taken from the *Holy Bible*, New Living Translation, copyright © 1996, 2004, 2007, 2013 by Tyndale House Foundation. Used by permission of Tyndale House Publishers, Inc., Carol Stream, Illinois 60188. All rights reserved.

Every Waking Moment is a work of fiction. Where real people, events, establishments, organizations, or locales appear, they are used fictitiously. All other elements of the novel are drawn from the author's imagination.

Library of Congress Cataloging-in-Publication Data

Fabry, Chris, date.
  Every waking moment / Chris Fabry.
    pages cm
  SBN 978-1-4143-4863-6 (sc)
1. Caregivers—Fiction. 2. Frail elderly—Fiction. 3. Mental healing—Fiction. 4. Dementia—Fiction. I. Title.
  PS3556.A26E94 2013
  813'.54—dc23   2013017344

Printed in the United States of America

19   18   17   16   15   14   13
 7   6   5   4   3   2   1

To Tricia, Nate, and
Annabel "Annie" Wren McMillan.
With love.

And to Elsie Young.

It is one of the most beautiful compensations of this life that no man can sincerely try to help another without helping himself.

RALPH WALDO EMERSON

When you are Real, you don't mind being hurt.

MARGERY WILLIAMS, *The Velveteen Rabbit*

Before

TREHA IMAGINED IT like this: A summer afternoon. Her mother's satin dress billowing. Fully leaved, green trees swaying. Crossing a busy street.

"Keep up with me, Treha," her mother said.

Looking into the sunlight, she saw the silhouette of her mother's face with beads of sweat on her lip and the wide-brimmed hat casting shade. Her mother not quite smiling but showing dazzling teeth. Deep-red lipstick. Like a movie star with a hint of concern on her face.

Momentum carried them to the sidewalk and the corner shop with the tinkling bell as they passed the red bricks and moved into the cool, sweet air smells and bright colors under a sign that said *Ice Cream*.

Her mother led her to the glass case that held the containers. Treha stood on tiptoes but wasn't tall enough to see over the edge, so her mother picked her up and held her, letting her hover above the colors. She pointed out the ones with dark specks and those with pecans and pralines or cookies or M&M's.

"Which one would you like? The orange? Yellow? Don't take all day now."

The man behind the counter wore a white apron and wiped

his hands and smiled. Behind him on the wall was a clock with a fish symbol in the middle and a second hand that jerked around the face.

Treha chose the pink, purple, and yellow all mixed together, and her mother put her on the floor. Treha studied the tile, the way the patterns worked together in threes. Triangles that made up squares that made up bigger triangles and squares. Black-and-white patterns she could see when she closed her eyes.

"Cone or cup?" the man said.

"Cup," she said quickly, like she knew the cup lasted longer. You got more ice cream that way and less all over you.

"You're a smart girl," her mother said, sitting her on a chair next to a round table. The top was green and smooth and cool to the touch. "And so pretty."

There was something in her mother's eye that she wiped away. Dust? A bit of water?

The man brought the cup filled to overflowing, with a plastic spoon standing at attention. Her mother paid him and he went back to the register, then returned to them.

"How old is she?" the man said, handing her mother the change.

"Almost two."

"Adorable. She's a living doll."

He spoke as if Treha weren't there, as if she were an inanimate object incapable of understanding words.

Her mother knelt on the tile arranged in threes, the design continuing to infinity. She dabbed a napkin at the corners of Treha's mouth. As hard as Treha tried to stay neat and clean, she always got the ice cream on her face and hands and dress. Maybe that was why it happened. She was adorable and a doll but too much trouble.

"I need to step out. You wait here, okay?"

Treha studied her as she took another spoonful and carefully placed it in her mouth.

Her mother kissed her forehead and whispered in her ear, "I love you, my sweet princess."

She said something with her eyes before she stood but Treha could not decipher the message. Something between the words, something behind the stare, interconnected but dangling, like a loose thread in an unwanted scarf.

The bell jingled behind her and Treha looked back long enough to see her mother disappear into traffic, lost in sunlight.

When she finished the ice cream, the man came to the table and took the cup. "Where's your mama?"

She stared at him with those brown eyes, wide like saucers. Milky-white skin untainted by the sun. Ice cream spots on her pretty dress that she tried to wipe away but couldn't.

"You want another scoop?"

She shook her head. Her chin puckered. Somehow she knew. The world had tilted a little. She was alone.

The man walked to the door and looked out. Scratched his head with the brim of the white hat, then put it back on.

Treha swung her legs from the chair and looked at the sign behind the counter, the lines that connected to form words she did not understand. Words on walls and hats and buildings and cars. Letters bunched in threes and fours and more to make sentences and stories. Her story. The one she didn't know. The one she tried hard to remember but never could. The one she had to make up.

CHAPTER I

ARDETH WILLIAMS was eighty-nine and her eyes were glassy and clouded. She stared straight ahead with a slight head tilt as her daughter and son-in-law wheeled her past open doors at Desert Gardens of Tucson, Arizona. The companion building, Desert Gardens Retirement Home, was a fully staffed facility featuring its own golf course, a spa, exercise rooms, and several pools. But this Desert Gardens offered assisted living and hospice, a nursing home with frills. It was billed on the brochure as a complete end-of-life facility located in the comfort of an upscale desert community.

Miriam Howard, director of the facility, followed the group closely, watching Ardeth for any response. She couldn't tell if anything was going on behind the opaque eyes. The old woman's body sat rigid, her hands drawn in. Her head bounced like a marionette's as her son-in-law pushed her.

Retirement was bearing down on Miriam like a semitruck trying to make it through a yellow light. It was a huge transition Miriam had dreamed about, but now that she could measure her remaining time in hours instead of days or weeks, she couldn't suppress the sadness. This wasn't her timing. But the decision had been made by the board and the new director was moving in.

She had developed a facility that actually cared for people inside the "compound," as some cantankerous residents called it. There was human capital here and she knew it. And she hoped the new director would learn the same. The woman was on the job already, learning procedures, the problem residents, soaking up the routine, uncovering the scope and magnitude of her duties.

"Aren't these flowers the prettiest?" Ardeth's daughter said when they reached the room. "It's so bright in here, don't you think? And clean. They'll keep it neat for you, Mom, and you don't have to do a thing. You always kept everything so tidy and now you won't have to worry about that. Isn't that great?"

The daughter didn't realize this was part of the problem. The same tasks that wore her mother down were the tasks that gave her structure and stability. Worth. When she could no longer do them and others were paid to accomplish things she had done as long as she could remember, life became a calendar of guilt—every day lived as a spectator, watching others do what she couldn't and being reminded with each breakfast made by someone else's hands. Miriam saw this clearly but could never fully explain the truth to families crunching numbers on the cost of warehousing the aged.

"You'll have a nice view of the parking lot, too," her son-in-law said, tongue in cheek. "All those fancy cars the employees drive." His hair was graying and it was clear he and his wife were having a hard time letting go, though they were trying to be strong.

He pushed the wheelchair farther into the narrow room and struggled past the bed.

"She can't see the TV facing that way," his wife snapped. She turned the chair around, jostling the old woman.

Miriam had seen this tug-of-war for thirty years. The walk of a hopeless family trying to love well but failing. Everyone watching a parent slip away shot flares of anger that were really masqueraded loss. Deciding what Mother would like or wouldn't was a seesaw between two relatives who were guessing. Love looked like this and worse and was accompanied by a mute, white-haired shell.

When Ardeth was situated, the man locked the wheels clumsily and patted her spotted hand as he bent to her ear. "Here we are. What do you think, Mom? Do you want this to be your home?"

Nothing from the old woman. Not a grunt or a wave of the hand. No scowl. No recognition. Behind the cataracts and age and wrinkles, there was simply bewilderment. And even a casual observer could sense the fear. Could taste it in the air. But this scene brought out Miriam's strength.

She sat on the bed beside Ardeth. In the early days, before she had learned the valuable lessons that came with running the facility, she would have spoken as if the old woman weren't there or weren't aware. Now, she gently put a hand on Ardeth's shoulder and spoke softly, including her.

"Ardeth will not just be a patient if she comes here," Miriam said. "She will be part of our family. Part of our village. And there are things she will contribute to the whole that others can't."

The daughter hung on every word. Mouth agape. Water filling her eyes.

Miriam continued. "What you're doing, the process you're going through, is a loving one. I know it doesn't feel like that.

3

You're having a hard time even considering this, and your heart is telling you to take her home, where she belongs."

The man crossed his arms and looked away, but the daughter nodded. "That's exactly it. I just want to take care of her. We're overreacting. She put up with so much from me; the least I can do is return the favor."

Miriam smiled. "That's a viable option. But if Ardeth was to stay with us, I want you to know that you won't be abandoning her. You're giving her the best care possible."

The daughter took her mother's hand. "I want to be here for her."

"Of course. And she knows that, though she can't express it."

The woman pulled a tissue from a full, decorative box on the nightstand and wiped at her eyes.

"Our goal is to give each resident the best care," Miriam said. "Late at night, early in the morning, all of those who work here strive to give the attention each person needs. If you decide this is the best, you can rest easy. Ardeth will lack for nothing."

A bead of saliva pooled at the edge of the old woman's mouth and gravity did its work. Her daughter leaned forward, taking another tissue to catch the bead as it ran down her chin.

"I don't want her to be in bed all day," the daughter said, her voice breaking, her tone accusatory. She caught herself and put a hand on her chest. "But that was happening at home. I hated leaving her in front of the television, but I have things to do and I can't take her with me." She was whispering now.

Miriam knew it was time to be quiet.

The daughter went on. "I want her to do the things she loves. Gardening and reading. She loves life. She loves our children. You only see her this way, the vacant stare, but there's a vibrant woman in there. Giving and kind. But she gets upset when she can't remember things and then she gets angry, and I can't . . ."

More tears. Head down and retreating to tissues.

Miriam scooted to the edge of the bed and leaned toward the daughter. Trust was her most important commodity. The family had to place their full faith in her and the staff. "I know exactly what you're going through, and I wouldn't blame you if you took your mother and got in the car and drove home. This is the hardest decision I ever had to make."

"You've done this?"

"Yes. My own mother. Of course, it was easier bringing her here, knowing I'd be working with her every day. But seeing her lose that independence, that sense of dignity—it felt like giving up. Like one more loss in a long line of them. And you want the losses to stop. You just want the old life back. The person you knew."

The woman nodded. "Exactly."

It was time for words again. Miriam felt the spotlight. The moment when things either came together or disintegrated.

"I want to be honest. As I look at you, I see that strong woman your mother was. Confident and caring and full of life. Only wanting the best for those you love. I want that person you knew to return. But the truth is, this may be the best we achieve. Today, having her here and comfortable and not agitated . . . that may be as good as we get. Are you okay with that? If this is as good as it gets, can you let go and rest in that?"

"I don't know what you're asking."

Miriam leaned forward, her elbows on her knees. "Your love for your mother is not conditional on her response. You love her for who she is. You don't love her because of the things she can do for you."

The daughter nodded.

"So no matter what happens—if she improves, remains like this, or if she regresses—her condition is not the point. We always hope and pray for progress. But if you don't get the response you'd like, are you willing to accept that and just love her? That's where I see you struggling."

The woman's face clouded. "You're saying I don't love my mother if I don't let her stay here?"

The man put a hand on his wife's shoulder. "Let's cut the sales job, Mrs. Howard. Your job is to convince us to spend the money Ardeth has saved and put it into this place so you can keep building your little geriatric empire."

Miriam pursed her lips. The anger wasn't new. She had heard much more creative and acerbic accusations. She disregarded the charge and focused on the daughter.

"Let me try again. What I'm calling you to do is to see reality. Not how things might be or could be, but how they are. This is the baseline we work from. And when you embrace that, not requiring change but accepting where you are, where she is, then wonderful things can happen. Your heart can rest. You won't feel guilty about what you've done or haven't done. You can simply love her."

The daughter thought a moment, ruminating on the words. Processing.

Miriam wished she could film this interaction for her successor—it was a classic scene she had seen repeated a thousand times with varying results.

"My biggest fear is that she'll fall. That if she stays with us, she won't be safe. But you can't guarantee . . ." There was raw emotion in the words. The daughter looked up, pleading, almost begging.

"Our highest priority is her safety and comfort. But our goal for Ardeth doesn't stop there—or with her surviving a few years. We want her to thrive. And in whatever ways she can integrate into our family, our community, we're going to help her do that. We'll give her opportunities to be involved at whatever level she's able."

Her husband leaned forward. His voice was high-pitched and came out nearly whining. "This is not making her part of your community. It doesn't take a village to care for my mother-in-law, especially when it costs this much."

Miriam turned to him with a smile. "If the best place for Ardeth is your home or some other facility, I would not want her to move here."

The old woman leaned in her chair, her body ramrod straight but listing like the Tower of Pisa.

Miriam addressed the daughter again. "You mentioned reading. What does she like to read? What music does she enjoy? We can provide recorded books and music. That adds such a quality of life."

The daughter's eyes came alive. "You could do that? When she was younger, she read *Little Women* to me. I hated it. Now it's one of the treasures of my life." She rattled off several other book titles and music from the 1940s—Benny Goodman, George Gershwin, Glenn Miller, and Tommy Dorsey.

"Oh, great," the man said. "You charge extra for CDs of the big band era?" He walked to the window and stood, looking out.

"My mother loved 'Indian Summer,'" Miriam said, ignoring him. "I still have some of those CDs. Bing Crosby. Frank Sinatra. The Andrews Sisters."

It was a rapturous look, the face of the daughter, and Miriam knew she had opened something, a pathway leading to a connection with another resident.

"I don't want her wasting away in an institution. She's gone downhill so quickly. It's hard to watch."

"The process is never easy. But you're not losing her."

"That's what it feels like. Even if she gets to read books and hear music, it feels like she's moving on without us." The woman's eyes misted and she dropped her gaze to the floor.

Footsteps echoed in the hallway and Miriam glanced up as Treha passed the room. Miriam called to her, and the young woman took three heavy steps backward in a modified moonwalk, her blue scrubs swishing, and stood in the doorway. She stared at a spot just above the floor and swayed, her brown hair gathered in a clip on top of her head, emphasizing her strong features—high cheekbones, a well-defined nose, dark brows and lashes, and ears that bent forward, as if her parents might have been elves.

Miriam spoke to the daughter. "This is a young lady who works with us. She would be one of the caretakers for your mother."

"It's nice to meet you," the daughter said.

The girl nodded and her cheeks jiggled, but she didn't make eye contact.

"She is a special young lady," Miriam said. "A very hard worker. Would you mind if I introduce her to Ardeth?"

The daughter spoke tentatively. "I suppose it would be all right."

The man studied the girl's name tag and tried to pronounce it. "Is it *Tree-ha*?"

"*Tray-uh,*" Miriam corrected. "Why don't you step inside a moment?"

The girl shuffled in, the untied laces of her black-and-white canvas Keds clicking on the tile. She glanced up at the woman and her husband and then quickly found another spot on the wall, her head swaying slightly.

"Treha, I want you to meet Ardeth. She may be coming to live with us."

Treha looked at the old woman instead of averting her eyes. She tilted her head to one side and leaned forward, speaking in a soft voice like a timid actress unsure of her lines. The words sounded thick and unformed on her tongue.

"Hello, Mrs. Ardeth."

The old woman didn't respond, and Treha took another step and angled her body away. She leaned closer as if trying a different frequency on the woman's receiver.

"Would you like to take Ardeth to the dayroom?" Miriam said.

Treha looked up, questioning with her eyes, asking and receiving something unspoken. She nodded, then gave Ardeth a light touch on the arm, the slightest feathery movement with a pudgy hand. There was no response.

Treha released the wheel locks and pushed the chair through the door with ease, gliding confidently, her body one with the chair and the old woman, as if they were made for one another.

"What will she do?" the daughter said.

Miriam tried to hide the smile, the inner joy. She didn't want to promise something Treha couldn't deliver. "Come with me."

CHAPTER 2

Devin Hillis crossed the half-full parking lot at Heritage Acres Funeral Home, Mortuary, and Cemetery and walked up the stone pathway of remembrance, with names carved into rocks along the wall, past the finely manicured lawn and rose garden, and into the main building. A receptionist greeted him warmly and asked if he was there for the Garrity gathering, and he nodded.

The service was nearing the end when he took a seat at the back of the small auditorium. The officiating pastor wore a black robe and sonorously spoke of the life of the departed as if he did not know the man well. Vague references to "the family" and his life as a "devoted father and husband." He mentioned the man's wife, but when he used her name, it sounded stiff, as if he were reading a cue card. He concluded with verses from the book of John—the story of Lazarus being raised from the dead.

"In what must have echoed in the heart of our Lord, he says to the sister of Lazarus, 'I am the resurrection and the life. The one who believes in me will live, even though they die; and whoever lives by believing in me will never die. Do you believe this?'"

He looked at the crowd. "Jesus asked this of Martha and I

ask it of you today. Do you believe this?" He looked strategically and dramatically about the room. "Your husband, your father, your grandfather believed this, and on the authority of God's Word I tell you, he is not here but is at this very moment in the presence of his Lord and Savior, Jesus Christ. And he is more alive now than ever."

Sniffles and soft sobs and nods of agreement. The man prayed. Devin shifted in his seat and glanced at his watch.

Then the lights dimmed and Devin held his breath as the screen above the casket came to life with words listing the birth and death dates of Martin Garrity. The music was a sparse mixture of piano and orchestral instrumentation that sounded like a Thomas Newman sound track. It evoked emotion but not too much. The plaintive tune had been composed and performed by his videographer and musical jack-of-all-trades, Jonah Verwer, and perfectly set the mood. The screen looked a little washed-out because the curtains on the right weren't closed all the way. It was all Devin could do not to stand and hold them together, but he kept his seat, transfixed by the scene he had imagined.

Music up. Screen dark. Garrity voice-over.

I was born in 1927. Grew up smack-dab in the middle of the Depression.

Tight shot of Garrity's face.

You learn a lot about life when you don't have much. And we didn't have much.

Still-shot photo of Garrity's parents.

My mother and father were hardworking. My mother made do with whatever he could bring home.

Photo of brothers at the swimming hole.

> **My brothers and I would go down to the creek and skinny-dip.**

Tight shot of photo of brother.

> **Ross was the only one who could float on his back.**

Tight shot of Garrity speaking, smiling.

> **He'd float there with his hands behind his head and yell up at us, "Last pickle on the platter!"**

The congregation laughed and exchanged glances as the image of Garrity lingered on the screen, smiling, wet-eyed, remembering his brother. The pause was perfectly timed.

As the viewers settled, Garrity's wedding picture flashed on the screen, and just as Devin had imagined, congregants glanced at the man's widow, then back, as if drawn by some unseen director.

Garrity voice-over.

> **In 1943 I met the love of my life. I saw her across a classroom in high school. . . .**

Cut to still shot of wedding ceremony/eating cake.

> **It was Latin class. Funny thing. My heart came alive studying a dead language. I couldn't take my eyes off of her.**

Garrity tight shot.

> **She wouldn't have anything to do with me. But a year passed and there was a dance coming up, the fall homecoming or some such thing.**

Still shot of yearbook picture.

I don't know how I did it, but I got up the nerve to ask. I about fell over when she said yes. She made me feel like a million dollars. Anytime I was near her. She still makes me feel that way.

An audible "Awwww" rose, mostly from women. People wiped at their eyes. Devin took it all in. It was one of those moments he could predict as they shot the video. The lighting, the crisp speech, the lines in the man's face, the timbre of his voice. Devin had chills as they filmed that day and had known exactly how to put it together. Now, he had chills experiencing the emotion of the room. It was a holy moment, the fruition of piecing together an old man's disparate memories.

When the music swelled at the end and the frame froze on Garrity's face, smiling and happy with the memories he had divulged, it was perfection. There was nothing left to say but good-bye. The family filed past the casket one final time with the still frame of the man on the screen above.

Devin rose from his seat and walked into the hallway, wiping tears. Tears celebrating the connection between life and art and how such things penetrated the soul. He had made a connection with the old man and had called from him something lasting, something of beauty. The perfect benediction. Martin Garrity had been here, had walked the earth, had a voice, had a story. His heart beat with love and concern, and that truth could be played over and over.

He checked his watch again and stood aside as mourners exited, smiling at cousins and distant relatives. A door opened and one of Garrity's sons moved toward the men's room. Devin followed and waited at the sink, washing his hands twice.

"Devin," the man said, glancing at him. "I didn't know you were here."

"I slipped in toward the end of the service. I'm sorry for your loss."

"That video . . ." He shook his head. "That was incredible. You captured him perfectly. The photos and music and him talking about his faith . . . My mother will talk about that for the rest of her life."

Devin beamed. "That was my hope. I knew the spiritual component was especially important to him. I couldn't be happier. It all worked so well."

The man dried his hands and shook Devin's. Then an awkward pause. Devin reached for the door, then turned. "I know this is a really bad time to talk about payment . . ."

"Yes, it is."

"I didn't do this for the money. That's not what—"

"My understanding was that you were making a documentary over at Desert Gardens."

"Yes, that's how I met your father. And when I saw him deteriorate, I thought we could use some of the footage . . ."

"To make a little money."

"No. It's not like that. But your father and I had an agreement." He left it there.

The man frowned. "You'll be paid, Devin. The death benefit from his company has been filed. My mother will use that to reimburse you."

Devin opened his mouth to speak again but decided against it. He opened the door and the man walked past him.

"You did an excellent job," he said.

Devin nodded and glanced at his watch.

CHAPTER 3

THE DAYROOM WAS A QUIET and secluded spot toward the north end of the building, down a long, tiled hallway. Across the hall was a room with a large-screen television and areas to park wheelchairs for "exercise" sessions. Pristine yoga mats were still in plastic and equally pristine dumbbells languished. Lining an end table by the television were dusty videos with covers featuring smiling octogenarians. *Strengthening the Core, Easy Elderly Pilates, Jane Fonda's Low-Impact Aerobic Workout, Move What You Can*—all in a similar state of neglect. There was no treadmill, but three exercise bikes sat idle by the large window.

Etched into the glass wall at the entrance to the dayroom on the opposite side of the hall was a mountain scene that rose like Everest. Trees with towering boughs spread above, inspiring, almost breathtaking in their grandeur and artistry. The old woman who was pushed past it didn't seem to notice.

The door was heavy and clunked when Treha tugged at it, making it open automatically. At eye level on the door, easily visible to anyone in a sitting position, was a quotation by Ralph Waldo Emerson.

Do not go where the path may lead; go instead where there is no path and leave a trail.

Treha waited for the door to fully open, then pushed the woman through, her shoelaces clicking. A fireplace with an oak mantel centered the room. It was flanked by two six-by-six-foot windows that looked out on the expansive lawn and an iron fence that surrounded the acreage. A flagpole at the far end of the property rose to heights that suggested the need for a beacon on top to warn incoming planes. The huge American flag that usually hung limp waved and flapped in the stiff breeze, rippling and fluttering.

Along the walls ran bench-like structures for larger meetings. They were empty now, but two ladies sat beside each other at a long table at the end of the room, choosing edge pieces from a puzzle box and speaking loudly, engaging in the conversation with grunts and chuckles and bodily noises forgiven without asking. One was Miss Madalyn, the one called the Opera Singer, and the other was a newer resident Treha hadn't met. On the other side of the room sat Dr. Crenshaw looking out the window, staring at the golf course grass—as if he, too, longed to be planted. He held a Bible on one knee and a folded newspaper on the other, and when Treha walked inside, he smiled and nodded and turned back to the view.

Treha maneuvered Ardeth's wheelchair safely up to the table, then took one of the woman's hands and rested it on top. She did the same for the other, and the skin on the woman's arms sagged, bearing the telltale flaking, cracking, and splotching of too many summers. Limp and compliant, she kept her arms exactly where Treha placed them as she stared at the wall.

Treha felt neither hope nor despair but something wedged

between. This was her job now, her calling. A resolution to life, as if she were scrubbing dishes or sweeping a floor she had promised to finish. She took short steps from one side of the table to the other, pulled out a chair, and sat. She placed her hands on the table, her index fingers nearly touching Ardeth's. The comparison was startling. On one side were wrinkled and blemished hands. On the other was clear, smooth skin. The old woman's nails were polished, but Treha's were cut to the quick, not clipped evenly but jagged and rough.

Treha closed her eyes and took a deep breath. When she opened them, her eyes shifted and reset, the involuntary movement of her life. Walls and floors blurring and leaning. A vibration that shuddered through nerve endings. Then the swaying and quick jump, the return of a typewriter carriage in her head.

She waited, closed her eyes again, shook her head slightly, and looked up. Still there. Still moving. But the room settled as she swayed to compensate. The eyes of the old woman were clouded, barricades of age and confusion, but she knew that behind the cloud were the words. Treha could feel them even if they couldn't be seen. Words floating, disembodied, perhaps only unformed letters and memories drifting like smoke.

Treha searched the old woman's eyes and saw a chasm of darkness, a shadowed veil suspended between the inner, unseen world and the self-evident one. She lifted a finger, and then her hand hovered over the wrinkled one.

There was no jolt of electricity, no sound or feeling other than the meeting of skin. But something happened. There was a reaching, a leaning response from the old woman's body, moving closer.

Treha sat forward and placed both hands on Ardeth's. The

ladies had quieted their chattering as if they could sense what was happening. Dr. Crenshaw turned his chair toward them.

"Mrs. Ardeth," Treha whispered. A pause. A stroke of the hand. She rubbed the woman's wrist as her head continued its movement. And then came a loosening of the muscles in the woman's arms and color moving through the pallor. Scales falling.

"My name is Treha," she said.

She let the words hang between them and leaned forward, closer, to see the woman's eyes, to see the storm that would release the rain.

"What is she doing?" the son-in-law said, his voice reflected by the glass wall with towering trees. Treha stared, eerily transfixed, as if preparing an experiment or to read the woman's fortune. "And why is she shaking her head like that?"

"She has a condition called nystagmus," Miriam said. "It's involuntary. She can't help it. She compensates by moving her head so the room doesn't spin."

The old woman's daughter glanced at the fireplace, the picture frames and blown glass and snow globes arranged on the mantel. She crossed her arms.

Miriam stood transfixed by the girl. "Treha has a gift."

"What do you mean?"

"An ability to . . . connect. I'm not sure what else to call it."

"She stared at the floor the whole time she was in the room," the man said. "I'd hardly call that a gift."

"She's unusual. I'll admit that."

"She looks like she can't even take care of herself. How can she possibly take care of others?"

"I don't like her," the daughter said.

"Treha is a very private person, as you can tell. I know more about her than most, but I still only know a little."

"What is she doing?" the daughter said. "Is she massaging her? Some kind of physical therapy?"

Miriam turned. "You and I think of communication as words and nonverbal signals. Stimulus given and received. But your mother is a labyrinth. A closed system. She's unable to break through the walls in her mind, and the longer she stays closed, the thicker the walls get."

"So you're saying she'll never come back to us? You haven't even evaluated her."

"I asked Treha to speak with your mother because she has keys to the locks. I've never seen anything like her."

"She's saying something," the woman said. "What is she saying?"

"Don't go inside yet. Let her work."

"I don't like this."

The husband stepped beside his wife and placed a hand on her shoulder. "We should leave."

"Give her just a moment," Miriam said.

"What if she upsets Mother? She gets uncomfortable in strange places. She'll never forgive me."

Miriam faced the glass. "I'll have Treha stop if you'd like."

The daughter wrung her hands and narrowed her gaze. "Yes, that's what I want. I want my mother out of there and I don't want her—"

"Wait," the man said. "Honey, look."

CHAPTER 4

DEVIN STARED out the window of the Bank of America office and watched the vintage Chevrolet Impala pull in. He placed it in the early 1960s. Rounded top. Whitewall tires. Sweeping lines and contours. Then it headed into a space outside the window and he noticed the double headlights and the wide grille. It nearly took his breath away. A 1959. He had seen pictures of his grandfather driving that exact model. Clark Gable mustache and white starched shirt and skinny tie. If he closed his eyes, he could watch it pull into the driveway and imagine his own father as a boy standing at the door, waiting.

Devin glanced at the newspaper on top of the magazines strategically spread across the waiting room table. On the front page were stories about an oil spill and the money being doled out by the company. A deadly virus had spread through several communities in the Midwest, but doctors were hopeful that it was now contained. And a lawsuit against a big pharma company was finally going to trial with doubts about whether a company like Phutura would ever lose. Lawyers, it seemed, were the only ones assured of making any real money these days.

"Mr. Hillis, sorry to keep you waiting."

The man was short and stout, a little teapot. He held out a

meaty hand and Devin shook it. Soft. A banker's handshake. The nameplate on the desk said, *Jeffrey Whitman, Vice President.*

"No problem. Thanks for seeing me, Mr. Whitman."

Devin could tell from the man's face and averted eyes that things weren't good. Whitman opened a folder, pulled out the paperwork, and pushed his glasses down. He spoke with a guttural rattle as if his nasal passages were blocked by marbles, and Devin wondered what it had been like on the playground when he was a child, what inhuman things the older kids did to him. The names they called him, the games they played without little Jeffrey.

"I've reviewed the loan application and talked with our senior vice president." He pushed his glasses back and looked up. "If documentaries are what you want to do, shouldn't you be seeking funding from other sources?"

Devin dug into his briefcase and handed the man a DVD in a white sleeve. "We're doing that. But watch this. I just came from a funeral—which is no reason to be excited, don't get me wrong. Death is final; it's dark and grim. But what I saw was a beautiful display of exactly what we're trying to do."

Devin described the service and the reaction to the video. Whitman looked puzzled as Devin scooted to the edge of his chair and put his hand on the desk.

"I'm a story collector. It's my passion. Most baby boomers—people in your age bracket—don't know their parents. They don't value their stories. And a lot of them are being forced to decide if they're going to connect with the previous generation or stay at a distance."

"How much were you paid for this video?" Jeffrey said.

"The total bill, if memory serves me, is somewhere between—"

"Not how much do you charge—how much have you been paid?"

"Well, we haven't been. Not yet. Out of deference to the family and their loss, I'm waiting for the death benefit."

"How long have you worked on that man's story?"

Devin thought about it. "I first shot video with Mr. Garrity a year ago. Maybe eighteen months."

"And this is your business model? Interviews? Story collecting for funerals?"

"No. The goal is to make films. Art that people years from now will watch and cry over. I want you and your family to go to a theater and come away changed. That's the goal. What I'm doing now is a beginning. This is how I'm going to pay for the documentary I'm making. Instead of getting a big grant, I'm working at it each day. Think of it this way: the people I'm interviewing are really investing in the future project, and the bank is just helping my business get off the ground."

"Why this retirement home? Why these people?" Whitman scratched his neck. "I know creative types like you. I have a brother who's a writer. Great mind, but he doesn't think in a linear way—he's all over the place. And financially, being all over the place is not good."

"I understand that."

"I've only seen one documentary in my life. It was about the guy who strung a wire from the South Tower to the North Tower and walked across it."

"*Man on Wire*. Great film."

"Yeah. It was fascinating. So why aren't you going after someone like that? Or an issue—illegal immigration. Gun control. Anything but old people sitting in a nursing home. I'm not saying we'd fund it, but it would be more compelling."

"I've studied film all my life. I've told you about the awards from my student work."

"This is not about awards; this is about money."

"Understood, and I see your point. My goal is a feature film. I've invested in the equipment."

"Using money from your parents' estate."

"Yes, and from my grandfather. That's how I wound up at Desert Gardens in the first place. I went to see him and met people with fascinating stories, like Mr. Garrity." Devin ran a hand throug his hair. "I don't have an agenda, but I know we're going to find the right thread, the right focus in the midst of all the possibilities."

"You're not going to find a man on a wire. Not in there."

Devin sat back, trying to figure out how to explain art to a number cruncher. The man asked if he'd given the film a title, and Devin told him.

"*Streams from Desert Gardens*?" Whitman repeated with a scowl. "Mr. Hillis, the account you have with us has dwindled. Your inheritance is almost gone. I've been waiving the checking fee because you haven't even been able to hit the minimum withdrawal on your credit card."

"Mr. Whitman, in ten years people are going to come to you and ask if this is the place where that filmmaker got his start. Seriously. I have an incredible guy working with me. Jonah's a genius. He's piecing together the documentary as we go, while at the same time working on these shorter pieces. We're advertising aggressively on social media and in some strategic areas . . ."

"You're advertising the documentary?"

"No, these short films about people's lives."

"Devin, you put up flyers in nursing homes. You have

seventy-five friends on Facebook. I'm one of them. I don't call that aggressive."

"It's a start," Devin said.

"Well, I'd really like to help you—"

"Look, all I need is someone to catch the vision, to understand what we're doing."

"Any teenager with a laptop can do what you're doing. The music, too. Free. I have a teenager of my own. And you want people to shell out thousands for—" he tossed the DVD onto the desk—"a family video?"

Devin put a hand up. "Indulge me. Five minutes." He raised his eyebrows. "Please."

The banker put the folder down and leaned back.

"Okay, thank you," Devin said. He rubbed his hands on the armrests. "I believe in the cosmic story. That all of us are connected—our lives, our relationships. Everything we do, everything happening in our lives, is like water on the planet. The oceans, lakes, rivers, rain from above, it's all flowing and gushing. It looks haphazard—rain, snow, a trickle here and then a monsoon. But it's not. All of it is ordered and managed, cascading around us. Through us. We are part of the cosmic story being told every day with each of our lives."

"What's the point?"

Devin stood and leaned forward, his hands on the desk. "We are preserving stories. We are connecting family and friends and neighbors and every person on the planet. The world is shrinking, Mr. Whitman. People are closer to each other than ever before, but with the explosion of information, we actually know less than ever. You know what your sister had for dinner last night because she put it on Facebook. But you don't know your sister."

The man seemed unimpressed, nonplussed. Devin took off his jacket and folded it across the chair.

"My belief is that everyone wants to make sense of their story. You, me, the old man in the nursing home, the doctor in the ER. Each wants to know there's a purpose, a reason we're walking the planet. And that's what we provide. Context. A record of having lived. Substance and meaning for every life."

"It's a DVD of old people talking."

"No. This is not a talking head." He picked up the DVD. "This is art. It's not something a kid can do on his computer after visiting Grandma. I mean, a talented teenager can do some amazing things, and I'm sure your son—"

"Daughter."

"I'm sure your daughter does amazing work. I might hire her as an intern this summer—that's the beauty of this: there are so many possibilities." His mind wandered and he had to close his eyes and rein it in, narrow his focus before he galloped off the reservation. "We're not cataloging lives or just collecting information. We're turning stories into a symphony. We're deciphering the days of this older generation or the young father with a terminal illness or a mother with breast cancer who has a few months to live or a child with a tumor whose parents want to hang on to life. Make sense of the pain. We're taking all of that and putting it into understandable bits of video and music and story. This is a holy endeavor."

"This is about your grandfather, isn't it?"

"What do you mean?"

"You're having a hard time dealing with his death. With what happened to your parents, I don't blame you. It's a tough thing to lose someone like that." Jeffrey picked up the DVD again. "I like your passion. I'm not trying to denigrate your idea. I hope you make a million. I hope you're the next Steven Spielberg."

Devin bit his tongue. He did not want to be Spielberg. He wanted to be better than Spielberg could ever hope to be.

"I appreciate how hard you've worked and what you're willing to do to fund your art. But this is a DVD that will go on the shelf and collect dust. And just as you have to represent your vision, I have to represent the bank's. In this economy, investing lots of money in an artistic endeavor makes no sense."

Devin took a deep breath and swallowed his pride. "I was drawn to this because of my grandfather; you're right. And I could be cataloging border issues or the drug wars or a thousand other more sexy subjects. But if this catches on, there are retirement communities and areas of the country—look at Florida. California. The Pacific Northwest. It's an untapped reservoir and not just because of the money. I can see this getting bigger, with reps on both coasts and in the Midwest. And the more stories we record and tell, the more word gets out, the more affordable we make it. The documentary will be the best way to publicize what we're doing. It will bring awareness to the project."

"Just like Tom Hanks did with WWII veterans," Whitman said, barely able to cross his legs.

"Exactly," Devin said. He lifted his thumb in the air like Atticus Finch at the jury box. "I've always heard if you do what you love, the money will follow. If you do something with passion that comes from deep inside, you'll never really work a day in your life. I could pitch you five different ideas that would make me a successful entrepreneur in a year or less. But I want to do something that lasts. I want to make a difference. These are the stories I was meant to tell. I can feel it. And if you'll help us, I promise you won't be disappointed."

When he finished, his hands were balled into fists.

"You really believe that, don't you?"

"With everything in me. This can't lose. And not only will we make money and get the documentary going; we'll make the world better. Isn't that what it's all about?"

Devin glanced out the window as the Chevrolet backed out of the parking lot and pulled away. There was something about seeing the taillights that both unnerved and invigorated him.

CHAPTER 5

THE TRANSFORMATION—and that was the only word that could adequately describe what Miriam observed—came slowly, as if a flower were opening. It showed in the old woman's eyes as she tilted her head like a dog hearing a strange noise. A train whistle. A siren. First came the head tilt, then a more precise stare, a studying of the force of nature near her. She leaned forward, as close to the girl as she could, dipping her head, her chest against the table.

The daughter opened the door and rushed into the room, leaving her husband behind. Miriam followed.

"Mrs. Ardeth, do you know where you are?" Treha said.

The old woman squinted and gave a hint of a smile. She tried to form words through an open mouth, her tongue moving.

"It's okay," Treha said. "Be patient. We have lots of time."

The words hung thick on Treha's lips, but they were said with such kindness. She didn't look up or acknowledge their presence. Treha locked on to the woman as if she were the only person on the planet.

Ardeth slipped a hand on top of Treha's. Then she did the same with the other and squeezed. The husband caught up as

Ardeth's tongue slipped forward. She struggled, squeezing her eyes shut, and spoke with the force of a bursting dam.

"Hoooo . . . mmmm." The word came out in multiple syllables, and when she finished, she sucked in air like she hadn't breathed in days.

"She spoke," the daughter gasped. She leaned closer. "What did you say, Mom?"

The woman looked up at her daughter, then back at Treha. It looked like the circulation was cut off to Treha's hands.

"That's right," Treha said. "You are home."

"Yessssssssss," Ardeth said, nodding. "Hoooommmme. Hoomme." She sat back, a look of confidence spreading. And then instead of many syllables, it was just one.

"Home."

The two ladies turned from their puzzle, their hands together, faces beaming. Dr. Crenshaw chuckled and shook his head and thumped his Bible on one knee. Behind him, the sun broke through the cloud cover.

"This feels like . . . home to me," Ardeth said, punctuating the words by raising and lowering Treha's hand. She laughed.

"I can't believe it," the man whispered. "I thought she'd never talk again."

"It's remarkable, isn't it?" Miriam said.

The daughter stepped forward to look at Treha. Miriam searched the girl's face for any hint of joy or sadness or longing, but there was only a blank stare.

"Treha, how did you do that?"

"How did I do what?" She said it sincerely.

"What you did. The breakthrough. You reached her."

Treha looked at Ardeth, then back to the daughter. "I just spoke to her. I showed her I would listen."

Ardeth held on to Treha's hands and studied her through glistening eyes. "You're a nice girl. Such a sweet face. You look like my granddaughter." She glanced up. "Celeste, she looks a little like Tiffany, don't you think?"

The daughter patted her mother's arm. Overwhelmed, overcome. "Yes, Mom. You're right—she does look like Tiff."

"Such a beautiful girl."

The husband touched Miriam's arm and the two retreated. "Does she work here full-time? Would she be seeing my mother-in-law regularly?"

Miriam smiled. "Treha is in high demand. She spends time with a number of people. I'm sure she would visit Ardeth."

The man looked back at the three, his wife now kneeling by the wheelchair. "Does it work like that for everyone? I mean, if she can break through to Ardeth . . ."

"It depends. I've seen people with mild dementia come alive, like today. I've seen Alzheimer's patients connect for a time. Even the most severely affected have some kind of response."

"How long does it last? She could go right back into herself at sundown, right?"

Miriam studied the scene, taking in the unity that had replaced the discord. Three separate individuals, in pain, uniting around the words of an old woman.

"It's not really up to us," Miriam said. "Or Treha, for that matter. It's up to the person she's reaching. You have to want to be reached. To respond."

The man's eyes searched the room for nothing in particular. "I'd like to see the contract, if you wouldn't mind."

Streams from Desert Gardens
scene 6

Wide shot of security guard Buck Davis in uniform, arms crossed, leaning back in his chair.

The day Mrs. Howard began was the same day I was hired. I told her she'd never regret it. I like to say she never would have made it this long if I hadn't come along. Been here every step of the way. We've grown up together. Not grown old, mind you, just grown up.

You learn a lot of things working at a place like this, if you'll let it teach you. It's just like anything in life—you have to open your mind. Have to see what's not there as much as what is.

Tight shot of Buck's weathered hands, then back to wide shot.

We had one fellow years ago, Mr. Pennington. He was some high-powered banker or investment man who made lots of money, but his wife had died and his children didn't want him around, so they put him here.

Every morning he would get up and have his breakfast, read the paper, and get dressed in his suit and tie. He'd head toward the front gate and right on out to the street. The first time it happened, we sounded the alarm and everybody got agitated until

34

we ran him down and brought him back. He wasn't too happy about it, either. This was a man who was used to being the boss. So we tried to explain he couldn't go walking off like that. He said he was sorry, that he was a little mixed up, and that he wouldn't do it again.

Still photo of Mr. Pennington.

Well, you know what happened the next day. Here he was again going toward the gate. So Mrs. Howard and I put our heads together and pretty soon we figured out he wasn't hurting anybody by taking a walk. It was actually doing him some good. So she would phone me of a morning and tell me when she saw Mr. Pennington was dressed and coming out of his room. I'd say good morning to him when he passed me and then I'd get in the car and follow him until he got tired, which was usually down at the Walgreens unless it was the summer. I'd pull up like I was his chauffeur and give him a ride back, ask how his day was. He'd reach in his pocket to give me a tip and tell me he forgot his wallet. And I'd say, "That's okay," and he'd go in and take a nap.

The next morning, same time every day, he'd be dressed and ready to go. Except for there at the end, he would be late by a few minutes or forget to put his pants on and we'd have to go to plan B.

Wide shot of residents in the dining hall as voice-over continues.

People are creatures of habit, every last one of us. You can make your rules and try to get everybody to follow in lockstep and control every little thing they do, or you can treat people with some dignity and go with the flow. That's what Mrs. Howard has always been good at. Taking people where they are and working with them to make this place a little like home.

Tight shot of Buck, misty-eyed.

I'm going to miss her. I thought maybe one day she would just move in here with her husband, but that's probably going to be a few more years, I guess.

CHAPTER 6

MIRIAM EXITED the dayroom but stopped abruptly when she saw Jillian Millstone peering through the mountain on the glass wall. The woman was stocky, with a matronly build and short hair that seemed a little too dark for her age. She kept each thinning strand under tight control and wore dark, slim-fitting pantsuits that made her look less attractive than she was, Miriam thought. She was unmarried, had no children, and seemed able to catalog every duty for the job except compassion. But the board of directors had made their decision and Miriam trusted their judgment. Even if they were making a mistake.

"Ms. Millstone, I was hoping I'd see you. We have a prospective member of the community I'd like you to meet. I was going to get the contract and go over it with the family."

Millstone held up a hand. "I don't want to interrupt. Are you certain she'll be staying?"

There was an edge to her voice. Miriam sidestepped it like dog waste on the sidewalk. "They seem impressed with the facilities and the people. There will be money concerns, of course."

The woman moved toward the door. "What is she doing?"

"Treha? What she always does. She's our one-woman welcome wagon."

No smile. No reaction. "That's not her job."

"No, we certainly don't pay her what she's worth."

"That's not what I mean."

"I'm sure you've been able to pick up by now that Treha is one of our greatest assets."

Millstone stared through the glass at the fuzzy images.

"Well, if you'll excuse me, I'll—"

"Just a moment, Mrs. Howard. Do you think it's proper? In your opinion and with your experience, do you think it's wise to have an untrained employee working so closely with the residents? She's a janitorial worker, is she not?"

Miriam nodded, but the woman wasn't looking at her. "I hired her because she does everything we ask."

"She's not scrubbing toilets and tile, is she? Most of the time she's engaging patients."

"She is the most beloved person on staff. Once we discovered her gift, I didn't give her as much to clean. We didn't want to waste her ability."

"You've supported this because the ends justify the means. If something works, don't question it—is that right?"

"Ms. Millstone, I'm not sure you fully understand what Treha offers."

The woman turned to face her. "I understand quite well. There is a liability issue. I'm surprised you haven't seen that."

"Well, that's absurd. Treha—"

"When something happens—and I mean *when*—this facility will be held responsible."

"You don't know her."

A glance through the glass again. "I understand you had a dog once. You used it for therapeutic purposes."

"Yes. Bailey."

"What happened to Bailey?"

"He grew old. We had to euthanize him."

"Not before he bit a child. Visiting a grandparent, as I understand it. How much did that family receive in the out-of-court settlement?"

"The child was hitting the dog with a cane. Bailey reared back to protect himself and one of his claws scratched the child—"

"There was a settlement, wasn't there?"

"Yes, we did take responsibility."

"And you were vulnerable because you decided taking in this animal was worth the risk."

Miriam smiled. "I'm sure you've seen the studies. You can't measure the reparative impact of an animal to . . . Bailey brought life to these halls. Smiles, joy."

"Many residents were traumatized. The attack made them question your judgment."

Miriam looked at the floor.

"If he was so therapeutic, why didn't you replace him?"

She didn't answer.

"The board told you not to bring another animal into the facility, didn't they? I would think patients deserve a life without ticks and fleas and animals that use the hallway as a restroom. Certainly seeing little children attacked can't contribute to their long-term well-being."

"Ms. Millstone, there is no comparison between Treha and an animal. There is no risk. And there's no end to the reward she gives."

"I was looking through the personnel files. What we know is alarming. And what we don't know, the unanswered questions—that's even more frightening. You obviously didn't take this into consideration."

"I think everyone deserves a chance."

"Agreed. And maybe even a second chance. In the proper context. With the proper education and supervision. And she has neither. That makes everyone vulnerable."

"You can't judge someone simply by reading a file."

"Isn't the safety of our residents the primary job? One day this girl will snap. She's a volcano ready to erupt. There's no predicting when that will be."

Miriam knew this was not the time or place for a battle over Treha. She wanted Millstone to understand, to realize how wrong she was. Perhaps over coffee she could get her to see. With a gentle, soft voice and a slight step forward, she spoke.

"I've learned a lot over the years that I could never learn in a classroom or from a book. Mistakes, yes. Lessons taught by the diminishment of each life. The medical community views individuals as patients to be cured. But when people age, they're not looking for a cure as much as they are for encouragement to continue. Our work here is not about curing. It's about the dignity of each person wheeled from breakfast back to their room."

Millstone studied her hands.

"Before coming here," Miriam continued, "I served in a VA trauma unit. I was frustrated with the care the patients received. There was a man, thin and hardly breathing . . . They were working with him to find a vein for an IV. I simply spoke to him. Calmed him while they worked. He had won the Congressional Medal of Honor. But he was just an old man in a wheelchair to me when I started."

"And your point is?"

"Value people not just for the income they provide us. Value them because of the lives they've lived. Value each person who pushes a broom or cleans a bedpan. And value the girl whose life is marred, yes, but who gives these people more than any doctor ever will."

Millstone smiled, sickly sweet. "And this is the Miriam Howard shorter catechism?"

Miriam's eyes narrowed; then she composed herself. "Ms. Millstone, you can run this facility any way you want. But you'll be making a big mistake if you hamper that girl from doing what God has gifted her to do."

She turned and walked briskly down the hall and didn't slam a door until she was in her office.

CHAPTER 7

DEVIN SLUNG his backpack toward the chair he had bought on sale at OfficeMax, and it rolled back on the plastic mat. The cherry desk and hutch had been 50 percent off. These were the only things that were "new" in the office. The rest came from Goodwill. A gray desk from a WWII battleship sat in the corner.

Devin had jumped at the chance to sign a year's lease in a strip mall that had seen its better days. Businesses had come and gone and there were several storefronts that had nothing but red For Lease signs in the windows. This office had previously housed a tax preparer who had moved to a busier intersection and hired a woman to dress up in a Lady Liberty costume and stand by a nearby stoplight twirling a sign. An insurance agent occupied the office before that, and the first tenant had been a carryout pizza restaurant. There were still sauce stains on the ceiling, and a doughy odor lingered in the carpet.

Instead of installing new walls and configuring the office the way he wanted, Devin had negotiated the rental price down a hundred dollars per month. And then he made Jonah a full partner. It was the least he could do since Jonah and his mother had done so much for him.

Devin studied the battered phone and the unlit message

light. The phone system was a leftover from the tax preparer, as were the plant and two tattered chairs that sat in what was termed the lobby.

Jonah Verwer stepped into Devin's office with one hand in the pocket of his khakis and the other around a twenty-four-ounce bottle of Mountain Dew Code Red. He was pudgy, dutifully carrying the extra weight of his sedentary life. He spent much of his day in front of a screen consuming high-sugar and immensely caffeinated beverages, along with fries and burgers from the dollar menu at a local fast-food restaurant. He was probably thirty pounds over what might be considered a moderately healthy existence, but Devin knew he wouldn't change until the heart attack twenty years down the road.

"Let me guess. The bank offered you a loan and you're frustrated because you don't know which editing software you want to buy."

Devin moved his backpack and sat in the chair that tilted a little too much to the left. "We didn't get it."

"Shocker. What excuse did he give?"

"The same. Bad business model."

"We have a business model?" Jonah ran his hand along the impressive collection of DVDs lining a dusty bookshelf. "So where do we stand?"

Devin told him about the Garrity funeral and how the family had responded. He tried to show grit and fight in the face of hurricane odds.

"Did you ask for a check?"

"Come on, it was a funeral. You think I'd ask to be paid when the casket is still open?"

"You should've held the video until they paid. Like a ransom."

"I'll remember that next funeral."

"They'll pay eventually," Jonah said. He leaned against the table that held Devin's printer, but it wobbled and he didn't sit. "Mr. Garrity was a peach. Sad to see the old guy go. He's been our best so far. Didn't even have to ask that many questions—I just turned on the camera and he took off."

"I wish you could have seen the reaction. Your music made it sing. It took you right there, you know? Just like I'd pictured. If that banker had been there, he would have written a check on the spot."

Jonah took a swig from the bottle and screwed the cap back on. "Sullivan dropped by." He burped.

Devin's shoulders slumped and he closed his eyes. "Did you let him in?"

"I tried pretending I didn't hear his knock, but it didn't work."

"What did he say?"

"He's ready to change the locks by the end of the week."

"Great."

"How much are we behind?"

"Two months. Three next week."

Jonah stared at the stack of bills on the desk. "What about the electricity? If they cut that—"

"I'm current with Tucson Electric. Well, maybe a month behind. I know we have to have juice in order to power the machines and the air-conditioning. We'll be okay."

Jonah turned toward the window overlooking concrete and asphalt and the finely manicured desert that had gone to seed. Some kind of thistle had sprung up in the wash and taken over. Tall and green and resistant to Roundup. "Even the eternal optimist has to come back to reality when they're changing the locks, don't you think?"

"You can't change the locks on a person's outlook on life," Devin said.

"Where'd you read that?"

"I made it up."

"Nice."

"You know what I'm looking forward to?"

"What's that?"

"The day that banker comes in here and stands right where you're standing. I can see it. He's going to stand right there and beg us to set up an account. No, he'll be crawling. Hands and knees. Offering an interest-free loan. 'Please let us give you money.'" Devin laughed, but it was more from worry than mirth.

Jonah turned the crank on the window blinds and the room darkened. "I want to be here when that happens. But it doesn't look like anybody's beating the door down right now. Clients or lenders."

There was an uncomfortable silence of men in transition. Men confronted with themselves and each other.

"I was thinking that . . . maybe it might be a good idea if . . ."

"A good idea if what?"

"If Sullivan locks the place up—"

"He's not going to lock us out. I'm going to pay him."

"But if he does, we lose all of this. I can't afford to be without my computer and camera. And you don't want to lose the new desk and your DVDs." Jonah pawed on the floor with a foot. "My mom was saying you could put your stuff at our place. Just until we figure things out."

"Jonah, what kind of image does that present? You and me working out of your mother's house? Come on. We've been there before. Have a little faith. We'll get through this."

"I'm trying to be responsible. The equipment's all we have."

Devin scowled. "Fine. Give up. Move your stuff home to Mother if you're scared. I don't blame you."

"It's just until we can get settled," Jonah said.

"No, it's not. It's giving up. If you take your camera and computer and stabilizer and tripods—you take that out of here and it's over. It's like a couple moving in together and one person says they need space. 'I just need my space. Give me space.' The other person moves out and it's over. Kaput. They never see each other again."

Jonah stared at the painfully thin carpet. "I'm not . . . What was her name?"

"It doesn't matter."

"If I don't take the equipment, it's over for both of us. He locks those doors and the property inside is his. I had a friend who worked over at a Chuy's when they closed, and the guy wouldn't even return the purse she left behind the bar."

"I told you, I'm going to pay."

"With what?"

"Garrity's family writes a check this week for sure. That will buy us more time."

Jonah thought a minute. "Devin, we've known each other a long time." He waited. "Agreed?"

"Yeah, we can agree on that."

"And I've been as committed to this as you. I've shot video of old people who can do nothing but drool and I haven't complained. . . . Okay, I've complained a little."

"Agreed."

"But I've been here every day. Well, almost every day. And I've worked my tail off."

"You've worked hard but you still have quite a tail."

"But there comes a point when you have to make a decision. When you have to see the truth."

"Which is?"

"Maybe it's not working. We could shoot this documentary another ten years and we wouldn't find what you're looking for. Even when we get a gig, like with Garrity or the weddings, they don't pay."

"The wedding paid."

"They gave us cake and the check bounced."

"It will work; trust me. Stop whining!"

"I'm not whining. This is the truth. Garrity was an anomaly. He was one in a million. Most of the people we've shot have been so stiff you couldn't tell if rigor had set in. They couldn't remember most of their lives and couldn't communicate what they did remember. That one woman was so nervous—"

Devin waved him off. "Her daughter told me she had a weak bladder."

"Weak? That's like saying Niagara Falls gets a little fast at the edge."

"I should have warned you."

"You should have bought me a raincoat. And galoshes."

"Jonah, this is part of the process. It's paying our dues. Remember when I told you we had to pay our dues?"

"I'm fine paying dues. I can work long hours for no pay. I can keep going without a steady check. For a while. I can set up a shoot and get the audio and sequence the music. But I don't think we're getting anywhere. You're a great visionary— you have ideas and you can see what is coming together on-screen—but old people are sometimes scared of you."

"We've gotten some great footage."

"That's meandering toward pointless."

"It'll come together. And maybe we'll hire somebody softer, more inviting, to do the interviews."

"Devin, we don't have money for rent. How do we hire another employee? Maybe we've reached the peak, you know?"

Devin leaned forward, his elbows on his empty month-at-a-glance calendar, his finger and thumb slightly apart. "We're this close to something big. I can feel it. Something with the shoot that changes everything. We can't give up. The people at Garrity's funeral, if they ask who did that, the phone will ring off the hook and we won't have time to tie our shoelaces. Then we'll finish the documentary and win an Academy Award."

Jonah stared blankly.

"Fine. Go unplug your stuff and leave." Devin stood and put out a hand. "No hard feelings. I'll get somebody else."

"I don't want you to get somebody else. Devin, I'm not your enemy."

He pointed a finger at Jonah. "Every time you talk about quitting, you're my enemy."

"This is the first time I've said anything."

"Then every time you entertain the *idea* of quitting, you're going against me."

"So now you're doing the *Minority Report* thing? You can get inside my head?"

"My *friend* is my coworker who believes in what we're doing. Somebody who buys the vision and runs with it, even when it gets tough. Have a little faith."

Jonah unfolded a chair that was leaning against the wall by the bookcase. It was left over from the pizza restaurant and had flour stains on the seat. He sat and the rivets whined.

"My dad said something to me a long time ago," Jonah said. "He said life is like a pretty girl who smiles at you and asks you to come to her house. It feels good to be with her. And you get all tingly and warm inside. And about the time you get up the nerve to ask her for a kiss, when you think she'll say yes, she plants a boot in your mouth. This is not an *if* but a *when*. It's going to happen. If it's not a boot, it's a sock full of nickels. Life swings it hard, and if it connects, the best thing you can hope for is to lose a few teeth."

"Your dad was Mr. Encouragement, wasn't he?"

"He was a realist."

"Is that why he killed himself?"

Jonah looked away.

"I'm sorry—that was a cheap shot. Keep going. I want to hear what life does next. Seriously. Can you at least cash in the sock full of nickels or does life take those with her?"

Jonah rubbed the fuzz on his chin, then gestured with a hand. "His point was you have to make the right decisions early."

"You mean like not going over to life's house?"

"No."

"Keeping her away from the sock drawer?"

"You have to decide how you're going to handle the boot because if you don't, you'll give up when things get tough. Just sit down and stop living because it's too hard. Life hurts too much. It kicks you in the teeth, which it did to him. And it's doing it to us."

"So you're illustrating irony here? Because giving up is exactly what you're doing."

"I'm not giving up. I'm trying to move forward. I'm making a good decision now so I don't have to suffer later. I keep the equipment instead of buying it back from the sheriff's auction."

Devin turned his chair toward the window.

"This business wasn't a bad idea," Jonah said. "It was good—"

"Leave."

"We shouldn't have set up the office. You should have saved the inheritance—"

"We can't present a professional image from your mother's spare bedroom."

"We don't have a professional image! Don't you see that, Devin? We don't have paying clients. We have a hundred hours of old people talking about life in the good old days."

Devin waved a hand. "Whatever."

Jonah walked to the door. When Devin turned, he saw something in the man's face he hadn't seen before. A resolve—defiance perhaps.

"You know what the problem is, Devin? I can't tell you anything. I can't talk about what's bothering me. Or what's wrong with the business. You don't want a partner. You, you, you—" he stammered. "You want a lackey, a camera operator. Some techie who can get the shots and call it good and edit and take your direction. But you don't want feedback. You don't want correction. You don't want to work *together*; you want a slave. You're the only one who can have an idea. And that's sad because I'm fully invested. I wanted to be part of this."

Jonah 's face was red when he finished, his voice raspy.

"Where'd that come from?" Devin said.

"I don't know. I guess I've been waiting. All the things I wanted to say but was afraid to."

"I should have told you to get out a long time ago. That was good."

"You think so?"

"There was real energy there. Like you were feeling it."

"You want me to try it again?"

"The 'you, you, you' part was impressive. It felt a little forced when you said 'slave,' but I'd keep it if you'd recorded it."

"I'm trying to get more passion in my life. You know, like living from the heart instead of the head."

"Your mom tell you that?"

"Yeah."

"She's right. It's working. You convinced me. It was really good."

"Thanks."

"And you're right."

"About what?"

"All of it."

Jonah lifted an eyebrow. "You think so?"

"Yeah, absolutely. I'm a narcissistic, overbearing, grandiose thinker who only wants to do things the best way because *my* way is the best way, and if you don't like it, hit the road. It's in my DNA. Passed from generation to generation. I don't see reality. Someone like you can."

"Someone like me? What does that mean?"

"Just that you're different; you complement me. My weakness is your strength."

"So you want to help me move the equipment?"

"No, give me a couple of days."

"Devin . . ."

"He's not changing the locks until the end of the week, right? Give me a chance to get the money. If it doesn't come in, I'll personally carry everything in here over to your mother's house and put it in her spare bedroom. And I'll do it from the heart, with passion."

Jonah took a breath and shook his head. "End of the week. That's it."

Streams from Desert Gardens
scene 4

Wide shot of medical certificates on wall. Tight shot of Dr. Crenshaw's name and his accreditation as an ob-gyn.

Crenshaw voice-over:

> The year was 1937—toward the end of the Depression, but there were still heavy pockets of despair and hopelessness.

Picture of a young Crenshaw in hat and gloves.

> Just surviving was the most anyone could hope for. Many children were sent to live with family members. Aunts and uncles who had means.

Wide shot of Crenshaw in his leather chair by the window. Early morning light.

> My mother had begun to cry, days on end. I was very young. Too young to understand. But it's here, in my memory. My mother stayed home that day with the other children and my father walked with me into town—he had sold the car. We got a ride from someone passing and they let us off in front of an ice cream shop. We couldn't afford ice cream. We couldn't afford *food*. But as a child you don't understand that.

My father took me inside and ordered an ice cream cone and handed it to me. Then he had me sit down in a booth across from a man and woman I had never seen. And while I ate my ice cream, he walked out the door.

I never saw him again. I never saw my mother. Or my siblings.

Tight shot of Crenshaw's pictures with his adoptive mother and father.

My adoptive parents couldn't have children. They made an agreement with my mother and father that there would be no contact after the ice cream shop. Years later I asked them about what had happened. I suppose they thought I would forget. Everything was hush-hush; you didn't talk about such things back then. You didn't bring it up because it meant you were ungrateful or you were trying to cause trouble.

My biological parents knew they couldn't take care of all of us children. I was the youngest of three. And they saw something in me, or so my adoptive mother said. They thought I had some intellect, a promise of something greater. My adoptive father was a medical doctor. My parents simply felt this would be better for me. So they gave me away.

Tight shot of Dr. Crenshaw's face, eyes moist.

I've helped many people through the years. I like to think I've saved some lives. I don't know if that's true. I like to think their sacrifice led to my success in medicine. But I often think of what it must have taken for them to make that choice. What led to that decision? Did they argue? Were there tears?

Struggle? I have no idea if they knew I became a doctor. Were they proud of me? Those questions have haunted me all my life.

Cutaway to Crenshaw's bare feet, his empty slippers beside them.

Cut to picture of adoptive father, mother, and Crenshaw at medical school graduation.

I've often wondered if I would have made that kind of sacrifice. Or what would have happened if they had kept me. Would I still have become a doctor? In God's providence or fate, would I have found a way into the medical profession, or would I have learned a trade, perhaps? Carpentry? Plumbing?

Tight shot of Crenshaw's face as a tear escapes.

Is life worth living if the children are hungry? If it doesn't improve, would it be better to stay together or separate? . . . A life hangs on these questions.

Fade to black.

CHAPTER 8

Before leaving each evening—and most nights she didn't leave until dark—Treha would visit Dr. Crenshaw, also known as Cranky Crenshaw. He had been one of her success stories, though the abyss he gravitated toward felt different from dementia. Not as much disease as disconnection and depression. It seemed there was a past cloud that hung over him, and Treha tried to be the warm air that pushed the cold front away.

She had no real clue of how it actually worked. All she knew was that some were locked inside themselves and couldn't break through without help. She wasn't sure where the keys came from, only that she had them. Each time she saw eyes open, she was given something. But what? Hope? A vision of the future? She lived in a world of possibility, where one day someone might call her forth as well. It was a little like the fairy tales of Rapunzel, trapped in the tower. Sleeping Beauty, waiting for the kiss. Perhaps her prince would come. She would awaken and find the world different, her mind repaired.

Or perhaps there was no one with a similar key for her.

She knocked lightly on the door and pushed it open. Sunlight faded on the lonely room and she saw his silhouette in the chair by the window, a well-read newspaper folded in front of him.

"Treha," Dr. Crenshaw said. It sent a warm feeling through

her. He tapped the chair beside him, identical to his own. "Come in and sit."

She kicked off her shoes and sat, drawing her knees to herself and closing her eyes. "All right. Ready."

"*X-T-E-R-E,*" he said, pronouncing each letter slowly.

As soon as he had said the final letter, she replied, "*Exert.*" In truth, she had known how to begin the word as soon as he said the first *E*.

"Good," he said. "How about *R-E-B-O-D*?"

"*Bored.*"

"No, try another. There are several—"

"*Robed. Orbed,*" she said quickly, without effort.

"Yes, it was *robed*. I should run a timer, my dear."

He gave her the next two words, which she solved just as quickly, and then a list of letters for the paper's final jumble below a cartoon that was supposed to help.

The old man laughed, his eyes twinkling. Treha squeezed her legs with her arms and watched him fill the blanks with a pencil.

"I have been working on this all day, staring at it, moving the letters around in my brain, and you simply hear them and fit them together. It's amazing."

She paused, not responding to the adulation. "How was your day?"

"Oh, it was full of excitement." He gestured with a hand, overdramatizing the words. "Way too much to talk about. If I told you all of it, we'd be here all night and my blood pressure would be through the roof." He chuckled, though he didn't receive anything back. "How about you, Treha? Anything happen to you today?"

"I like hearing about you."

He folded the paper neatly and she noticed he had made

marks and notes on the front. He put the paper on the small table between them. Sitting back, he took a breath as if gaining momentum.

"All right, let me see. At breakfast the oatmeal was tepid and the orange juice was warm, so I mixed them together. I was doing it to disgust Elsie, of course. I called it 'orangemeal.' And just to get her goat, I tried it, and it turned out not that bad."

"So you're eating again."

"I had some toast and the orangemeal, and for lunch I managed to down the mystery meat of the day and some yogurt. Oh, and the Lovebirds were back. Though she's not doing well. She's using oxygen now and seems more pale. You probably heard about it. He brought her a rose, a single red rose. I have no idea where he found it—probably took it from the garden— but the other women swooned when he wheeled himself up to her. He gave her the rose and kissed her on the cheek as she ate. It makes me sick the way those two carry on. Like teenagers."

"I think they are sweet."

"Yes, you would. You haven't seen as much life as I have. There is a fine line between sweet and nauseating." He smiled and shook as he laughed. "The Opera Singer was in rare form today—tuning her voice, running the scales. Then Hemingway arrived and thought he was in Pamplona. He was ordering drinks for everyone, saying the great DiMaggio would be coming soon, and then his eyes grew wide and he said the bulls were coming. He actually got out of his chair and put his ear to the floor and yelled that they were coming down the corridor and we needed to clear the dining room."

Crenshaw imitated the man perfectly but Treha did not smile. She simply burrowed her head further behind her knees and watched.

"Did the bulls show up?" she said.

"Yes, the bulls in the white uniforms with the syringe. I suspect he's off his medication again." He looked at her in the fading sunlight and leaned forward, making something in his arm or his back pop. He frowned. "My bones sound like a bowl of Rice Krispies."

"You should stretch more," Treha said.

"No amount of stretching will stop the popping and snapping inside, my dear. I need an oil change. A transmission flush. A complete overhaul." He took a deep breath. "Let's not talk about me tonight. Let's talk about you."

"There's nothing to tell."

"Au contraire. There's much to learn. Much to know."

"I could tell you what I did today, but it would bore you."

"No, I don't mean about today. I mean about your life. Where you've been. What you've done. What you've seen. You never talk about it."

"I told you, I don't remember much."

"I don't believe you. You remember everything. The things you read. The things told to you. How could you say you don't remember?"

"Maybe I don't want to remember."

"Aha, now you're getting closer to the truth, I think."

She gripped her legs tighter and lowered her head where he couldn't see her.

"Close your eyes and let me ask you some questions. If you don't know the answer, say you don't know. Or make something up. If you can ask me questions, it only seems fair that I should do the same with you."

She closed her eyes but they still moved behind the eyelids. Her fingers were engaged now, typing on some unseen keyboard. She bit her lip, tearing at a chapped area. Crenshaw got like this frequently, asking questions about her past. It almost seemed to her that he wanted to tell her something, reveal something hidden, but what could he know?

"Tell me about your parents. What do you remember?"

Her head moved slightly left and right. "I only remember my mother in the ice cream shop. The color of her dress. A little perfume. And her walking across the street."

When he didn't speak, she opened her eyes and found him staring at her with condescension. "That's not nice, Treha. You can't take another person's story and make it your own."

"You said to make something up."

"You know what I mean."

She sat all the way back. "All right. I remember my mother taking me into a jewelry store. Or maybe it was a watch repair shop. And she left and I never saw her again."

"You're hopeless, you know that?"

"Hopeless?"

"Go ahead. Give me synonyms for the word *hopeless*. Thirty seconds. Go."

She closed her eyes again and rhythmically, without hesitation, spoke the words that passed across the synapses. "*Hopeless. Despairing. Miserable. Depressed. Downcast. Disconsolate. Dejected. Melancholic. Wretched* . . ."

He interrupted. "What about this: 'The wretched refuse'? Does that ring a bell?"

"'The wretched refuse of your teeming shore. Send these, the homeless, tempest-tost to me, I lift my lamp beside the golden door!'"

"Emma Lazarus," he said, beaming. "You are amazing," he whispered. "Simply amazing."

"Remembering the words is not amazing. The words are amazing."

"True. But most people are not able to remember like you." He looked at the floor, at the slippers beside his chair. At the bed and the television and desk and nightstand, the circumference of his limited world. "I was reading earlier today," he said, picking up a dog-eared book. "A sentence jumped out of a novel at me. Arrested me. I thought of you."

"What did it say?"

He flipped to a bookmarked section. "Here it is. 'Scared money can't win and a worried man can't love.' Marvelous, isn't it?" He read it again. "What do you think that means?"

She sat, unmoving except for her eyes, mulling the words. "The first part has something to do with gambling. If you want to win, you have to risk. Put your money where your mouth is?"

"Good." He nodded. "And what about the second part? 'A worried man can't love.'"

Her head swayed like a blind performer's, with no concern for who noticed. "If you worry, you can only think of yourself. You can't love someone else."

"Why not?"

"Because love is not about what you receive. It's about what you give."

"How do you know this, Treha?"

She shrugged. "There are some things you just know."

He turned his head to look at the ceiling for a moment. "That's very insightful. Maybe that's why it jumped out at me. It brought back all the mistakes. Things I regret."

"What regrets do you have?" she said.

He waved a hand and the splotches on his skin shone in the

dim light. Other signs of unwanted age too—the weary movement, the misshapen nails, the telltale wrinkles and sags.

"There are things in my life I would like to do over. I used to look at my life as a long tunnel, a hole in the side of a huge mountain that I entered and couldn't see the light on the other end. It felt like it stretched forever. But now I can't see the light behind me. And the rest of the tunnel is very short, I'm afraid."

"Can you see the light ahead?"

"Yes, and I think it's a train." He studied her as if to see any hint of joy or laughter. "When I read that sentence, I saw for an instant what has held me back."

"From what?"

"From living fully. The choices you make when you are younger . . . there is no way to undo them. You can ask forgiveness. You can beg pardon. From others you hurt, from God, even. But there is no way to erase what happened. There is no way to untie the knots of a life. There are so many strings and they're pulled together so tightly." He held up his arthritic hands. "With these, you can't get the threads apart. And you can't distinguish the individual strands with your eyes because you can't focus. Do you understand?"

She nodded. "What is it you would like to erase?"

"Little decisions. A thousand things I said or did. To my children. My wife. My patients. Little decisions always lead to bigger ones, of course. You take a wrong turn on a road and you can quickly head in a direction you shouldn't go. But there aren't many off-ramps to life." He remained in that far-off place, reflecting. Then he returned and ran his tongue over his dentures. "I was talking with Elsie. She said you have memories of your mother. Do you recall this?"

"I recall telling Elsie, yes."

He dipped his head and waited like some wizened prophet.

"My mother was not a nice woman. I became angry with her. Very angry."

"About what?"

"I don't know. It may not have actually happened. It could be a memory I've stolen."

"True. But I think you know the difference between what is real and what is imaginary. What actually happened and what has been appropriated."

"I'm not as sure as you."

"You know you were not left in an ice cream shop. You know that is my story."

Treha remained silent.

"Why do you think you do this?" Crenshaw said. "You co-opt these shared histories. Do they give a structure to your life? A past, a way to become comfortable?"

"If you say so."

"I'm asking about your childhood. What is the real story?"

"Why is it so important?"

He seemed frightened by her stare. It felt like he was trying to open a cellar door on some unimaginable horror in her life that made her numb. She looked out the window at the fluorescent lights of the parking lot.

"I'm not sure," he said. "Perhaps I'm trying to expel the fear so that I can love well."

He smiled and Treha chewed on her thumbnail. She put a foot on the floor and then the other and then brought them both back to the chair.

"I don't remember my parents. I don't think I ever had any."

"How could that be?"

Staring at the floor now, her head swaying, eyes moving, her right hand typing and left thumb in her mouth. She slipped her feet into the open shoes. "I need to go."

"Treha, don't be upset."

"I'm not upset. I need to go."

Crenshaw nodded. "I understand. Treha, what would you say if I told you . . . ?"

"Told me what?" she said.

"What if I told you I need you to mail something for me? An important letter?" He struggled to stand and she told him to stay seated. "It's on the desk. The one addressed to Calvin Davidson. Do you see it?"

She nodded and put the letter in her pocket and walked to the door, shoelaces flapping.

"Will I see you tomorrow?" he said.

She spoke to the door. "Of course."

≈

After she left, Crenshaw reached for the light, pulled the switch, and sat in the dark looking out the window until Treha rode past on her bicycle. He sat in the dark with the truth. He could not remake his life. But he could deal truthfully with it. And he could force others to do the same. He could let the truth do its good work in her life.

Something inside rose, a whisper that said an old man could not make a difference. That no one would believe him. Digging up the past would bring scorn. Doing such a thing showed ingratitude. He shook the voice away and stood, shakily, and walked to his nightstand, pulling the bookmark, a business card that said, *Life Reviews—Devin Hillis, President.*

He sat on his bed and caught his breath as he picked up the phone and dialed. A message said to leave his name and number.

"This is James Crenshaw. I am one of those you spoke with for your documentary. From Desert Gardens. I need your help. I want to enlist your services for something important. A story that needs to be told."

Streams from Desert Gardens
scene 9

Wide shot of Ardeth Williams sitting in wheelchair in her room, plumping her hair.

I don't know what you want me to say.

VOICE OFF CAMERA: **Just tell us your story. When did you come to Desert Gardens?**

Oh, not very long ago. I'd been sick for a time and living with my daughter and her husband. And they thought it best for me to be in a place where . . . They both have jobs and I was at home by myself and couldn't manage.

VOC: **Did you want to live here?**

I can't say for sure. I hadn't thought of it, really. I suppose if you'd asked me, I'd have wanted my independence. But after coming here, that first day, the world opened for me.

VOC: **What do you mean?**

Well, it's hard to explain. I think I had almost given up. And coming here made me want to keep going. It was meeting her that did it. The girl, you know.

VOC: **What girl is that?**

The one who looks like Tiffany, my granddaughter.
I get them mixed up sometimes, there's such a
resemblance. Treha. That's her name. She comes to
see me and I look forward to her visits because . . .
she doesn't expect anything. Most of my life people
have expected things. You, coming here and making
your movie or whatever it is you're doing, I can feel
it. You've come here with a purpose, recording an
old geezer like me. I don't know what it is you want
and I don't pretend to care. That's another thing age
does for you: it makes you not care about what other
people think. My daughter expects me to be the
old me, the mother she remembers. My son-in-law
expects me to kick the bucket before my money
runs out.

But that girl. I think it's the first time I ever felt
like someone didn't *need*. She was just there one
day. Showed up and sat with me. She was patient.
Like it didn't matter how long it took. She was going
to be there.

I don't know that I've ever had that before.

CHAPTER 9

TREHA ARRIVED early the next day, riding her bike in the cool September morning air. The day would heat up and be oppressive by the time she rode home, but not for those in cars with air-conditioning, only for people like her who had to walk or ride a bike or the bus.

She avoided Dr. Crenshaw's room. As soon as she passed the post office near Desert Gardens, she'd remembered the man's letter and that she had forgotten it in the pocket of her other scrubs.

She avoided other residents and cleaned a hallway that had been waxed, arranged rarely touched books in the library, and dusted the dayroom mantel. Late in the morning she tired of the busywork and found Ardeth Williams, the new resident. The woman sat in her wheelchair with the television on and the volume loud enough to obscure low-flying jetliners or passing tornadoes.

Treha turned down the volume and the woman glanced up. "Tiffany. I didn't know you worked here."

Treha didn't correct her. "How are you today, Mrs. Ardeth?"

"I suppose I'm all right, now that you're here."

"Do you need anything?"

She peered closer, leaning forward. "You're not Tiffany."

"My name is Treha."

"Such a nice girl." The old woman looked around for someone else. "You look like my granddaughter."

"Would you like to go for a walk? I think you would like the view of the garden."

Treha released the brake even though the woman told her she didn't want to go outside. She placed Ardeth's hands on the armrests and pushed her slowly toward the hall and then past an attendant's station.

"There goes Mrs. Williams," a nurse said, smiling. "Hey, Mrs. Williams."

Ardeth nodded and waved as if she were the queen of England. Treha looked for Dr. Crenshaw but didn't see him. They made a lap around the south wing and stopped by the window near the garden. Ardeth delighted like a child, patting her hands as she watched the fountain shoot water and saw the colors of the flowers planted in a mosaic.

As Treha returned Ardeth, Mrs. Howard's voice came over the intercom. "Treha, could you come to my office, please?"

A few minutes later, Treha peeked inside and Mrs. Howard smiled and motioned her to sit. There were empty boxes stacked in a corner of the room and several full boxes of books by the shelf.

"I've been meaning to have a little talk before I leave," Mrs. Howard said, crossing her arms. "You know there is a new director. Ms. Millstone."

"Yes. I have seen her."

Mrs. Howard seemed to be searching for the right words. "There may be changes after I leave. I have done things a certain way, but I don't pretend it's the only way. Or the best way. I don't want you to be surprised."

"What kind of changes?"

"The board has given her carte blanche. That means—"

"I know what it means."

"Yes, of course you do."

"It means free reign. She can do what she wants."

"Exactly."

"You think I should be wary of her?"

A look of concern clouded the woman's face. "Treha, I've tried to explain to her how valuable each worker is here. Ms. Millstone may have a slightly different vision. I was thinking, if you could try to put your best foot forward, connect with her, that might be a good start."

"Does she have a problem with her brain?"

Mrs. Howard smiled. "Not the kind of problem you are used to. Let's just say her vision is limited."

"Compared to you."

Mrs. Howard stood and held out a small piece of paper. "I don't want to see you get hurt. Keep this. It's my home number. If anything happens, call me. We can talk it out, work it out."

Treha nodded and took the paper.

"Do you promise you'll call?"

Treha nodded.

Mrs. Howard leaned against the desk. "Treha, I've been trying to understand your gift. Trying to put it into words. And I think what you offer is safety. The residents feel safe talking to you. You listen. You validate."

Treha stared at the floor.

A deep breath. "At some point, you'll need to stop listening, though."

"I don't understand."

"You listen but never tell. Do you think it's because no one is safe enough to speak with?"

Treha looked up, teeth clenched. "There's nothing to tell. I have no story."

"Oh yes you do, my dear. You have a—"

The intercom blared and a breathless voice said, "Mrs. Howard, come quickly. It's Dr. Crenshaw."

Treha followed Mrs. Howard, her mind whirring like a hard drive. *Dead. Deceased. Departed. Lifeless. Gone. Late. Passed away.* This was all she could think. Synonyms. She wanted to give him a riddle or just sit and talk and feel warm inside.

When they reached his room, a group of residents had congregated and Mrs. Howard asked Treha to help them. Treha looked inside as Mrs. Howard entered the room. The man was lying still in his bed with staff around him.

CHAPTER 10

AT A TIME like this, Miriam knew her two greatest allies were procedure and protocol. Everything that happened at Desert Gardens could be broken down to those two components. Fulfill the list of duties assigned and things would go more smoothly. Showing control and composure provided residents with comfort.

Treha stood by the door to Dr. Crenshaw's room like a faithful dog waiting for its master. Miriam's heart ached, but she had to focus. She put a hand to the man's neck and felt a slight pulse. His eyes were fixed on some place on the ceiling, staring at infinity. His left side seemed to be wracked with spasms.

"We called the paramedics," a nurse said.

"Good. Call Chaplain Calhoun as well. Ask him to come immediately."

If she recalled correctly, Dr. Crenshaw had a son who had accompanied him years earlier. They would need to contact him too.

The paramedics arrived and took over, stabilizing Dr. Crenshaw and then lifting him onto a gurney. Miriam stepped into the hallway and put a hand on Treha's shoulder as she stood with the residents watching the scene, too scared to ask questions. The girl's eyes moved but there were no sobs. No contorted face. No tears.

"Treha, these things happen."

"Is he dead?"

"No."

"What's wrong with him?"

"We're not sure. The doctors will help him. It looks like he may have suffered a stroke."

Miriam felt a shudder run through her as Jillian Millstone noiselessly entered the hallway. Her face also showed no emotion.

"There are two men here with camera equipment." Millstone said it almost as an accusation. "They say they were here to talk with Dr. Crenshaw. Do you know about this?"

"That's Devin and Jonah," Miriam said. "I'll speak with them."

Millstone glanced at the residents gathered. "Shouldn't we disperse the crowd?"

She spoke as if they were protesters at an illegal gathering or cattle too close to the killing floor.

"No, this is an important time. They need to know what's happening."

Miriam walked toward the exit and found the two men, Jonah shooting video of Dr. Crenshaw being wheeled to the waiting ambulance. She signaled to Devin that she would be right with him.

She returned to find even more residents spilling into the hallway near Dr. Crenshaw's room. She knew each by name. Some hadn't encountered paramedics yet; they were newer to the facility. Others were long-term and watched the proceedings as if anticipating the next moves of a running back.

She spoke loudly enough for them to hear but with a calm tone, the art of every good administrator. Show authority without being authoritarian. Sound the alarm without alarming.

"Everyone, please give me your attention. I have news about one of our friends."

The people stood or sat like mannequins. This was like a reality show they watched on television except they couldn't adjust the sound.

"Dr. Crenshaw became ill a few moments ago and the paramedics were called. He is in very good hands now."

Miriam noticed Elsie with her wheeled walker, clutching a rolled-up paper towel that she dabbed at her nose.

"Is he dead?" Hemingway shouted from the back of the group.

"No, he has a strong pulse, and if I know Dr. Crenshaw, he will make it through this. He's a fighter, and he's been through many setbacks. I'll call members of his family right away and let them know. Let's keep him in our prayers."

"What do you think happened?" Elsie said.

Miriam placed a hand on her shoulder and spoke softly. "I know how much he means to you."

She nodded.

Miriam spoke again so all could hear. "I'm not sure. He may have had a stroke. We'll just have to wait and see. As you know, getting the person treated quickly after a stroke is important. I don't think we could have acted any quicker, so at this point we must leave things in God's hands."

There were tears in the hall and shaking heads and many far-off stares. A nurse relayed the news that the chaplain was on his way.

"I've asked Chaplain Calhoun to join us," Miriam said. "If

you would like to talk with him or just be in a quiet place, you can move to the chapel. He should be there shortly."

"He's such a dear man," Elsie said, choking on the words. "I was just talking with him at breakfast."

Elsie turned to Henry, half of the Lovebirds, who had wheeled himself down the hall to see the commotion. The man began to speak of deaths he had experienced in the war, in "the big one," as he called it.

Miriam found Devin and Jonah, and both seemed shaken. The two had been shadows around Desert Gardens for months, recording residents, talking with the staff. Devin had first come because of his grandfather and, after the man died, continued his visits and interviews.

Miriam had wondered at first if Devin might be an opportunist, someone who preyed on the elderly, no different from contractors who promised a new roof or a paved driveway and then drove away with the down payment. But that fear was put to rest when he spent an hour in her office explaining his vision, in a seemingly unstoppable, passionate defense of his thesis about the power of stories and the interconnectedness of humanity. She couldn't help catching his excitement. She had given them free rein after seeing some of his student work from the University of Arizona and talking to two of the references on his résumé, who had given glowing reports. And at a meeting with the residents, everyone voted in favor of letting them record their "movie." Now they were recording not just the memories, but the dark side of the work, the loss.

"Did Dr. Crenshaw say why he wanted you to come?"

"He left a message. Said he had something important to say. A story that needed to be told."

"They say timing is everything," Jonah said. "Should I put the equipment away?"

"No," Devin said. "You mentioned the chaplain was on his way. Could we record people's reactions, from a distance? We won't be intrusive. Maybe they want to talk about Dr. Crenshaw. What he means to them. We could use it at his memorial, if it comes to that."

Miriam looked at Jillian Millstone, who was near the office on the phone. She put a hand on Devin's shoulder. "Be discreet."

She turned and saw Treha holding Elsie's hands. The woman wept and Treha simply held on.

"This is going to be hard for the girl, isn't it?" Devin said.

"You mean Treha?"

"Yeah, Dr. Crenshaw mentioned her. Said they spent a lot of time together. I've never spoken with her, though."

"I'm sure it will be hard. But Treha will be a help to the residents. She's quite gifted."

"What do you mean?"

"Perhaps we can talk later. If you'll excuse me."

❧

Devin and Jonah stayed at Desert Gardens for two hours, asking people to tell them about Dr. Crenshaw. When Chaplain Calhoun arrived, they moved their equipment to the chapel and recorded the impromptu service. The man read several portions of Scripture to try to comfort the little flock and then spoke individually with residents.

Devin couldn't help watching Treha. She stayed near Elsie the most, but she was like the flower petals and the old people were the bees. The girl was short and heavy, pear-shaped, with pale skin that was even more pale when compared with her dark scrubs. Her brown hair was pulled back so tightly that it seemed to draw her face upward, accentuating ears that jutted like an elf's. She stared at the floor mostly. Or the walls. And there was a sway to her, a movement of the head and body like the world had become unstable and she was compensating.

She was the type of person you might see in a family photo and never notice. Not because she was hiding, just because she looked lost. An extra in one of life's B movies. That was probably why Devin had never really noticed her before. He had seen her but never *saw* her.

Her tennis shoes remained untied, which was unnerving to him, but as she spoke with the residents in the chapel, Devin asked Jonah for the camera. From across the room he centered on the shoelaces and followed her around the room. Then he focused on her face—the dark eyebrows, the eyes the color of some exotic ocean, sparkling blue-green. Despite the extra weight, she had a square jaw and high cheekbones. No earrings, no studs, no jewelry of any kind.

The more he focused on her, the more uneasy he became, as if he were a voyeur. Something was missing with Treha. Something wasn't quite right. And then it hit him. He hadn't seen one smile. In fact, there was no emotion at all. She took in the grief and solemnity of the crowd, absorbing it, but showed none herself.

A cinder block of a woman walked past the chapel, dark shoes squeaking on shiny tile. She looked out of place, out of her element. Proper and collected as she passed the grieving, she paused and stared at Devin, then quickly walked toward him.

"You're still here," she said.

He wanted to affirm her powers of observation but just nodded, unsure how to answer.

"I was told you were leaving. I think it's time."

He kept his voice low, almost a whisper. "We have an agreement with Mrs. Howard. We won't be much longer."

A scowl that tried to turn itself into a smile. There was something behind it, something powerful he couldn't decipher. "We've had plenty of excitement for one day."

She walked away and Devin lingered in the room, watching Treha, catching some of the conversation around him. Miriam had mentioned that Treha had a gift. The way old eyes came alive around her gave him an idea. And the more he watched, the more convinced he became.

Streams from Desert Gardens
scene 15

Wide shot of Chaplain Calhoun in the empty chapel, hands folded. A cappella voices singing a hymn underneath.

> I don't get paid for this—I wouldn't accept it if they offered. I was pastor of a church nearby for many years and some of the people who live here now were in my congregation. I hold services each week and laugh with them when they have a birthday and cry with them when they lose someone they love. We walk through the pain together, sharing the comfort we've received.

Wide shot of Calhoun with residents, sitting in dining hall.

> Growing older is not much fun. It's the slowing down that gets to you. Elsie calls it "vigor mortis." You just can't do what you used to do, what you worked your entire life for. You try to arrive at some goal of rest or retirement. But contentment is what you crave, and that's a funny thing. Most of us live decades trying to grasp it and we come close, but there's always something in the future, something that spurs us to hope things will be different. That they'll improve. And you miss so much when you're caught in that struggle.

Handheld shots following Calhoun down the hallway, stepping into a room. Voice-over continues.

The people here know the truth. Old age teaches you in a very unkind way that things won't necessarily get better. Not in this life. In fact, you can pretty much count on things degenerating.

Being content is not a lack of ambition. It's being able to rest and relax and know your worth doesn't come from what others think of you or even what *you* think of you.

Tight shot of Calhoun.

I had a friend who had a tumor. It shouldn't have killed him—it was benign. It was where it was located next to his brain that made all the difference. If it hadn't grown, he would still be alive. But it did grow.

The last weekend of his life, the family got together and took him to his favorite place, a cottage in the mountains. They all got in the hot tub and he sat there next to his wife and children. He could barely talk by then, but he whispered to her, "If I die tomorrow, I'll die a happy man."

And he did. The very next day he slipped away.

That's what we're longing for, no matter how old. That moment when we look around and can truly say, "I'm okay with this. No matter what happens, I'm more than okay. I accept it and I embrace it."

That's what I try to help the people here do. And the funny thing is, they've helped me more than I've helped them.

Fade to black.

CHAPTER 11

TREHA RODE HER BICYCLE in the dark, wishing she knew which hospital Dr. Crenshaw was in. She hadn't asked and was sure they wouldn't let her see him if she found him. They only let family members visit people in the hospital. That's what she had heard. She imagined what it would be like, him lying there with tubes and machines hooked to him, and her gently touching him and waking him. Maybe tomorrow she would ask Mrs. Howard.

She wound her way home and pushed her bike up the stairs, into her one-bedroom apartment, and sat, listening to the bugs skitter among dirty dishes. The air-conditioning had stopped working the week before and simply blew tepid air. The only relief at night was to open the front door, which was not a good idea on this street.

She opened the freezer and ran her hand over the ice caking the walls. Like the surface of the moon. There was nothing there but an empty ice cube tray, so she left the door open. Some people ran their oven in the winter to warm themselves, or so she had read, so why couldn't she cool her kitchen like this?

She stuck her head inside, breathing in the frigid air and letting it out to see her breath like in the movies where people walked in the moonlight. Maybe this was what it felt like in a morgue. When the blood stopped, did the skin get this cold?

There wasn't much in the refrigerator. Sliced cheese. A few eggs and wilted kale and flaccid carrots. She wasn't hungry anyway.

The events of the day roiled like thunderheads and her fingers typed on ice and her eyes moved. She could feel it building, something inside.

If she had checked on Dr. Crenshaw earlier instead of just standing around, she might have saved him.

She turned to her unmade bed in the next room, her cover gnarled like a snake. Behind it was the closet with empty hangers, skeletal in appearance, dangling over the full hamper. She needed to change scrubs but none were clean.

She glanced at the corner, the books on the shelf she had assembled herself. There were some from the library, a few she couldn't return because they meant so much, and some she had bought at Goodwill or the thrift store. Books were friends and pages were scenes of lives she would never experience except through paragraphs. Letters and white space that deciphered life. Riddles and romance and mysteries of the heart. She picked one and put it under her arm, then grabbed the hamper. At least the Laundromat was air-conditioned.

Treha jammed her clothes into a mesh bag and put the book inside, then pulled the drawstring tight and slung it over her shoulder. She closed the freezer and rummaged in a kitchen drawer for spare change, coming up with enough quarters for the washer and dryer. She hoped.

The laundry was awkward, so she left her bike. She locked the door and carried the sack to the decaying stairs. Concrete that was new in the 1980s was now cracked and brittle.

Halfway down the steps, she heard the familiar click and pop of gum in a child's mouth and caught the aroma of lemon as strong as furniture polish. Lightning Lemonade. Bubblicious mixed with the heat of the evening, and she stopped, wondering if she might avoid him.

"Is that you, Miss Treha?" came the voice. High-pitched but tinged with oncoming hormones.

Treha descended and peered between the stairs, yellow light bleeding through and marsupial eyes watching her. She took a deep breath.

"Going to the Laundromat?" the boy said.

"How did you guess?"

The boy laughed and bounced into the light, hands and arms hanging on everything he could touch, leaning and twisting in the night.

"You're funny," the boy said. "I knowed you was going to the Laundromat as soon as I heard you come out. Sure came home late tonight."

He pulled a high-intensity flashlight from a pocket and nearly blinded her when he clicked it on.

"Turn that off. Where did you get that?"

He nodded across the street. "Liquor store." It came out "licka stow."

"And where did you get the money, Gavroche?"

He pointed it at the ground and turned it off, his face fully in the yellow streetlight. Ten years old. Maybe eleven. Round head, the size of a basketball. Hershey-colored skin. Short hair, down to the very nub of the scalp, and teeth so white they flashed like a beacon. He wasn't from Arizona; she knew that. He talked with anyone who would pay attention and it was clear he was too trusting.

"My name ain't Gavroche. Why do you call me that?"

She didn't answer.

"You shouldn't come out here without a flashlight, Miss Treha. You never know what's gonna be crawling around in the desert—that's what my daddy said. It's almost October, but critters are still out."

"This is the city."

"Just because there's concrete don't mean things can't crawl. I heard snakes like to lay on the slabs at night to get warm. I'll go with you."

"Stay here and wait for your mother."

"She don't get off till eleven. Plus, my daddy said you should never let a lady go out alone after dark. If he was here, he'd walk you to the Laundromat. I know he would."

Treha kept walking, hoping the indifference would discourage him.

"My name's not Gavroche; it's Du'Relle. You know that, Miss Treha. Why you call me that?" He had the flashlight on and was moving it back and forth in front of them on the sidewalk, jiggling it so much it made her head hurt.

"Because you remind me of him."

"He somebody you know?"

"No, he's a character in a book."

"Oh, I get it. The book in the laundry bag?"

"No, from another book. You wouldn't know it."

"Try me. I mighta read it. My mama reads to me at night sometimes late after she gets home. If I can stay awake."

"Trust me, you wouldn't know the book."

"Well, what's he like? Is he handsome? Does he turn into a superhero?"

"It's not that kind of story."

"That's what I want to be when I grow up. Captain America. But not the Hulk. I mean, I'd be okay with smashing stuff, but

I don't think I'd want to split my pants every time I had to save the world. I don't see how he keeps his pants on if he grows that big, do you? Your underwear probably wouldn't come off because there's elastic in it, but I guess you can't show superheroes in their underwear in a comic book or parents will boycott it."

They were silent for half a block, Du'Relle smacking the gum. Finally he said, "What kind of story is it?"

"What do you mean?"

"The one with Gavroche. Is it the kind where there's animals? Because my teacher read one to us last year about this boy and he saved up his money for a long time and sent it off and there were these two dogs that came on a train he taught to chase rabbits and coons and it was a sad ending—I won't spoil it, but I just about bawled my eyes out."

"*Where the Red Fern Grows.*"

"That's it! You read it? Man, that was the saddest book I ever heard. But it felt kinda good at the same time, you know? Like you was hunting all night with the boy in the story or sleeping in the woods. I guess you have to wade through the sad parts to see what happens, but I swear if I woulda wrote that, I'd have stopped before . . . you know, the blood and guts."

He walked with his arms out like he was flying a plane through the crosswalk.

"I wonder if those dogs went to heaven. Do you think animals go to heaven?"

"I don't know."

"Well, I know you don't *know* because who can know something like that for sure? I'm asking you what you think."

"I told you, I don't know."

"You can guess. Like a baseball game. Who's going to win the World Series? You have to guess. That's half the fun, don't you think? And then finding out the answer and whether or not you was right."

"Questions that don't have an answer aren't worth asking."

"Really? So how do you know that?"

She didn't answer.

"Okay then, what about people? Do people go to heaven when they die?"

She stopped and turned. "Can we talk about something else?"

He stared at her as if trying to read the words that hung in the air. "Sure, I'll talk about whatever you want. How about that story with the fellow you get me mixed up with? What was his name again?"

"Gavroche."

"Yeah, Gavroche. Is that a sad story?"

She walked a few more steps before she answered. "I'm not in the mood to talk tonight, Du'Relle."

"Something bad happen at the old folks' home? Did somebody die? No wonder you don't want to talk about heaven."

"My friend Dr. Crenshaw was taken to the hospital."

"He's like your best friend there, isn't he?"

She nodded.

"That's too bad. Sometimes old people get sick and hang on and on, like my grandmamma—she was in her eighties and had the 'beaties, and they'd take her to the hospital in an ambulance and then she'd come home and go back. That was when we lived in North Carolina, before we moved here. She had to have her foot cut off and then she up and died."

The Laundromat was ahead in a strip mall flanked by a secondhand furniture store and a Walgreens. The light from the Laundromat bathed the parking lot, and moths flew in formation, covering the windows. Every time the door opened, a swarm flew inside.

"You're going to miss that old man, aren't you, Miss Treha?"

She stopped. His eyes were as big as saucers. Pleading for something she couldn't give. Something she didn't have herself.

"He's not gone yet."

"Right. Well, I can talk to you about stuff if you want."

Only he didn't say *stuff*; he said another word. "Don't use that kind of language."

"Sorry, Miss Treha; I didn't mean to cuss. I just thought maybe I could give you some of the riddles like he did. I remember you told me about him playing games with you and s—" He stopped himself. "And stuff like that."

They walked across the parking lot.

"I got one. The letters is *S-G-U-R-D*."

"You can't just spell it backward; it has to be mixed up. Spelling it backward makes it too easy."

Treha grabbed her book and turned the bag upside down into the first empty washing machine. She liked to be at the front, where she could see everything, especially this time of night. Three women folded clothes at tables around the room. A disheveled man with a Diamondbacks hat and red shorts read a newspaper next to the Coke machine by the restrooms.

The boy watched her dump the clothes. "Aren't you going to put any soap in? It won't get clean unless you use soap. That's what my mama says."

"I can't—the soap hurts."

"That's the first time I ever heard of soap hurting a person. What does it do to you?"

"Rashes. Bumps on the skin. And it itches."

She put the quarters in the slots and water sprayed. Just as she started to close the lid, she saw a piece of paper sticking out of a pocket and remembered Dr. Crenshaw's letter. She grabbed the wet envelope and put it on the table to dry, then found a plastic chair and sat with her book.

"What's that?"

"A letter I forgot to mail."

Du'Relle ambled back to the vending machines and explored the circumference of the room before returning and pulling himself up on the table. He swung his legs, black matchsticks. He wore no socks, just dirty tennis shoes with the emblem of some animal whose ears and face had worn off long ago. There was a hole at the end of the right shoe, where his big toe stuck through. The shoelaces were a broken, distant memory.

"People say when you get older, you're supposed to get closer to God, you know? Because you have less time to live, I guess. I don't think you get close to God just because you get old. That's like saying everybody who's a kid has fun all the time. That ain't true. They's plenty of old people meaner than snakes. And they's teenagers who want to know about God. Those folks that come by and take me to church in they little bus—that fellow who drives it ain't much older than you and he does it. So thinking about God doesn't have anything to do with your age, that's what I think."

"I didn't know you went to church."

"Yeah, every Sunday the little bus comes. Mama works Sundays, so I go by myself. And then Wednesday nights they have this thing where you memorize Bible verses and play games and . . . stuff. The people are nice and they usually have cookies . . ."

He stopped midsentence and glanced behind him. Treha followed his gaze out the window and saw three hooded figures.

"Huh-oh, this don't look good." Du'Relle jumped down

from the table. "We should get out of here and come back when your clothes are done."

She patted the plastic chair beside her. "Sit."

"Miss Treha, you don't understand. These guys are—"

She focused on him like a laser and clenched her teeth. "Sit."

The boys entered the Laundromat and something else came with them. A presence? A feeling? Treha stared at her book, cross-legged in the chair, and Du'Relle stared at the floor.

The three were loud, laughing and snickering. The leader was the shortest of the three, squat and built like a bowling ball with his pants sagging. Her peripheral vision caught his glance and then the man looked at the other women. Then came cursing and more laughter as they walked toward the restroom. The man with the newspaper held it higher, blocking his view.

The three entered the restroom, but one exited again, skinny, with cornrows in his hair and his hands under his armpits. Waiting his turn like a hanging bag of bones, with the shifting eyes and feet that showed a child with a full bladder. Scared and trying to act tough and hardened when he simply had to go to the bathroom.

Bowling Ball exited along with the other, who kept his hoodie pulled tight. Cornrows quickly disappeared into the bathroom.

Bowling Ball walked to the front and stopped near Treha. "Hey, little lady. I've seen you before. You live around here?"

Treha didn't speak, didn't look up.

"That can't be your kid; he doesn't look a thing like you. You babysitting?"

"Looks like she's not gonna answer you, dawg," Hoodie said.

"Aw, she's just a scared white girl. Judging us by appearance. Ain't that right, big girl?"

The Laundromat was eerily silent except for the *sludge-sludge* of water in washers and the tick and rattle of dryers.

Bowling Ball grabbed the book from Treha. She didn't react, just kept her head down.

Du'Relle jumped. "Give it back!"

Treha calmly, evenly took Du'Relle by the arm and guided him back to the seat. "Sit."

"You leave her book alone, creep!" Du'Relle said, spit flying, fire in his eyes. Thin muscles tensing.

"Calm down, little man," Bowling Ball said. "All I'm looking for is a little respect."

Hoodie cursed. "She's as fat as you are, dawg. What you been eating, girl? Everything?"

"And why you move your head like that?" Bowling Ball said. He looked at Hoodie. "You see that? It's like watching a tennis match, back and forth, back and forth."

Cornrows came out of the bathroom and slowed as he approached. "What's going on?"

Bowling Ball looked at the book cover, then back at Treha. "You a college girl? Or you just trying to act smart?"

She didn't move, except for the regular motion. "You don't get respect by imposing your will. Respect is earned."

The three moved back an imperceptible distance, visibly shocked at the voice, at the resolve.

"You wouldn't be saying that if you knew who you were talking to," Cornrows whined.

Bowling Ball edged closer and made a gun with his hand, thumb up, index and middle fingers together, and put them against her temple. "I can put a cap in your skull right now and walk away and never think twice. You understand me?"

"Hey!" the man in the red shorts yelled. He stood, the paper dangling by his side. "Get on out of here. Give her the book and get out."

The women kept folding, heads down.

Bowling Ball cocked his head sideways like he couldn't believe what he was hearing. He took a step toward the man. "You telling me what to do?" He pulled the sweatshirt up, revealing the butt of a gun.

"We're asking you nicely. Just leave. Let us do our laundry. Let her read her book."

"Man, these people need to be taught a lesson," Hoodie said.

Treha closed her eyes. Something stirred inside, the old feelings, the old increase in heart rate she had managed to keep reined in. She spoke again, and the words were the release. "You act like you don't care that your pants are dragging on the ground, but you do care. You want to look tough." She glanced above them and their eyes followed. "When the police watch the surveillance video from the camera, they'll see that you've violated your parole. And they'll come looking for you."

Bowling Ball leaned close, his voice like gravel. "You have no idea what I can do to you." He slammed the book into her chest. "Take your eyes back, Jane."

He glanced at the table and saw the wet letter. Treha lunged for it as he grabbed it. The letter tore in half as she ripped it from his hands.

"Fat and stupid," Bowling Ball muttered.

The others laughed as they walked out of the laundry and into the night.

It was nearly eleven when Treha and Du'Relle walked home, the clothes still damp and stuffed into the mesh bag. Du'Relle trained the flashlight in a circle, hitting the pavement as well as the buildings.

"How you know about guys like that?"

"I read a lot."

"How'd you know the big guy had been to prison?"

"I didn't. I guessed. If he hasn't been to prison, he's heard stories and doesn't want to go, in spite of his bravado."

"His what?"

"Bravado. It means false courage. He was sure of himself because he had a gun."

"You like to take chances, don't you?"

"No, I don't. But I don't like bullies. Especially when the person being bullied is me."

"Well, next time let me handle it."

They walked through the moonlight and the jiggling high-intensity flashlight. Du'Relle was quiet, deep in thought. Finally he spoke.

"Why did he call you Jane and say that about your eyes?"

"He saw the title of my book. He thought it said *eyes* on the front, but it doesn't."

"What's it called?"

"*Jane Eyre*. It's a novel."

"What's it about?"

"A woman named Jane Eyre."

He shrugged. "She go to the Laundromat a lot?"

Treha sighed. "It's about a girl who is orphaned and falls in love with a man who is married, and she won't compromise."

He rolled the words around and she saw his lips moving, saying, *"Compromise."*

"What's that mean?" he said.

"Compromise is when you know something is wrong but you do it anyway. And you make yourself think it's okay."

Du'Relle nodded. "So you like that book?"

"It's my favorite."

They walked farther. When they came within sight of the apartment, Du'Relle said, "How can you read if your eyes move like that?"

"You can do whatever you want if you want to badly enough."

"Is that why you don't go to college? Because you didn't want to go bad enough?"

They crossed the street.

"You ask too many questions."

"I'm not trying to."

"Let me ask you a few."

"Okay."

"When is your father coming home?"

Du'Relle hesitated and the flashlight went off. The string from the bag cut off Treha's circulation, so she shifted the clothes to the other shoulder.

"Mama doesn't talk about it. I think they're having problems."

"You think they're getting a divorce?"

"Maybe. I don't know. I hope not. He's all the way over in 'ghanistan and they talk on the computer sometimes."

He moved into the shadows as they came to the stairs and the fractured concrete that led to her apartment. Du'Relle leaned against the railing as if his tour of duty was complete.

"You were brave back there," he said. "Standing up to those guys. You didn't look scared."

"That's because I wasn't."

"How could you not be scared? I was ready to pee my pants."

A car pulled into the parking lot, one headlight out and the other so cloudy the light was a muted brown. The engine knocked and pinged and sputtered after Du'Relle's mother turned off the ignition.

"Good night," Treha said. "Thank you for walking with me."

"Good night, Miss Treha," the boy said. He flipped on the flashlight and ran to the car, arms swinging. When he reached it, he opened the door and hung on to it until his mother climbed out.

Inside, Treha stared through the plastic window blinds that were always slightly askew. There were voices in the night, the sounds of late-night television programs and laughter. They passed through the walls and vents and down corridors. Passing sirens and car alarms.

She watched and listened, then reached into her pocket and pulled out the letter. She would never have opened it. It was a crime to open other people's mail. It pained her to think she had let Dr. Crenshaw down and hadn't mailed it like she said.

She turned on the light and pulled the ripped page from the envelope.

Piecing the thick paper together, she studied the man's "doctor's scrawl," as he called it. The words were tiny and slanted upward on the unlined page. Some were smudged by the water and others were almost illegible because of the shake of the man's hand, but after a few moments she relaxed and followed the scribbling.

Dear Calvin,

It has been many years, but I know you'll remember me and our working relationship. I now live in Tucson, at a retirement home where they do everything but think for me. Unfortunately, thinking is all I do these days. I can't seem to find release from the deeds of my past. I don't say this as an accusation or to cast aspersion. I'm sure you have a perspective on the situation now that we can both look back on it.

The lawsuit has added to my thinking on this, of course. I've read about the legal action and the prog-ress in the case against the company. I believe my information might help the plaintiffs. I know it would damage Phutura.

My intent is not to blame or stir up trouble. I'm simply wondering if you have similar misgivings. I've come to the point in my life where I can see more clearly. I suppose age will do that. It would be easier to forget, move on, and put all that behind. But the truth has a way of hang-ing on to you. I've experienced a change deep in my soul. I'm no longer concerned about ramifications. I want to make things right.

There is one other reason for contacting you—a young lady I've found. You will remember the test case that was abandoned. This girl is remarkable but impaired. I believe we are culpable. I will explain further if you call me. Perhaps we could talk. My contact information is at the bottom of this letter.

I hope this reaches you and that you are well.

Sincerely,
James Crenshaw, MD

Treha let her eyes rest, as much as they could, on the sen-tence that said, *a young lady I've found.* Could he be talking about her? Was she the "impaired" person he described?

She studied the letter as if it were a word puzzle. Did he know something about her life that she didn't? If so, how? And if he died or was in a coma, how would she ever get the infor-mation from him? He was leaving a riddle, a life jumble, and she couldn't decipher it.

Streams from Desert Gardens
scene 12

Wide shot of Miriam Howard's office.

Miriam rummaging through books, putting them in boxes.

Close-up of nursing textbooks.

Close-up of Miriam's hands.

Some people talk about hating going to work. I feel sorry for those people because I've never felt that way, at least not here. I get to speak into the lives of some amazing people, courageous men and women who choose this as their final address.

The people who come here are like family. It's a very spiritual place. A caring place. I brought my own mother here when she couldn't take care of herself, although it was an arduous process to get her to consider it. She put up a real fight after my father died, but it was the last fall she had that helped her see: She wasn't safe. She couldn't do it anymore.

So she came here and made friends, much to her surprise. And she thrived and was a real part of the community in those last few years.

Wide shot of Miriam pulling into the parking lot, getting out, walking to the front door.

There's a flutter in your heart when you know you're going to see someone you love. And each morning as I drove up, I could see her through the window of the front room. Just sitting there waiting, reading the morning paper. I would pour us both a cup of coffee and we'd sit together and talk about the news and whatever was on her mind. Most of the time it was memories she had of my father or some concern she had about her finances. How she was going to pay the bill for the lights we kept on in the hall. She'd ask me that every day: when was she going to get the bill for those lights we kept on all day?

Toward the end, her mind wandered and she couldn't hold those thoughts. She would repeat herself time and again. The same stories. The same memories. The same questions.

Still photo of Miriam and her mother.

Watching someone grow older teaches you things about yourself. Things you don't anticipate learning. Things you never wanted to learn. Like how to be patient with the woman who diapered you, how to answer her questions ten times in the same sitting without getting huffy.

I remember the day she took a turn. I didn't see her when I drove up, and she wasn't in her usual place. I walked to her room and found her sitting on the bed, staring out the window, without a stitch of clothes on. She was in some other place.

I used to wonder what it would have been like if both my father and mother had been here. I like to think they would have been a lot like the Lovebirds.

Shot of Lovebirds kissing in the dining hall.

It's not easy to say good-bye to family. It's not
easy turning the page on your life. There's real fear
about . . . the routine. How it will change. What that
will be like.

CHAPTER 12

Miriam awakened at the first sign of sunlight through the bedroom window and lay still next to her husband, Charlie. It was a dog's name. Or an uncle's, maybe. And that was exactly what he had become—an old dog, a ubiquitous uncle with a perpetually empty stomach. It had crossed her mind more than once that it would be to her advantage if she were to put him to sleep, just like an old dog, but the authorities didn't look kindly on euthanizing a spouse and she probably would miss him. She needed someone to bring in the salt for the water softener.

They had moved from the north side of the city shortly after his retirement from Raytheon. Both had wanted to be closer to the country and have a little more privacy. They agreed on this but not much else.

Miriam made a mental list of what she needed to do before she left for the day, then a mental list of what Charlie would do. She would make the coffee and shower and get ready. He would awaken and pour the first cup and turn on Bloomberg in the kitchen to watch the futures crawl across the bottom of the screen. Other men watched football or NASCAR or were glued to the University of Arizona sports schedule. This time of year was high and holy because of college football and the end of the baseball season. Other men followed batting averages and box scores. Charlie's passion was the stock market, and he seemed to get a little depressed on the weekends or holidays when the market was closed. After the opening bell, as he sat studying his portfolio and opening e-mails from subscription services that told him what was going on behind the scenes and how he could take advantage of rising or falling gold or oil futures, he would turn on his conservative talk radio. She wasn't sure which was worse: the mind-numbing cacophony of the stock market or the shrill, cutting voice of Rush Limbaugh. Charlie loved him, had even called in and spoken with him after the shooting in Tucson. Then it was Hannity, and the afternoon ended with a re-air of Glenn Beck. The conservative trinity.

She watched the rising and falling of his chest and listened to his slightly clogged nasal passages. What would life look like when she was home all day? He would retreat into his office, the third bedroom at the back of the house, and probably stay there. They would find some kind of rhythm; she was sure of that. They always had. There was a chance they would grow closer, that their relationship would deepen, but there was also a chance it would snow in September.

Miriam turned her head, scanning the nightstand and the half-finished mystery novel she was working through. It was a diversion that kept her mind from focusing on things she couldn't change and might not want to.

Years ago she'd had a sit-down with Charlie, a confrontation. She told him this was not what she had signed up for, that marriage was meant to be more than what they had become. To her delight, Charlie had responded, had actually moved toward her. It was easy to accuse him of going through the motions, of just changing for selfish reasons, but the truth was, his movement had forced her to respond, had forced her to look at herself. She thought of herself as the catalyst for good in their marriage. But his response had shown her own issues, her own retreat. She knew he liked her to do little things, like make him a sandwich. She had stopped that, mainly because she didn't want to be his mother. Let him get his own food.

So she feigned contentment and they carried on with their lives, their careers, their home empty, void of children and any measured love. They were faithful to each other, and to outsiders, their relationship looked fine—close, even.

As she lay in bed, something in her heart stirred, but it was not hope. It was more a crushing reality pressing down. A feeling that as she looked at the mountain of happiness and contentment above them, this was as high as they would climb. She wished she had convinced him they should have children. They could have adopted. She would have been such a good mother.

Such old, useless, dried-up feelings, she thought.

More tired than when she fell into bed the night before, Miriam gained momentum and rolled her feet to the floor, trying not to disturb him, and made coffee, showered, and dressed. She would get something to eat at the hospital as she checked on Dr. Crenshaw.

As she was leaving, Charlie hobbled from the bedroom with his EIB baseball hat pulled low, the wrinkled khaki shorts he always wore hanging to his pasty-white knees. Black socks halfway up his calves and moccasins worn through. He did not have an ounce of pride about his clothes. She loved and loathed his self-confidence, his ability not to care what others thought, the way he had settled into himself.

He poured a cup of coffee. "You were late last night."

She nodded. "I'm heading to TMC."

"Somebody sick?"

She told him about Dr. Crenshaw. Charlie had fallen asleep before she had come home the night before. As she spoke, his eyes glazed while a reporter gave the latest unemployment numbers. He raised his mug again and drank, then told her to drive carefully.

"Will you be there this afternoon?" she said.

His face betrayed him. He hadn't remembered. A milestone in her life and it wasn't even on his radar.

"It's fine," she said. "There's no pressure."

"Oh, I wouldn't miss your big send-off. I'll be there. What time is the party?"

She told him, though it grated on her that she had to remind him. She had to remind him of everything. Names. Dates. Bills due that he forgot. She had given up on her birthday and their anniversary, and it was hit or miss whether he would expend the energy to get her something, whether he would look at the calendar and remember. He'd always been this way. Something about that side of his brain. He'd been a brilliant engineer, a meticulously scrupulous worker who could cross every t and dot every i, but he couldn't remember her birthday.

He took another sip of coffee. "Maybe we could go out to eat afterward. To celebrate. Sizemore's?"

Sizemore's was a buffet-style family diner that sat next to a Dress Barn in a strip mall. All you could eat. Miriam hated it. She hated the fried food, the tables and booths, the clientele, the aroma. But Charlie loved the senior discount and the variety. Fish or steak and all the mashed potatoes he could eat. Just once she wanted to go somewhere nice. She wanted to be whisked off her feet and taken to a restaurant with white tablecloths and well-dressed waiters instead of being part of a herd waiting for another slab of ribs.

"That would be nice," she said.

Miriam navigated the parking garage at Tucson Medical Center near the university and walked toward the horseshoe driveway. It was early, but the heat of the day rose as the sun spread shadows from the Rincon Mountains in the distance. Exhausted hospital workers passed her on their way home or to get their kids off to school. The end and the beginning right here in front of her.

As she neared the revolving door, she noticed someone sitting cross-legged on the pavement, arms around knees, a bicycle chained to a bench behind her. The woman's head swayed.

"Treha?"

She turned and shielded her eyes from the sun. Sheer bewilderment on her face.

"Treha, what are you doing here?"

The girl stood. "I came to see Dr. Crenshaw but they said I couldn't go in because I'm not related."

Miriam hugged her, but Treha stood with limp arms. "Come with me."

They walked to the front desk, where Miriam presented her identification and asked for two visitor passes. The older woman at the front scrolled through a screen to find the room of James Crenshaw, and when she hesitated, Miriam's stomach clenched.

"When I left him last night, he was in ICU—I assume he's still there."

"Oh, I see him." The woman handed over the badges, and Miriam gave a sigh of relief, leading Treha to the elevator.

"That's quite a bike ride for you all this way, isn't it?"

"It's not that far."

Miriam had a vague idea of where Treha lived, a hazy concept of the apartment and neighborhood and the dangerous traffic she navigated with each dark ride home. They rode up to the ICU and Miriam talked with the head nurse while Treha stared through the observation window at a row of beds and curtains. There were other rooms near the nurses' station and Miriam assumed Dr. Crenshaw was in one of them.

"We've seen no signs of improvement since last night," the nurse said. "The doctor scheduled tests later, but only if he's up to it."

Miriam told the nurse they hadn't made contact with the family but that she had been approved to make decisions in lieu of next of kin. She handed the paperwork to the woman.

"Who is she?" the nurse said, looking at Treha.

"A friend of Dr. Crenshaw. She works with us at Desert Gardens."

"Is she . . . ?" Her voice trailed as she searched for the word.

"She's like a daughter to him. I know he would love to see her."

"He's shown no reaction. No response at all. I don't think it would be . . ." The nurse made eye contact and saw the look on Miriam's face. "All right. If you think it would help, you can go in."

Miriam took Treha by the arm. "Would you like to see him?"

Treha's face showed surprise and perhaps a little hope. It was the most emotion she had seen from the girl.

The nurse led them down the hall to the room, and Treha stared at the lifeless body with the tubes and monitors. A ventilator hooked to a large plastic tube made his chest rise and fall.

Treha looked at Miriam, her eyes moving, her body swaying.

"You can touch him. Talk with him, if you'd like. See if you can make a connection."

Treha gingerly walked to the bed and put a hand on the man's arm. She touched his hand and squeezed it, but there was no response. She bent over him and spoke his name, rubbing his shoulder, struggling to get around the wires.

Miriam watched Treha's face. Her lips moved but Miriam couldn't hear the words. The girl's face inched closer, straining, trying to break through. Miriam watched for any sign of change—a more rapid heartbeat or a difference in the breathing, fluttering eyelids or some hand or foot movement. There was nothing.

Finally Treha turned from Dr. Crenshaw and said pitifully, "He's not there."

Miriam tried to smile and put a hand on Treha's shoulder. "I'm sure he can hear you. You simply can't see his response."

Treha looked back at him. "He gave me a letter to mail. I forgot about it."

"Don't be too hard on yourself about a letter."

"I let him down."

"Do you still have it?"

She nodded.

"We can just mail it today. There's no harm in that."

Miriam put an arm around her and led her out of the room. She spoke briefly with the nurse, giving her a card with her contact information and asking her to call with any change in the man's condition. Treha paused at the nurses' station and looked back at the room as if she had forgotten to do one last thing, make one last try.

In the elevator, Miriam told Treha to wait at the front and

she would give her a ride to Desert Gardens. Miriam navigated the tight garage and got in line in the horseshoe, waiting for a van to unload a disabled passenger. She put her emergency flashers on and parked in front of Treha, but when she hit the button for the back hatch, she noticed something was wrong.

"Treha, where's your bicycle?"

Treha's voice was soft, her eyes vacant. "It's not here." She held up the clipped chain.

"Maybe the security guard moved it."

Miriam spoke with the man, who said he hadn't touched the bike and that it wasn't supposed to be there in the first place. She tried to keep her composure, tried to shove down the anger and outrage, and made her way back to Treha.

"I wasn't sure we could get that bike in the back anyway," Miriam said. "Come on; we'll file a police report later."

Treha shook her head. "They don't care about bicycles." No emotion, simply fact. "I should have been more careful."

"It's not your fault how the world is. You locked the bike; you did everything you could. Some people don't have an ounce of decency."

Miriam thought of stopping at a thrift store near Desert Gardens and finding another bike, then thought better of it. She wanted to rescue, help the girl find her way, do something for her, when that might not actually help Treha. She pushed the urge aside.

"Tell me about the letter," Miriam said. "It really bothered you, didn't it?"

Treha nodded.

"There's a post office up ahead. Do you have it with you? We'll drop it in the slot."

Treha pulled a torn page and envelope from her pocket. "A man at the Laundromat ripped it last night."

"Are you worried that Dr. Crenshaw will be upset?"

Treha looked at the street ahead. "I read it."

"And you think he'll sue you?" Miriam said it with a smile, but Treha didn't react.

"I think he was writing about me," she said. "I wanted to ask him. I have to find out what he meant."

Miriam pulled into the parking lot at Desert Gardens and took the letter from the girl. She read it, then studied the address on the envelope.

"What does it mean?" Treha said. "Do you know what Phutura is?"

"It's a major pharmaceutical company." Miriam folded the letter and tucked it into her purse. "It's clear Dr. Crenshaw was upset about something, something this Mr. Davidson will know about. I'm sure there's an explanation."

"What does he mean about the lawsuit?"

"I'm not sure. There are lawsuits filed all the time. You know how he kept up with the daily news—nothing got past him."

"Do you think he is talking about me at the end?"

Miriam turned in the seat. "Treha, Dr. Crenshaw cares a great deal about you. We'll find out what this means. Let's take it a step at a time."

Streams from Desert Gardens
scene 3

Music up.

Fade in from black to sign of Desert Gardens, Catalina Mountains in background.

Switch to unstable camera shot panning from security guard window through entrance, showing reception area.

Cut to hallway shot.

Cut to dining hall and people seated/talking.

Music swells, then goes under voice-over by Elsie Pratt.

> I came here—what was it? Twenty-five years ago now. It's the most beautiful place in the country, as far as I'm concerned, and I've been a few places. My husband said something about Tucson being a good place to retire, and my first reaction was "It's too hot. It's too close to the Mexican border. Too many cowboys. I don't want to live in the desert." I had all these excuses.

Still shot of Elsie and Harold wedding photo.

> So he let it go and then I saw this brochure on the kitchen table one day. It looked like the most

beautiful place in the world with mountains all around and lemon trees and soaring palm trees.

Cut to Elsie speaking/gesturing.

I said, "Harold, what's this?" And he said, "It's a brochure." And I said, "I know it's a brochure, but where is this place?" Do you know what? He had put that brochure where I could see it but he didn't say a word about it because he knew moving to a place like this would have to be my idea. So that's what he did. He let it be my idea. Just waited for me. Isn't that something?

Fade to black.

CHAPTER 13

ELSIE PRATT sat at the empty table, her food untouched, watching the parking lot for Miriam. No one had said anything about Dr. Crenshaw. The workers Elsie questioned shook their heads. If anyone would know, it was Miriam. She cared.

Elsie hadn't slept well and couldn't get the memory of the emergency workers wheeling her friend away out of her mind. She couldn't bear to think of them ending this way.

Perpetually jovial, outgoing, loquacious even, Elsie had fallen into the abyss of silence. She kept the television off in her room, unable to endure the noise and laughter and commercials. She couldn't even bring herself to turn on the local Christian radio station. At breakfast she stared out the window at birds flitting from branches of a lemon tree, heat radiating from the east-facing window. She took her Bible with her each morning, but today it lay closed before her, next to the cold oatmeal.

When she saw Miriam pull into the parking lot, she hurried, as much as a woman of her age could, to the lobby.

"Aren't you going to eat anything, Elsie?" one of the workers said as she passed.

Elsie waved the Bible at her. "Not hungry today."

She waited until Miriam walked inside, followed by Treha in

wrinkled scrubs. Miriam kept moving toward the office. Treha, however, came to Elsie, calm and subdued.

"Have you heard anything of Dr. Crenshaw?" Elsie said.

"I saw him in the hospital. He didn't respond."

Elsie looked at her hands, wrinkled and worn, knuckles swollen and fingers pointing in directions they weren't designed to go. She felt the ravages of age in every inch of her body. "What do the doctors say? Was it a stroke?"

"I heard something about tests. He's in intensive care."

Tears came to Elsie's eyes and she thought they were as much for Treha as Dr. Crenshaw. The girl would be just as affected by his death but would never show it. And then the tears flowed, like a stream leaking through her mind. The waters had backed up with debris and now they came with force over her, an emotional tide.

"He was so taken with you," Elsie choked.

Treha watched, coaxing her, willing the overflow.

"I didn't expect it. I think that's what's killing me. With others, you know it's coming. You treasure every moment. Then people get sick and go downhill and don't make it back from a fall or a long illness. A life deteriorates and comes to a slow end. But it was so fast with Jim. I didn't get to say good-bye."

Elsie shook with emotion, and Treha leaned forward and clasped her hands, not too tightly, just enough. A warmth spread through the old woman.

"There are so many changes," she continued. "And old fogies like me don't do very well with change."

"You don't know what will happen. And you're not an old fogy. Whatever that means."

"You know what it means. You probably know the etymology of it."

Treha stared. She did, Elsie could tell.

"It describes everybody in here," Elsie said. "Everybody whose life is not their own because they have to depend on others. I can't make my own breakfast. I can't have hot coffee because I might burn myself. My food is tepid. The oatmeal is cold. I take medicine that's given to me to make me go to the bathroom and medicine to stop me from going to the bathroom. I take medicine to regulate my blood pressure and other pills to regulate other medicine."

"But you are a fighter. You are a survivor."

"Longevity is not a fruit of the Spirit. I don't want to survive; I want to live. I want to stop feeling like a baby someone has to care for." She waved a hand. "How can I make someone so young understand?"

Treha's eyes shifted and she stepped back.

Elsie looked away. "Listen to me, all wrapped up in myself. That's where the grief leads you, back to yourself and your problems. There's a whole lot more suffering out in the world than the temperature of my coffee and oatmeal, isn't there?"

"I don't blame you. Tepid coffee is the worst. Maybe you should put ice in it."

"Would that it would be hot or cold," Elsie said, chuckling. A bright girl in a dim package. Jim had tried to loosen her with his games and riddles. He had tried to pull her out, to bring her into the open like she was able to do with others. Treha's gift was to help flowers bloom, to free chained minds. But the girl herself remained closed tight like a desert rose in the winter.

"He always believed you were special," Elsie said. "When he talked about you, his eyes lit up like Christmas."

"Dr. Crenshaw?"

She nodded. "He knew a lot about people. How to treat each patient with dignity. You knew he was an ob-gyn?"

"He never talked about his career. At least not with me."

"He worked with pregnant women. How many babies that man delivered, God only knows. He was a real success. You wouldn't know that from seeing him here. I'm not saying anything negative about this place—but I think his family wanted rid of him."

"I miss his word games."

Elsie smiled. "He loved to find new ways to challenge you. It challenged him as well. He said you were so fast that it was incredible to watch, the way your mind worked. He said he could see your neural pathway opening up. There was something about you he had never seen. He thought your linguistic power would one day help you conquer the world."

Treha looked away as Elsie continued.

"He said you could do anything you wanted. You could be more than what you are here. Perhaps a writer. Did you know he thought that about you, Treha?"

"I'm going to miss Mrs. Howard."

"Yes, today's her last day, isn't it?" Elsie said. "But you're not listening to me. Jim—Dr. Crenshaw—he told me that you have great potential. You have the ability to become—"

"He sent a letter before he became ill."

"A letter? To you?"

Treha shook her head. "To a Mr. Davidson. He said things about me, I think."

Elsie leaned forward. "In the letter? What are you talking about, child?"

Before she could answer, there were footsteps on the freshly waxed floor. A *squeak-squeak* of pressed rubber. Elsie looked up, thinking it might be Miriam, but saw Ms. Millstone staring at Treha as if Elsie didn't exist.

"I need to see you right away," the woman said. No emotion, no feeling.

Treha kept her eyes on Elsie as if looking for some kind of permission.

"Come back when you're finished," Elsie said. "I want to hear more about that letter."

"Ms. Langsam, I said I need to see you," Ms. Millstone said firmly.

The girl nodded. Elsie smiled at her and reached for her hand, but she was gone.

Streams from Desert Gardens
scene 11

Fade in from black to shot of Gaylen Reynolds, aka Hemingway, standing at his writing desk.

Close-up of ceramic cats on the desk, the windowsill, the bed behind him.

Tight shot of his hands as he gestures over the manual typewriter.

> People don't understand. How hard this is. They think anyone can write. Anyone with an idea in their head and a computer. Or a pen. Or that you put your fingers over the typewriter and the music starts and you follow it. That's the belief, but it's not like that at all. Writing is work. It's like digging a trench on a hot day with the sun beating down on you and everything inside screaming to get to the shade and get to a drink of water.

Cut to the books lining the shelves, all copies of Hemingway novels.

> He was an old man who fished alone in a skiff in the Gulf Stream and he had gone eighty-four days without taking a fish. Do you remember that one? Do you know what it took to get that from the well? To drag that up from the waters?

It's harder than warfare. In war, a man dies like a dog. With writing, your critics tear you to pieces and treat you less than a dog. It's insane that anyone would put themselves through such a thing. But if it's in there, if you truly have something to say, if you truly have a story to tell, you have to keep going, you see? You have to show up each day and do the work you were called to and then stop while there's still fuel in the tank. I've always said that. Never empty the well—you have to stop when there is still water left to pull.

They won't let you have the drink here, you know? They said I could keep my cats but not the Scotch, and to be honest with you, I'd rather have the Scotch. Just a glass of wine would loosen things up. Do you think you could sneak something in to me? Just a small bottle, it wouldn't . . .

Cut to the ceramic cat by the coffee mug.

Mary should have been back by now. She knows how worried I get when she's gone this long. You never know who's listening in on your conversations—the IRS or the FBI or some other government agency that wants more taxes. They'll bleed you dry.

Close-up of Hemingway typing, showing the nearly blank page in front of him.

The biggest fear of a writer is running dry, you know. Of getting to the point where the words are all jumbled and locked away and you can see them right there, almost hold them in your hand, but you can't

reach them, can't get them out, and when you do,
they don't come in the right order.

That's why I need to get back to Finca Vigía.
There are manuscripts waiting for me, in a bank
vault. But I'm here. Trapped like a rat. Waiting for
the end. Waiting for destruction.

Extreme close-up of Hemingway, just the eyes.

I've always believed you can destroy a man but you
cannot defeat him. Defeat happens in here, deep
within, a place you can't touch from the outside.
God's little garden, as someone said. The heart . . .

Now if you won't promise to bring that bottle,
you'll have to excuse me.

*Camera moves out of the room, into the hall, and Hemingway
closes the door.*

CHAPTER 14

TREHA NOTICED a darkness to Ms. Millstone's office. It wasn't just the closed blinds and the dark color the walls had been painted, nor the soft, green glow from the banker's lamp on the desk. It was the deep-brown carpeting that enveloped her. Her head began the familiar spinning that signaled some reaction, perhaps to the glue used to adhere the carpet or the chemicals used to clean it. She tried to take a deep breath as she entered.

The familiar pictures and artwork she'd come to relate with Mrs. Howard were gone. Empty bookshelves were filled. Treha counted three clocks, all with precisely the same time. She noticed a single sheet of paper on the desk, like a to-do list. A framed motivational print hung across from the desk. It had the word *Excellence* above a quote that made managing the facility seem like a climb up Mt. Everest. The photo showed a snow-capped mountain and climbers. Treha wondered what defined the top of her mountain.

"Close the door, please," Ms. Millstone said.

Treha obeyed, then sat in the fresh leather of an overstuffed chair and tried to calm her heartbeat and the spinning. Her fingers were typing, moving across the invisible keyboard on her lap.

"Well, this is not going to be easy for either of us, so I might as well get to the point. We're letting you go."

It took a moment for Treha to form the words. "Excuse me?"

"Your time at this institution has come to an end, Ms. Langsam. I'd like you to gather your things."

"I don't understand. What did I do wrong?"

Ms. Millstone picked up a file. "I don't want to go through the accusations. I'm simply willing to move ahead."

"What accusations?"

"In your file there are certain incidents that crop up."

"What incidents?" Treha said.

The woman took a deep breath and glanced at one of the clocks. "You're upsetting the residents."

"The residents love me."

"Yes, well, there are those who say you may have contributed to Dr. Crenshaw's stroke."

Treha sat still, eyes focused on Millstone's desk, like she was at the Laundromat again.

"Is that a possibility? Did you do something to him? Other residents say he seemed distressed after seeing you the evening before last."

"I don't know what you're talking about. I visited him like I do every evening before I leave."

"Correct, and others say he was agitated after that. If this got back to the family, that a staff member was upsetting him, they would ask questions." She adjusted her glasses and opened the file. "If this were the only complaint, I might overlook it, but here's one from Mr. Reynolds, saying you stole something from his room. From his desk."

"That's Hemingway. He filed a report that I stole his manuscript and the carbon copies and that I won't give them back."

"That sounds malicious to me."

"He's not malicious; he's mixed up." Treha ran her hands along the armrests of the leather chair and let her fingers sink deeply. "It's easier for him to think he is someone else."

"There are others who feel uncomfortable with you. Coworkers. I am concerned about how much free rein you have."

"Mrs. Howard said I was a great asset."

"Well, Mrs. Howard is leaving, isn't she?" Millstone folded her hands on top of the page. "Ms. Langsam, it's time for you to spread your wings instead of staying in this cage."

"I've done nothing wrong. I've helped everyone I could."

"You're unqualified. If you simply did your job, the janitorial work, I might have a different opinion, but this is not what you do."

"I talk to them like they are real people. They feel safe with me."

"Yes. And what about Elsie? Tell me about your conversation just now. What were you speaking about?"

"We were speaking of Dr. Crenshaw. They were close. She is hurting."

The woman smiled. "We have counseling services available to the residents. You are not qualified."

Treha's eyes continued in a wider arc. "I am her friend."

"Well, I can't afford to hire *friends*. I need qualified workers."

"Some of them are talking for the first time in years."

Millstone closed her eyes. "I'm aware of your 'gift.' I'm sure you'll be able to use it elsewhere."

Treha looked at the carpet and thought of Mrs. Howard's words. How she was supposed to make a connection with the woman, if that was possible. She locked eyes with Millstone.

"My bicycle was stolen this morning. This is the only job I have. Please. I'll do whatever you ask. I won't speak to anyone."

The woman's body grew tense and she leaned forward, elbows on her desk. "Would you please stop that movement? I'm getting dizzy watching you."

Treha closed her eyes. "I'm sorry. I'm not doing it on purpose."

"It's unnerving." She stood, came around the front of the desk, and leaned back, her feet almost touching Treha's.

"If this is about money, you could lower my salary."

"This is not about . . . This is about what's best for the residents."

"That's all I've ever wanted."

A heavy sigh. "So you'll stick to cleaning floors? You'll do the janitorial work without interacting with anyone?"

Treha nodded. "If that's what it takes to let me stay." She looked up again, then saw the revulsion in the woman's face and lowered her eyes.

Millstone crossed her arms. "All right. Here's how it will work. You'll be on probation. I'll give you one more chance. But if I find you talking to the residents or interacting in any way, just one infraction and you'll be asked to leave. Do you understand?"

Treha nodded and typed *thank you* on the unseen keyboard.

She glanced at *Excellence* as she exited, her head light from the glue and paint. She looked back at Millstone as the woman turned to her to-do list.

Without glancing up, she said, "I'll be watching you, Treha."

Streams from Desert Gardens
scene 19

Wide shot of Miriam Howard, standing in front of the half-eaten cake, a microphone to her mouth.

> I knew this day would come. But I had no idea it
> would be this difficult. I've always looked forward to
> my retirement. And I still do. But it's come so quickly.
> I've heard people talk about the brevity of life—I've
> heard some of you talk about it.

Cutaway shots of residents watching, wiping tears, smiling, adjusting hearing aids.

Cut back to Miriam.

> There's a proverb that says, "The afternoon knows
> what the morning never suspected." That's the truth.
> But it doesn't describe how quickly the afternoon
> gets here. It felt like morning such a short time ago.
>
> It's been a pleasure to serve you. A joy to be your
> friend. Some of you knew my mother as she came to
> live here. And I think of her and of all those who are
> not here today, friends we've known and loved and
> cared for. I like to think they're looking down on us
> and wishing they could have some of this delicious
> cake we've enjoyed.

Cutaway of laughter and smiles. Back to tight shot of Miriam.

When I was younger, I wanted to conquer the world. I wanted to find cures for diseases. I looked at a place like this as necessary, but not attractive. But an opportunity opened for me and I went through that door. Buck came along at about the same time and we've walked through this together. And I want you to know I wouldn't have missed it.

Cutaway to Buck Davis, wiping away tears.

Thank you for loving me and accepting me. I have a feeling you haven't seen the last of me. And I know you're going to enjoy the leadership of Ms. Millstone and the experience she brings to this job. I hope you will welcome her as you have welcomed me.

From the bottom of my heart . . .

Tight shot of Miriam holding the microphone away.

Cutaway to her husband, Charlie, watching from the corner.

Cut back to Miriam.

Thank you . . . for the honor of allowing me to serve you for a little while. God bless you all.

CHAPTER 15

MIRIAM'S VOICE trembled as she spoke, which was a new sensation. This job was so old, so routine, that emotion surprised her. But as she scanned the room, her astigmatism compounded by the tears, she saw blurry faces, treasures in wrinkled bodies, and it hit her, what she was about to do, the step she was about to take.

Devin and Jonah had shown up with their camera, much to the chagrin of Jillian Millstone. This "passage" was something they wanted to document. Seeing Millstone's glare when she gave them permission to film, Miriam wondered what would happen to their project.

Most surprising was that Treha was nowhere in the room. Where had the girl gone?

Millstone stood surveying her kingdom, as if Desert Gardens were now her manifest destiny—which it was. There was a foot-tapping quality to her as she stood in the back, waiting for the festivities to end.

Miriam had officiated many farewells and birthday parties but had never seen this much emotion, even at funerals. Residents hobbled to the microphone or it was taken to them and they spoke of her as if she were a member of their family.

Listening to their halting thoughts and heartfelt expressions was like watching a continuous loop of *On Golden Pond*.

Elsie launched into a poem about Miriam that she had worked on for several months. Miriam was captivated by the power of the old woman's words. Elsie included a healthy dose of spiritual fervor, getting in several mentions of Jesus and how Miriam had been his hands and feet. Miriam smiled, watching the reactions of some who were not as spiritually attuned as Elsie, as well as others who nodded and drank in her words. This was vintage Elsie. It was like watching a geyser spout, a naturally reoccurring phenomenon. Elsie also managed to work Miriam's mother into her soliloquy, which made Miriam tear up. The woman had been such good friends with her mother during her stay.

Miriam spotted Charlie in the corner, eating a piece of cake and watching the festivities like he was looking for the stock crawl. His head bobbed from his carrot cake to whoever was talking.

When it was over, when the words had all been spoken and the people shuffled back to their rooms and staff members came to store the sound system and fold chairs, Charlie came to her.

"That was some send-off, wasn't it?"

She smiled. "It was, but I can't find Treha."

"Who?"

"Treha, the girl I've told you about."

He motioned with a finger. "The one with the eyes? I think I saw her at the end of the hall. Looked like she was cleaning the floor."

Miriam found her doing exactly that, and Treha kept working as Miriam spoke. "I missed you at the party. Did you get cake?"

She shook her head.

CHRIS FABRY

"Treha, what's wrong? Why won't you look at me?"

Head still down. "I can't."

"Why not?"

"I'm not supposed to talk to anyone."

"Who told you that?"

"Ms. Millstone. I tried to do what you said and make a connection. She was going to fire me and then said I had to do my job and stop talking to people."

Miriam wanted to curse but thought better of it. She also wanted to grab Jillian Millstone by the shoulders and shake some sense into her.

"How are you getting home tonight?" she said.

"Walking, I guess."

"No. Charlie and I will give you a ride. I just need to check on a few things and call the hospital about Dr. Crenshaw. Your shift ends in thirty minutes, right?"

The girl nodded at the floor and kept scrubbing. Miriam wanted to rip into Millstone, but on the walk to the office, she cooled. A confrontation would probably only make things worse for Treha.

Miriam located her last boxes of books and office material in the hall and asked Charlie to load them, which he dutifully did. She stepped into the office, taking in what Millstone had done. Her footprints weren't even out the front door and the paint was fresh on the walls. She scanned the immaculately decorated room, the muted lighting, felt the thick carpeting underfoot and wondered why she hadn't done this long ago. She had cared too much about the bottom line, the cost of something so extravagant.

The only thing out of place in the room was in the corner behind the door, three full boxes. She recognized the clock and

Dr. Crenshaw's framed medical license, his diplomas, and his patented brown slippers. Everyone chided him about how worn those had become.

Millstone's actions were against protocol, cleaning out a resident's room before it was time, and Miriam wanted to educate the woman on the rules she obviously didn't understand. Unless she knew something Miriam didn't. A wild thought raced through her mind and she glanced toward Millstone's desk to see if there was a call slip from the hospital or some other communication about Dr. Crenshaw's condition.

She saw nothing but lingered near the door as the contents of the third box caught her eye. Neatly packed to the brim were word puzzles and spiral notebooks one on top of another. Behind the books were manila file folders pushed tightly together. She saw one titled *Taxes*, another that said *Life Insurance*, and another that said *Investments*.

She opened a folder titled *Memories* and saw loose pictures of the man's childhood. Black-and-white photographs of his unmistakable smile. He had a sheepish grin and a way of holding his head that had followed him through life. She put the photos back and returned the file to the box. And noticed another with the heading *Treha*.

Miriam's heart skipped a beat. Crenshaw had taken an interest in the girl, but what could he be keeping in a file about her? Perhaps notes about her mental prowess, how many seconds it took her to unscramble words? She opened the folder and peeked inside. There were several pages filled with Dr. Crenshaw's scrawl. Toward the back were more official-looking papers, like medical records.

"May I help you?" someone said behind her.

Miriam closed the folder and turned to see Jillian Millstone.

"I was just saying good-bye to the old place. I noticed Dr. Crenshaw's things here. Have you heard anything more about his condition?"

"No, but I'm assuming from how he was when he left that he won't be returning."

"Doesn't that seem a bit premature?"

"Perhaps it is, but I don't see that it's your concern now, Mrs. Howard. You're off duty."

"Well, you don't just walk away from someone you've had a relationship with for years."

"Maybe that would be best for you. Let go. Move on with your life. I'm sure you'll find a . . . hobby."

Miriam gritted her teeth. The audacity. The woman was so clinical. Go by the numbers. What Miriam had tried so hard to make into a community, Millstone would turn into a warehouse in a week.

"The protocol for personal belongings is that—"

"I'm aware of the rule, Mrs. Howard. This is not your concern any longer." She took a step forward. "You've had a good run here. We'll take care of things now."

Miriam stared at the woman. There was something dead in her eyes. Some spark that hadn't come about or had withered long ago. She tried to shake it off but couldn't.

"I want to make one more appeal on behalf of Treha," Miriam said.

Millstone smiled. "Please don't. You're free; don't you understand? These people are in good hands. Walk out that door and rest peacefully. You're not responsible."

"There's a folder here with Treha's name on it . . ." Before Miriam could finish, before she could even ask, Jillian Millstone put a cold hand on her arm.

"Let it go, Miriam."

The sound of her first name made Miriam want to dry heave. She looked back at the box, then quickly made her way out of the office and down the hall.

CHAPTER 16

Miriam was still reeling from the encounter with Millstone when they walked into Sizemore's on Oracle Avenue.

Charlie had shrugged when Miriam suggested they take Treha and said, "Might as well keep the party going." But she knew he would care about the money, how much he would have to pay for Treha's meal.

Walking into the restaurant felt like giving up.

The place was not so much crowded as bunched in the line to the buffet. As they worked their way through, someone behind them said, "Mind if we join you?"

Miriam turned to see Devin and Jonah smiling sheepishly.

"We kind of followed you. I hope you don't mind."

"Not at all. The more the merrier," she said, looking at Charlie and seeing the questions about who would pay spin in his brain.

The five worked through the buffet line, Treha staying close to Miriam. Then they sat at a circular wooden table and threw out small talk about the party and Miriam's final day. Treha ate with her head down, barely looking up from her plate of salad and chicken that she'd arranged meticulously, not allowing one to touch the other. Devin seemed fascinated by her.

Miriam told them she had called the hospital and Dr. Crenshaw was still clinging to life, but the test results hadn't given any good news. He was resting comfortably. Her guess was that this was as good as he would get, but she didn't reveal this.

"What are you going to do with all your free time, Mrs. Howard?" Jonah said. He had two glasses of soda in front of him and a plate that looked like a gastronomic Everest. She guessed Charlie would say something about Jonah "getting his money's worth" on the drive home.

"Keeping Charlie in line will be a full-time job," Miriam said, glancing at him. Charlie didn't break stride with his corn on the cob. "I have some volunteer work I may do at TMC. I might write a book about my experiences at Desert Gardens."

"I'd read it," Devin said.

There was an awkward silence until Jonah said, "The reason we followed you is because of our project." His face turned grim. "If you hadn't intervened, I don't think Millstone would have let us in the door. But now I think we're done."

Treha looked at him, then back at her plate.

"What were you doing over there in the first place?" Charlie said.

Jonah motioned with a french fry toward Devin, who wiped his mouth.

"I'm a big believer in the power of stories. Individual and collective. We were capturing people at Desert Gardens rehearsing their lives, showing how one person's story touches another and how it feeds the rest of us, makes us better. Instead of discounting those on the margins, those our society says aren't important, we need to celebrate their stories. Ask more questions. Learn and grow and honor them."

Charlie cocked his head. "That's it? You've been working on old people's stories? Doesn't sound like much of a plan."

Miriam gave him a look, which he didn't see.

"A documentary is an organic thing."

"So's a cucumber, but you still have to plant it. You don't have a script? You can't just record people talking. I mean, how do you know when you're done?"

"Good question," Jonah said, making it to base camp three.

"What we're doing is different," Devin said. "The script is life observed. We look for story lines and drama in the everyday."

Charlie scowled. "I get up every day and brush my teeth, but that would make a boring movie. Why not shoot people painting a wall? In the end, at least you'd have a wall painted."

"That's our next film," Jonah said, deadpan. "It's a thriller. We're calling it *Dry Hard.*"

Charlie didn't smile, didn't get the joke. He picked a piece of corn from his teeth and said, "Who wants to watch old geezers? The whole reason we put people away is because we don't care about their stories. We don't want to hear them."

"Charles," Miriam said.

"It's true. I don't want it to be true, but it is. We don't want to see them, so we pay other people to care for them. So they won't be in our way, hold us back."

Miriam reached out to touch him, but he pulled back. She saw it then, just as starkly as she saw it at Desert Gardens. It wasn't just in the gray hair and stooped shoulders or the wrinkles or shuffling feet, in the canes, walkers, and wheelchairs. Age showed most in the eyes, in the hunched-over inability to see or perhaps to even look. Set and immovable. Veins and yellowing of the whites. The color of the irises faded too. She remembered

Charlie's eyes vibrant blue as the ocean. Now they were dull puddles, graying just like the sky and his hair.

"It's okay," Devin said. "But, Charlie, you're making my point. My thesis is we don't realize what we're shutting out, what we're losing. Our hope is, by creating a film like this, it will awaken people."

Charlie took a sip of coffee and shook his head. "I'm not seeing it. I appreciate your concept. I applaud it. Not many young people would go to the trouble. But who's going to watch? And how do you know—? You could collect stories from now till kingdom come and not know you're done."

Jonah held up a pudgy hand as if he wanted the floor. "A few years ago, a group decided to make a documentary about firefighters in a New York engine company. A guy was going to shoot a day in the life of these men. The fresh rookie right out of the academy, the grizzled veteran who'd seen it all. They just happened to be shooting on September 11 when the call came in about the North Tower being on fire. They didn't plan any of what happened. But you can bet they knew when they were finished that they had something riveting. Something amazingly human and tragic."

"You're saying you're waiting for a terrorist attack at Desert Gardens?" Charlie said, eyebrows raised.

Jonah smiled and grabbed the nearly empty bottle of Heinz and patted it until some spilled onto the plate.

Devin continued, his eyes on fire. "We've followed several residents and the changes they've been through in the past few months. Dr. Crenshaw was one of them—we have interviews with him going way back. Elsie is another. And we've talked with you, Mrs. Howard. I thought several times that the hook to bring all of this together was you—your transition to retirement."

Miriam gave him a startled look.

"It's true. The residents are watching you handle this change. They know there's something unfair here. They're so attached to you and they can't understand this switch to Millstone, who is less than warm."

"She's as warm as this pudding," Charlie said.

"This is the thread that runs through the stories: handling change, taking what life throws at you, responding with grace, fighting back when you have to, or being content. Knowing things might not get better. And that they're probably going to go downhill. I wanted to follow these threads, but if we have no access to Desert Gardens, we have to go another direction."

He glanced at Treha, who seemed in another world. Her head swayed as she ate, and Charlie was studying her typing fingers. Then she looked around the room and rose.

"The restroom is straight to the back," Miriam said, and Treha headed for it.

As soon as she left, Devin leaned forward. "I'm sorry we horned in on dinner tonight, but I wanted to broach something with you. I'm not sure . . ."

"Go ahead," Miriam said.

"I've been thinking. What if our focus is something else? Someone else?"

"Who?" Miriam said, following his eyes toward the bathroom. "Treha?"

"That might be a short movie," Charlie said. "Without much emotion."

Miriam studied Devin. "What are you thinking?"

"You mentioned her gift. I think I saw it in the chapel. What if we captured her calling someone back? What if we told her story?"

Miriam put down her fork. "I don't think that's a good idea."

"Why not?"

"Several reasons. I won't see her exploited, for one. And if you were to catch what she's able to do on video, you'd have the whole world knocking at her door."

"Exactly," Devin said. "This would be big."

"But you'd change everything. You'd change *her*. She couldn't handle that."

"How do you know?"

"What are you two talking about?" Charlie said.

Miriam held up a hand to him, a signal she hoped he would interpret.

"If you've trusted us with the residents at Desert Gardens, why wouldn't you trust us with her?" Devin said.

"She's different. You show Treha in action and that will go viral. You'll turn her into a cliché, a video of an idiot savant. I won't have that. She'll be invited onto TV shows and hounded by desperate family members. You'll kill the thing that makes her special."

Devin sat back and gave a puzzled look. "I know you feel responsible and that you care, but what if she wants to do this? What if she wants to tell her history, how this gift came to her?"

"She doesn't know," Miriam said.

"What do you mean?"

"I mean she doesn't know her history."

"Time-out," Jonah said. "I'm with Charlie. What does Treha do?"

"She brings people back," Devin said. "Dementia, Alzheimer's patients—she makes a connection and gets them talking again."

"You've seen this?" Jonah said to Miriam.

Miriam nodded.

Jonah rubbed the stubble on his chin. "If you're worried about people discovering her identity, we can make her anonymous. Block her face or blur the image. Change her voice, her name. Shoot from behind her. There are all kinds of things we can do."

"But if you can't go back to Desert Gardens, what's the point?" Charlie said.

Devin glanced at the bathroom and leaned closer. "Maybe she's been the story all along. All this footage has prepared us for *her* story. Where she came from. How she developed her gift. And we meet someone with dementia or Alzheimer's."

Jonah gestured wildly, suddenly fully engaged. "What about Crenshaw? That would be the perfect bookend—we interviewed him, we saw him wheeled away, and Treha could wake him up. Does she do comas?"

Miriam was glad someone was interested in Treha, but not this way. She felt protective of the girl and had questions of her own. Questions about Dr. Crenshaw's file and the man named Davidson. "I don't think Dr. Crenshaw will be returning."

When she said it, she knew from their faces that Treha was there, that she had heard. Treha sat, glancing around the table, wary.

"Think I'll get a little dessert," Charlie said, scooting back from the table. "Got my eye on that banana cream pie."

"Yeah, I'll join you," Jonah said.

Miriam looked at Devin and tried to communicate. She couldn't allow something as pure and innocent as Treha to be used.

They finished the meal and Charlie paid the bill. Devin said he would leave the tip and Charlie let him.

As they exited, Devin put a hand on Miriam's shoulder and

pressed a business card in her hand. "Please think about it," he whispered. "I really want the best for her."

Charlie drove them to Treha's apartment and the girl got out without thanking them for dinner or the ride. Just walked up the stairs.

Charlie shook his head. "She may have a gift, but she could use some manners to go with it."

Miriam ignored him and rolled down the window. "Treha, I'll be by in the morning to give you a ride to work, okay?"

"You don't have to do that."

"I know, but I want to. I have some unfinished business there. I'll pick you up at six thirty, okay?"

Treha nodded. A boy appeared from the shadows, dark face but white eyes wide. He watched Treha go into her apartment and then watched them drive away.

"You sure you want to get up that early on your first day of retirement?" Charlie said. "Seems like you'd want to sleep in."

Miriam didn't answer, her mind racing as they drove. Charlie turned on the local talk station and a younger voice assaulted them with conservative views, a little more hip and faster paced than the ones during the day.

"I'm sorry to do this, but could you turn around?" Miriam said.

"What?"

"I want to go back to Desert Gardens."

"We're halfway home. Can't it wait until morning?"

"It probably could, but humor me. It'll keep me up all night thinking about it. I won't be long."

He sighed and made a U-turn at the light, and they were nearly broadsided by an oncoming SUV. The driver laid on the horn and made Charlie pay for his indiscretion. Charlie took it in stride, just grumbled. He pulled up to the loading and unloading zone.

"Stay here. I won't be a minute."

"I'll pull to the parking lot," he said. "Don't want them to think we're terrorists." He turned up the radio as she closed the door, and the voice boomed through the glass.

At the front door Miriam found Buck in his position, faithfully watching the black-and-white monitors and cracking pistachios. His full name was Buckner Theodore Davis, but he had asked her to call him Buck because everyone did.

"I thought that was you, Mrs. Howard," the man said through the small window at the side of the entrance area. It reminded her of the guard in *The Wizard of Oz*. He chuckled and moved stiff-legged to the front door, unlocking it and ushering her inside. "Did you forget something?"

"I did. Figured you'd let me in. Did you get a piece of cake?"

"Boy, did I. That was tasty as all get-out. I hope you don't mind—I'm taking an extra piece home to the missus."

"How is Vera doing after the surgery?"

"Oh, she's slowed a little, but she's getting better. Day by day, you know."

Miriam nodded. "Tell her I asked about her. And I hope she enjoys the cake." She paused as she looked at the reception area. "Ms. Millstone isn't still here, is she?"

"No, ma'am, she left about an hour ago. Just got on her broom and took off." He chewed like there was still a nut trapped somewhere, and she saw the twinkle in his eye. "Is there something I can help you with?"

"I left something in her office. I meant to take it with me and it slipped my mind. Of course I've already handed over the keys to the kingdom. Would you open the door for me?"

His eyes betrayed him. He must have thought of the consequences of such an infraction.

"I don't want to put you in a bad position," she said. "If you'd rather I come back tomorrow, I suppose I can just—"

"No, no. I'm sure it's all right. If she was here, she'd let you in. I think if you work at a place as long as you have, you're entitled to visit any room you want."

Keys jangled as they walked the hall. Miriam smiled and waved at a staff member at the desk. Buck flipped on the light in the outer office and mumbled something about the keys, then tried two before he found the right one.

Miriam turned on the light and Buck lingered in the outer office, watching but not watching. She knelt at the box behind the door and found the file marked *Treha*.

The folder was empty.

Her head went light. She rummaged through the files surrounding it, but the pages she had seen, the handwritten notes by Dr. Crenshaw, were gone.

She put the file back and closed the door behind her.

"Didn't find what you were looking for?"

She shook her head, thoughts filling her mind. Bad thoughts. She put a hand on Buck's arm. "Maybe it would be better if Ms. Millstone didn't know you let me in tonight."

Buck paused, but something playful showed through the lines and wrinkles on his face. "Why, the only reason you came back here tonight was to make sure Vera got her piece of cake, Mrs. Howard."

He laughed and she gave him a hug and walked to the parking lot, where she found Charlie asleep. She was going to peck on the window but didn't want to startle him, so she opened her purse to get the remote and saw Devin's card beside the letter to Mr. Davidson.

Miriam stood outside the car, thinking. What was the connection between Crenshaw and Davidson? What did they know about Treha that she didn't? She stared at the letter and the card in the light of the parking lot until she heard the door lock click.

Charlie drove her home without a word.

CHAPTER 17

TREHA WOKE at first light, as she always did. No matter how long it took her to get to sleep, no matter how late into the night she read—and some nights she read all night—when the sun peeked through the blinds that didn't close, her mind whirred. She showered and looked at herself in the small bathroom mirror and the bad thoughts returned. *Ugly. Fat. Nobody likes you. Misfit. Why are you going to work? Nobody cares about you.*

She dressed in the same scrubs she had worn the day before and opened the refrigerator. How could she keep weight on when she didn't eat much? She had wanted to bring home a few scraps from the restaurant the night before, but they didn't allow it. "All you can eat" meant all you could eat at the table. Her stomach growled and her mind raced. She thought of Dr. Crenshaw's letter. Perhaps he would awaken today and tell her about the man Davidson.

She brushed her teeth and sat on the top steps, watching the parking lot and the street beyond as people began their day. Men in trucks passed, women in uniform, and kids with backpacks and jeans riding low and halter tops doing the same.

She heard the familiar *pad-pad* underneath her a second before Du'Relle stuck his head around the corner.

"Hey, Miss Treha."

"Shouldn't you be getting ready for school?"

"What do you mean? I am ready. You don't like my outfit?"

The boy loped up the steps, wearing baggy shorts and a long T-shirt, hanging on to the railing and leaning like a gymnast.

"Don't do that—you'll fall."

"You sound like my mama. I'm not going to fall."

"Your mother is smart. You shouldn't take chances."

That made him lean farther and Treha wanted to grab him and pull him back, but she stared at the street instead.

"How come you haven't left for work?" Du'Relle said. "Usually you're gone by now."

"I'm waiting for my ride."

"Your ride? Since when did . . . ? Hey, where's your bike?"

"I don't have one anymore."

"What are you talking about? You and that bike have been together ever since I've known you. You're like Siamese twins."

"Someone stole it."

Du'Relle cursed and Treha gave him a stern look.

"Sorry, Miss Treha. But that's about the meanest thing I ever heard, somebody stealing a bike from someone like you."

What did he mean, *"someone like you"*? Did this waif of a boy feel pity for her? That was what she felt for him with his father gone and his mother working two jobs until late.

"That makes no sense," Du'Relle said. "Did they take it from your apartment?"

She recognized Mrs. Howard's car pulling into the lot and walked past him, tugging his shoulder. "Don't lean over the railing."

"I'm real sorry about your bike, Miss Treha. I'll keep my eye out for it."

Treha got in the car and Mrs. Howard smiled and leaned forward. "Is he a friend of yours?"

Treha told her his name and that he was a pest, but a nice pest. "He keeps me company even when I don't need it."

Mrs. Howard drove toward Desert Gardens, talking about the weather, her retirement party, and Dr. Crenshaw's condition, which hadn't changed. She grew serious as they neared the facility.

"Devin asked me something at dinner that I dismissed, but I was awake a lot last night thinking about his question. He wants to interview you. To follow your story like he has others at Desert Gardens."

"What does he want to know?"

"I think he wants to tell your story."

Treha didn't respond. She wanted to say she didn't have a story. She had taken other people's stories.

"Devin has a desire to follow you and perhaps film you bringing someone back."

"Do you think I should?"

"I don't know. I have reservations about it. But last night I tossed and turned and decided that I shouldn't be making up your mind about such things." She opened her purse and pulled out the letter Crenshaw had written to Davidson, handing it back to Treha.

"I can't speak to anyone at Desert Gardens. And Ms. Millstone won't let them in."

"I plan on talking with Ms. Millstone. That's part of why I'm going back today. . . ."

Mrs. Howard kept talking but Treha didn't hear her.

Somewhere inside, in some place touched by the books and stories she read that told her what a mother and daughter should be like, she wanted to scoot close and hug the woman, to put her head on her shoulder and cry or laugh. But she couldn't. This was a fence she couldn't climb, and even if she tried, there was razor wire at the top.

Treha glanced at street signs and jumbled the letters of the road they were on. *Oracle.* Dr. Crenshaw would quiz her, get out his stopwatch and ask her to make as many other words as she could in a minute. At least four letters.

Lace. Real. Clear. Coral. Lore. Care. Race. Coal. Role. Oral.

"Treha?" Mrs. Howard said, jarring her from her word trance. "Would it be okay with you if I talked with Ms. Millstone? About you? About your future at Desert Gardens?"

Treha nodded, staring straight ahead.

"You can think about the interview with Devin. Maybe let me know later."

When they arrived, Buck was just getting off his shift. Ms. Millstone had moved him to overnight as one of her first executive decisions. He tipped his hat to Treha and Mrs. Howard as they entered.

"Now don't give me that look, Buckner," Mrs. Howard said.

The man laughed. "Then don't you call me that. Only my mother calls me that. Just surprised to see you back so soon."

"Well, the world is full of surprises." She turned to Treha. "Go ahead and clock in. I'll catch up with you a little later."

"You have a good day, Treha," Buck said warmly.

He and Mrs. Howard spoke as Treha walked to the employee room behind the reception area. She swiped her card and turned to her locker. On the outside was a note written in heavy black ink.

Treha, I want you to wash the floors in the dayroom. Put out the yellow signs so no one slips. See me afterward. JDM

She looked at the initials and wondered what the woman's middle name was. *JDM* was on the bottom of all her notes, all her paperwork. Initials that stirred something inside Treha. Something like fear.

She found the mop and yellow signs and filled the rolling bucket with warm water and soap. She pushed the contraption down the hall, trying not to slosh when she crossed a bump. Past room after room, she tried not to look, but as she heard familiar voices, familiar sounds, it became more difficult. The *click-click-ding* return of Hemingway's typewriter. Then a high voice running through scales. *"La la la la la la la la. Do do do do do do do do."*

As the noise faded, she pushed past Ardeth's room and heard whimpering. It was faint, almost imperceptible over the sound of the wheels under the bucket. Something like a soft sob.

Treha stopped and backed up slowly, pulling the bucket by the mop handle. The door to Ardeth's room was slightly ajar and Treha leaned close to the opening. "Mrs. Ardeth?"

No answer. Just the noise. Like the weeping of a frightened child. Treha pushed the door open. The room was dark, but light from the hall showed Ardeth on the floor, holding up a hand, reaching out.

Treha rushed to her and took her hand. "You're okay now. I heard you from the hallway."

No words from the old woman, just emotion and distress. She was a child who had lost her way, who had fallen and wanted help.

"Mrs. Ardeth, can you get back in your bed?"

Her mouth opened, but not to answer. The pain had taken over, had brought bewildered eyes and a vacant stare.

Treha began stroking Ardeth's hand and arm, rubbing her shoulder. The old woman's muscles were tense and shaking, but after a few moments she began to relax and the arm went limp.

The voice cracked and sputtered. "Tiffany?"

"It's Treha, Mrs. Ardeth. How did you get down here?"

The woman looked around and the movement made her gasp. "I can't remember."

"Where does it hurt?"

"All over."

There was an emergency button on the wall, but Treha couldn't reach it. When she moved, the woman grabbed her arm more tightly and held on.

CHAPTER 18

MIRIAM DECIDED not to speak with Jillian Millstone about the empty file until after she'd had a conversation with Elsie. If there was anyone who would know about Dr. Crenshaw, it was her. The two of them were an item around the facility, though they tried hard to conceal it. Neither wanted to become a point of conversation, an aged cliché.

She signed in at the front and spoke with the receptionist briefly, skirting the reason for her return. The Lovebirds were in the dining hall, leaning close to each other and talking as if a jet plane were nearby getting ready for takeoff. An intimate conversation about bowel movements spoken at levels that made others look at them with furrowed brows, and Miriam couldn't help but smile. The overflow of loving each other this long was both glorious and maddening. Not so much the topic of conversation but the fact that they were still in love, still growing toward each other rather than away.

She quickly moved down the hall as Charlie came to mind. Why couldn't Charlie be like *him*? Why couldn't they be lovebirds? She was willing to draw closer and give her heart to a man with such commitment, but his heart had become filled with stocks and bonds and retirement funds and figures. There had to be more to life, more to a marriage than the bottom line. Life was not measured in a bank statement.

"Miriam?" someone said. She glanced up to see Elsie with her three-wheeled walker, heading the other way.

"I was just coming to see you," Miriam said. "Are you headed to breakfast?"

"I thought I might get a little something. You want to join me?" Her voice rattled and crackled but the sound was heavenly to Miriam.

"Why don't you let me get it for you and bring it to your room?"

"No, I try to avoid cocooning. I usually eat with the rest of the herd."

"Please, Elsie." Miriam caught the woman's eyes and tried to communicate. "I'd really like to speak with you alone. If you don't mind."

Elsie's eyes softened. "All right."

Elsie gave her usual list for breakfast: English muffin, no butter, a bowl of oatmeal, a small fruit cup, and a glass of orange juice. Miriam quickly retrieved it from the dining hall, skirting the staff and residents, then hurried back.

Elsie's room smelled of talcum and rose, maybe cinnamon or clove with a hint of mint. An elderly person's potpourri to overcome the other smells of alcohol and cleaning solution. She sat in her easy chair, stately and queen-like. Behind her was a faded quilt with tiny markings all around, words and numbers Miriam couldn't decipher. The blinds were open to let in the full light of the morning. At her side was a nightstand with a lavender-colored lampshade that cast light on a Bible so worn and falling apart it looked like it might have been printed by Gutenberg himself.

Miriam placed the food on a tray that pivoted over the woman's easy chair and Elsie smiled. "I didn't order toast."

"That's for me," Miriam said, pulling a chair from the nearby desk.

"Boy, this is service," Elsie said. "You never did this while you were running the place. Maybe you can come back here every day."

"I wasn't planning on coming back at all, but circumstances changed."

"What circumstances?"

"Well, Treha, mostly. She and Ms. Millstone are not getting along."

Elsie ground her teeth. As long as she had known her, Miriam had never heard Elsie utter a bad word about another human being. She suspected that was about to change. The woman's back creaked, literally creaked as she leaned forward and lowered her voice. "I've been trying to pray for that woman, but she is going to be the death of this place. You can see it in her face. My guess is she probably believes in evolution. That we crawled up from the slime, survival of the fittest and all that. She treats us like single-cell organisms. What I can't understand is why she came here if she doesn't like old people."

"She's very competent, and I believe she means well. . . ."

"Means well, my foot. She has no business here. I wouldn't let that woman babysit my turtle if I had one. If it was dead, I wouldn't let her bury it."

Miriam stifled a smile. "Well, we have to deal with what is, and she's here now. She's in charge. We have to live with it."

"No, *you* don't have to live with it; you're retired. *We* have to live with it. Treha does."

Miriam nodded and told the woman about the dinner the night before, that Devin and Jonah might not be allowed back.

"See what I mean?" Elsie said. "Those boys have brought life to this place. Letting us tell our stories and remember. How is that hurting anybody? Millstone is a nursing home Nazi if you ask me." She took a bite of oatmeal and chewed as if it were required.

"But there's a twist in the story. Every ending means a new beginning, right?"

"You're asking me?" Elsie said.

"Isn't that what you believe? When God closes a door, he opens a window?"

"Listen, honey, God has closed doors and windows on my fingers. You won't find that window-and-door thing in the Bible, though I suppose it's generally true. He redirects us through the circumstances. I believe that. But I prefer to lean on Proverbs 3:5 and 6." She recited it, punctuating the "trust in the Lord" and "lean not on your own understanding" parts.

"I wish I had your faith, Elsie."

The woman cocked her head. "Now what is *that* supposed to mean?"

"I wish I could trust in God the way you do."

"Fiddlesticks."

"No, I'm serious. I believe. I just don't know if it makes any difference. God seems awfully disinterested in my life. But your faith is real and vibrant."

"Like I have something special, right? You don't know how many times I hear that kind of thing and it drives me up a wall. I don't have some pipeline to God that's unavailable to every other human. I only have a tiny smidgen of faith—" she held out a pinkie and measured the fingernail—"but God says if you have faith as big as a grain of mustard seed, you can move mountains. Uproot trees. It's not my faith that's the key, or how much of it I have; it's where I place it that matters."

Miriam nodded. "You're right; you're really nothing special."

Elsie threw her head back and laughed. "I've heard that, too."

Miriam finished her toast and brushed the crumbs from her fingers. "Not having access to the facility has given Devin a new idea. He's interested in following Treha's story. Finding out more about her. Showing her gift. At first I was dead set against it, thinking they might try to exploit her, but the more I've thought about it, slept on it, the more I think this might be good."

"Treha's story," Elsie said vacantly, staring at the tile floor. Some light seemed to enter her face. "Now there's a movie I'd like to see. Sometimes I wish I knew what she has been through in her life and then other times I don't think I could handle it."

"I know a little. The trouble is, I don't think she knows much more than that."

"Jim used to . . . Dr. Crenshaw would say that Treha listens to stories here and makes them her own because she can't remember her past. She's a memory stealer. But she doesn't do it to be mean; she does it to fill in the gaps."

"That's the real reason I wanted to talk with you. Dr. Crenshaw."

Elsie put her spoon down and stopped midchew on the oatmeal. "He's not gone, is he? You didn't wait until now to tell me . . . ?"

"No, no, his condition is critical, but he's still with us."

A look of relief flooded her. "I hadn't wanted to ask. I thought in the hallway that you wanted me to come back here because he was gone and you were just working up to telling me." Tears filled her eyes. "I don't know what I would have done if . . ."

Miriam put a hand on her arm. "We'll keep praying, Elsie. Even if I don't feel like God is listening. We'll just keep using the little faith we have, right?"

A tear stair-stepped the woman's wrinkled cheek. "I don't want him to suffer. I really don't. I know he's old and in pain. I know he wouldn't want to live hooked up to machines. His body's tired and worn-out. And I know his soul is at peace. But I sure would like to tell him good-bye."

More tears and the napkin went to the eyes. Miriam put an arm around her, thinking it might take the woman a while to recover, but Elsie took a deep breath and jabbed her spoon back in the oatmeal.

"I don't like it cold," she said, her mouth full.

"I don't want to upset you with any of this."

Elsie waved an arthritic hand. "I've been thinking of him every moment. Alone in that hospital. That verse going over and over in my head—the one people use to say God won't give us more than we can handle, 1 Corinthians 10:13. They think temptation and the hard stuff of life are the same. I don't believe that for a minute. He does give us more than we can handle. He lets us go through deeper waters so that we cling to him; that's the whole point of having faith. If we could handle everything, there would be no reason for us to need God."

Miriam listened. Once Elsie got on a roll, it was best to let her continue. And truth be told, she liked hearing the strength of Elsie's faith.

"I'm not big on claiming verses. You hear people say that a lot. 'I claimed this verse or that verse for such and such,' as if they have God's arm behind his back because they read something and can remember it. I'll tell you one thing: he knows a lot better than I do what I need. And he knows the same for Jim, too. But if I were to claim a verse for him—and I've been praying this for him every day for the last six months—it would be from Ephesians 1, where Paul says, 'I pray that your hearts will be flooded with light so that you can understand the confident hope he has given.'" She punctuated the "confident hope" with a wag of her finger. "I don't know if he has a heart problem or a brain problem or something else, but God knows how to flood us with light and understanding. He knows all that's wrong and what it'll take to fix us."

She put her head back against the chair and pushed the tray away.

"I didn't mean to upset you."

"No, you didn't. I get tired so easy these days. Just getting up and getting dressed makes me want to go back to bed, but then it takes so long to go to sleep. I just lay there and doze and wake up and the deep sleep feels so far away. It's like going to a party but you have to always watch through the window; you never eat the cake or get to wear the hat. I'm not complaining— I know this comes with the territory. They say age is a state of mind. Don't you believe it. It has very little to do with the mind in my case. It's my hip and my joints and my bladder. Gray hair is a crown of splendor nobody wants. You can look that up in Proverbs 16, the EAV, Elsie Authorized Version."

"How did you learn so much about the Bible?"

"Only one way to learn and that's to open and read it. Ask questions. Listen to others who know it better than you do. And stay away from the people who think they have God figured out or who say they know the code. You have to come to the Bible humbly and admit you don't know everything—that's the key. Most people come to me with a Bible question or two they want answered. Hemingway always wants to argue; he's cantankerous. That's fine; let him argue. The Lovebirds never ask questions; they just live 1 Corinthians 13."

Miriam chuckled and glanced around the room. There were framed Scripture verses and knickknacks on pressboard bookshelves. A snow globe here, a Precious Moments figurine there. It had the cluttered look of an old woman who had reached her final dwelling place and was going out with as many trinkets as she could gather. The TV was dark but the radio was tuned to a Christian station that played a soothing strings version of some old song Miriam couldn't quite place. It sounded like sanctified elevator music.

"You live your whole life collecting things that collect dust," Elsie said. "And then you realize you're collecting dust too."

"Dust will never settle on you, Elsie. Your mind goes too fast."

She put her hand on the Bible and looked up. "You said you wanted to talk with me about Dr. Crenshaw. And Treha. I think I know what you're going to ask, but you need to understand something. When I give my word, I don't go back on it. Integrity is the only thing they can't take away from you. They can tax you living or dead, but they can't take integrity."

"Did Dr. Crenshaw tell you something in confidence about Treha?"

She looked at her hands.

"Elsie, you were a good friend to him. I think Dr. Crenshaw knew something about Treha, didn't he?"

Down the hallway came a quick beep, the distress signal from one of the rooms. Instinctively Miriam rose and moved toward the door. She knew this wasn't her job, but she couldn't help it.

"I'll be right back."

CHAPTER 19

THE ONLY WAY Treha could hit the button was to let Ardeth slump to the floor, so she'd grabbed the pillows from the bed and placed them under the woman's head. After she reached the button, she returned to Ardeth's side. "It's going to be okay, Mrs. Ardeth."

"No, it's not. I heard it snap. When I fell, I hit bone. This is the end, Tiffany."

"It's not the end," Treha said sharply.

One of the nurses was the first to find them. She tried to help Treha get the woman in a comfortable position. Ms. Millstone rushed to the phone and dialed the EMTs, then seemed paralyzed by the situation.

"Treha, you need to move that bucket out of the hallway now," the woman finally snapped.

When Treha moved, Ardeth gave a yelp of pain.

"Let's just hold her position right there," the nurse said. "No sudden movements."

Millstone turned and propped the door open, then pushed the bucket out of sight down the hallway. The nurse spoke to Ardeth, assured her help was on the way, then told Treha she was doing a good job. "We're going to make a nurse out of you yet."

Instead of Millstone returning, Mrs. Howard came into the room and knelt to take Ardeth's hand. She didn't ask questions, just spoke kindly and gently, and Treha felt the woman's response—a relaxing of the muscles.

"Her leg is shaking," Treha said.

Mrs. Howard nodded. "Did you see her fall?"

"No. I was pushing the bucket down the hallway and I heard her crying. I found her like this."

"My bones are so brittle," Ardeth said.

"It's all right, Ardeth. Help is on the way." Then to Treha, she said, "You did a good thing. You got her help when no one else heard her."

"But I'm not supposed to talk to anyone."

"The only reason you talked to Ardeth was to help her. No one will have a problem with that."

Treha felt a presence in the room before the shadow covered them. She looked behind Mrs. Howard to see Ms. Millstone looking down, hands on hips.

"Get up from there," Millstone said.

"I think we should wait for the EMTs," Mrs. Howard said.

"I'm not talking about Mrs. Williams; I'm talking about Ms. Langsam."

"But she's keeping Ardeth comfortable. There will be more pain if you move her."

"I want you out of here now," Millstone said.

The nurse and Mrs. Howard held Ardeth as best they could as Treha slipped from underneath her. There were sirens in the distance that were drowned by Ardeth's cries. She reached out and Treha patted the woman's hand.

"To my office," Millstone said. "Go."

Treha walked out of the room and saw the mop and bucket

at the end of the hallway. "Do you want me to mop the floor in the—?"

"To my office!" Millstone shouted.

More crying and moaning from Ardeth. The ambulance pulled up to the front and the EMTs rushed through the door. Treha pointed them to Ardeth's room and they hurried down the corridor with their equipment in tow.

Treha walked into Millstone's office and waited, unable to sit for fear it wouldn't be approved. From the hallway she heard murmurs of curious residents. She finally sat on the floor with her back against the wall and, as much as she could, stared at the bookshelves, the spines in perfect symmetry.

She drew her knees to herself and hugged them, breathing in the glue and new carpet. It was even stronger down here but she didn't want to sit in the leather chair and have Ms. Millstone scold her.

When Millstone finally arrived, she flipped on the light and glared at Treha. "Why are you in the dark? And why are you sitting down there? Get in the chair."

Treha obeyed while Millstone took a folder from a stand on the credenza behind her.

"Is the address we have on file your current one?"

"Yes."

"That's where we'll send your final check."

"But I pick it up here."

"Ms. Langsam, you're not employed here any longer. I told you the rules and you violated them. End of discussion. It's all documented, very carefully."

Treha looked at the page, upside down. "I didn't talk with anyone. I just tried to help Mrs. Ardeth."

The woman was busy signing things, then turned the file

around. "Sign here and initial these pages. This says you understand the reasons for termination. It's standard procedure."

"Don't sign anything, Treha," someone said behind her. Treha
turned to see Mrs. Howard in the door. She stepped inside and
moved toward the desk. "You have no right treating her this
way. She helped Ardeth. You should be giving her a medal."

Millstone glared at Mrs. Howard, but before she could
speak, the office manager appeared. A petite woman with large
glasses. "Mrs. Williams's daughter is on the phone for you, Ms.
Millstone."

She glanced at Treha before picking up the phone. "This is
Jillian Millstone. Thank you for returning my call. I wanted to
inform you that your mother has had an accident. A fall . . . No,
she's all right. They're transporting her to the hospital now. . . ."

Mrs. Howard turned to Treha and whispered, "This is not
fair. There's no way she can legally terminate you for helping
someone who fell. Don't sign anything. Do you understand?"

Treha nodded. Mrs. Howard scanned the credenza behind
Millstone as if she were looking for something.

Millstone hung up the phone, then picked it up again and
dialed three numbers. "Mr. Davis, would you—? I'm sorry;
that's right. Mr. Drennan, would you come to my office immediately?"

"Jillian, don't do this. Treha was helping you. She's an asset
here, not a liability."

Millstone came around her desk and pointed at Mrs.
Howard. "You are no longer welcome here. Find another place
to meddle." She picked up an envelope behind her.

"How can you be so insensitive?"

"And how can you be so hard of hearing? We don't need you.
Why don't you understand?"

A younger security guard walked in, keys jangling, a grim look on his face. "You wanted to see me, ma'am?"

"Escort Ms. Langsam to her locker and then out of the building." The woman handed the envelope to Treha. "This is a restraining order. You are not to come within one hundred yards of the building after today. It's all in there. You can read it."

Treha took the envelope but left it sealed. She looked at Mrs. Howard, then back to Millstone. "Why do you hate me?"

"I don't hate you. Now follow Mr. Drennan and get your things."

The security guard stepped inside, touched the brim of his hat, and nodded. He put his thumbs in his belt and stood dutifully, glancing at Treha.

"Can I say good-bye to them?" Treha said.

Millstone shook her head.

"Just to Elsie?" Treha said flatly.

Millstone glanced at Drennan and the man took Treha's elbow as if he had done this type of thing before, as if the movements were choreographed.

"Come with me," he said.

Treha typed with the fingers of her free hand. She glanced at *Excellence*. Her head was light because of the glue and some sort of aftershave Drennan wore, or maybe it was his deodorant. A sweet and sweaty bouquet that followed him out the door as his keys jangled.

Treha glanced back at Mrs. Howard. "Would you tell them good-bye for me?"

Mrs. Howard nodded.

As she passed the front desk, there were averted eyes, inner conflict at seeing a coworker banished. Nothing to say but go back to your duties as assigned and hope it didn't happen to you.

The contents of her locker fit neatly into a white kitchen trash bag. Treha stared at it on the floor of the empty locker. This was all the space she needed to house her life. There were extra scrubs and a hairbrush and below were a couple photos the residents had given her in the past few months. A roll of duct tape. A pair of headphones that didn't work.

"I'm sorry this is happening," Drennan said.

She picked up the bag and handed him the roll of tape. Her last gift. "I don't need this."

"Okay," he said. "Thanks."

Treha closed the locker and walked outside, shoelaces dangling. He didn't hold her elbow. He didn't have to.

CHAPTER 20

Miriam knew this was not the time to have a confrontation with Millstone. Besides, she knew if she said anything, it would end with her jumping over the desk and wrestling the woman to the ground. She had heard all the tricks of counting to ten, and she had used many with some of the more belligerent residents, but turning her back and walking away was the only real coping mechanism now. She walked out the front door and the security guard pointed to the front gate, where she found Treha by the sidewalk.

"Is this one hundred yards, do you think?" the girl said.

"You're fine. Treha, don't let her get to you. This is not over."

Her eyes seemed to be going full tilt now, her body swaying.

"I need to tell Elsie what happened. I'll call her, and then we'll leave together."

"You can go back and see her," Treha said.

"Are you sure you're all right?"

She nodded. "Tell her I'm sorry I won't get to talk with her anymore."

"You'll get to talk with her again. Trust me."

Miriam walked briskly inside and went to Elsie's room, halfway expecting Millstone to slap her with a restraining order too.

She found Elsie still in her chair, her eyes closed. When she turned to leave, Elsie spoke.

"I was praying, not sleeping. Tell me what happened."

Miriam told her and Elsie pursed her lips and shook her head.

"This may be my last chance to talk face-to-face for a while," Miriam said. "Millstone has drawn a line and I think I'm on the other side of it."

"It's moments like this that make a God-fearing woman want to learn a few good curse words."

"Elsie, what can you tell me about Dr. Crenshaw? What did he know about Treha's past?"

Elsie looked out the window. "He was torn up about something concerning her. Regrets. I never figured it out, but I did help him find forgiveness. Physically Jim Crenshaw was a mess. He'd abused his body for decades. But spiritually he was worse. He was adrift."

Peace in the Valley. That was the song she had heard on the radio earlier. How had she remembered? Something about sorrow and sadness and trouble leaving because there will be peace in the valley.

"What regrets?"

"He said he had done things as a doctor he wasn't proud of and wanted forgiveness. I told him he could have that."

"And you think this had something to do with Treha?"

"This is the part . . . Jim said he was the reason Treha came to work here. He found her."

"That can't be. As I recall, she answered an advertisement. She had printed it and carried it with her when she showed up on our doorstep."

"Do you know how she found it?"

"I assumed it was online or Buck put it on a board at a grocery."

"Jim sent that to her. He suggested she apply."

"But how would he have known her? Or where she lived?"

"I never asked."

Miriam's mind spun. "Elsie, did he keep a file on Treha? Things written down that might help?"

"Not that I know of. Why?"

"I thought he might have mentioned it. Did he ever talk about a man named Davidson?"

The old woman shook her head, making the skin under her neck jiggle. "I think he didn't share more because he was protecting somebody."

"Who?"

"I don't know. Maybe himself. Maybe me. Maybe he was just so ashamed of what he did that he didn't want me to think less of him. I told him there was nothing he could do that would keep God from loving him. And if he was good enough for God, he was good enough for me. But that didn't help."

Elsie reached for the quilt behind her and pulled on a yellow strand that had gone rogue. "This was given to me by the ladies' missionary society at my church. For years we would make care baskets for missionaries in Africa, India, Burma—they call it something else now." She pointed a crooked finger at a panel. "Each of these little squares has a verse reference. Like this one here. Isaiah 40:8. 'The grass withers and the flowers fall, but the word of our God endures forever.'"

"Do you know all of these by heart?"

"When the mind is sharp, I can get pretty close. Here's Psalm 119:11." She closed her eyes and lifted her right hand like some conductor ready to lead a biblical orchestra. "'I have hidden your word in my heart that I might not sin against you.' That one is a comfort, but the truth is all the hiding in the world doesn't keep you from sin; it just lets you know it's there."

Now Miriam understood the straight and curved lines on the patchwork that had made no sense when she saw them upside down. Like her life. And Treha's. "It's beautiful," she said.

"No, it's full of flaws. Missed stitches and crooked squares fashioned by arthritic hands. That's what makes it priceless to me. It's more meaningful because every time I look, I see those ladies working and talking and laughing and praying. We solved a lot of the world's problems in those sewing circles. The beauty is in the flaws. I tried to tell Jim that."

"He wouldn't listen?"

"He listened and I think he understood." Elsie touched a few more panels like she was caressing the face of a friend. "I don't know everything Jim did, but I saw a tortured soul set free."

"What do you mean?"

"He was cool to my faith at first. Stayed away for a while, didn't want to hear it. I can take rejection as long as you're really rejecting the message and not my bad breath or the way I'm presenting it. As time went on and we built trust, he came around and wanted to know what gave me hope."

She touched another panel. "'Always be prepared to give an answer to everyone who asks you to give the reason for the hope that you have.'"

"Your recall is amazing."

"That's not the important part. The important part comes last. Give people the reason for the hope you have, 'but do this with gentleness and respect.'" She punctuated each word with a finger on the quilt. "If only Millstone could follow that. And if Christians would wrap their truth like that, I expect we'd give the truth to more hungry people."

"I appreciate what you're saying. I believe, but I struggle with it."

"Mmm-hmm. I've known since we met that you're searching for more than retirement. You're searching for something you can't find anywhere but in here." She pointed at Miriam's chest.

Miriam stared at the quilt and the squares. In their imperfection they somehow seemed perfect, placed in the design by loving hands that cared about an old woman alone in a room with cheesy music and a faith so real she could taste it.

"What about Jim?" she said. "What happened?"

"We were sitting at the breakfast table. I remember as clear as you sitting right there. He wasn't eating his grapefruit. His coffee was cold. Just staring off. I said, 'Jim, you look like you've come to a decision.'

"'I sure have,' he says. And he gave me that smile of his and I knew what had happened."

She pointed at another square on the quilt. On it was stitched *Ezekiel 36:26*. Elsie closed her eyes again. "'I will give you a new heart and put a new spirit in you; I will remove from you your heart of stone and give you a heart of flesh.' That's what happened. We prayed together. We cried together. And God began to work in his heart to change things. To help him deal with his regrets."

"That's why he had hired Devin to come record him."

"That's right. And then he was gone. He was reading his Bible, soaking it in, asking more questions . . ."

Elsie yawned and Miriam stood. "I'll leave you to get some beauty rest."

"Too late for beauty, my dear. I'll settle for sanity and continence."

Miriam put a hand on her shoulder. "Thank you, Elsie. Hang in there with Millstone."

Elsie clasped hands with her, and Miriam was surprised at the fierce grip. "You take care of that girl."

Streams from Desert Gardens
outtake 1

Camera shaking, being positioned.

Shot of empty office, empty chair. Devin walks into shot and turns.

What's that?

JONAH (OFF CAMERA): **New lens. Sit down—I want to try it out.**

Devin sits.

How much did that cost? And where'd you get the money?

VOC: **You don't need to know everything. Just talk.**

About what?

VOC: **I don't care. Anything. Why we're doing this.**

Why? We're doing this because we can't *not* do it. That's the best answer. We're doing this because this is what we were made to do.

VOC: **We were made to have a failing business?**

We're not failing. Don't you see? Some of the biggest breakthroughs came when everybody thought something was a failure.

VOC: **Give me one example.**

I don't know. The lightbulb. The coffeemaker. Are you done?

VOC: **No, stay there.**

Camera zooms and refocuses.

VOC: **What makes a good documentary?**

Well, it's certainly not letting the director get in front of the camera. You're supposed to stay out of the way. Be seen, not heard. A good documentary presents the illusion that you're simply watching life. And the viewer is not really *watching*; they're participating in the process, discovering as the camera discovers. When you achieve that, you know you have something special.

VOC: **Preach it.**

A good film draws you in because it feels like life. That's what we're doing at Desert Gardens, showing real life.

VOC: **Turn left a little. No, my left. There. This looks really good. So keep going. Why did you choose this place, these people?**

My grandfather was here. I would come to see him and listen to the stories of my family. After the crash—

VOC: **Say more about the crash. For our viewing audience.**

My parents . . . You know this. My parents died in a plane crash. A private company plane. They weren't

rich or anything, just headed to a conference. Plane went down and I was alone. A pack of wolves took me in, though.

VOC: Is that why you do this? Connecting with other people?

I've never thought of it that way, but maybe. This kind of fills in some pieces for me. But it's more than that. More than some psychological catharsis, if that's what you're saying.

VOC: Hey, I'm just testing out a new lens.

Will that work on a long shot?

VOC: That's what it's for.

CHAPTER 21

DEVIN SAT in his car counting bricks in the wall surrounding the massive home of Calvin Davidson. He hadn't seen the old man yet and he was running out of gas because he had to keep the air conditioner running. It was about five degrees warmer here than in Tucson.

He had searched for the man's phone number but it was unlisted. He had the address because Miriam Howard had given it to him. She had warmed to his idea of telling Treha's story and suggested he try to find some information about Davidson, so that morning he'd gone all in and driven two hours and now here he was. Waiting.

Devin wasn't sure how this man connected with Treha and Dr. Crenshaw, but it seemed important to Miriam. And that was enough for him. Because this idea about Treha was golden. So he had to get Miriam to trust him, give him access now that Desert Gardens was closed to him. This was a way to prove he was fully invested.

It was one of Devin's strengths—tenacity. Or maybe foolishness.

When he'd first pulled up, he rang the bell and passed the time waiting by reading a paper taped to the front door.

A lawn care company had left it and the date of service was the day before. Apparently Davidson's slow-drip sprinklers were operating, though some plants in the xeriscape were in distress, and the company would need access to the control panel inside the garage—could the occupant please call to set up a service appointment? Davidson's phone number was scribbled at the top of the bill and Devin programmed it into his phone.

He'd dialed as soon as he returned to the car but received no answer. He was hoping to hear Davidson's voice, but a machine told him to leave a message. Devin had, though now he thought it might have been a mistake. He had hemmed and hawed at why he wanted to see the man.

A text came from Jonah: Any geezer activity?

Devin replied: Zilch. Saw a neighbor walking. Said he hadn't seen Davidson in a week.

Detect any odors?

Somebody is barbecuing.

Do you like your Davidson medium or rare?

Not funny.

Hang tough.

Devin noticed the gate opening in his rearview and a UPS truck barreled through. He had followed a garbage truck into the subdivision, past the slow-moving gate, and wound to the Davidson property on at least two acres along a side street. Devin's heart skipped a beat when the truck's brake lights shone in front of him; then the truck moved to the next house, and the man in brown shorts with wraparound sunglasses and gelled hair knocked on the front door. A woman answered and signed for the package and life went on.

The truck gave Devin an idea. He drove back through the

gate—getting out was a lot easier than getting in—and twenty minutes later he was back at the same spot where his car's slight coolant leak had left a yellowish-green spot on the pavement. He parked and pulled out the book-size box and some tape he had bought at Office Depot. He didn't want to make it too hard in case the man had arthritic fingers.

He opened the spiral notebook he kept with him and took three runs at the message. The first two tries felt too desperate. Phrases like *please call* and *I need to talk to you* covered the page. It sounded pathetic and he didn't want that. He wanted to draw the old man in with a hook, make him yearn to know who had sent the box. He told himself this was okay, it was for a good cause, though he wasn't sure.

Devin pushed the thoughts away and wrote, this time finding something mysterious and inviting.

Your house is being watched. Call this number. I can help.

He wrote his cell number beneath the words but didn't sign the note. He folded the page twice and placed it in the box, writing *Calvin Davidson* on the front. The sun was fully up when he propped the box against the door and rang the bell. He retreated to the car and watched the front windows to see any movement of drapes or shutters. His view was partially blocked by mesquite trees whose brilliant-green branches had taken over.

An hour later, bored out of his mind, Devin was so hungry he could hear his stomach speaking another language. He checked his phone to find the nearest restaurant and looked once more at the box by the front door.

He was gone a few minutes and returned with two chicken

sandwiches, waffle fries, and an iced tea. Devin shook his head when he saw the box was gone.

We have activity, he texted Jonah.

You dig him up in the backyard?

Not funny. Stay tuned.

He unwrapped the first sandwich and ate ravenously, the prospect of finally breaking through stirring his appetite. In the middle of the second sandwich, the phone rang. The number was restricted. He tried twice to unlock the cell but his greasy fingers slipped. On the third try he answered and glanced at the house as he tried to swallow and talk.

"Yes?"

Silence on the other end. A *click-click*—or maybe *cluck-cluck*. Like someone's dentures. He decided to go for it.

"Mr. Davidson, thank you for calling." Firm, confident. Exuding strength.

He had always believed you could tell much about a person by their voice. Not just word choice and demeanor, but also the actual vocal print. The human voice was unique to each person—like a fingerprint.

He knew next to nothing about the man on the other end, but when he heard the first words from Calvin Davidson's mouth, Devin knew he had discovered gold.

"Are you with them?"

Four words. Crackling, like hot water poured over ice. Also deeply resonant, as if coming from some underground cavern. Davidson sounded like an actor Devin's mother had loved. She would point him out in films when Devin was younger, and now the man was typecast as the grizzled, confused old man.

"Who are you? What do you want with me?"

"Mr. Davidson, don't hang up. I'm a friend."

"You are no friend of mine."

What richness. Texture. And the syntax—not the colloquial *you're*, but *you are*. Devin couldn't wait to get a microphone on the man and watch the meters dance.

Careful not to sound needy. Let him hear poise.

"Your home is being watched." Of course, Devin was the one watching. "I'd like to help you—"

"Surveillance. You tell me nothing I don't already know. They come at night. When I try to sleep. They can sense me sleeping. Or maybe you're one of them."

"No, I'm not one of them."

"They've planted listening devices in the ceiling. My phone. They're engineering plants now, modifying them genetically to listen in on conversations."

Devin waited, took a breath. "Sir, my name is Devin Hillis. I'm not your enemy."

"And who are you with, Devin Hillis?" Davidson spat his name as if it were a curse.

"I'm not with anyone. I mean, I own a company called Life Reviews. We produce video presentations, make films—documentaries."

"Documentaries. Do you think people care about the truth these days? We can't discern the truth from the lies being told us."

"Sir, a friend suggested I contact you. Her name is Miriam Howard."

"I've never heard of her."

"She runs a retirement home—at least she did until a couple of days ago."

"You're not taking me there. I won't go. I know that's why they're listening, so they can trap me. So they can have me committed, put a white jacket on me."

"That's not why I'm calling. One of her residents knew you. He wrote you a letter and she wanted you to have it."

Silence on the other end except for the wheezing rasp, as if he were exerting himself. Devin looked at the front windows of the house but there was no movement.

"You're with the government, are you not?"

"What?"

"Or are you selling something?"

His voice was a bubbling cauldron of contempt. Wonderful. At least there was passion.

"I'm not selling anything. I'm here to help."

"So you are from the government. Here to help yourself."

The call cut off and Devin cursed. He'd felt he was making a connection with the man; then the line went dead. He redialed.

A sharp tap against the window.

Devin glanced over to see the barrel of a handgun. Square and ancient. Behind it, a wrinkled hand gripping the revolver. A face full of wrinkles and derision.

Poise suddenly left Devin, along with composure and control. The gun jerked toward the ground twice, and Devin interpreted this correctly and rolled his window down. He noticed the cordless phone in the man's other hand.

Calvin Davidson wore a blue cardigan sweater and plaid pants. They looked thin, like pajamas. His face was neatly shaved up to the thin mustache, which reminded Devin of his grandfather's, though Davidson had missed a patch under his chin and the skin around it was blotchy and red as if he had been scratching with fingernails that were just a little too long for a person with all his sanity. His eyelids were puffy, like wrinkled cotton balls.

The man's mouth was open as if his dentures were giving

him pain; then he gnashed his teeth. "They can't trace this. Every gun sold these days has a number, a trail to follow."

Devin nodded.

"Not this weapon. It was taken from a German soldier in the Ardennes Forest. It's a relic, like me. But even relics can have life. Do you understand?"

The old man leaned down farther. His eyes were green and clouded, but there was fire behind them. Like a rumbling volcano ready to spew ash. Devin gulped, and as hard as it was not to stare at the gun, he kept his eyes on the man's face.

"You don't need to use that, sir."

"Do you think a firearm that is seventy years old, give or take, could actually work after all this time?"

Good question. Devin tried to answer, but his mouth could only form the word *I* and no sound came from his lips. He looked at the barrel and the wrinkled finger wrapped around the trigger.

Davidson put the phone in his sweater pocket and the antenna stuck out. Then he grabbed the back of his head and rubbed. "Microwave towers are strong here. A man can't think straight. A man might pull the trigger."

"I'm sorry," Devin finally managed. "I didn't mean to bother you. I'm only trying to contact you."

"Spying is not contacting. Sending cryptic messages in boxes, calling my unlisted number—this is at the very least harassment. The authorities would agree with me."

Devin held up both hands. "I only wanted to talk."

The gun in his face now. The man's pitch was low, air traveling over the vocal folds and the vibration slow and grating. But his face and the veins in his neck tensed.

"They have ways of controlling the mind. The medicine

they give, the contaminated water, the messages they send through television, subliminal advertising, even during sports—messages in the end zone."

Women have higher voices because they have shorter vocal cords. But men's voices can rise in moments of stress and great emotion. Fear, excitement, and joy also affect the voice.

Which was why Devin wanted to scream like a schoolgirl.

He put the car in gear and held his foot over the brake. "The man's name is Crenshaw. The guy who sent you the letter. James Crenshaw. He was a doctor."

He had hoped this would snap the man out of his stupor, that he would show recognition and invite him inside, to laugh and say it was all an act. Instead, Davidson squinted, his eyebrows bushy with several rogue hairs branching out like the mesquite trees. He put both thumbs on the hammer and with great effort pulled it back.

"I'm leaving," Devin said.

His cell beeped with a text message as he accelerated. Jonah, asking for an update.

Contact made, Devin texted as he drove through the gate. Need a new icebreaker.

CHAPTER 22

MIRIAM TOSSED and turned, dozed awhile, then finally gave up before daylight and rose to make coffee. She couldn't get Treha or Desert Gardens off her mind. The scene with Jillian Millstone after Mrs. Williams was taken away haunted her.

She called TMC to check on their conditions and found that Ardeth Williams had a broken hip. No change with Dr. Crenshaw. Miriam wondered about the man's family, but that was out of her hands now.

Charlie shuffled into the kitchen, seeming oblivious to her struggle. He poured a cup of coffee and flipped on the television, and she couldn't take the noise, so she got dressed and told him she was going for a walk.

"Where you going?" he said, still staring at the TV.

"I don't know. Around the block."

Maybe she should get a dog. That would force her to exercise more. But the prospect of feeding it and cleaning up after it made her think again. After all, she had Charlie.

The streets were busy. Neighbors hustling off to work and school, mothers busy with children, men with honey-do lists on pads by their steering wheels and fiddling with cell phones.

The ground was flat here and she set out a good pace to get

her heart rate going. Step by step, she thought of Treha. What would her life be like a year down the road? Her job skills were limited and she had even fewer relational skills. How would she find her way?

Perhaps this path Devin offered was a good one. Miriam had asked Treha about her life, about her history, and the conversations always led to walls. It wasn't that the girl didn't want to talk. She would gladly dive into her past, but it was a dive into an empty lake, so she borrowed water from other cisterns and filled her life with theirs. It was like asking Charlie a question about his feelings. He had lived his entire life trying not to have feelings. Treha really didn't know about her past, and this pushed Miriam's walking pace, as if the energy expended here could propel her closer to the girl.

In their first meeting, Treha had almost wandered in off the street with the application. For some reason Miriam had seen more than the shifting eyes and head movement and dirty scrubs. There was intelligence here—she could tell by the way Treha filled out the application for the low-level janitorial position. Most applicants got stuck somewhere between lines ten and twenty. But Treha wasn't fazed by the task. Her writing skills, spelling, and comprehension surprised Miriam. She had an excellent vocabulary and tiny but legible handwriting, though she grasped the pen in an awkward way, sticking it between the third and fourth fingers of her left hand and steadying it with her thumb.

Miriam stopped at the corner and glanced at her watch, realizing she had been walking longer and farther than she expected. A half block away was a park with a paved walkway that ringed the property. Artificial turf on an empty field near the phantom playground equipment. The picnic tables under the gazebo were also empty of all signs of life, painted an off-yellow that made the whole area seem bright.

She picked up her pace and her breathing evened. The air this close to the mountains felt clean and pure, part of why they had wanted to move to this side of town. When she passed the baseball field, she was at full steam and feeling good, actually breaking a sweat, surprised at the way her body was working. She wouldn't win any marathons, but the neck- and backaches she sometimes felt this early weren't there. Perhaps if she spent less time in the car, her muscles wouldn't tense. Maybe the exercise would help her sleep as well. If she could get Charlie out here, it might mean a resurgence to their sex life.

She smiled. There was only so much exercise one could do.

Perhaps it was the movement, the increased blood flow or oxygen to the brain, but in a flash Miriam again saw Treha clutching the application. She had given one paltry reference and Miriam hadn't checked it. . . . No, she had—she had called the number but hadn't connected with the woman Treha had listed. And it didn't matter; there had been something about Treha, something she intuitively trusted.

Now she wanted to open that personnel file and fish it out. Of course, she couldn't do that, and her memory wasn't good enough to recall the reference.

Why was she so consumed with this girl? Why would her thoughts not turn toward something or someone else? Was it the impending boredom bearing down on her? The repressed mothering instincts dormant for so long?

She turned toward home, bits and pieces of conversations she'd had with Treha running through her mind. Questions that filtered through as she showered and cleaned the dirty dishes Charlie had left in the sink and put a load of laundry in and stripped the bed. She wasn't averse to domestic work—she had been doing this her whole married life—but the feeling she had at noon was that there was something more important to do.

She wanted to call Treha, but the girl had no phone. She was lucky to have an apartment of her own. Miriam decided to pay her a visit.

She could have just stuck her head in the office door and told Charlie where she was going, but that felt like giving him too much control. She didn't want to send the message that he had a right to know everything she was doing and thinking every minute. So she jotted a note and put a magnet over it on the refrigerator.

Running an errand, back in a couple of hours.

He would call if he needed something. They were both going to have to learn this dance, this new-normal setting on life.

She drove to Treha's apartment from memory, taking a wrong turn and reaching a dead end at an ancient brick house with iron bars on the windows. She made a U-turn and back-tracked to find the correct street and finally saw the apartment in the distance. As she parked, she heard a noise she thought at first might be her car, then saw the boy tossing what was left of a tennis ball against a concrete wall. He watched her warily as if he were the security guard.

"You looking for somebody?" *Thwop-smack*, the ball against the wall and in his hand again.

Miriam got out. "I'm here to see Treha."

"Oh, I remember you were here the other night dropping her off." *Thwop-smack*. "She ain't here." *Thwop-smack*.

"Do you know where she is?"

"Maybe. Who's asking?"

She held out a hand. "I'm Mrs. Howard. I work with her."

"You mean you used to," he said. "She got fired."

"You must be Du'Relle."

He shook her hand vigorously, as if he'd been trained by someone in the military to do so, and looked at her with wide brown eyes. "We look out for each other, me and Treha. I watch her back; she watches mine."

Precocious child. "I just need to talk with her."

Thwop-tick-tick. He missed the ball and ran into the parking lot after it. As he crawled under an old Camaro, he said, "She told me she was going to Goodwill. Try to find another bike. Hers got stolen."

Thwop-smack.

"Do you know what's wrong with her eyes?" he said. "They move all around and I don't want to ask her because my mama says it's not polite to ask people stuff like that."

"Your mother is a kind woman." *Not very present, but kind.*

"I ain't never seen her smile. One time I had her come over to my house and we watched this comedy movie. Man, it's the funniest thing I ever seen. I about bust a gut every time I watch it. But she sits there and her face is frozen. Not even a twitch of a grin—I watched her the whole time. She just looked at the TV like it was some *CSI* show. But I've seen her stand up to gangbangers. She don't take nothing from nobody."

"I'm not sure why Treha is the way she is. That's a good question."

Thwop-smack.

"Well, my mama says everybody's different in their own way and you can either try to make them into who you want them to be or you can accept them and deal with what you got."

"Your mama sounds like a philosopher."

"She's pretty smart."

"Could you tell me where Goodwill is from here?"

Thwop-smack.

"Go down that way to . . . Aww, it'd be easier for me to show you. It's not that far." He moved toward her car.

"You shouldn't get in cars with people you meet for the first time."

Thwop-smack.

"Fine. Suit yourself." He pointed the ball with a long, gangly arm. "You go down about, I don't know, seven or eight streets, and go left. Then there's a Walgreens on the corner. I think it's two—no, that's a CVS and then there's a Walgreens. Anyway, you turn there . . ."

The rest of the directions were incomprehensible. A series of turns marked by fast-food restaurants and a Fry's near a Dollar Tree and a check-cashing place and the Goodwill was in the next plaza.

Thwop-smack-shrug.

"Hope you find her, ma'am."

Miriam stopped at a Kwik Mart to get directions and finally found the Goodwill in an area Du'Relle had not described. It *was* near a Walgreens, but what in the world isn't?

The store was a cornucopia of clothing and cast-off items on racks. There was an odor of mildew and dust and a smell she could only associate with a childhood memory of her grandfather's house, a Proustian moment when she could close her eyes and see the old man at the stove cooking eggs and onions and then wandering onto the front porch for a game of ringtoss, the rings made of heavy rope. He had seemed ancient then, but she realized he was no older than she was now.

Along the front wall of the store were bookshelves filled with paperbacks and some hardcovers. Romance novels, mostly, but some mysteries and popular nonfiction. It was clear many wanted nothing more to do with Tom Clancy, John Grisham, and Nora Roberts, though the books seemed to have been well read.

In the far back corner was what was loosely termed *Sporting Goods*, but Treha wasn't there. The only bicycles were for children, and they were in surprisingly good condition.

Miriam found a woman wearing a blue vest with a name tag and asked if she'd seen someone fitting Treha's description. The woman shook her head. Miriam asked where else in the area she could buy a used bike and the woman told her about a second-hand sports store four blocks away, pointing like Du'Relle.

"Across from the Walgreens," the woman said.

Miriam found bikes chained outside in a line and spotted Treha checking tags, gesturing and speaking to a portly man with a mustache and shaved head. She wore her greenish-blue scrubs. Her skin was milky white and ghostlike, and from this vantage point, the curious shape of her ears was accentuated. The man behind her seemed disinterested at best.

"You know that's twice as much as you should charge," Treha said. "I could buy a new one for that."

"Be my guest," the man said. "If you can find a new one for $225, snag it. I'll go $200, but that's it. I'd lose money if I go lower."

"You could be arrested for that."

"For what?" the man said.

"Robbery. I don't know who is worse, the person who cut my chain and rode off or you. I think you may be worse because you see me."

Bald Guy looked up at Miriam. "Can I help you with something?"

Miriam shook her head. "Treha, I'd like to speak with you."

Treha turned and froze like a farm animal might notice a human in the pasture and fix a gaze. If there was emotion behind the stare, Miriam couldn't detect it. It took the girl a moment to process Miriam standing there, but she turned and spoke again to Bald Guy.

"I told you, my bike was stolen. The one I bought here last year. You should give me a break on the price."

"You're right; I should. Just because you had your bike stolen. I've had seven bikes stolen from here in the last month. Now am I supposed to charge you more because I've had some bad luck? I'll go $200."

Treha looked back at Miriam. "What are you doing here?"

"I wanted to talk. See how you were doing. Are you looking for a new bike?"

Stupid question. Of course she was.

"You need more time; that's fine," the man said.

"Do you have the money?" Miriam said. She thought she would have been able to read the look on the face of anyone else on the planet, but she couldn't discern Treha's response.

"I have money, but not what they're asking for these."

"All right, I'll have pity on you and give you the returning-customer discount," the man behind her said. "I'll go $190, but that's it. That's as low as I can go."

"Have you had lunch yet?" Miriam said.

Treha shook her head.

"They have a deal at the sub place. Let's go there."

Treha looked at the man and then nodded. He called after her in the parking lot that the price would go back up if they walked away, but they kept going.

They ordered two six-inch sub sandwiches with soda and

chips and sat in a booth in the room that looked like it had been taken over by someone who only knew how to paint in yellow and black.

"How did you find me?" Treha said.

"Du'Relle. He's something. Seems to like you quite a bit."

Treha chewed her food, her head swaying, fingers working on the sandwich. "He asks too many questions."

"I'll bet that's what you say to Du'Relle about me."

Anyone else would have smiled, but Treha stared.

Miriam nodded. She hoped Treha wouldn't think the same of her when they were through. "Are you interested in the bike at the store?"

"He's charging twice as much as he should," she said. "I could buy a new one for what he is asking."

"Why don't you?"

"Because the new ones don't last. They're not made as well."

"We have neighbors who have garage sales, children that are grown who leave behind bikes. I might be able to find you one for much less. Free, even."

They ate in silence for a moment, Treha staring at the table. "I would like that."

Miriam didn't know how to broach what she had come to ask. Was it enough to have simply found Treha, to spend time with her?

"Treha, now that your time at Desert Gardens has come to an end, what do you want to do? Do you have anything in mind?"

Treha looked up from her food, her eyes dancing. "I want to know why."

"Why you were let go?"

"Why I am the way I am."

"I can help you with that if you'd like. But it may not be easy. It might be painful."

"I don't care," Treha said.

"Then let's start with this. Your coming to Desert Gardens. How did you find out about the job? Was it online or did you see a help-wanted ad?"

"I got a letter. There was an application inside."

"Who was it from?"

"The envelope had *Desert Gardens* on it. No one signed it. I thought it came from you."

"Was it just the application?"

"No, there was an ad and a note. Something like 'Dear Treha, we want you to work for us. Fill this out.' Something like that."

"Do you remember the reference you gave? I think you only had one person listed. I never talked to her."

"Why not?"

"I tried to call but we never connected. Besides, I could tell you were perfect for the job. Do you remember who you listed?"

Treha shook her head, but Miriam wondered if it was the truth.

"Why do you want to help me?" Treha said.

"I would hope you know by now how much I care. And now I have a lot of extra time on my hands. We both do. It would make me feel good to know I'm doing something constructive." Miriam leaned forward. "You've learned the histories of many people at Desert Gardens. Maybe it's time to learn yours."

"I don't think it will be a very nice story."

"We won't know unless we try." She smiled at the girl and wadded the wax paper that had held her sandwich.

"There was a place near the interstate where I stayed. Before I moved to my apartment."

"Is that the reference you gave?"

Treha nodded. "James 127 House. I listed the woman who ran it."

Miriam's heart quickened. "Do you remember her name?"

"Vivian Hansen."

"Do you remember where the house is?"

"I'm not good with directions."

Miriam's cell rang. She looked at it but didn't recognize the number. "I should take this."

"Miriam, this is Devin Hillis. I thought you should know I've made contact with Calvin Davidson."

The news stunned her. "What? Devin, I asked you to find out more information, not—"

"I'm sorry. I wanted to show you I'm serious. I drove up to Scottsdale because he had an unlisted phone number."

"You *drove* there? When?"

"This morning, early. Miriam, I really want to work with Treha. I can't explain this feeling, but something says we need to follow her story. I thought if I could find information about her, you'd see how serious I am."

There was no denying his commitment. . . . "What happened with Davidson?"

"The old guy's a paranoid kook. Thinks people are tapping his phones. Probably has a date set for the apocalypse. Lucid in some ways, but in others . . . He kind of lives like a hermit in a big house. Wants nothing to do with the outside world."

"You knocked on the door and found all this out?"

"He shoved a gun in my face and told me to leave. So I did."

"What do you want from me, Devin?"

"She trusts you. You can help us."

Miriam glanced at the girl as she gathered bits of lettuce with her fingers and ate them. "I don't know."

"I'm just going to let her tell her story or help her discover what that story really is. If it leads nowhere, at least we tried."

Miriam was beginning to feel the same way, but she didn't want to tell him that. "I'll call you back," she said.

CHAPTER 23

THE ANSWERING MACHINE came on when Miriam called home, and she spoke as if Charlie were listening, asking him to answer. He always had an ear to the phone, the TV, the radio. When he didn't answer, she hung up and walked toward the car. Treha was waiting.

Her cell rang. Charlie.

"You need something?"

"I'm trying to find an address. Do you think you could look it up?"

"Sure."

She told him the listing and he quickly found a website and the address and phone number. The location was northwest of Tucson in the town of Marana. He gave her the exit from I-10 and the cross streets. "Looks like it's out in the boonies. Farm country. Why are you interested in this place?"

"Treha used to live there." She hesitated, then forged ahead. "Charles, what would you think of having Treha stay with us for a few days? In the guest room. It would only be temporary."

"What for? I thought she had an apartment."

"She does, but I may be spending more time with her."

"I don't understand it, but I guess I don't have to. It's fine."

He said it without much emotion, but she could hear the lingering questions. He didn't trust her. He didn't value her opinion, her heart.

"I'll be a little longer than I thought," she said.

"Take your time."

James 127 House was a ministry run by Vivian Hansen and her husband, Jake. Their vision came from a message their pastor had given at the local megachurch from James chapter 1. Before that, the couple had been on short-term mission trips across the border and had been drawn to orphans. They'd even tried to adopt two boys from Russia, but when that fell through, they decided God had other plans. That was twenty years ago.

Miriam gleaned all of this from the brochure in the entryway of the home before she met Vivian. During that morning message at the church, their focus had gone from orphans to orphans and widows. The spark had come at the same time, God invading with a combination ministry to children who had no parents and lonely widows in grief.

Jake, who was a contractor by trade, building houses in a market that didn't need them, had focused his energy on their five acres in the middle of farms and subdivisions. He took a three-bedroom house and expanded the three-car garage to two levels and the 2,500-square-foot home suddenly jumped to nearly 5,000. He built another garage with a small apartment over it behind the house and their ministry began.

The first girl who had come to them was now in her twenties, married with children—there was a picture of Vivian and Gabriella on the back of the brochure. Miriam was touched by the stories of those who had come through the house, the testimonials. It crossed her mind that Devin and Jonah should set up shop here.

When Vivian saw Treha, her eyes lit. She gave the girl a hug and wouldn't let go, even though Treha didn't return it.

"I hope we're not intruding," Miriam said.

"Not at all—it's so great to see you! I've wondered how you were doing, Treha. I've been praying for you."

Vivian gave a quick tour of the main house, which was just like the pictures. The ministry vision hadn't changed. There was a young widow with two children living in the apartment over the garage. Four other children lived with the Hansen family, including two boys of their own. The most recent family Christmas picture on the refrigerator incorporated everyone. There were smiles all around, but even the casual observer could detect pain behind the snapshot. For a house with that many people in it, things were relatively quiet.

Vivian's "office" was her kitchen table and she offered them something to drink. Both said they were fine. She sat and looked at Treha with fascination. "So tell me what you've been doing since you left us."

Treha gave a thumbnail sketch of her life at Desert Gardens with a little of the drama that had unfolded. Miriam picked up the story and explained their relationship.

"I'm so glad to hear this," Vivian said. "I'll bet you fit in with the people at Desert Gardens. I was really concerned when you moved away, but you seemed ready to make a new start."

Miriam spread her hands on the table. "We're trying to connect the dots of Treha's past. She has very little memory of her early life, her own family. We thought you might be able to help."

Vivian gritted her teeth as if she needed to apologize. "We

try not to pry. If children want to talk, we're here. Many of them have come from the foster system and don't want to. You were fostered for a time, weren't you, Treha?"

Eyes shifting, head weaving, staring at the table. "I don't know."

Vivian rose and went to a built-in desk on the other side of the kitchen island stove. There was a corkboard above the desk with notes and a calendar filled with scribbled writing—doctor's appointments and phone numbers all scattered under a Bible verse at the top. She pulled out a plastic box of papers and files divided by year, unclasped the top, and riffled through the pages.

"This is the best I can do. The last place Treha lived before coming to us is listed here." She handed a folder to them and Miriam studied the forms inside. They were from a state program in Arizona with the words *Department of Economic Security* emblazoned at the top. Toward the bottom was the name Treha Langsam and a list of symptoms and disorders the child had been diagnosed with, including "violent behavior." She was described on the back of the report as "unreachable."

"My understanding was that Treha had been in a series of foster homes from early childhood. The state doesn't give us information about that."

"Did anyone ever come looking for her?"

"No. We had her all to ourselves from the time she arrived."

Miriam looked at Treha. "How old were you when you came here?"

A slight shake of the head.

"You were about ten, right, Treha?"

Miriam forged ahead. "Did you notice any of these symptoms after Treha moved here?"

Vivian folded her hands. "There were several outbursts early on, but we learned to cope. Avoid the triggers. Treha, do you remember any of that?"

She shook her head.

"What were the triggers?" Miriam said.

"Sensory things. Noises. Other children being too loud. We gave her certain clothes to wear—a nice jumper outfit, a dress with ruffles—but if she didn't like them, she wouldn't put them on. It may have been the color, the fabric, or a combination. Now that I see you wearing scrubs, it makes me think you always did best in cotton."

Miriam nodded. This must have been why Treha was wearing scrubs when she first came to Desert Gardens.

Vivian continued, "It's our policy not to turn anyone away. We've had to improvise a time or two when we've come up against things we've never experienced. But once Treha came, and she saw our commitment to her, she integrated."

"Did she go to school?"

"I used to teach middle school, so I homeschool. Piecemeal education. We have some who are only here for a few months. Others stay for years. My goal for Treha was to have her get her GED before she left, and she exceeded my expectations. She was a great reader before she ever came here. Must be in her genes. Do you remember taking the test?"

Treha nodded.

"She was off the charts. We were so proud when she did so well."

"Did you ever notice any special abilities she displayed while she lived here?"

"Like what?"

"The way she is with people who are different."

Vivian thought a moment. "There was a little autistic boy we cared for. His father had passed and he and his mother moved in. One day we couldn't find him and the mother got worried. He was in Treha's room, having a conversation. Now this was a boy who could hardly say his own name. And he was sitting there talking with her like . . ." Her voice trailed as she remembered the scene. "It just astounded us."

Miriam glanced at Treha. Her head was down.

"She was always good with words, too. She could memorize like nobody I've ever seen. Such a bright thing. Others couldn't see it, of course."

"But as far as her history goes, you can't shed any light," Miriam said.

"No. But I do have the person's name from Child Protective Services who suggested Treha come here. She's a friend. She knows how to identify and place children who have fallen through the cracks." Vivian handed her a scrap of paper with a phone number and the name Sharon Gavineau. "I doubt Sharon knows any more than I do, but it wouldn't hurt to talk with her."

She looked at Treha again, cocking her head to one side. "Treha, we've missed you. Jake will be sorry he didn't get to see you. I'm so glad you came back to visit."

"Thank you."

Vivian took a picture of the two of them to show her husband and prove Treha had actually been there. Then she pulled Miriam aside and whispered, "Thanks for taking an interest in her. I'll be praying you find the answers."

It was a silent ride back to the interstate. Clouds were forming above the stately Catalinas. Miriam wondered about the lease on Treha's apartment and if she'd be able to pay the rent. How would she get another job? It really would be easier if Treha came to live with her for a few days, but she wasn't sure if the girl would balk.

Treha interrupted Miriam's thoughts. "I heard what the man said on the phone."

"Excuse me? What man?"

"The documentary man, Devin. I heard you talking to him."

"How could you hear what he said?"

"It's not hard; the voice comes through. Maybe it's my ears—I don't know. I heard him talk about Mr. Davidson. The man Dr. Crenshaw wrote to. I want to talk with him."

"All right. But if you heard the conversation, you know this Davidson fellow threatened Devin. I don't think you'll be talking with him anytime soon."

"Threatened him how?"

"He had a gun. You didn't hear that part?"

"He is scared."

"You bet he's scared, and he's not going back there."

"Not Devin. I mean Mr. Davidson is scared."

"Well, I don't care how he feels; I won't put you in that position."

"You aren't putting me in any position. I want to speak to him."

"How do you know he won't pull a gun and shoot you?"

"I don't. But I believe I can get through to him."

Miriam glanced at the girl and she looked the same—her facial expression was set, her eyes moved—but there was something off, something different now. Something present that hadn't been there. Treha had gone along with whatever others had told her. Now something was rising, a will of her own.

And Miriam wasn't sure she liked it. It was easier to deal with a compliant Treha.

"I suppose I can talk with Devin and see—"

"Let me use your phone," she interrupted. "I'll call him. He wants to interview me. He will agree." She held out her hand.

"Treha, is there anything you're not telling me?"

"About what?"

"About any of this. About your past. About Dr. Crenshaw—he was the one who contacted you about the job at Desert Gardens, wasn't he?"

"I don't know what you're talking about."

Miriam could tell she had stepped over the line, had turned to accusing rather than questioning, and she regretted it. She took the phone from her pocket and handed it to Treha.

CHAPTER 24

DEVIN HAD TO HOLD the phone away from his ear because of the volume of Jonah's voice. It was early, at least for Jonah, and he was always cranky when Devin called.

"Why in the world would you go back to Scottsdale? Do you have a death wish?"

"*She* wants to go," Devin said.

"*She?* Since when do you take orders from anyone? I can't even get you to pay me, but *she* speaks and you jump. What's up with that?"

"Jonah, listen to me—"

"If *she* wants to go to Scottsdale, let *her* go. *She* can ride her bike."

"She doesn't have a bike—it was stolen."

"Then let her walk. It'll expand her life expectancy."

"Jonah, calm down. This Davidson guy wasn't that crazy."

"Devin, he pulled a Luger on you."

"It wasn't a Luger."

"It was a gun from some German foxhole. It was probably loaded with the Führer's hollow points. And don't tell me Davidson's a bad aim. The guy is not stable. He probably has a medicine cabinet full of bottles he can't even open. Anyone who's been off their medication can do damage."

203

"You sound like you know. Are you not telling me something?"

"Acid reflux is all I have."

"I want you to come with us."

"*What?* I thought you were calling to get the camera. Devin, this is crazy."

"I need you to shoot the whole thing."

"*Shoot* is the operative word, but we're not the ones who'll be shooting—we'll be dodging. Do you want me to bring the first aid kit, too, the one with all the bandages? Maybe a little morphine to dull the pain?"

"Did you watch *Saving Private Ryan* last night?"

"No, that was two nights ago. Devin, we don't need this right now. We need a paying gig. You haven't answered the phone in a couple of days. Maybe there's something waiting. Something we could use to pay the rent."

"I know this is hard for you to believe, but I need you to trust me. If you've ever trusted my instincts—"

"Let's see—this whole Desert Gardens idea was a sure thing, as I recall. You estimated we'd get a hundred contracts at five grand each. That's the last sure thing I remember."

"Jonah, this is it. I can feel it."

"Devin, I'm numb from the number of times you've said you can feel it. I *can't* feel it."

"Meet me at the office."

"We don't have an office!"

"What are you talking about?"

"I'm sorry. I didn't want to tell you last night. There's this little piece of paper on the door and the locks have been changed. But I'm sure you felt that."

"What about the equipment? Our stuff?"

"When you didn't come in yesterday, I got scared and loaded the computers and equipment in my car. But I didn't touch your stuff. I assume you have your laptop with you."

"Yeah. Wow, I didn't think Sullivan would do that."

"It happens when you don't pay bills. I told you he was serious."

"Okay, I'll pick you up at your mom's house."

"Devin, it's over. This is the third strike."

"No, this is a setback. It's a hurdle. It's every story we've ever recorded that's worth telling; don't you see?"

"I'd say it's more than a hurdle."

"I'm not letting this stop us. We move forward."

"I'm okay moving forward, but Davidson feels like a bad idea. What do we do while we're driving up there for two hours, watch her eyes go back and forth?"

"Now you're being mean."

"I'm being real. It's like watching a human windshield wiper. She gives me the willies."

"You don't have to marry her—I just want you to shoot her. Film her, I mean. I don't care what you do on the way. Listen to your iPod. Sleep. I'm here at her place now. I'll be there in about forty-five minutes."

"You've been talking to me all this time while you're driving to her apartment?"

"No, I'm at Miriam Howard's place. Treha's staying there for some reason."

"I hate you."

"No, you don't—you love me. And you're going to love what happens with this. You're going to read a long, flowing tribute to me one day at the Academy Awards and tell me how much my friendship and mentoring have meant to you and how you would never have realized your dream without my tutelage."

"Tutelage?"

"Trust me."

"We're going to get shot."

"No, we're not. Be ready in forty-five."

Devin rang the doorbell and Mrs. Howard answered. Charlie was behind her with a coffee mug in hand. He raised it and nodded, which felt like as much communication as Devin would get from Treha for the next two hours.

Mrs. Howard stepped outside and closed the door behind her. "I'm concerned, Devin. I don't want anything to happen to her. Or you."

The world was suddenly filled with nervous Nellies. They hadn't been concerned about her riding a bike to work through gang-infested neighborhoods, but an old man in Scottsdale was going to be her undoing.

"I understand. Believe me, I won't take any chances with Davidson."

The woman pursed her lips. "I'm looking into her past and some things are becoming clearer. Not all of it is rosy. Some of it's disturbing."

"Disturbing?"

"Treha looks innocent, an agent of good in a bad world. But a tame tiger is fine until it gets angry or hungry. Or both."

"What are you saying?"

"I think we're dealing with someone neither of us understands."

"You think she'll go Stephen King on me? You know, start a fire or tip over buckets of blood?"

She didn't understand the reference. "I'm just telling you to be careful. She's been in a stable environment and I think that's why she hasn't regressed."

Devin wanted to ask what *regressed* meant, what Miriam had uncovered, but the tiger opened the door and stepped out in her scrubs. She didn't look at Devin, just headed for his car.

"I think I should go with you," Miriam said.

"We have room, if you don't mind equipment at your feet."

"No," Treha said. "I want to do this alone."

Miriam was going to respond, but Treha opened the passenger door, got inside, and buckled.

"You want me to bring her back here?" Devin said.

Miriam nodded. "Call me. Tell me what happens."

Devin got in the car and prepared for the silence. He reached for the radio but was surprised when Treha spoke.

"Tell me about Mr. Davidson."

Devin described him, the house, the neighborhood, his gun—everything he could remember. Treha drank in the information.

"The trick will be getting him to trust us. And maybe you'll have more luck."

"Is he sick?"

"Yes. Dementia, perhaps. Paranoia. Talking about the government. He's not drooling yet, but he's close. He may be a black-helicopter conspiracy theorist. Wouldn't surprise me if he leaned that way."

"Black helicopters?"

"It's how some deal with uncertainty. They make up theories about water contamination and that Wi-Fi is bombarding us with hidden messages. They think the government attacks citizens and starts earthquakes and floods."

"So he spoke with you."

"If you can call it that. I wouldn't classify it as a conversation, per se. It was more like me saying hello and him giving the theory of relativity. In Swahili." A pause as Devin pondered how much to tell. "He brought a pistol to the car. Waved it around and said I was harassing him. I understood that part."

Devin tried to keep his mind on the road but the questions were getting to him. A sign straight ahead said *Photo Enforcement.*

"Why are you helping me?" she said. "Why are you going to this trouble?"

A light flashed in his rearview and he cursed under his breath. He didn't need another Tucson traffic ticket.

"I have a theory, Treha. Things happen for a purpose. People meet, they come together at just the right time. If you're paying attention, good things come. I'm looking for an opportunity to watch you break through to someone like Miriam says you can. I have a good feeling about you and Davidson. We're picking up my camera guy, Jonah, and then we'll head to Scottsdale." He leaned over and opened the glove compartment. "In the meantime, here's some paperwork. It's a release form that says we can film you, interview you, and use the material we get."

She looked at the pages, her head swaying. "I can't read this in a moving car."

"Okay, that's fine. We can talk about it later."

"Is there payment?"

The question took him aback. His first thought was how Jonah would kill him if he offered this girl money.

"We're actually not fully funded right now, but as soon as we start the editing process, I'm expecting investors to come alongside." *Not sure who that might be, but it sounds good.*

"You didn't answer my question," she said.

"How much do you want?"

"How much do you pay someone in a documentary?"

"I don't think people usually get paid—I mean, we could work out a percentage after we recoup our initial investment."

"What does that mean?"

"It means if you invest your time with us now, you'll get paid back later if the movie is a success."

"Okay," she said.

They pulled up to Jonah's house and parked. "Jonah is a little sensitive about the money thing right now. So let's not talk about that on the way."

She looked at him with those wandering eyes and for a moment Devin wondered what he had gotten himself into. Was there any way this girl could salvage his business, his movie, his dreams?

Jonah got in and put the camera equipment beside him.

"Got everything?" Devin said.

"Oh yeah, camera, batteries, memory card, bulletproof vest—I think I'm set."

CHAPTER 25

MIRIAM WATCHED Devin and Treha drive away, feeling she had lost something. The emptiness wasn't just that Treha was gone; it was more. She went for a walk, then halfway down the block turned around and came back to the house and dialed the number Vivian had given her the day before.

Sharon Gavineau had a pleasant voice, but she was all business and seemed standoffish when she realized Miriam was asking about a past client.

"I understand the rules of confidentiality," Miriam said. "But I have a young lady here, Treha Langsam, who has no idea where she came from. Vivian Hansen thought you might be able to put some pieces of the puzzle together."

Her response was firm but kind. "I remember Treha. I knew if anyone could help her, Vivian and Jake could. I'm glad to hear she's progressed and is able to be on her own. But as far as her puzzle goes, I'm afraid I don't have information. I don't have pieces . . . I don't even have the box. I applaud you for wanting to help, though."

"Is there someone you can suggest?"

"I'm sorry, Mrs. Howard."

Miriam hung up. Another closed door. She decided to go

on and not think about Treha, not try to play bloodhound on the trail of her past.

She went to Treha's room. The girl had packed an overnight bag. Literally, a plastic bag from Ross with drawstrings. One pair of scrubs lay on the floor, and another in the bag. Both the same color as the pair she'd worn to Scottsdale.

Miriam picked up the dirty clothes and was thinking of washing them when she noticed something in the morning sunlight. Treha had left her apartment key on the dresser. A single key on a lanyard that said *Arizona Wildcats*. She put the clothes in the washer with another load and returned. Farther down in the bag she found a clean pair of socks and underwear and at the bottom a copy of *Jane Eyre* with a $1 Goodwill sticker. She sat on the bed and opened to the bookmark, about halfway through. There were underlined passages and dog-eared pages. She couldn't tell if this was Treha's work or the previous owner's, but the book moved her. Such a lonely girl reading about an orphan passed from family to family, looking for her place in the world.

Inaction bred hopelessness, so Miriam put the book at the bottom of the bag and dialed the hospital. Ardeth Williams had made a turn for the better, it sounded like, and the hip surgery had gone well, though it would be a long rehab. She spoke with Ardeth's daughter, who was glad for the change but disgruntled with Desert Gardens. Miriam couldn't blame her and told her how sorry she was about what had happened.

The on-duty nurse in ICU said Dr. Crenshaw's condition had not changed, and Miriam could tell from her voice that she had very little hope he would ever awaken. His son was there, or had been, and they were simply waiting for the inevitable.

Through the wall Miriam heard the telltale voices of financial wizards giving opinions about the market. Like the weather forecasters who predicted sunshine, unless there were clouds and rain. It all seemed endless, a financial merry-go-round that never changed, never went anywhere, just kept going up and down and round and round, and she wanted to get off, wanted Charlie to get off and walk in the real world rather than the world of numbers.

She tried to lose herself in the news of the day, checking her computer, but all she found was useless information about celebrities breaking up or getting back together or a child swallowing a Civil War medallion alongside other reports of genocide and human trafficking. As if all of those were equal.

She wound up on Facebook, which felt equally empty. Smiling people who had met for coffee or dinner having a wonderful time at the beach or the mountains. Pictures of weddings and graduations, children and grandchildren and puppies. Facebook was an online billboard that only reinforced the pain of her life, the truth of her loneliness.

As much as Miriam tried to think of something else, Treha kept coming. She felt confident that uncovering the truth would help the girl. Discover the past and it would eventually unveil the future. Dr. Crenshaw had somehow found her, so why couldn't Miriam? From the conversations with Vivian and Sharon, it was clear the hoops through which Treha had jumped in the foster care system were now closed, the information hidden. So what was the next logical place? She could return to Desert Gardens and paw through Jillian Millstone's office . . . No, she couldn't do that.

The next logical source was Treha herself. Perhaps the girl possessed information she didn't realize, couldn't decipher. Records she had in the apartment. Clues. Perhaps Treha was hiding from herself. Perhaps she really didn't want to know her past.

Miriam couldn't invade the girl's space any more than she could waltz into Desert Gardens. She couldn't intrude without asking. Pilfering wasn't ethical or loving. It would be a breach of trust. If Treha ever discovered it . . . what would she do? Pout? She never showed emotion. Except in the past, if Vivian and the foster care documents were right.

She walked to Charlie's door and peeked in. He was staring at the computer screen, feet up on the desk. Across the room, mounted on the wall, was a TV perfectly placed where he could watch both at the same time with a simple head tilt. She wanted him to talk her out of the trip. Talk some sense into her.

She decided the risk was worth it. Treha would never know. And besides, she wasn't doing this selfishly; she was doing it for the girl. To help her.

Miriam grabbed her purse and drove to Treha's apartment, turning the radio up loud and trying to drown the guilt with music from the eighties. She sang along as loudly as she could, remembering the feelings the lyrics stirred. But the guilt returned when she parked, and a bigger twinge overcame her as she walked up the concrete stairs and heard a pitter of feet behind her. Du'Relle.

"Treha's not here," the boy said.

She tried to think quickly. How could she get him away from the apartments? Perhaps send him on an errand to a store. Anything to keep him from seeing her enter the apartment. Anything to give her enough time to search.

"Why aren't you in school?" she said.

"I'm sick today."

"You don't sound sick."

"You can ask my mama. She told me I should stay home."

"Well, if your mother says you're sick, then I suppose you are."

"We got bad news."

Now he was engaging her, leaning against the railing, feeling with both hands along the metal, reaching out for something. She didn't want to encourage him, but she couldn't think of anything to say other than "Is that so?"

"My daddy's not coming home no more."

This stopped her. She studied his face. "I'm sorry to hear that. Where is he?"

"He's over in 'ghanistan. But he's not coming back. These men in uniform came here last night and I told them Mama was at work. I knew he had died, but they wouldn't tell me. She says they're having a funeral and we get to keep a flag."

Miriam's knees gave way and she sat on the stairs. "You poor thing." She was at eye level now, and there was no emotion on his face.

"They told Mama last night at work but she didn't tell me till I got up this morning." He pointed at the apartment behind him, on the bottom level. "She's in there crying."

Miriam didn't know what to say. It was clear the boy was in pain but was more worried about his mother than himself. He was hanging on the railing, almost to the point of falling, it seemed, and she wanted to grab him and hug him and take the hurt away. Like she had done with her own mother. But the hurt was there no matter how hard she hugged, no matter how much she loved or cared. She could only hope to soothe it and make it a bit more bearable. This was the equation of pain: doing the work alone is unequal and impossible. There must be team lifting, like they suggest for appliances.

"I thought they was going to split up," Du'Relle continued. "I thought that was the worst that could happen, them getting a divorce. Then I woke up today. I asked her why he had to die and she said we can't know the answers to some questions, that only God does."

"Your mother's right again," she said.

Miriam looked at her purse and thought of Treha's key. Somehow getting inside the apartment didn't seem as important. And then she thought of what Devin had said about stories intertwining with each other and what we learn about ourselves from hearing others' stories. Was it enough to listen? Was there a response required?

"What does your mother like to eat?" Miriam said. "If she could have anything she wanted, what would it be?"

"I expect if she could have anything, it would be her mother's fried chicken, but you'd have to fly to North Carolina to get that. Around here, I'd say she likes Chinese. There's a little place over that way that we go to sometimes on Sundays because they have this special and you get an egg roll with your fried rice or whatever. But we haven't been there in a while."

"What's her favorite dish?"

"Mama, she likes the kung fu chicken, but I like chicken fried rice. With that sweet red sauce they make. I pour that over it."

Miriam smiled at the boy's mistake, but she couldn't stifle the emptiness she felt for his loss. This day would mark the rest of his life. How would he remember it? His mother's tears? Waking to news of his father's death?

She put a hand on his head, cradled his cheek, and told him what a brave young man he was and that it was okay to cry if he needed to.

"I already done that, but I figure I'll wait till Mama goes to work to finish."

"What time does she leave?"

He told her, adding that his mother worked the evening shift.

Miriam told him to go back to his mother and sit with her. She would return soon with some lunch for them.

She found the Chinese restaurant in the general direction he had pointed, just a little hole-in-the-wall place with a few tables and a view of the kitchen occupied by a thin man wearing a dirty white apron and a disposable paper hat that should have been disposed of weeks ago. She ordered the fried rice, kung pao chicken, egg rolls, and then something for herself. She absently handed her credit card to the woman behind the register without hearing the total, signed the receipt, added a tip, and waited a few minutes for the brown bag.

Du'Relle was nowhere in sight when Miriam returned. She thought of leaving the feast by the door. Then panic struck and she wondered if the boy might have lied. Perhaps his father would come to the door and she'd feel duped. Or he was just making up the story to cover his truancy.

She knocked on the door and a middle-aged woman opened it a few inches, just enough for Miriam to see her dark complexion and red eyes.

"Can I help you?" she said.

"I was speaking with Du'Relle earlier and he told me of your loss. I'm so sorry."

The door opened a little wider.

"I'm friends with Treha, who lives upstairs."

The woman looked at the brown bag, then back at Miriam's face. "What did Du'Relle tell you?"

"About your husband. I brought this for you. For lunch. I know you may not feel like eating, but you can refrigerate it."

The woman held out a hand. "I'm Samantha. Come on in."

Du'Relle appeared behind her and looked at the bag, then retreated to the kitchen.

Samantha took the bag from Miriam. "This is kind of you. You don't even know us."

"I know enough," she said. She touched the woman on the shoulder and forced a smile.

"Please, stay and eat with us. If you're a friend of Treha's, you're a friend of ours."

Miriam smiled and stepped inside.

CHAPTER 26

TREHA LISTENED to the two men banter as they drove toward Scottsdale. Jonah sounded truly fearful of Davidson. Devin was acting like the brave one, but she could tell he was also uncomfortable. She closed her eyes when Devin chose some music. She hadn't slept well at Mrs. Howard's house and the music and the noise of the road lulled her.

As she slept, she dreamed, and the dream was static, calm, with no movement of the eyes to make the scene shift. Treha liked to dream because this was the only time she saw the world without the motion. If she could dream her whole life, she would.

Her mother came to her, or a woman she supposed was her mother, and took her by the hand, sunlight silhouetting her face and brown hair curling. She was thin, and Treha liked this because it made her think she would not have to be fat all of her life and that one day someone would see her as something other than damaged.

Her mother led her to a building with glass windows lining the front. Inside, she could see flower arrangements and beautiful vases and stands to hold the displays of roses and daffodils. She thought it must smell heavenly in there.

Through the door and color exploded, the greens and yellows and reds, deep red, deeper and darker than she had ever imagined a flower could reach. And blue and violet and white, the palette of God himself all over the walls and into the coolness of the next room, where the flowers were kept until they were cut and sold.

The hallway became dark but the smell of the flowers lingered. Then through another door and along a corridor that angled slightly up, a ramp of sorts for something with wheels. Grooves in the carpet on either side of her footsteps.

Treha opened the next door by herself. Her mother was gone, and she stood alone in a room that smelled of wood and metal. The fresh flowers were replaced by silk ones and around the room were caskets with prices printed above the open lids. Treha turned to retreat, but there was no door. She ran the circumference of the room feeling the walls, moving between the caskets and searching for a way out. At the front of the room, where the light was brightest, sat one closed coffin, and Treha was drawn there, though she didn't want to be. She navigated the room again looking for another way out but came back to the front, back to the closed coffin where the light shone like the sun.

She stepped to the box and looked down, hands trembling, and as she reached for the lid to lift it, her eyes began the motion again, the back-and-forth, unyielding motion. She lifted the box open.

And screamed.

"Treha, you okay?" Devin said.

She sat up quickly and looked out the window, trying to figure out where she was. Concrete abutments and cactus designs and green street signs overhead. *Scottsdale—6 miles.*

"Must have been some nightmare," Jonah said from the back.

She nodded and brought her feet onto the seat to hug her knees tightly to her chest. The music was still on low and the air-conditioning gave her a chill. This was how it always happened. Her mother led her into the room, through the flowers, through all things living to all things dead. And before she could see who or what was in the casket, she awakened, frightened, alone, and her life in constant motion again.

Was it her mother in the casket? Was it someone Treha loved, someone she knew? Was it Treha herself? For some reason her subconscious kept her from seeing this, from deciphering the truth from the dream. Sometimes it was a graveyard. Sometimes an airport, though Treha thought it strange because she had never been in an airport before and had nothing on which to base her view of what the train would look like that delivered her to the terminal, with the dead end and no doors that opened and how all alone she was.

They made a few turns, moved through areas of the world she had never seen, grocery stores nearly hidden from view, shrouded by shrubbery and facades of stucco and brick, landscaping and high walls. Devin slowed as he drove past a gate and pointed out the subdivision where Davidson lived. They could park a few streets away and walk, but Jonah wasn't fond of the idea.

"If we're going to be gunned down, we might as well park close to the house."

Devin frowned and glanced at Treha.

When a white Valley Cab pulled up to the gate, Devin followed it inside and turned at the first street, around a densely wooded cul-de-sac. There were mimosa and ash trees that seemed to have taken over the street, surrounded by rock walls and fencing that gave privacy to even the most reclusive. Treha imagined backyards with pools and hot tubs and tennis courts, but she couldn't see from the front.

Devin made a U-turn and backtracked to park on the street. "That's his," he said, pointing to an estate two houses down.

The three of them sat, trancelike, looking at the home. The shades were drawn and there was no movement except for birds that flitted from ocotillo to hydrangea in the front yard. Several large boulders flanked the walkway leading to the front door.

"Get the camera and mic her," Devin said to Jonah. It wasn't so much a command as an informal to-do list that Jonah acquiesced to immediately. He asked Treha to turn slightly and clipped a small wireless microphone on the V of her top. When he had the camera out and ready, Devin told him to roll.

"Here?" Jonah said.

Devin turned and gave the man a look, then glanced back at the Davidson home. "Why do you always wear those scrubs?"

"I like how they feel."

"So it's a comfort thing."

Treha nodded and heard the whir of the camera from the backseat. Jonah had on black headphones that said *Sony* on the earpieces.

"I thought you were going to record me talking to Davidson."

"We'll do a little of both if you can have a breakthrough with him. What are you thinking about?"

"I'm not thinking about anything."

"Are you scared of the old man?"

"No. I'm hopeful."

"About what?"

"That he will have answers about Dr. Crenshaw, about what he wrote in the letter."

"Tell us about that, Treha. What letter are you talking about?"

She glanced at Jonah. A red light stayed lit on the front of the camera.

"Dr. Crenshaw wrote a letter and it was opened by accident. Mrs. Howard and I think this man, Davidson, may know something about a mistake Dr. Crenshaw said he made long ago."

"Did you know Dr. Crenshaw before Desert Gardens?"

"No."

"Then what kind of mistake could he have made?"

"I don't know."

"Tell us more about your relationship with Dr. Crenshaw," Devin said.

She did the best she could, telling him about the word games and riddles the man gave. She didn't like talking, but Devin asked good questions that made the conversation easy, and he was bright, though a bit quirky and locked in on the task. He had a long face, dark hair and eyebrows, a bit of chin stubble. His hair was silky, parted in the middle, and was the kind that fell into place with a simple whisk of the hand. She could almost predict the frequency of the hand through his hair.

"So this letter is a big deal to you."

"I want to know if Dr. Crenshaw was talking about me."

"How old are you?"

"I'm twenty."

"And you haven't gone to college, right?"

She shook her head.

He seemed a little nervous now, unsure of himself. "Miriam Howard spoke highly of you."

Treha didn't answer.

"She said you have an incredible ability. A way to connect

with older people. Which makes me wonder why Desert Gardens would let you go."

"A new person is running the facility."

"Downsizing?"

"No, she said I was upsetting the residents."

"Upsetting them how? Mrs. Howard said you were a great employee. The residents love you."

Treha didn't answer.

"So what do you do to wake them? Is it a technique? Do you put some kind of spell on people?" He motioned with his hands, fingers moving all around. She looked at him and he smiled; then it disappeared when she didn't respond.

"I didn't mean to offend you."

"You didn't."

"You don't have to give away trade secrets. I'm not going to steal them. If you slip something in their Ensure before you talk, I won't tell anybody."

She sat with the silence between them. The leather car seats were aged and cracked, but she could tell the man took pride in his car, kept it clean and emptied the trash. There were no used cups or wrappers strewn about.

"People respond to touch."

He turned toward her, a look of relief on his face. "Really?"

Jonah snorted. "If you'd have given him a hug, he would've tossed the gun away and started talking."

Devin frowned. "I think this guy needs something more than a hug."

It was easier to speak with Devin looking forward, with both of them focused on the house rather than on each other. "Older people become isolated. They draw inward. And they are starved for human touch."

"Does it matter what type of touch?"

"I put a hand on an arm or shoulder. Or rub their back."

He turned to study her but she kept her eyes on the house.

"You must think about this a lot."

"I don't think about it at all."

"How did you figure it out? How do you know what to do?"

"I just know it."

"When did you know you could do it?"

"Not until Desert Gardens."

"So you didn't do this when you were younger?"

"When I was younger, I didn't know older people."

"Who *did* you know when you were younger? What's your story, Treha?"

"I don't have one. Not one I can remember."

It felt hard to breathe in the silence that followed and she wondered if she had said too much. But Devin seemed to understand and process the words.

"Mrs. Howard said when you talk, it draws them out. Like a butterfly coming out of a cocoon. That's what we want to see."

"Why?"

"That's what movies are about. Asking questions. Discovering. And I think it's fascinating. If you can really do this, we should bottle it. People would pay big money. They'd come from every continent. You'd be a spiritual guru."

"Is that what you want? To sell what I can do?"

"No, I want your story. I want to tell it well and to discover the backstory as well."

"Backstory?"

"What happened before, earlier in your life. How you acquired this ability." Devin cleared his throat and ran a hand through his hair. "Are there people you can't reach?"

"Some have gone too far, at least to get them to speak. But sometimes a smile is enough."

"Enough for who?"

"Enough to let me know they hear me, they know I'm there."

"Are there different categories of people you reach? Aren't some stuck in their childhood? They think they're living back in the Depression?"

She nodded. "I met a man who had not spoken in several months. He was bedridden and couldn't communicate with those caring for him. I rubbed his hands. He opened his eyes and his mouth began to move. Several minutes later he tried to get up."

"Must have scared you."

"I wasn't scared; I was concerned he would fall. I told him to lie down but he said, 'I need to milk the cows.' I told him there were no cows. 'They are full; they need to be milked. Can't you hear them?'"

"What did you do?"

"I hit the alarm and held him down until help arrived."

"So you can't always be sure how they'll respond?"

She shook her head and a flash of memory from her childhood came back that she didn't want, hadn't asked for.

"I guess that's the downside of having the gift," Devin said. "Can I ask you a different question?"

"Yes."

"Have you ever smiled?"

She glanced at him, then stared out the windshield again. "Perhaps when I was a girl."

"Why don't you smile?"

"Perhaps there is nothing to smile about."

"Or you could just not be able to. Have you ever tried? Even a fake smile?"

CHRIS FABRY

She perfunctorily pulled the edges of her mouth up to show her teeth. Then she resumed her deadpan.

"At least we know the muscles work," Jonah said.

A white mail truck drove past the mailbox and parked by Davidson's driveway.

"Hey, this looks interesting. Get a shot of this."

The window came down in the back and Jonah pointed the camera toward the carrier walking up to the house. "Mailman doesn't seem scared of the old guy's gun."

"It's not a mailman," Treha said.

"What?" Jonah said.

"It's a woman."

"Yeah, okay, mail lady, then. Sorry." Jonah zoomed in and watched through the camera. "Hey, I think I got something. The woman rang the bell twice and knocked on the door. It's like a USPS code or something."

The carrier returned to the truck and drove away. A moment later the door opened a few inches and someone retrieved the package sitting outside.

"Okay, this is great," Devin said. "We know he's there."

"We know *someone's* there; we don't know who," Jonah corrected.

Treha grabbed the door handle.

"What are you doing?"

"I'm going to use the secret code." She opened the door and stepped out.

"Will you be able to get the audio signal from here?" Devin said to Jonah.

"Should be fine."

Devin locked eyes with her. "We'll be listening. Be careful, okay?"

CHAPTER 27

MIRIAM HAD NEVER seen a human use so much sweet-and-sour sauce. Du'Relle ate his fried rice in a bowl like cereal.

He finished before Miriam was halfway done with hers and asked if he could watch TV. Samantha suggested he go to the corner store and get a candy bar, handing him some change from a jar by the door. Du'Relle was instantly out the door, his worn-out shoes slapping the concrete. With him gone, Samantha spoke freely.

"We were having troubles before he deployed, Du'Relle's father and me. I don't think either of us thought we would make it. That's one of the reasons I transferred out here. I wanted things to be different when he came back. I wanted to show him I could make it on my own, instead of him calling the shots. I guess that was a way of preparing me."

"Did you get details about what happened?"

"They told me about the attack and how Wayne was protecting his men, but I don't remember much."

"That's something to hang on to. His selfless nature."

"I halfway wonder if he didn't go out there and put himself in the line of fire on purpose."

"Why?"

"We had a fight three—no, two days ago. If I'd known that was going to be our last conversation, I never would have ended it that way."

"You can't hold yourself responsible, Samantha. We all have regrets."

Miriam watched the woman compose herself and thought of her own life, her own regrets. Things she would do differently if she had the chance.

"Du'Relle looks like he's adjusted to the move here."

"He has problems in school sometimes. I have to work evenings, so he comes home to an empty apartment. I worry. Been trying to get on the day shift, but there's a few in line ahead of me."

"Where do you work?"

Samantha told her and Miriam recognized the hospital across town. "I don't get home till late."

"Du'Relle seems to have latched on to Treha."

The woman smiled. "That's been the bright spot. He follows her around like a puppy and says he's taking care of her. She seems okay with it."

"Do you know her very well?"

Samantha shook her head and waved a hand in front of her mouth. The kung pao chicken was a little spicy. She took a drink of water and continued. "I thought she worked at a hospital or at some vet clinic when I first saw her. You say you work with her at a nursing home?"

"It's a modified retirement center and nursing home. I just retired but have taken an interest in her. That's actually part of why I'm here. We're trying to piece together some of her past."

"I'm sure she appreciates the help." Samantha looked at the front room and rose, bringing back a picture of her husband

and setting it on the table. "I think about Du'Relle and what he's going to go through without a father. Maybe sometimes it's better not to know your past."

"Where will the funeral be?" Miriam said.

"Back in North Carolina. That's where his family lives. The military will fly us there after the arrangements are made." She wiped a tear away and then put her head in both hands. "I want to be strong for Du'Relle."

"It's okay to grieve. It's a huge loss. Even if there was trouble between you two. It's not just his death you're dealing with but the death of the two of you together, the death of a dream."

"You sound like you've been through this before."

Miriam thought of her life—losing her mother, losing one of her best friends to cancer, losing the dream of children. "Nothing compared to what you've gone through. Is there anywhere in this area you can go? Any family or friends? I know that can be a tremendous help."

"We're alone here. But that's okay. I don't think I want to be with anybody right now. I talked with my sister on the phone for a long time this morning. That helped."

Du'Relle came back from the store with a Snickers as big as his forearm and turned the TV on in the living room. Miriam took the empty plates to the sink but Samantha said she couldn't let her do the dishes. "You've done enough just bringing this food in and talking with me. You were a gift from God today."

Miriam gave her a hug and wrote her phone number on a scrap piece of paper. "You call me if you need anything. A ride to the airport or help with Du'Relle . . ." She paused. "You know, I just met someone who helped Treha a long time ago. The family ministers to widows and orphans." She pulled out the brochure for James 127 House. "Call them. They're great people and might have resources for you and Du'Relle."

Samantha took the brochure and smiled. "Thank you."

Du'Relle ran up to Miriam at the door, burying his face in her stomach and hugging her tightly. "Thank you for the Chinese, ma'am."

Miriam walked to her car and stood beside it for a minute, taking in the pain she'd just experienced. She glanced at Treha's apartment. Since Du'Relle was occupied, she figured she might as well take a quick look.

CHAPTER 28

Treha walked toward the front door, then decided against it. The man would hear the knock and know something was amiss. She moved to the side gate and spoke into the microphone. "I'm going to try something else. Forget the doorbell."

The home was flanked by a hedge that grew through the wrought-iron fence running the property's perimeter. The gate at the side was too high to scale, but Treha looked through at the backyard. She pushed on the gate and to her surprise it was ajar. She imagined Devin and Jonah listening, telling her to stop and come back to the car, but she kept walking.

Following a stone walkway, she saw that the backyard was a series of rock gardens and desert plants. In the middle of the oasis was an inground pool, empty except for a spot in the deep end, where sludge and debris had collected.

Behind the pool, away from the house, was a smaller building. A rock path stretched from its front door to the main house's back porch.

Something clicked on the building and Treha froze, waiting for an alarm or a watchdog. When nothing happened, she walked across the patio to the main house's back door, passing a grill and a built-in fireplace. She could see into the kitchen, where a light was on over the stove, but the door was locked when she tried it. She moved toward the other side of the house, looking for any movement, passing another door with a shade pulled low. The yard was eerily quiet as if even the birds knew to stay away.

At the far end of the house she found an unshuttered window that looked into a room filled with shelves of books that reached from floor to ceiling. To the right was an area with dusty wineglasses suspended from a rack above a sink. To the left were two overstuffed chairs sitting back-to-back.

A shadow moved near the door. Treha cupped her hand to the window, but the room was empty.

"Can I help you?" someone said, his voice gruff.

She turned slowly and looked into the face of an elderly man with a finely trimmed mustache. His white hair surrounded his face like a mane. He wore a striped shirt and a solid blue tie pulled tight to the collar. The tie was wide at the top and flared at the bottom and she decided it had been in and out of style several times in the man's life. His skin was blotchy and pale, and there were bags under his eyes. In his hand he held a pistol that, from his swaying arm, looked heavy. His eyes darted as if he was having a hard time focusing.

"It would help me if you put that gun down," she said.

The man looked down at the gun as if he'd just realized he was holding it. Then he raised it higher, seeming unsure and a little confused.

"You tripped the alarm when you came through the fence." He checked his watch. "You have perhaps three minutes before security arrives."

"Three minutes to talk to you?"

"You have three minutes to escape."

"I don't want to escape. I came to speak with you."

Eyebrows raised. "Not to steal my wallet? A painting from my library?"

"I don't want anything you have."

Whiskers raised now and an impish grin. He looked her over from head to toe and she could feel his judgment. "Then why would you try to get into my house?"

"I came looking for you, Mr. Davidson."

He pulled his head back. "How do you know my name?" His eyes were wild again as he glanced at her clothing. "You're with them, aren't you? The people with the white coats. You've been listening to me."

"I'm not with anyone in a white coat. And I haven't been listening."

His muscles tensed and his movements became jerky. "I won't let you take me away. Do you understand me?" He held up the gun and she reached out to touch his arm.

"I'm not taking you anywhere, Mr. Davidson." Her voice was controlled and soothing. "Relax."

She heard a screech of tires. Davidson turned and waved a hand over his head. "It doesn't matter now. I hear them. I hope you convince the authorities you just wanted to talk. Good luck."

Someone called her name from the other side of the fence. Was it Devin? She heard voices of men at the front, followed by the doorbell and the squawk of a radio.

The old man walked toward the small building near the pool, toddling like a child searching for invisible handrails. A man came through the house quickly, heading for the back door. Another came through the side gate in a uniform with a shield on the shirt pocket, keys jangling.

"She's by the back door," Davidson yelled over his shoulder. "She didn't steal anything yet."

Treha didn't move as the man at the gate intercepted her and cuffed one hand, then pulled the other behind her and did the same. The other guard took longer, moving through the house and finally exiting. "All clear."

Treha watched the old man open the door to the small building and turn back to look at her. He stared at her shifting eyes and she tried to reach out to him somehow, with her hands behind her. Finally she whispered, "Dr. Crenshaw sent me."

"That's enough, miss," a guard said, grabbing her wrists. "Explain it to the police."

She walked stiff-legged to the fence, tugged along by the guard. He pushed instead of pulling at the gate, then realized his mistake.

"What did you say?"

Treha saw Davidson near the edge of the pool, no longer looking for handrails. He didn't have his gun and his face had softened as if there were questions in his mind.

"We've got her now, sir," a guard said. "We'll handle it."

"No, let her go."

"What? Sir, she was trespassing."

He put his hand to his head and scratched as if he had forgotten something. Then he smiled and turned his hand like a conductor leading an orchestra. "It's my mind. I'm not thinking clearly, you see. It happens to us old fogies." He laughed, but it was not a real laugh.

"Sir?" the guard said.

"Leave her. Take those handcuffs off. I'm sorry, my dear. I didn't recognize you."

"You know her, sir?"

"Yes, yes, just take them off, please. Let her go."

"What's her name, sir?"

"Her name?"

"If you know her, you must know her name."

"Yes, of course. It's on the tip of my tongue. . . ."

"Treha," she said.

"That's it, Treha. Yes. Treha. Now if you'll take those off, please. Let Treha go."

The two guards looked at each other, then uncuffed her. Treha glanced at her wrists and rubbed them as the guards lingered.

The old man moved toward her and took her by the arm. "Come inside and we'll have some tea." Under his breath he said, "Keep walking. Don't look at them."

"Are you sure about this, sir?" one of the guards called after him.

"Thank you for your service, gentlemen! I'm sorry to have troubled you."

The gate clanged behind them and the man let go of her arm. He walked past the pool and entered the small building, leaving the door open behind him. The ceiling was much lower here than in the main house. There were carpets strewn on the tile in a haphazard way around an easy chair with worn arms. In the corner was a small refrigerator and a kitchenette and Treha noticed a burnt toast smell. Davidson disappeared into the next room as Treha closed the door. He returned with a folding chair, placing it next to the recliner. His gun was in his front pocket, making his pants sag.

"Please, sit. Can I get you something?" His face was softer now, his eyes more inviting.

"I'm fine."

He walked to the kitchen and returned with a mug of hot water and a tea bag. "Would you like a slice of lemon? It's fresh from the tree."

"That would be fine."

He sat in the folding chair and exhaled as if he had just run a marathon. "So, Treha, how do you know Dr. Crenshaw?"

She placed the tea bag in the water. "He's my friend. I worked with him at Desert Gardens."

"In Scottsdale? Jim lives here?"

She shook her head. "No, in Tucson. But he is in the hospital now."

The lines in his forehead were suddenly gone. "What's wrong with him?"

She told him what she knew and the old man's eyes clouded. He seemed to float in and out of worlds, the real one and his own.

"You said he sent you. What do you mean?"

"He gave me a letter to mail. It was addressed to you." She pulled the torn envelope out and handed it to him. "I meant to mail it, but it got ripped, and when I read it, I knew I had to speak with—"

Davidson raised a hand to stop her, then put a finger to his lips. He stood and lifted one of the blinds to look out on the lawn.

"What's wrong?" she said.

He pointed to his ear and mouthed, *"They can hear us."*

"Who?" she whispered.

He waved her forward, opened the front door, and walked outside. She followed into the light and he stopped by the empty pool.

"I had to drain this because they put an injection in the

chlorine. It wasn't safe any longer. They're listening to everything. That's why I moved to the casita, but I still hear the noise on the phone. I've heard the men with their microphones. I saw one of them the other day. Found him by the road in his car. I don't think they've planted devices out here. But I can't say for sure. Don't say anything you wouldn't want them hearing."

"Who?"

"Phutura. I used to work for them. Now they've made me a prisoner in my own home." He stepped closer. "They'll come for you next. If they knew you had this information, they would come for you."

She had seen this look before. The fear and paranoia mixed with a degeneration of the faculties, like gasoline on a fire. Fear eating fear, using itself as an accelerant.

"Treha!" someone said behind them. It was Devin, his head just over the wall on the other side of the house. "Are you all right?"

Davidson reached for his gun. "Who is that?"

"He is with me. His name is Devin. He records the stories—"

"That's the man in the car. He's with them. I should have shot him when I first laid eyes on him." He turned. "And if you're with him . . ."

He grabbed her by the arm and led her forcefully to the gate. "I should have let the guards take you when I had the chance."

"Stop; you're hurting me."

"I knew it. You're one of them."

"I'm not one of anybody," she shouted. She wrenched free of his grasp and stood still. "I'm trying to find out the truth about my friend. About me. And if you would listen, you might be able to help."

"The truth? You want to know the truth? They killed him.

That's right—they killed Crenshaw, and if he's not already dead, he will be. If you know what's good for you, you'll stop asking questions."

Davidson opened the gate and pushed her through. Devin and Jonah were just arriving on the other side. Jonah pointed a camera at them and Davidson sneered.

"Are you all right?" Devin said.

Treha nodded and looked back at the old man, whose mouth moved in a whisper. "You must leave. It's begun now and it won't stop."

"Mr. Davidson, please talk with me," Treha said.

He pulled her close and spoke in her ear, his voice sending a shiver through her.

"You have no idea the danger you are in. Leave now. Before it's too late."

CHAPTER 29

As SOON as she stepped inside the apartment, Miriam put a hand over her heart and said aloud, "Oh, Treha." It was as much a prayer as anything.

It wasn't just the squalor, the emptiness of the rooms, and the overflowing trash can; it was the darkness and loneliness. Hopelessness, really. That, added with the heat of the room, made the oppression heavy enough to cut with a knife.

She moved to the no-frills refrigerator and opened it, though she didn't know why. Maybe it felt safe, like she would find something to encourage her inside, but she found it nearly empty, except for some off-brand cheese and butter. The pantry had canned peaches, macaroni, and spaghetti sauce, along with a half-eaten bag of Doritos, but that was it.

"Oh, Treha," she whispered again.

She flipped on the light and spotted a mesh laundry bag near the front door. Next to it, on the tile, there was sand and a little mud, and Miriam guessed this was where Treha had parked her bike.

Her stomach clenched and she fought the nerves or the Chinese food as she made a quick sweep of the apartment.

A small television sat on a makeshift stand in the living room area with a cover on the floor in front of it. Miriam imagined Treha curled up watching a nature video on PBS, a survival-of-the-fittest scene with wayward wildebeests being chased by lions, her eyes swaying as the predators devoured their meal. Or maybe Treha watched *Jeopardy!* and got all the answers.

Miriam wanted to go to her car. If she stopped now, she wouldn't disturb anything, and she wouldn't need to ask the girl's forgiveness. She could simply call this a mistake and retreat. But something pulled her further into this strange world.

There was no desk to look through, no filing cabinets, no stacks of newspapers or magazines. In Treha's bedroom she found a small bookshelf, the pressboard kind you put together with a screwdriver. It was full of paperbacks, and as Miriam knelt to get a better look, she saw they were mostly classics. All worn and dog-eared, marked up. Some of them barely had covers. *David Copperfield. Madame Bovary. The Wind in the Willows. The Red Badge of Courage. Moby Dick.* Great books with great words strung together in amazing ways, filtered through the mind of a damaged young woman.

The bedroom also had a twin mattress on the floor. No sheet over the mattress, no case on the lone pillow at the head, just a single red cover thrown over it that made it look like Treha slept on top instead of underneath. As Miriam suspected, her closet was equally barren. Treha had one hooded sweatshirt. One pair of sweatpants. And in the corner a pile of socks and underwear that looked like they had been dumped from the laundry bag and left to die.

Miriam made a mental list of things Treha didn't have. A vacuum. An iron or ironing board. A phone. A computer. Washer and dryer. Alarm clock. If she wanted to load Treha down at Christmas, she could think of a hundred practical gifts. Food to stock her refrigerator. Some shampoo and conditioner. But did Treha really need any of it? She was living as simply as a person could live, not by choice, but because she didn't know any other way.

And then the questions. Had Treha ever had a boyfriend? Had she ever had a friend, other than someone like Du'Relle and his mother? Did anyone else in her life know about her gift?

Miriam went back to the bookshelf and studied the spines. There was one without a title and when she pulled it out, she realized it was not a book at all but a small photo album. A shudder shot through her and she retreated to the kitchen, where the light was better. She opened to the first page and there was Treha at three or four—the awkward stare, the pointed ears accentuated by the Buster Brown haircut. The casual observer would simply see a child looking for a toy, but Miriam saw more. All the days between this photo and today. And then the ones to come. It was creased down the middle as if it had been tossed away and someone had retrieved it.

She turned the page. Empty. She turned the next one. Empty. She went through the rest of the book, looking for any trace of the girl between that vulnerable age and today, but found nothing. She had seen the Facebook photos of young people obsessed with themselves, taking pictures with their computers or holding their phones at arm's length and mugging. There were thousands of pictures chronicling the lives of teenagers and early adults and Treha had one photo of herself.

One photo.

Miriam turned back to the picture, removed it, and flipped it over, hoping beyond hope that there would be something written. A name, an address, a phone number, some clue.

It was blank.

She turned it back over and studied it. The room Treha was in didn't appear to be a home. The setting was out of place— more like an office. A cubicle desk and chair behind her. A filing cabinet. A calendar on the wall, blurry but distinguishable.

Miriam replaced the book where she'd found it. She looked through drawers in the kitchen and bathroom but other than the dishwasher and refrigerator instruction booklets, there wasn't so much as a scrap of paper. The utility closet didn't even hold a broom.

Miriam opened the blinds fully to let in some natural light and knelt in front of the bookshelf again, more comfortable than when she first arrived. It almost felt like she was getting to know Treha better. She scanned the rest of the shelf. Perhaps she had missed something. Some papers shoved between books. A birth certificate. A key to a safety-deposit box or a train station locker that would reveal everything.

She didn't find any of that. But in opening the books, she did find a clue as to why Treha had so many classics—multiple copies of some. In the front of *Jane Eyre*, she read, *To Connie on your 15th birthday. This book has meant so much to me and I hope you'll enjoy it as much as I did. Love, Mom.*

Almost every copy was inscribed as a gift to someone and then cast off like a bad Christmas sweater. Or perhaps the people had perished long ago and the books had been donated. However they had been jettisoned, the fact that Treha now had them made Miriam think Treha had not only appropriated the stories of people at Desert Gardens; she had also chosen these books, given as gifts by someone else, for her own. The only things she truly owned were these.

Miriam opened a tattered copy of *Huckleberry Finn* and read another inscription: *To Frank, may you always have a heart like Huck. I'll be cheering your ride down the Mississippi. Pap.*

Miriam wondered where Frank had gone and why he had let go of such a heartfelt gift. Each book was a story within a story, tales told to young and old that kept giving and returning.

At the end of the final row, the largest of the three because of the way the shelving was situated, shoved up against the end of the bookcase and a copy of *Ethan Frome* inscribed to *My dear Cecilia*, was a pristine copy of *Goodnight Moon*. It did not have the same wear and tear as the other books on the shelf and when Miriam opened it, her breath caught, not because it felt like the book was opening for the first time, but because something fell out and she simultaneously spotted the word *Treha* inside the cover.

To Treha, it said. Miriam could not believe her eyes. Was there another human being on the planet with that name? She looked at it again and wondered if perhaps Treha had bought the book for herself and written the message. But Miriam had seen her handwriting, had noted the slanting, miniature left-handed scrawl. This was not it.

To Treha,
Though you can't read it yet, I hope this book will bring
you comfort and let you know there is someone who loves
and cares for you. Keep it to remind you that my prayers
will always be with you.

Love always,
Kara

Miriam read the note again, examining each cursive line, every consonant and vowel. Was Kara Treha's mother? It was given when she was too young to read. . . . But who was this phantom?

She looked at the piece of paper that had fallen to the carpet. It was a business card with the name Kara Robbins at the top. Underneath was the title *Children's Advocate*. There was a phone number with an area code she didn't recognize and underneath that were the words *Family Support Services*. The rest of the card was blank.

Miriam pulled out a card of her own from her purse and on the back she wrote down the name and number. Now her heart rate increased as if she had uncovered some hieroglyph of Treha's past. She put the card in the front of the book and flipped through it to make sure there was nothing else written inside. She only found Margaret Wise Brown's words and Clement Hurd's illustrations. It was a popular book, she knew, but she had never actually read it. She never had a reason. No children to tuck in at night, no little eyes to coax to sleep with the tucked-in bunny and the cow jumping and the great green room.

She closed the book and put it back where she had found it. The carpet was as comfortable as a concrete slab. With the natural light showing, she noticed a few bugs crawling up the wall.

Miriam retrieved her purse and locked the front door behind her. Before she started the car, she gazed at Du'Relle and Samantha's place. The blinds were closed on the tiny window that faced the parking lot. If all the hurt in the world were laid end to end . . . No, forget all the hurt in the world. If all the hurt from the hearts that dwelled in just these two apartments were laid end to end, she had no doubt it would encircle the earth.

And that didn't count her own heart.

CHAPTER 30

DEVIN'S FIRM conviction, his overriding principle, was that telling the story led to life. Following the next step, the next chapter, the next memory propelled them forward.

He was beginning to question that principle.

Treha sat in the front with him, and Jonah got in behind them with the equipment, sweating profusely.

"I think we dodged a bullet—no pun intended," Jonah said. "This is the kind of guy who shows up at a government office one day and opens fire and his neighbors can't believe it and everybody's looking for why. There's no why to crazy. It's just crazy. We could have been part of a big headline. 'Three Killed in Deadly Rampage.'"

"Tell me what you know about Phutura," Treha said. No emotion. Not paying attention to anything but the drum of her fingers and the movement of her eyes.

"Please don't tell me you're going to try to make sense of what he told you," Jonah said. "He's crazy."

"Phutura is a big pharmaceutical company," Devin said. "Big as in billions of dollars every year."

"Go; just drive away from here before he finds his stash of grenades and lobs one toward us," Jonah said. "I'm applying at

Target tomorrow. You don't pay me enough to risk my life. In fact, you don't pay me at all."

Devin looked at Treha. "He really thinks there's someone listening to him, doesn't he?"

She nodded.

"Can we go now?" Jonah said.

Devin started the car. "Did you get through to him? Can you tell?"

"I don't know if he has dementia or disease. There's definitely paranoia. But there's something different. . . ."

"Devin, she's not a doctor; she's a janitor. No offense, Treha."

"His fear is very deep. I can sense that."

"I don't understand," Devin said.

"I don't understand why we're not moving," Jonah said.

"You think he's actually being watched?" Devin said.

"We're here, aren't we?" Treha said.

"Yeah, but *you're* the reason we're here. I don't have a hidden agenda or a black helicopter."

"He told me I was in grave danger." She looked down at a crack in the leather seats. "What if he's right?"

"Great, now we've got two of them," Jonah said. "Buckle her up and keep her away from sharp objects."

"Treha, the guy probably thinks the president is reading his e-mail. Or the attorney general. Every time the air conditioner kicks on, it's another government plot to poison him with refrigerant. I'm surprised he lets the postal service get that close to his house. Surely you ran into this at Desert Gardens. Come on, you're scaring me."

She stared out the windshield, her jaw set. Devin's phone buzzed and he answered it.

A pause. "Mr. Hillis, I need to speak with you."

Devin plugged his Bluetooth in and held his other ear. "It's good to hear from you, Mr. Davidson."

"Hang up!" Jonah said.

"A question for you. Where did you get her?"

"Treha?"

"Yes."

"At the retirement home. We sort of found each other."

"Do you have any idea where she is from? Where she grew up?"

"No, but she's right here. I can ask."

The man paused and made a noise—perhaps rubbed his face. Devin couldn't tell. "Why me? Why do you . . . ? Are you working for those monitoring me?"

Devin took a breath. "No, sir. My partner and I are working on a documentary that features Dr. Crenshaw and others from Desert Gardens."

"And you came to me because . . . ?"

"We're focusing on Treha now. Telling her story and looking for answers about her life. We think you might have information."

A long pause. "I don't see how that could be possible."

"Mr. Davidson, if you could give us fifteen minutes—just ten, even—I think we could get some answers."

The line went dead. Devin stared at the phone.

Then Jonah screamed like a girl. "There he is! I told you we should have left!"

Calvin Davidson opened the door behind Devin and almost fell into the seat, his pistol out. "Drive away, now," he said, his eyes dancing. "They'll be here any minute."

Devin glanced at Treha. Jonah was pressed up against the other door, acting like he wanted to jump out.

"This is much more serious than you realize," Davidson said gravely. His color was off and he was breathing heavily.

"You'd better buckle up," Devin said. The man's hands were trembling. "Jonah, help him buckle up."

"Why me?"

"I can do it myself," Davidson said.

He fumbled with the seat belt, and Devin thought Jonah had plenty of opportunities to take the gun from him, but was glad he didn't. A misfire could be disastrous.

"I apologize for my rude behavior, but there are some things you don't understand."

"Maybe you could fill us in," Devin said.

"Or maybe you'll just fill us with lead," Jonah said, wiping his face.

"I don't want to harm you. I want to protect you. And myself. It's just that I get befuddled in the head." He waved a hand. "I'll answer your questions, but not here, not where they can hear me."

"Have you taken your medication?" Jonah said.

Davidson threw back his head and laughed. "Now that is funny. If I'm treating you kindly, like a human being is supposed to, I must be on medication."

Devin looked in the rearview at Jonah, trying to tell him with his eyes to shut up, to humor the old man. Not to tick him off. They started driving through the affluence of Scottsdale with this man who seemed like he hadn't been out of his house in years.

"Do you have a phone?" Davidson said to Jonah.

"You want to call your therapist? Be my guest." Jonah reached in his pocket gingerly and handed the phone to the man. Davidson rolled down the window and, before Jonah could protest, tossed the phone out.

"Hey!" Jonah sat forward, his mouth agape, looking first at

Davidson, then at Devin. "You just . . . That was my iPhone! Stop the car, Devin!"

"Don't stop the car," Davidson said. "Keep going."

"You've got to be kidding me!" Jonah said. "Do you know how much that costs? All of my contacts are on there!"

"You can buy a new phone. You can't buy a new life."

"If we're in that much danger, we should get to a police station," Devin said.

"No, not the police," Davidson said. "They may be part of it."

Jonah was still openmouthed, looking behind them. "The conspiracy theories are flying as fast as the phones. You owe me a new iPhone, man!"

"They can trace you with your phone," Davidson said. "If you want to stay alive, listen to me. Do what I tell you."

"Stop the car, Devin," Jonah said. "This is crazy. Let me out. I'm not staying in here with . . . He'll throw the camera out next."

Davidson shifted in his seat and Jonah grabbed the camera bag. "Don't you dare! You don't touch this."

Davidson shook his head. "You're incorrigible. You don't see what's coming."

"Who are we dealing with?" Devin said. "Who's listening to you?"

Davidson looked back. "The company. Whoever they've hired. They want me silenced."

"What company? Phutura? What do you know that's so important to them?"

"Keep driving. You don't need to know this. It will only put you in more danger." He lifted a hand toward the front. "I need your phone as well, Mr. Hillis."

"No way. Don't let him have it," Jonah said. "He'll chuck it into the cheap seats."

Davidson still had his hand out, waiting. "Do you have a phone?" he said to Treha.

She shook her head.

"Look, just take out the battery," Devin said. "There's no way for them to track us."

"That's not true. . . . They can still track you." Davidson looked confused.

"Not if your phone isn't communicating with the towers," Jonah said. He held out a hand and Devin gave him the phone. Jonah powered it down and removed the battery. "Why didn't you tell him that before he threw mine out the window?"

"We'll get you a new phone," Devin said.

"Great. You know, if they had geriatric Olympics, you could get the gold in the iPhone toss. You actually put some backspin on it."

Davidson's face was stern, his teeth clenched. "They will find me."

"Who?" Devin said. "Tell me who we're running from."

"Young man, are not the years I have lived enough reason to respect me? Do you see the lines in this face? I've paid the price for your respect."

They came to a red light at a large intersection.

"We need to go somewhere they won't expect. Somewhere far from here."

"How about the Apple Store?"

"Jonah, please." Devin gave him a frustrated glance.

"Take me to Tucson. I want to see Dr. Crenshaw," Davidson said.

"And when we get there, what are we going to do?" Jonah said.

Devin drove under the interstate and Davidson gave him a

tired look. "When we get to safety, after I've seen him, you can set up your camera and record my testimony."

"Testimony?" Devin said.

"You mean like a religious conversion story?" Jonah said.

"I'm not talking about religion. I made promises years ago, when I was younger. Things I would not reveal. And if I testify about those things, it will cost them millions. Billions, even."

"And this has something to do with Dr. Crenshaw?" Treha said.

"It has everything to do with him."

"He is comatose," Treha said. "He can't speak with you."

"If you want answers to your questions, take me there."

Streams from Desert Gardens
scene 23

Shot of home in Plainfield, AZ.

Cut to family room, where Corrine and Kelsey Wells sit on a couch.

Tight shot on family portrait behind them.

> CORRINE: **That picture was taken last year, before Kelsey started high school. We had homeschooled her up to that point but we all agreed she was ready. She loves volleyball and runs cross-country. And she's musical . . . artistic.**

Tight shot of Kelsey's eyes and her nystagmus. Return to shot of Corrine and Kelsey.

> KELSEY: **I can't . . . hold the guitar or the flute . . . anymore. My hands . . .**

Tight shot of Corrine holding Kelsey's hand. Then back to full two-shot of them.

> CORRINE: **In this little high school, there are two dozen kids who have the same symptoms. Six students have committed suicide. And there are anger and rage issues in students who were perfectly normal before they came to this school.**

Cut to home videos of Kelsey playing volleyball, with most of image grayed to highlight #12. Slow motion of Kelsey spiking the ball and high-fiving teammates.

CORRINE (VOICE-OVER): **She was so excited to be on the volleyball team. The students welcomed her and voted her the captain.**

KELSEY (VOICE-OVER): **Because I'm tall.**

CORRINE (VO): **(Laughs.)**

KELSEY (VO): **We won the district championship . . . and I wanted to go out for the JV team this year . . . but I got sick.**

Linger on video of match point in district finals and girls celebrating on the court. Tight shot of Kelsey smiling.

Two-shot of Kelsey and Corrine watching the video, Corrine wiping away tears.

CORRINE: **Yeah. That's so painful to watch, isn't it?**

KELSEY: **We won.**

CORRINE: **You sure did. . . . That was a year ago. It happened so fast. We've been looking for answers, reasons why she's been struggling, and we finally made the connection between what happened with Phutura—the spill.**

KELSEY: **We have to go to court. A different court, not volleyball this time.**

CORRINE: **That's right. And we're going to win, aren't we?**

Tight shot on Corrine brushing hair from Kelsey's face and pulling her closer to kiss her forehead.

CORRINE: **We're going to get you all better, baby girl.**

CHAPTER 31

MIRIAM STARED at the computer screen. She'd never been very good at searching for things. Not like Charlie. Her search felt like a logjam on a swollen river. There was so much information swirling but so many barriers to get to Treha's past.

She had dialed the number on the card for Family Support Services and spoken with a disinterested desk worker. She asked for Kara Robbins and was met with a pause.

"I'm following up on a case and trying to track down information. Is Kara in today?"

"Hold, please."

Music on hold. Words she couldn't understand set to music that would never speak to her. She was growing more and more like her mother, the songs from the past blocking anything new.

"This is Marie; can I help you?"

Miriam asked for Kara, explaining briefly and guardedly about an old case.

"I'm afraid you're about ten years too late. Kara left some time ago. Is there anything I can help you with?"

"Did she move to another job?"

"She started a family. She's a full-time mom now. What's this about?"

"I found her business card at a friend's house. We're looking into her past and I thought Kara might help."

"Who's your friend?"

"Her name is Treha Langsam."

A pause. "No, doesn't ring a bell. How long ago would this have been?"

"It could have been fifteen, sixteen years ago."

"That was before my time, and honestly, even if I knew, we aren't at liberty to talk about confidential matters. I'm afraid I can't help you."

Before Miriam could formulate the next salvo, the phone had clicked and she sat in silence. She hit the search engine button and typed the name in again, but she came up empty.

Charlie wandered past the room, heading toward the kitchen, but paused, peering over her shoulder. "What you looking for?"

An innocent question, but she felt it was an intrusion. She didn't pry into his online habits or searches. Maybe she should. Who knew what he was looking at all day back there.

"It's about Treha. I'm looking for someone who knew her when she was young."

"Why don't you type the name into Facebook?" he said.

She hadn't thought of that.

"Type her in and see what you get."

He continued to the kitchen and Miriam typed in the name, coming up with people from Belvedere, Ohio; Kalamazoo, Michigan; St. Louis, Missouri; and more. She studied them all but none looked like they were old enough to have children. She clicked on *See More* and several others popped up—one from Arizona. Kara Robbins Praytor lived in Clarion, Arizona, originally from Scranton, Pennsylvania. Studied at Penn State. Degree in criminology. Previous employer was listed as "social work." Her photo showed an African American with a pleasant face, big smile, and two children who hugged her neck so tightly it looked like they would leave a mark.

Miriam clicked Kara's name but found her personal information blocked, although there was a link to a blog. It had a creative title and looked artistic, with a series of impressionistic photographs on the header. Miriam scrolled through the posts—a haphazard mix of observations about current events or adventures in potty training. The woman wrote unashamedly from a Christian perspective. Her words weren't heavy-handed but winsome, and there was something about the way she seemed to genuinely live out what she believed that drew Miriam. There were no political diatribes, no mean-spirited slams against other faiths or groups of people. This woman simply wanted to honor God with everything she did.

Partway down the impressive list of past topics, the title "Shoelaces" piqued her interest. She clicked on the entry.

In my other life, the one I left to start this grand experiment called motherhood, I was a social worker. (Sometimes I wonder if that job prepared me for motherhood better than any seminar or parenting book.) I tried to help moms figure out how to feed their children. I tried to help kids escape abusive parents or houses filled with animals, filth, and meth. I saw some horrific things but I made a difference. At least I like to think so.

It's hard not to focus on what I've given up to be a mom. I have less free time, less disposable income, less conversation with adults, and at the end of the day I'm exhausted and feel I haven't done anything meaningful. It's easy to believe I haven't changed someone's life, just diapers.

Still, I don't miss the commute or the office politics—with apologies to former coworkers—or the temptations of those glazed donuts every Friday morning. What I miss about my old job is encapsulated in one face that walks in on me at the strangest moments. I will call her Julie because I'm not allowed to give her real name. She was almost five at the time. She came to me in tattered shoes, with a stare that compares to Superman's laser vision. She was a poster child for abandonment, for everything wrong with the world.

That is not why I think of her today, nor why I think she comes to me in my dreams. Her shifting eyes haunt me.

I was privileged to take her to the shoe store. We were going to pick out a pair of sneakers. I measured her feet, showed her the styles available in her size on shelves above her line of sight. I pulled thick white socks over her feet and watched her glide along the shelves. She gravitated to a certain pair—pink with white flowers, as I recall—and then she would wander to sandals or tap shoes or the dainty sneakers with Velcro and try them on. Each time she would return the shoes to the box and walk back to the pink sneakers. She looked up at me as we stood there, staring long and deep into my eyes, as if there were an ocean of pain and hurt inside. She drew me in like a magnet, like a tide pulling at the beach, and I couldn't help kneeling beside her and putting a finger to her temple and tapping lightly.

"What's going on inside there?" I said. "What are you thinking?"

She spoke in a whisper too light and airy to discern, but I could read the lips and hear her heart.

"Do you have a mother?"

"Yes, I do," I said.

"What's it like?" she said.

Children will ask the height of the sky or what God is like and they don't really expect an answer. They know somewhere deep inside that there are questions that can't fully be answered. They simply want you to hear them, to care.

Julie wasn't looking for a single answer to the mother question but for a life full of things she had never experienced. So I told her. I told her everything. It came pouring out—the way my mother used to wake me in the morning before school, the smell of the kitchen with heavy bacon fat that sizzled in the skillet, the peppermint candy she ate just before church, and how she would pull me up on her lap in my grandmother's rocking chair and read to me. She had been breastfed in that chair, and so had I, and years later my sons would be as well.

Julie listened, not dutifully or waiting to speak again, but drinking in my words until my well ran dry. People walked around us—climbed over us is more like it—for twenty minutes there on the floor of the shoe store, and each time I finished, she asked another question.

I think about her in my unguarded moments. I see her in my children, in some discovery they make. Like learning to tie shoelaces.

It was getting dark and time to leave, so I had Julie try on the pink shoes. The laces were in place but not tied and I could tell by the way she looked at them that she didn't know how. I told her about the bunny ears and recited the poem my mother had taught me, the sad rabbit whose ears were too long and needed to be tied in a bow. She stared at the laces, then at me, processing the information. I told her to try. Instead, she stood, walked the length of the aisle, and came back.

"Do you want me to tie them?" I said.

She shook her head.

"You could trip and fall if you don't. You don't want to let them flop around."

"It feels better this way," she said.

"You don't have to be scared of not knowing how to tie them. Do you want me to teach you?"

She shook her head and sat, taking the shoes off and putting them in the box.

"Then what is it? Why don't you want them? Why do you keep coming back to them?"

"If I tie them, the job is over. There's nothing left to do."

I still don't know exactly what she meant by that. At first I thought she meant that she'd get more attention from people with untied laces—that grown-ups like me would tie them for her and maybe tell her a story or two about their lives. But now I don't think that's what she meant. I think there was more behind her words.

We like to think of life as a series of knots we tie and move along. We do what we're told, follow the rules, and soon we're secure in the rhythm of life. We don't question. We don't even think of the questions. And when the laces flop, we feel insecure about the lack of pressure against the sides of our souls. Support allows us to relax and inhabit life. But this child philosopher was showing me something I couldn't see, something I couldn't begin to understand. That there was more than simply feeling okay about myself or okay about walking ahead. Or walking away.

Every time I tie my child's shoes, every time I tie my own, I think of this. I think of Julie and the way she walked out of the store that night with shoelaces flopping, holding my hand and looking down at them like she had freed the bunny. If I close my eyes and wait, I see her walking today, grown-up, that piercing stare and those questioning eyes.

Somewhere she is walking and I hope she feels freedom. Sometimes when we're at the park or walking on the track at school, I'll untie my shoes in her honor. It feels like the least I can do.

Miriam sat back. She hadn't taken a breath. Could "Julie" be Treha? She had to be. The shifting eyes and flopping shoelaces were a perfect match.

She typed Kara's last name and town into a phone directory and a James L. Praytor came up. Her heart beat a little faster, then fell when she saw the number was unlisted.

She pulled up the blog again and looked for an e-mail address, a way to contact Kara, but there was only a section for comments.

Kara, I stumbled onto your blog during a search for someone I think might be Julie. Very moving post. I have some urgent questions for you. . . .

Don't give too much away or appear to be a stalker. Don't gush about the blog either.

If you could call or e-mail as soon as possible, I would appreciate it.

Miriam typed her e-mail address and phone number, clicked the Send button, and immediately felt she had done something wrong, hadn't given enough information. Then again, maybe she had sounded too desperate. She could have said she was Julie's real mother but she didn't want to lie or manipulate.

Now she would wait. An hour, a day, a year. Who knew how long before the woman responded? It was out of Miriam's control, just like life. Day after day of waiting and hoping and trying not to feel but feeling all the same. Putting a fishing line in the water and sitting and watching for life to give a nibble. She had settled for this. Life's nibbles.

"You come up with anything?" Charlie said, stopping as he passed the room again. He had a ham sandwich in his hand and a paper towel for a napkin underneath. Crumbs fell like raindrops and Miriam tried not to look down.

"Actually, yes. I think your suggestion about Facebook helped."

He nodded and chewed, pointing with the sandwich at the screen and beginning a sentence that he stopped when she looked away. She hated watching him eat. The sounds, the slurping of the soup, the smacking lips. She couldn't stand the noise, the sight of the bread stuck to his teeth. There were so many things she couldn't stand. And she felt bad about it, but you can't train revulsion; it simply comes when it will.

Charlie ran his tongue across his teeth. "I meant to tell you,

I saw a news report about some kids. Strange stuff happening. I think you'll be interested."

Charlie was a news junkie, particularly of the death-and-mayhem variety. It didn't matter if it was a bus crash in Spain or a tsunami on some remote island in the Pacific, Charlie had to tell her about every missing person or missing limb he came across at some of the most inopportune times. Like during meals.

"They have this rapid eye movement," Charlie said, moving his hand back and forth in front of his face. "Brain stuff. Kind of like the girl . . . What was her name again?"

"Treha?" she said.

"Yeah. Like her. There's a bunch of people involved in a lawsuit against a company they say is responsible. Phutura Pharmaceuticals."

Phutura, Miriam thought. *They're cropping up everywhere.*

"I owned some of their stock when it was four dollars. Should have held on to it. You should watch the video."

She asked him where he'd seen the report and he said he would e-mail the link. She usually wasn't interested in the things he found online. Cartoons of Maxine. Jokes about old age and bad marriages and mothers-in-law. YouTube videos of military tributes and air shows and memorials of 9/11. Ceremonies during a storm at the tomb of the unknown soldier. Plus the passed-around threads of the aged, the cute and heartwarming stories of life with wrinkles and grandchildren along with the political jabs at the president or Congress or both. Charlie's favorites were the stories of things in the "good old days." When gasoline was a few pennies a gallon and you didn't have to get a home equity loan just to go to the grocery store. He would stare at pictures of childhood artifacts, memories that sparked some kind of feeling for him, and marvel at how much things had changed. How much the world had gone crazy.

Charlie seemed content to go with the flow, move from one day to the next, seeing what life might toss their way and whiling away hours behind the computer or fiddling with the drip-sprinkler system and adjusting the timer for the precise setting that would make everything green that was supposed to be green. It was his inner engineer always trying to surface. But why couldn't he treat their marriage that way? Why couldn't he narrow down on their relationship like he did the garage door opener or the PCV valve he was always changing in the car when the Check Engine light went on?

She didn't know and she had grown not to care. Charlie was Charlie and that was all there was to it. Take him or leave him. A lump of hardened clay. Every attempt to change him and make him the man she wanted left her frustrated and cold. Distanced. And this was as good as it was going to get.

Though she had to admit he was good to have around when you needed the recycle bin stacked perfectly or the satellite TV programmed, and his coffee did taste better than hers because he had a knack of measuring to the very grain, it seemed. But it is hard to see the good in a person when all you can see is what isn't there.

Miriam checked her e-mail and found the link Charlie had sent without any accompanying message. Just the link. Why send more? Why send an encouraging note saying he was look-ing forward to their new life together? *I love you more now than ever.* Or just *I like you, sort of.* Was that so much to ask?

The link was from a reputable news organization and not from the far right or left. The long story described a commu-nity baffled by strange reactions in teenagers and some adults who had developed eye conditions, problems with anger, and even suicidal tendencies. Students at a small high school were being accused by some of manufacturing their symptoms—head jerks, hand movements, intense anger issues, and behavioral abnormalities. Tourette's syndrome without the profanity. The story was alarming and Miriam couldn't imagine what the parents had been through with their sick children, but it wasn't until she watched the accompanying video that something clicked.

A ninth grader's face filled the screen. As the boy spoke, his head jerked to the right and his eyes twitched. "I don't have any control over the way my eyes are moving, and it's scary, you know?"

The report switched to the boy's mother, in tears, chin quavering. "Ryan was a straight-A student. Tops in his class. He was a finalist in the state forensics competition last year, oral interpretation."

"The family moved here one year ago," the reporter said gravely. "And Ryan's grades and health plunged as a result."

"He's not making this up," the mother said. "Something is wrong here."

The reporter was shown walking on a pastoral hillside near the sprawling complex of Phutura Pharmaceuticals. "In the class action lawsuit against the pharmaceutical giant, the plaintiffs contend that Phutura allowed toxic chemicals to seep into the groundwater near the school, affecting anyone who drank the water. Parents say they have the medical proof they need to convince a jury that Phutura caused their children's problems. But the company says that's simply not true."

Ezra Hollingsworth, vice president of Phutura, sat in a

leather chair behind a gleaming cherry desk with a look on his face that, to Miriam, exuded smarm.

"I find it more than ironic that people in this community have lived here for decades—they've breathed the air, they drank the water, they raised crops—and suddenly there are mysterious problems. I truly sympathize with the parents of these children, and it's human nature to want to blame. But we followed every FDA and EPA guideline to the letter. As a company, we're simply not at fault."

A panel of parents sat in front of a dark background, hands folded, mostly looking down. Solemn-faced. "Our children are the most vulnerable," one mother said. "If we can't protect them, who can we protect?"

Miriam read the report again, then looked at the still picture of one of the young girls. Such suffering in the world to so many innocent people. If they won the lawsuit, if the company was forced to pay them for damages, what difference would it make? Their lives were shattered.

And Treha . . . her symptoms were frighteningly similar to those young people's, but could there be a connection? Would Davidson be able to explain it all?

CHAPTER 32

THE LIGHT WAS FADING in the west and an orange glow hit the walls of the Howards' house as the car bearing the four travelers pulled to a stop. Treha got out and walked toward the front door, followed by Devin and Jonah carrying equipment, and a stiff-legged Calvin Davidson, who still carried a gun, though at a slightly different angle.

Devin had finally convinced the man that he would never get the gun past the front desk at the hospital and that seeing Crenshaw would simply endanger him more. He'd suggested they go to Miriam's home, where Treha was staying. Davidson agreed, but when Jonah further suggested they call Miriam from a pay phone at a Dairy Queen near Picacho Peak and ask her to open the garage so the car could disappear inside and not be seen by a drone, Davidson said to keep driving.

Throughout the drive Davidson had continued his sometimes-lucid, sometimes-rambling assessment of the world. He had canceled his Dish Network because "they" were watching him through the television. There were terrorists plotting an assault on the water systems of the United States and a corresponding electromagnetic pulse that would take them off the grid simultaneously. Infrared cameras looked through walls.

Cameras in the sewage system came up through the pipes to look in people's bathrooms, and no one cared. Why terrorists would look in Davidson's bathroom Treha couldn't decipher, but his fears seemed less rooted in these conspiracies than in another more pressing menace.

Treha rang the doorbell and Miriam answered, looking happy to see them but confused when she saw Davidson. And even more confused when she saw his gun.

"Please come in," Miriam said to the group. "Mr. Davidson, it's a pleasure to meet you."

Charlie was in the kitchen, hands in his pockets, sizing things up as he leaned against the silverware drawer, a puzzled look on his face.

Davidson glanced Miriam's way. "I wish the circumstances were different. Have you heard anything more about Jim's condition?"

"Dr. Crenshaw is still in ICU. There's been no change."

"And there will be none," Davidson said. "They won't allow it. In a few hours or a few days his heart will stop and the problem will be over. But they will still have to deal with me."

"What are you talking about?" Miriam said. "And why are you holding that gun? You have no enemies here."

The woman spoke in a way that was reassuring and inviting. Treha could tell her years of experience at Desert Gardens had trained her well for such a confrontation.

Davidson looked at Miriam, then glanced at Charlie. "Do you have Wi-Fi going in here?"

"Yes, sir."

"I can feel it. Unplug it. Quickly. Don't just turn it off; unplug it from the outlet. They have ways of monitoring you can't begin to imagine."

Charlie went to a cabinet in the kitchen to show Davidson the wireless router and unplugged it. Miriam offered to make them something to eat, but Davidson waved her off. "We're not hungry."

"I'm starving," Jonah said. "I'll take anything. A piece of bread. Moldy cheese."

"I have no idea how much time we have, but we can eat later. Set up your camera. We need to get started."

"I'll make you something while you prepare," Miriam said, putting a hand on Jonah's shoulder. "What's the urgency, Mr. Davidson?" she said as she opened the refrigerator.

"The urgency is I won't be here much longer. And the truth, what Jim was talking about in that letter, what we've covered for so long, needs to be told." He turned to Treha. "*She* needs to be told."

"Why me?"

"Because you're part of this. More than you know."

Jonah fitted the old man with a microphone, running it behind him and up through his shirt so the black cord wouldn't be visible. The wireless microphone was still clipped on Treha's scrubs. Miriam placed a sandwich near Jonah while he focused the camera, and as soon as it was running, he wolfed it.

"We're rolling," Jonah said through the sandwich.

"All right, where should I begin?" Davidson said.

Something took over that Treha couldn't explain. An inner sense, a knowing that she needed to ease the man into the truth.

"Tell me about your health. Are you sick?" she said.

"Do I look ill?"

"What about medication? Have you been prescribed anything?"

"Is there anyone my age who isn't on medication? That's part of the problem."

He sounded agitated, scattered. She tried to bring him to himself. "Tell me about your childhood. When were you born?"

He pursed his lips and looked at the floor. "I was born in 1932. My mother had complications after birth. The doctor was not skilled or perhaps was not as interested in a poor woman. Two months later she died."

He said it matter-of-factly, as if he were reciting the names of the presidents or the capitals of all fifty states.

"I was passed around in the community, a small town in northern Ohio, to whatever nursing mother was available. It wasn't such a bad deal getting all that attention from so many women. But as a child there was a void. A missing piece."

"Your mother."

"Yes, and my father, too. He took my mother's death very hard. He retreated. From life. He worked hard but wasn't home much." Telling this seemed to calm him a little, relax his muscles.

"What did your father do?"

"He worked at a mill. He tried farming, but the weather would take out a crop and you were left with nothing. There was work in the mines to the south, but he knew that would kill him. The mill was dangerous but you didn't have to climb into the earth for a paycheck every two weeks."

"Did he blame you?"

"For what?"

"Your mother's death."

He waved a hand. "No, I don't think so. It must have occurred to him that I was the reason he no longer had a wife, but I don't think he held back his love for me because of that."

"Do you know anything about your mother?" Treha said.

"I don't remember anything, if that's what you're asking. But I know she was beautiful from the picture I have. I know the perfume my father bought her, even though he could barely afford to feed us. She would sing songs from her childhood as she worked around the house. And she loved flowers. Lilies and dandelions and anything with color. She came alive when her children brought her flowers. Clover or weeds, even. Everything about her embodied life and love. And she was a very smart woman, even though she had little education."

"How do you know about her if you were an infant when she died?"

"Sister told me. She had the most vivid memories. The other children had foggy recollections. They would get things mixed up, attribute some saying to my mother when it was actually an aunt or a teacher who said it. That's the way children are, I suppose."

"Is your sister the one who took care of you?"

"Yes. Well, all of my siblings did. There were four who were born before me. Two boys, two girls." He looked at Treha as if he wanted to hold something back, to construct some kind of dam here in the story or turn away, but he kept opening. "My brothers and sisters also grew up without a mother, you see, and they had to fill in the missing pieces for each other. No child should have to do this, but it was all we knew."

"Tell me about this sister of yours. The one who cared for you."

The old man smiled and lines formed on his face, making him look like a kindly lion. "She was the oldest. She was ten when I was born, when Mother died, and she stayed home with me; she stopped going to school. I don't know if this was something my father asked her to do or made her do. Part of me thinks she did it of her own accord and he allowed it."

"What did you do all day, when the children were at school?"

"I suppose we played little games. But the thing I remember the most is her reading to me. I was reading before I ever set foot in the schoolhouse. It was her example, her finger following the words on the page from left to right, that accomplished that. She told me much later that one day she didn't put her finger on the page. She wanted to see what I would do. And I put my finger there and followed the words. She said it was then that she knew I was special. Even though I grew up without a mother, I felt special to someone. We grew quite close."

Treha watched the man's eyes twinkle and she followed the light.

"What was her name?"

"Evelyn. But I couldn't say the word as a child. I said 'Eleven' and everyone would laugh. So I called her Sister." His eyes darted as if searching for his childhood in the recesses of the mind. "It's funny what you remember when you talk of these things. I can still smell the aroma of the meals Sister cooked for us. And see the way she . . ."

"The way she what?" Treha said.

"How she looked out the window every day. There was a longing in her. For something out there, something on the horizon she couldn't see." The twinkle was gone and in its place was wetness at the memory. "She died several years ago. She was the first of us to go. The first to part after my father died. And now I am the only one left."

He leaned forward. "You asked if my father held me responsible for my mother's death." He shook his head. "But I felt responsible for Sister not going to school. For never having the life she could have had."

"She didn't go back to school?" Treha said.

"By the time I was in first grade, she was a young woman. When I went to school, she began working, first cleaning houses for the women in town and babysitting their children. And then she went to work at the mill. She and my father would go off together each morning, very early, before the sun came up." He sat back. "I don't like to think of those days. It was a difficult time for the family, but the struggle and the hardship make you strong. You know? You don't realize it at the time, but the pain propels you. Too many people today think that life is supposed to be easy. We look for the easiest route to get from one place to another with the machines they place in the cars and the Internet telling you which roads to take." He waved a hand again. "I guess it's all good for us and helpful. But there is something you miss about struggle and hardship by having everything laid out for you on a piece of paper or on a talking box telling you every turn."

He looked up from his diatribe, like a turtle realizing his head is out of the shell. "I suppose I'm sounding like a cranky old man now."

Treha pulled him back to the past. "You did well in school?"

"Yes. And I credit Sister. She read books to me. She explained everything she knew about science and how plants grow and the wonders of the world. I asked her so many things. She said once that my spine was formed in the shape of a question mark."

The two sat in silence, Davidson folding his wrinkled hands and staring at them and Treha sitting ramrod straight.

"Where did your education take you?" she said.

"To the university. I studied chemistry and wanted to find some cure—like Jonas Salk did. In school I was given an internship with a small company which was called Stonegate at the time. Eventually it became Phutura Pharmaceuticals."

"Is this how you met Dr. Crenshaw?"

Davidson glanced at the camera. Then a dip of the head. "Yes. I met him through Phutura. He was part of some drug trials we conducted. I like to think we helped many people over the years, even though there were regrets."

"Did Dr. Crenshaw contact you recently?"

The man looked as if he had been punched in the gut. "I know he wrote me a letter that never reached me."

"Did he call you? Send another letter? Some other communication?"

Davidson shook his head. "No."

"What did you do together?" she said.

He moved his mouth to swallow and struggled for a moment. He seemed stuck, somehow.

Miriam spoke. "Mr. Davidson, would you like something to drink? Water? Coffee? Or something to eat?"

"Yes, coffee, please. Thank you. And maybe if I stand and stretch a little to get my blood and old bones moving again."

CHAPTER 33

MIRIAM POURED the coffee as Mr. Davidson glanced around the kitchen. He was still holding his gun but Miriam hoped he might put it on the table while he drank. Maybe forget about it.

"She's very good at this, isn't she?" Davidson said.

"Treha? Oh, I think she has a gift."

A grimace from the old man. Perhaps something in his memory bank that had overdrawn him.

"What's wrong, Mr. Davidson? Is there something I can help you with? Maybe something you know about her that's hidden?"

"We're all hiding something, aren't we? The best of us, the worst of us."

"Earlier you seemed to think we were in danger. You talked about being monitored. What did you mean?"

Davidson acted as if he were hearing the words for the first time. Then his face changed and he put a withered hand on Miriam's shoulder. "I'm just a silly old man with a confused mind. My story isn't important."

"I think it is. I think it's important to her."

He nodded. "Where did you find her? When she asks questions, I feel as if I am under some kind of spell. Perhaps it is her captivating eyes. Or that she reminds me of a granddaughter. I almost get lost speaking with her, running through the fields of my youth. It's as if she's forcing me to remember. Not coercing, but something akin to drawing blood for analysis."

"That's a good analogy. I've seen her work with many people. She calls them from wherever they are. She brings them out. Like she's calling you out to play, like your sister."

He smiled at the mention of her. "I wish I could show you a picture. I have them at home in photo albums. In one she is fifteen or sixteen, in her uniform, as she called it. What she wore every day to the mill for many years. It was all she had. Her hand was bandaged in that photo. She had lost a finger in an accident. I believe she missed a half day of work."

"Those were different times," she said.

"Yes, it was a difficult life. But you did what you had to do to survive. Just like now."

He strained as he sat at the table. Miriam had poured half a cup of coffee, anticipating his shaking hands. He still nearly spilled it as he lifted it to his lips with his left hand. He set it back down, put the pistol on the table, and picked the mug up with his right hand.

"Why are you so interested in her? In her past?" Davidson said.

Miriam sat next to him, as near to the pistol as she could get, and cradled her own coffee mug. "She's like a daughter to me. A daughter I never had. And I think there is help for her. Hope for something better."

"She is impaired?"

"You've seen her. The eyes, the body movement, the disconnection."

"The gift."

"Yes. I think there is more in life for her, and I wonder if, perhaps, you have a key to help us unlock that."

He put the mug down and pushed his tongue under his dentures and stared at the tablecloth. It was the perfect chance for her to grab the pistol; she saw it there like ripened fruit.

Her cell phone rang. Davidson looked up.

"Excuse me," Miriam said, glancing at the screen. The number was listed as private.

"No, don't answer it," he said.

"I have to—it might be about Treha."

He put a hand to his head. "I forgot to have you shut them off when I came. I don't know what I was thinking."

Miriam moved past Davidson into the small hallway leading to her bedroom. Behind her, she heard Treha and the others go to Davidson, try to help him.

"Miriam, this is Kara Praytor. I saw your message on my blog."

"Thank you," Miriam said, catching her breath. "I'm surprised you called so quickly."

"What's this about?"

Miriam collected her thoughts. It sounded like the others had Davidson under control, so she continued. But what to say? If she asked if she could call back, she was afraid the woman might balk.

"Kara, I'm trying to piece together some information about the girl you wrote about in your blog. You called her Julie."

A pause on the other end. "Oh. Are you related to her?"

Miriam closed her eyes. "No, but I think I know her."

Kara hesitated. "I'm sure you're legitimate, Miriam, but I'm not comfortable talking about former cases. Plus, that was a really long time ago."

"I understand. And if this were just my curiosity, believe me,

I wouldn't trouble you. I'm trying to help this girl by finding out about her past, why she's damaged. And then give her hope for how to move forward."

"You say you know her. What is her name?"

"Treha Langsam."

Silence on the other end. "Treha. Oh, you don't know how I've prayed for that girl to find a friend. How is she? Where is she?"

Miriam told her as quickly as she could about Treha's life and about her gift. "Through the years she has co-opted the stories of others, people at the retirement home where she worked. She stole their stories because she has no past she remembers."

Sniffling on the other end but a smile in the voice. "I can't believe this. She's come back to me. Is there a way I could talk to her? Hear her voice?"

Miriam said she was sure there was, but that Treha was involved with something at the moment. "She's here with me. Staying at my house in Tucson. Can you tell me anything about where you found her? Where she came from?"

Miriam listened to the woman for a moment and then ran to the kitchen for a pad of paper and a pen.

CHAPTER 34

To Treha, the old man seemed more tired when he sat down in front of the camera again. That wasn't supposed to happen after you drank coffee. He still carried the pistol, which didn't concern Treha as much as it seemed to bother Jonah and Devin.

"Rolling," Jonah said.

Davidson leaned forward. "Before we begin, would you mind if I asked you a question or two?"

Treha blinked but didn't answer.

"I'm told you have a gift for this, for drawing people out as you have done with me."

"People can become locked away in their minds. I help open the door."

"You must have been highly valued at your workplace. Desert Gardens."

"I was, but then I was let go."

"Why? If you have so much to offer, why would they jettison you?"

Treha turned to Devin. "You wanted me to ask him questions."

Devin smiled. "It's okay; we want to hear." He whispered something to Jonah.

"I don't know why," Treha said, facing the old man again. "The person who runs the facility said I was a danger to the residents, which isn't true."

"A danger?"

"She said there were things in my record. She didn't want to take the chance of me hurting someone."

"Have you ever hurt anyone, Treha?"

She didn't respond.

"Have you ever lost your temper? Do you remember anything like that?"

"Perhaps when I was younger."

"How did getting fired make you feel?" Davidson said.

Treha shrugged.

"It sounds like you enjoyed working with Dr. Crenshaw and the others."

"I did."

"And when you were let go, you didn't feel anything? No anger? No pain?"

She didn't answer.

"Surely you felt something. If you had friends there, you must miss them. You must feel a certain injustice in being treated this way."

Treha gripped the arms of the chair, digging her fingernails into the soft leather. "They told me not to come back, so I didn't."

"You must be upset that you can't use your gift. Are you angry?"

Treha glanced back. They had focused the camera on her profile and suddenly she felt awkward. The intensity of the old man's gaze stirred something inside she didn't like.

"Treha, do you ever get angry? Are you ever happy or sad?"

She looked away from him and stared at a spot on the floor, her jaw clenched, muscles flexing.

"I'm sorry if I'm making you uncomfortable."

"You're not," she said, her voice tight. "Can we get back to you?"

The old man cradled the pistol in his lap. "Tell me something that makes you angry or upset. Or happy. Do you have a happy memory?"

She looked at her fingernails. "My mother took me to an ice cream shop when I was a little girl and let me order a bowl. I sat on the chair and she told me to stay; then she walked out the door and never returned."

A whisper behind her and she turned.

"That didn't happen to you," Devin said. "Dr. Crenshaw told us about that when we interviewed him."

"Is that what drew you to the people at Desert Gardens?" Davidson said, his voice calm and reassuring. "Were you shaping a history of your own from the stories you heard? Because you can't remember? Or don't want to remember?"

"I answered your question."

"With a fabrication," he said. "You told me someone else's story."

"I don't eat ice cream," Treha said. "Now you know why. Can we continue?"

"What else did Dr. Crenshaw tell you?"

Typing now, her fingers flew across her lap. "He talked about his life. Where he grew up. His family. His wife. How he came to the facility. He gave me riddles, word games, because he knew I was good at them."

"Did he tell you anything about his work?"

"He was a doctor."

"What kind of doctor?"

"Obstetrician. Gynecologist. He worked with mothers having babies."

"Yes, that is how I came to know him as well. I worked for Phutura developing medicines. I sometimes asked him to help me find willing participants for my research. This is why I believe he wrote to me. Did he talk to you about this?"

"No."

"And you didn't ask? You never wondered why he was so interested in you?"

"I was interested in what he wanted to tell me. I don't like to pry."

"But you're prying into my life."

"You don't have to say anything you don't want," she said evenly.

He dipped his head and there was a slight smile.

"You're trying to make me angry," Treha said.

"I'm looking for emotion."

More typing, but Treha didn't speak.

"What really happened to your mother? She didn't leave you in an ice cream shop."

Mrs. Howard stepped into the room. Treha glanced up and saw a look on her face that seemed both weighty and relieved.

"I don't know my mother. I never knew her."

"Pictures? A name?"

She shook her head.

"And what about your father? Brothers and sisters? You had to have a childhood. What was it like?"

She shook her head again.

Davidson's eyes wandered like a man who has gone on a

journey home and sees something that sparks a memory. He sat back, his arms limp, the gun dangling.

"What is it, Mr. Davidson?" Devin said. "Are you all right?"

Davidson looked at Treha and instead of paranoia she saw recognition, sure knowledge of the past.

"The answer," he whispered. He pointed an arthritic finger at her.

"What?" Treha said. "What answer?"

"The riddles he gave you. He wasn't looking for something inside you. *You* are the answer. You are the question he had. The question I have held at the back of my mind for many years." Tears rose in the old man's eyes. "I'm so sorry, Treha."

The coffeepot gasped in the next room. Otherwise the house was still. All eyes were focused on Davidson.

"What are you sorry about?" Treha said softly, inviting.

Davidson wiped his face with a hand. "Treha, I believe Dr. Crenshaw found you—I don't know how, but he did—because he must have been under a weight of guilt about what happened. And this is why he sought you out, suggested you work there. The quizzes, the riddles, the word games you played—these were not happenstance; they were engineered."

"Why?"

"Because he wanted to observe the effects, I believe." Davidson looked at Devin and Jonah. "This is important for you to get. I want you to hear every word."

Jonah focused the camera and nodded at the old man that he was ready.

Davidson leaned back and spoke toward the camera. "I worked for Phutura Pharmaceuticals for many years before starting my own company, an independent laboratory. At Phutura, there was pressure on us to perform, to come up with new products, new medication. There was competition from other laboratories and a great deal of money involved.

"By accident my experimentation led to what I thought was a breakthrough. That's the way it happens. You are looking for a medication that will stimulate the pancreas to produce insulin, for example, and you come upon something vastly different but just as important.

"My research held great promise and potentially huge profits for Phutura. We focused on an antidepressant, antianxiety medication. I won't go into the technical information, but from a layman's point of view, it was perfect. Safe enough for even a pregnant woman to use. Or so we thought. The delivery system was supposed to get the medication to the prefrontal cortex more effectively. But instead it penetrated the limbic system. It did what we wanted, but in the wrong place." He put a hand to his forehead as if in pain. "We discovered this with the laboratory animals."

"So this was not a legal trial you were conducting?" Devin said from behind Treha.

"No."

"Keep going," Treha said.

"Everything was going well in the laboratory. Everything seemed to be in line. But I was using two separate control groups of laboratory animals, and I realized there were problems. Certain symptoms I didn't anticipate."

Treha glanced back as Jonah adjusted the camera for a tighter shot of Davidson's face.

"The animals, in the initial stages, showed amazing response. The medication calmed them, took away hyperactivity, but also allowed them to focus and narrow their mental acuity. I conducted tests on the brains of the animals. I was elated about the possibilities, but after a few weeks I noticed a degeneration."

"What type of degeneration?" Miriam said.

Treha looked at her, but the questions coming from different sources didn't seem to bother Davidson.

He pursed his lips. "Nystagmus. Aggression. When stress chemicals stimulate the limbic system inappropriately, the result can be anger and rage. I knew then that human trials were out of the question." He looked again at Treha.

"So you told Phutura about this?" Miriam said.

"I told the director of research immediately. A man named Hollingsworth. He's still with the company, though in a higher position. He was disappointed, of course, but I considered the problem solved. I had lost valuable time and energy on this research, but no one was hurt. Phutura assured me nothing further would be done with the medication."

"They lied to you."

"Yes. To my face. While I was shutting down the research, discovering the drawbacks to the medication, Phutura went ahead with the development. Another team was given my notes, my research, and they continued working.

"But this is not the worst of it. Not only did they continue the research; they went behind my back and found a medical doctor who would introduce a human trial. A test subject who could never be traced, in case something went wrong."

"Not Dr. Crenshaw," Treha said.

Davidson nodded. "Yes. Jim Crenshaw. When I discovered this, I went to Hollingsworth. We had a heated conversation. I threatened to go to the authorities. To the media. I told him I would report the company. That I didn't care what happened to me."

"How did he respond?" Miriam said.

"He turned on me like a wild animal. He threatened my

career, told me I would be the one prosecuted. That the company would disavow any knowledge of what I was doing and that Crenshaw would go along with it. Would implicate me."

The man's face clouded and he looked down. "And then he did what those in power will do. He offered money. If I would keep things quiet, it would all go away. No one needed to know. I would be set for the rest of my life. My family wouldn't have to worry. All of that."

"And you accepted," Miriam said.

"Yes. To my shame. And the research on this medication ended. No more women were subjected to it. But they continued to test the delivery part of the active medication, thinking it might be useful in other medications. That research did not end until two years ago. And then the company dumped the waste." He sighed. "The truth is like a toxic spill, in a way. It is a dangerous thing. And it will come to the surface one day. The truth is always there, haunting you, hovering over you. Always ready to return."

"The truth being what?" Devin said.

"The damage done to the fetus, the unborn child of the woman involved in the human trial, was unconscionable. They never considered the possibility that this medication would be a teratogen—would hurt the unborn. Of course I didn't know the identity of the test subject. Jim Crenshaw did. I never knew the results, but I feared all these years that someone would come forward. And I also feared that no one would. That the company would not be held liable.

"Then I heard of the lawsuit, the schoolchildren who have developed abnormalities. This might never have come to light if the company had ceased development and disposed of the medication properly. But somehow it got into the groundwater near the school. Apparently the school is on its own water system, separate from the nearby town. I don't know why, but the truth is coming back, coming to the surface. Obviously the lawyers for those parents and children have a link to Phutura, but there's no way for them to identify the drug or know about its effects. If their legal team ever found this information, there would be a huge settlement. It could bankrupt the company."

Davidson leaned forward. "This is for the authorities. In case something happens to me. I want you to know the truth. This is why my house was bugged and why they are listening even now. I know I sound like a crazy old man, but I'm not. You will find that all of the records of my work for Phutura have been destroyed. There is no paper trail to me, but I'm swearing in front of these people now, there were human tests done, unauthorized human tests."

"Tell me about the tests," Treha said.

He set his jaw and nodded. "You deserve to know. . . . Many people in developing countries will agree to undergo trials without knowing the risks. And some in this country are desperate enough that they will agree to almost anything. When I uncovered what was happening and confronted Hollingsworth, I also went to Crenshaw and discovered he was using a young mother, her pregnancy well along. She was taking the medication for anxiety and depression and it was actually helping her. There were special circumstances with her case—I'm not sure of the specifics. Dr. Crenshaw said there would be no problem, that no one would be able to trace the child. I couldn't believe it."

"Was that me?" Treha said.

The man nodded again.

"Why would it never be detected?" Miriam said.

"The mother was giving up the child at birth. It was a blind adoption. Dr. Crenshaw was helping facilitate that. I don't know much else except that Treha's mother was told the medication wouldn't harm her child." The man's voice was grandfatherly. "Jim Crenshaw must have tracked you down."

"But why?" Devin said. "If he lied to Treha's mother—and if the company paid you off—they paid off Crenshaw, too, right? He was opening himself up for trouble. He'd want to keep her as far away as he could."

"Yes," Davidson said. "That is what I would have thought too. I've remained silent all these years, kept quiet and moved to the estate. But something must have made Crenshaw want to take a chance on finding Treha."

"He went through a spiritual change—a transformation," Miriam said. "I spoke with Elsie, one of the residents. Dr. Crenshaw confided certain things to her."

Treha sat forward. "He played games with me. He asked questions. He probed my mind with riddles and problems."

Davidson spoke softly again. "I suppose you were part of his coming to himself, this spiritual awakening. He couldn't bear not knowing the truth. And the truth will do strange things to you. When he made the connection between you and the research, the effect it had on you, he couldn't help but try to make amends."

Treha looked at the floor, her eyes pivoting, the room moving with the gentle swaying she had known for as long as she could remember. And the more she looked, the more questions came, and her heart rate accelerated.

"What about me?" she said. "If you know all of this about medication and laboratory animals, why can't you use that knowledge to help me?"

"I wish I knew how to help you," the old man said. "All I can ask is that you forgive me. Forgive all of us who were involved. And I will do everything I can to see that you are compensated."

"Compensated? Is that what you think I want?" She was shouting now, though she didn't realize it until the old man recoiled in his chair. But she couldn't help it. "You think I want their money? I don't want their money."

"Treha, please," Miriam said, reaching out to her.

But Treha moved backward and pulled away when Devin gently took her by the arm. "Don't touch me. Leave me alone."

"We'll get you help," Miriam said. "I promise you that."

"You heard what he said!" Treha screamed. The old man covered his ears as she let out a piercing yell. Her eyes raced, her mind on fire. Everyone in the room moved toward her and she wanted them away, wanted them to stand back.

"Treha, I know we can help you. Please calm down," Miriam continued louder, trying to break in.

"I don't want your help!" she shrieked. "I don't want to answer your questions." She pointed at her eyes. "I want this to stop!"

Treha ran for the door and opened it, but the outer door was locked. They were rushing for her and she wanted out. She balled her fists and beat them hard against the glass until it shattered and something sprayed in her eyes, and the light through them was red. Someone grabbed her and she beat at him and wouldn't stop until the sirens came and something stung her arm and then she fell asleep.

CHAPTER 35

Treha awoke to white light and the smell of fresh sheets. The first thing she felt was the difference in the clothes she wore, and she didn't like it.

"Where are my scrubs?" she mumbled.

When she tried to wipe the drool from her mouth, she couldn't reach because her arm was restrained to the railing of the bed. She let her eyes adjust and saw the TV on the wall. She was in a real bed, surrounded by a curtain. And beside her in a chair was Mrs. Howard, sleeping. Her head was tilted to the side, her mouth open, and it looked like a very uncomfortable position.

Treha pulled against the restraints again, not in anger or rage, but like a child who might awaken in a car seat, confined. There was pain to her struggle and Treha noticed she wasn't just restrained; she was bandaged about her wrists. She tried to remember what had happened.

The glass. The window must have cut her. She remembered screaming and the frightened looks on their faces, even Devin and Jonah. And Mr. Davidson . . . She remembered seeing him, distraught, trying to get to her, but it was someone else who grabbed her from behind—Charlie. It had to have been him, the one riding on the periphery the whole evening. He had grabbed her arms and held her down until the paramedics came.

She tried to relax, to close her eyes and just rest. There was a dull ache in her head, her reaction to the medication they must have given. She wanted to push on her temples—that was what made her feel better when a migraine came—but she couldn't. So she gave in to the truth, the reality. She stopped struggling.

And went back to sleep.

CHAPTER 36

Miriam awoke and found Treha sitting up, her eyes open and moving, a blank expression on her face. She pulled herself up in the chair, wiped her mouth, and yawned, but the girl didn't acknowledge or turn toward her.

"How are you feeling, Treha?" Miriam said.

No response.

"You caused quite a stir last night. Let me look at your arms."

The girl didn't move, didn't blink. She just stared straight ahead as Miriam checked the bandages. The restraints were a precaution so she didn't tear the stitches if she had another episode. This wasn't the psych ward; Miriam hoped it wouldn't come to that. They'd given her a powerful sedative that had knocked her out for the night.

There was the usual seepage and draining of the wounds and stitches, but Miriam felt confident the girl would be okay. Scarred, but intact. She shuddered thinking about the violence, the sight of Treha flailing her arms at the broken glass, the shards digging deeper. The spray of blood. If Charlie hadn't been there, hadn't grabbed her and held on with all his might, who knew what might have happened.

"Are you hungry?" Miriam said. "I can get the nurses to bring you something."

No response.

Miriam stepped into the hallway and let the nurse know Treha was awake. The nurse followed her back to the semiprivate room that Treha had to herself and inspected the bandages. Breakfast had already been delivered, so she carried Treha's meal to the tray table beside the bed.

"Can you take these off?" Treha said to Miriam. "How do they expect me to eat?"

Miriam leaned down. "They wanted to make sure you don't hurt yourself again."

Through all the movement of her eyes and head, Treha caught her gaze and communicated more in that look than Miriam could in a lifetime of talking. Her face said more than Charlie had ever said to her.

"All right, we'll take them off," Miriam said. "But if you get violent, we'll have to move you to a different place in the hospital."

"I know. The crazy floor."

Miriam smiled and untied the left arm, and Treha squeezed at her temples. When the right arm was free, Treha pushed herself all the way up in bed like she was ready to eat, so Miriam moved the tray over her lap. Treha drank the orange juice in one gulp and picked up a spoon to try the oatmeal. Miriam thought this was a good sign.

"Do you remember anything about last night?" she said.

"I remember Davidson telling me I would always be this way."

Miriam cocked her head. "Treha, we don't know that."

"The damage was done before I was born. There is nothing you can do to reverse that."

"That could be true. But there may be something we can do. We can't really know until there are tests."

"Tests cost money. I don't have health insurance."

"Don't worry about that. Let's just get you better. The good news is, now we know what happened. Mr. Davidson will be able to talk with the doctors and tell them what you were given and how it may have affected you."

"It doesn't matter. I'm not going to change." The girl took a bite of toast and crunched it, the crumbs falling on her hospital gown. She didn't brush them away, just kept chewing. "It's not so bad knowing."

"What do you mean?"

Treha stared out the window, chewing the toast, focused on nothing. "The stories I read. My favorite books. There is always someone looking for something else. Something more. Reaching for a goal. And I've wondered if I could do that. In some ways I didn't know I was asking the question."

"What question, Treha?"

"Can I get better? Will I always be . . . the way I am?"

"There is so much we can try. I think once the doctors look at you and begin to understand—"

Treha interrupted her. "It's better like this. It's better to know there will be no change. I can live with that. Move on with my life."

No emotion. No screaming or yelling. Just total submission.

Instead of arguing, Miriam sat back. She thought of her own life, her own circumstances.

"What are you thinking?" Treha said.

"That maybe you're right. Maybe it's better to give up. Just go along with whatever life hands you. Life deals the cards. You take them and don't ask questions. It's much easier that way, isn't it, Treha? Not to have to fight or struggle anymore. I understand."

"I don't think you do."

Miriam rose and walked to the door. "I don't suppose you'll be wanting to stay with me. Now that you've discovered this. You'll want to go back to your apartment. Find another cleaning position. Something that will pay the bills."

Treha didn't answer.

Miriam stopped at the door and turned. "I have a confession to make. I went to your apartment. I had lunch with Du'Relle and his mother. I didn't plan any of that; it just happened. They've had a loss in the family."

"What loss?"

"Du'Relle's father was killed. He's not coming home."

Treha stared at her as if she couldn't comprehend the news.

"This is what life does, Treha. It deals the cards. We can't choose that. We can only choose what we do with them."

"Why did you go there?"

"I went looking for answers. I thought I might find something about you. That's my confession. I went into your apartment and looked around. I used your key to get in. You can sue me if you'd like. I'm guilty. I wouldn't blame you."

"I don't want to sue you."

Miriam smiled. "I didn't think you would."

"I want to pay you for the broken glass."

"You just gave Charlie a project to work on. I never liked that door. We're replacing it." Miriam took a step toward her. "I did find something. It fell out of one of your stories, one of your books. A woman named Kara. Do you remember her?"

No recognition on Treha's face.

"You met her when you were about five years old. She took

you to buy a pair of shoes. Anyway, I made contact. I asked questions. And last night, while you were speaking with Mr. Davidson . . ."

"You had a phone call."

"Yes."

Treha sat up a little higher.

"If you've decided this is your life, that it can get no better, you probably don't want to know what else I discovered."

Treha pushed the tray from the bed.

"We've located your mother."

The eyes moved back and forth over the landscape of the room, and Miriam wondered what was going on behind them. After a few moments, Treha spoke.

"Where?"

"She's in Arizona. Not far from here. I haven't called her. And I won't, if you decide you don't want to see her. I can understand that decision."

There was a knock at the door and Devin stepped inside with a small bouquet of flowers. "I hope I'm not interrupting."

He had no idea what he was interrupting.

"Come in," Miriam said.

He handed Treha the flowers. "You look good. Are you feeling all right?"

"Better."

"I'm glad. You had us scared."

"But Jonah got some good video, I'm sure."

Devin smiled. "We're shooting more with Mr. Davidson. He's explaining more about the drug you were given when you were a baby. And how the students at that school got sick from it."

"Is he still here in Tucson?" Treha said.

"He's staying at our house," Miriam said. "Until he feels well enough to go home."

Treha ran a hand along her injured arm and spoke toward the wall. "Mrs. Howard just told me she's found my mother."

Devin turned. "Seriously?"

Miriam nodded.

"I want to see her," Treha said.

Miriam smiled. "All right. We can arrange that."

Devin's head moved from Miriam to Treha and back again. "I have to get that . . . I mean, is there any way you'd allow me to film that?"

"Let's get her well enough to leave here before we decide," Miriam said.

"Right," Devin said. "Well, there's something else that's come up I wanted you to know about. I'm sure you won't be able to join us, but—"

"What is it, Devin?"

Miriam listened as Devin described what he and Jonah had planned. Treha's eyes wandered, but Miriam thought she could see a flash of resolve on the young woman's face.

CHAPTER 37

DEVIN HELPED JONAH carry the equipment into the Phutura
Pharmaceuticals media room. It was here that they announced
breakthroughs, new FDA approvals, and held conference calls
with investors. And there were many investors in Phutura. After
a sluggish few years and a hit from the competition, the stock
had doubled each of the past two years and the company had
bright prospects for the future. Any good news about the lawsuit and the stock would jump. But from what Devin could
discern, investors might be jumping ship soon.

The company offered its own camera and equipment to use,
but Devin wanted to keep the footage consistent. The interview
that would've normally taken months to set up had been hast-
ily arranged by Calvin Davidson. The old man's history with
Hollingsworth carried extra weight. Devin hadn't actually lied
about the content of the questions, but it was clear that Phutura
believed this would be a sympathetic interview that would help
any damage done to their sterling reputation. His hope was to
get Phutura on camera for use in the documentary. And something even better.

An aide was sent to see if everything was prepared, and soon
after, Ezra Hollingsworth strolled into the room. The man exuded

presence as if he were royalty and everyone should bow or curtsy, though it was clear he tried to be unassuming as he acknowledged Jonah behind the camera and shook Devin's hand.

"Thank you for agreeing to this, Mr. Hollingsworth," Devin said. "This is going to add so much to our production."

"I'm glad to accommodate. Tell me again about your documentary. I understand you've been interviewing people who have used our medication."

Devin held up a piece of paper so Jonah could white-balance the camera. "We've mainly been collecting stories from older people who live at Desert Gardens in Tucson. As a filmmaker I try to follow the stories we gather, and several people have mentioned Phutura as a thread we wanted to follow. I think you'll be fascinated."

"I look forward to seeing it." He glanced at his watch. "Why don't we get started. Do you have an idea of how long this will take? I have a meeting in—"

"Fifteen minutes, tops," Devin said.

"Perfect." He sat in the overstuffed chair strategically positioned in front of the Phutura logo. An identical chair waited across from him, as well as a small table with a tasteful plant in the center.

"I just need one more thing," Devin said, looking around. He brought a stool from the other side of the room and placed a smaller camera on it, aiming it at the empty chair. A cable ran from both cameras to some equipment in front of Jonah. Devin hit the On button on the smaller camera.

"That's good," Jonah said. "It's out of the shot."

Hollingsworth studied the smaller camera.

"This is for the two-shot, so we can do a cutaway in editing if we need to," Devin said.

Hollingsworth waved a hand. "Understood. I've done a few of these over the years."

"Yes, I'm sure you have." *But none like this,* Devin thought.

Hollingsworth signaled the control room at the back with a twirling finger. "I hope you don't mind if we film as well. We like to keep a record of everything for our files. Just in case there are any discrepancies."

"Of course," Devin said, fitting him with a microphone. Jonah tested it and signaled he was ready. Then Devin walked toward the door. "Our interviewer is Treha. She'll be asking the questions."

A pause. "I was under the impression that you were going to be—"

Devin walked out, hearing Jonah say something to Hollingsworth, reassuring him. Laughing a little and lightening the mood. Jonah had his downsides but he was able to work on the fly better than anyone, as long as someone wasn't holding a gun on him or tossing his phone out the window. His editing on the documentary in the past week had been incredible. Give the guy a case of Mountain Dew and some potato chips and he was good for several days. The footage of Dr. Crenshaw they had taken months earlier now took on deeper meaning. Conversations that had seemed rambling and incoherent from early in their shooting suddenly made sense with the Phutura revelations.

Devin found Treha in the lobby sitting on a plush couch, her fingers typing away. The receptionist stared at her, mesmerized. Treha wore a pantsuit and a long-sleeved blouse and kept pulling at her collar as if it scratched her. Miriam had taken her to a salon, and her hair framed her face in a way that made her look thinner.

"Are you ready for this?" Devin said.

Treha nodded, gathering her three-by-five cards and following him to the room. Hollingsworth stood and shook hands with Treha, glancing at the bandages that were slightly visible underneath her sleeves. She gave a practiced smile, something Jonah and Devin had worked on as they drove to Phutura. It looked more like the expression of a pet that yawned or panted in a way that looked like a smile.

The two sat and Devin fitted Treha's microphone, then took his place, behind Treha but out of the shot, his stomach swirling, heart racing. Deep breath. Jonah gave him a thumbs-up.

"All right, Treha, we're ready when you are."

She paused a long, uncomfortable moment, and Devin was about to tell her again to go ahead, thinking she hadn't heard him, when she spoke.

"Mr. Hollingsworth, I understand you have worked with Phutura for some time."

"That's correct." A big smile. He crossed his legs and Devin thought he could see his reflection in the man's leather shoes.

"You must be proud of what the company has accomplished over those years."

Just as they had practiced, an easy first question to get him talking, get him comfortable with her staccato delivery and style.

"Yes, I'm quite proud of the people we've helped. It's easy to get caught up in the numbers, but a company like ours does not gauge success in dollar signs or units sold or anything of the sort. Success is changed lives. Just like our company motto—'Changed lives for your future.' Success is the heart patient who gains freedom from implanted devices and begins to live a normal life. Success is . . ."

Hollingsworth gave more examples of success, which

sounded hollow given the information Devin knew. But it was the perfect setup for what was to come.

Keep talking, he thought.

"But the help you've given people comes at a cost," Treha said.

"Yes, absolutely. For every medication we develop, there is much research, hard work, and frankly money expended. Many of our projects never reach the shelves. For many years I worked with research in the company and I think this knowledge has helped me lead. Someone who has been there and knows the ropes, so to speak. I know the struggle of developing a new medication, something we think will help people, only to find we can't go further. Some would say that money is wasted, but I don't feel that way. Everything works together; every success is buoyed by some mistake, some research that fails, and we learn and we grow and we get back on our feet and move forward. That's the hallmark of this corporation. We will not be defeated by temporary failures in our research and development. We will learn and help people change their lives."

Devin had given Jonah the progression of the documentary— where they would begin, each transition, each musical cue— but now he could see everything falling perfectly into place. Even the future interview with Treha's mother, the emotional reunion that would bring tears to viewers. But this would be the crowning moment, when the injured, innocent young woman faced the man responsible for her injury. They would build up to this section and work it into the whole as a crescendo. Finally the little guy confronting the big guy.

The sound track in Devin's mind began playing the requisite music—electronic, fast-paced, edgy, chance-taking chords propelling them forward. Treha asked one more innocuous question, which Hollingsworth caught and ran the length of the field with, then spiked in the end zone, a Cheshire cat smile plastered on his face. He looked like he had just been named most valuable pharmaceutical executive of the year.

Treha checked her notes, then looked up, her head swaying. "A spill occurred two years ago that your company took responsibility for."

"Yes, that's true. I don't see what this has to do with—"

"And the EPA approved the cleanup of the spill. You did everything required."

"Quite right."

"But you didn't tell the EPA about the experimental drug that was mixed in with the other material in that spill."

The man blinked hard and uncrossed his legs. He looked at the camera, deliciously vulnerable. Devin raised his eyebrows and shrugged, lifting his hands as if he had no control over the force of nature that was Treha.

"Do you remember the development of a drug for depression that you could give to pregnant women?"

"How do you . . . ?" He lowered his voice. "I would be careful how you accuse, young lady."

"The students near the spill have developed mysterious illnesses."

"None of which has any connection—"

"Illnesses that mimic the side effects of the drug you were testing."

"There is not a shred of evidence linking us with those . . ." Hollingsworth grabbed the microphone and began to unhook it. "This interview is over." He looked at Devin. "You misrepresented yourself."

"We have information about the students," Treha said, her

voice growing stronger. "Documented by the researcher who worked for you. Calvin Davidson."

Hollingsworth tossed the microphone to the floor. "That old crackpot's testimony would be laughed out of court after the first question."

"We have information that Dr. James Crenshaw gave an experimental drug to a pregnant woman with the full knowledge of Phutura officials."

Hollingsworth got to his feet, shrugging off the accusation. "I have no idea who or what you're talking—"

"With *your* full knowledge," she said.

"You have nothing," he spat, pointing a finger at her.

"And we have the child," Treha said softly.

Hollingsworth stared. "What did you say?"

"We have the child." Softer now, almost to herself. "We have the child. The one the drug affected."

He drew close, scowling. "You have no such thing because there never was a human test."

"We have the child."

He moved to leave, but Treha stood and blocked him from the doorway. "We have the child."

Hollingsworth squinted, trying to follow her eyes. Then a look of recognition. "There was no child," he said.

"Yes, there was. I was the child. I am the child. My name is Treha." Her jaw set and she raised her voice, the veins in her neck jutting, her head swaying in time to some different drummer. "My name is Treha Langsam and I was the child."

Hollingsworth studied the girl with equal amounts of fascination and derision. Finally he looked at someone in the control room. "Call security! They don't leave the building with this video."

"You won't be able to stop us," Devin called after him.

Hollingsworth turned.

"You can take our video, take our equipment, but you can't take the truth away. It's going to come out."

There was a visible sneer on the man's face. Jonah followed Hollingsworth with a tight shot.

"What do you want? Did you come here to threaten me? To threaten the company with these hollow accusations?"

"We came for the truth. We came to show you what you did to her." The emotion in his own voice surprised Devin.

"I am the child," Treha said softly.

Two security officers arrived. Hollingsworth ordered all of their equipment confiscated. The men took the camera Jonah was holding as well as the smaller camera on the stool.

"The plaintiffs in the court case are seeing the video we have of Davidson confessing to what happened," Devin said.

Hollingsworth ignored him. "We'll return your equipment, but not the video. Now take this freak and leave."

Jonah jerked free from one of the guards. He was a good foot shorter than Hollingsworth, but he stood on his tiptoes and yelled, spittle flying from his mouth, "She's not a freak. She's the best human being I've ever met in my life, you low-life piece of medical waste."

Devin took Jonah by the arm. "Settle down, tiger. Come on. We knew we'd never get out of here with the video."

The security guard escorted them to the front entrance and out into the parking lot. As they drove away, Devin looked at the second-floor window where Hollingsworth stood, watching them.

"Did you get the backup?" he said.

"Right here," Jonah said, pulling the external drive from his pocket. "Good call on recording from the splitter. We got both cameras and all the audio."

Treha stared at the road and typed with her fingers.

"What did you think of my diatribe?" Jonah said.

"Not bad. I liked the 'medical waste' thing," Devin said.

"I wanted to say something else. A little stronger. I wanted to tell him Phutura wouldn't even be able to sell aspirin after the lawsuit's over. Couldn't figure a way to work it in. Kind of felt forced, you know?"

"I think he was impressed with your vocab."

"Did you see me get in his face? I was like right up there—this close. I think some of my spit went into his eye. Man, it made me feel so powerful, like I was arguing with an umpire over a blown call at home plate."

"You were good."

"I've always wanted to do that, you know? Get in the bully's face and yell. Make him feel some of what he makes others feel."

Treha turned around, her eyes searching his face. "Did you really mean what you said about me?"

Jonah looked in the rearview at Devin, then back at Treha. "Well, yeah. I mean, how could anybody not like you, Treha? Him calling you a freak . . . He has no idea who you are, what a big heart you have."

"You're the best thing that's ever happened to us," Devin said, his voice catching as he glanced at her.

She turned back to the road and watched the signs flash by.

Devin smiled wide enough for both of them.

Streams from Desert Gardens
scene 31

Outside courthouse. Wide shot of lead attorney for plaintiffs, Jerilynn Caruthers, on bench in sunlight, with shaded trees in background.

We had a good case. I thought we had enough to show the jury that Phutura was negligent and had directly impacted this community and needed to make restitution. We had dramatic testimony prepared—we had video; we had the kids who had been affected with mysterious illnesses and tics symptomatic of a toxic exposure ready to take the stand and tell their stories. We'd spent thousands on soil samples. We had done our homework.

But there were those on the legal team who had real doubts. And certainly the attorneys for Phutura, this vast array of suits, gave us no indication that we could prove our point, no indication that they wanted to settle or even entertain the possibility. They fight these kinds of cases every year and have never lost.

We had to show a direct causal link between the research fifteen years ago and the toxic dump that happened two years ago, and match that with the illnesses of the students. Despite having good evidence, we never felt like we could tie it all together and show conclusively that Phutura held the smoking gun. Show, without any doubt, *why* this exposure had done so much damage.

Until Treha.

Tight shot on Caruthers.

You can write the history of this case BT and AT—before Treha and after Treha. That girl—young lady, I should say—changed everything. She gave us the link to the chemical compounds in the water, the drug test that went awry. And then with her own symptoms, which were dramatic . . . We knew if we got her before the jury and had the admission of the Phutura researcher, Calvin Davidson—this was the difference between a desperation three-point shot from downtown at the buzzer and a slam dunk. There just wasn't any question what a jury would do with that, and Phutura knew that and wisely settled. The EPA investigation that was triggered created more problems for the company. I know the interview that showed up on YouTube with Ezra Hollingsworth presented more than a PR nightmare for him and is the reason the investigation led the company to fire him.

Cut to B-roll footage of Ezra Hollingsworth leaving corporate headquarters with reporters surrounding him.

Back to tight shot of Caruthers.

I've argued a lot of cases. I've been involved in class-action suits, personal injury cases. Some we won, some we lost. I've never experienced someone so innocent and pure affecting the outcome of a legal proceeding. The truth came to us, without our knowledge, and changed or at least greatly influenced the outcome of the case. The film about Treha will show the world that the truth will eventually rise. And we hope she finds a way forward.

CHAPTER 38

MIRIAM PARKED her car in front of a double-wide trailer off a dirt road. There were many of these types of roads in Arizona, where the blacktop and covenants ended and the chain-link began. Chicken wire ran around the entire front yard and a large black dog prowled at the gate. Devin was in the backseat trying out a new piece of equipment, a wireless microphone that had better reception. Jonah was home editing their footage, working to shape it with the music he was also composing.

The woman's name was Janice Sadler. She was twice divorced and somewhere back there she had been a Langsam. On the phone she sounded rough and grizzled, a hardscrabble woman who carried a chip on her shoulder and probably for good reason.

"We're finally here," Miriam said.

Treha nodded, staring at the house.

"You may not be able to use this; you know that," Miriam said to Devin. "This will be a private moment, and if Treha doesn't want this in the film, it won't be."

"Understood," Devin said. "In fact, we'll need the permission of the mother at some point too. We'll have to get her signature if we do use it."

"Are you ready?" Miriam said to Treha.

She nodded.

"Which makes you more nervous, the trip to Phutura or this?" Devin said.

Treha stared at him, then got out of the car. She walked with Miriam to the gate, and the dog barked and snarled. It was overweight by at least twenty pounds and appeared to have lost eyesight in one eye, if not both.

"Like I said, she knows I'm coming, but she doesn't know you're going to be with me. And she doesn't know what this is about. I expect her to be surprised."

"I understand."

Miriam reached for the gate latch but Treha stopped her. "I want to go alone."

"Oh," Miriam said, taken aback. She tried not to show it. "Yes, that's fine, Treha. That's probably a good idea. I'll wait in the car. If you need me, just wave. Or call. I'll be able to hear through the microphone. Is it okay with you if we listen?"

"Yes."

Miriam wanted to hug the girl, kiss her forehead, say something that would change what she assumed was about to happen. She wanted to prepare her more for this meeting and the fallout from it. But maybe Treha was right. Maybe this was something she needed to do on her own. She had met with the legal team for the plaintiffs in the Phutura case by herself. They had paid for her to undergo testing, the blood and neurological work at the hospital, and she had done that alone. She could do this, too.

Treha hesitated and Miriam asked what she was thinking.

"What do I call her?"

"Her name is Janice. I think that would be a good start."

Treha nodded and walked through the gate, past the barking dog, and up the wooden steps to the porch. It was enough to tear Miriam's heart out. Treha looked out at a broken swing set and Miriam could almost read her mind. Had she played here? Had she known any animals the family had as pets?

Miriam wanted to take away her pain and hurt, the loneliness and uncertainty. But there are some things even a friend can't bear. This was also the equation of pain, she thought. Some things had to be done alone.

Treha reached out to knock, then held back, looking at the car. Miriam opened the driver's side door and sat, closing the door with a clunk.

"That takes an incredible amount of courage," Devin said.

"Yes, it does. You don't know how much I wanted to tell her that her mother was dead. After talking with the woman, I wanted to spare Treha this. She has enough trouble without that woman as her mother."

Devin was shooting video of Treha knocking at the door, balancing the camera on the headrest and shooting through the windshield. He took off his headphones and turned up a small speaker on the receiver so Miriam could hear.

When Treha knocked, there was more barking inside, higher-pitched, and a small dog ran out through a hole in the front door and jumped on Treha, dancing and yipping.

"Can I help you?" a woman said through the screen. Her voice was gruff with more than a little twang. "If you're selling something, we don't have any money to buy. You best move on down the road. There's some Mormons on the next street that seem to buy everything. All the football players selling their discount cards to the car wash and burger place. I don't get my car washed and don't have the money for cards or magazines."

"I'm not selling anything," Treha said, barely audible through the speaker over the barking dogs.

"What's that?"

"I'm not selling anything," she repeated.

"Well, what in the world do you . . . ?" The woman's voice trailed like she had seen something she hadn't expected. "Wait a minute." The door opened and she stepped outside. She wore pajama pants and ratty slippers with a bathrobe wrapped tightly around her. "Punkin? Is that you? . . . Why, it is. How in the world did you find me? And what are you doing here?"

The woman shielded her eyes from the sun and looked at the car.

"My friend Mrs. Howard helped me," Treha said.

"Land sakes. Is that the lady who called me?"

Treha nodded.

"She never said anything about bringing you." The woman cursed and gave a heavy sigh. "You might as well come in. As long as you're not looking for money. If that's what you're here for, you might as well go over to—"

"I don't want money."

"All right." Janice said it in one syllable and it sounded like "ahhite." She opened the door. "Jee-miny, those eyes of yours used to give me the willies. I remember now. Get in here before the dog beats you to it. Come on."

Treha disappeared inside and Miriam could only imagine what she was seeing. She closed her eyes and listened as the little dog barked and scampered about until it settled down.

"Is this where I lived? Where you raised me?"

"No, that was . . . another place down the road a piece. You remember any of that?"

"I think I was too little."

"You were a handful is what you were." Rattling of papers. "You sit there. You want something to drink?"

"No, I'm fine."

"Well, I could use something, now that I've seen your face again. You're about the last person on earth I expected to be showing up at my front door." The woman's voice grew distant. "I heard they put you in an institution. Locked you away. Is that right?"

"Not that I know of," Treha said. Her voice was soft now, mousy.

"What was that?" the woman said across the room.

"I don't think I was put in an institution. I went to live in foster homes. That's what I'm told."

"You're told? Why can't you remember?"

"I don't know."

A clink of glass. "Well, I half wondered if somebody would come here and tell me you were dead or something worse. I just don't want you coming back blaming me because I kept you as long as I could. It's a miracle I put up with all the shenanigans as long as I did. It was superhuman, to tell you the truth. The screaming and crying and throwing stuff. You were a real hell-raiser is what you were. Demon child, my husband called you. Ex-husband now. And then to watch your eyes go back and forth like that was like riding on a riverboat that never settles down. Made me seasick to feed you a bottle."

"How old was I when you . . . let me go?" Treha said.

"About four, four and a half, probably. I felt bad about it, if you want to know the truth. But I couldn't take it no more. You get to a point where you have to think of yourself, you know? And it liked to tear our marriage apart having you with us."

"There is a reason why I acted the way I did."

"I'm sure there was. Some doctor give you a diagnosis? They give you some pills?"

"Not yet. I'm waiting to find out what they think is the matter."

"Well, you seem to have settled down all right for now. It looks like you've become a nurse of some sort. Is that what you do?"

"No, I wear this because I like the way it feels."

"Well, you look like a nurse." The woman swallowed several times—probably downing her drink—and sighed afterward.

"Janice . . ." The word was thick on Treha's tongue but she regained her composure and kept going. "I have a question for you about Dr. Crenshaw."

"Dr. who?"

"Dr. Crenshaw. The man who prescribed the medication you took for depression. Do you remember him?"

A pause. "I don't remember no doctor prescribing anything for me except some antibiotics when I come down with pneumonia a couple years ago. And how in the world would you know what doctor I had?"

"It's a long story, but a friend of mine was your doctor before I was born. He prescribed medication that hurt me."

"Back up, back up. You talked to a doctor who treated me . . ."

"When you were pregnant with me. Your obstetrician was Dr. Crenshaw."

"Honey, I ain't never needed no obstetrician. I ain't never had no kids. That's how come I got you."

A long pause.

"Do you think I'm your real mother?"

"That's what Mrs. Howard said."

"Mrs. Howard evidently don't know everything. Didn't anybody ever tell you? I guess they wouldn't have. Your mother gave you up as soon as you was born. Me and my husband adopted you. I'm not your—what do they call it . . . ? Birth mother . . . Biological—that's it. But we took you in and treated you like our own, until we couldn't care for you anymore with all the behavior problems."

"My name. Why did you name me Treha?"

There was a noise as if someone was getting off a creaky piece of furniture. "You stay there. I might have something for you."

Miriam looked at Devin. He had the camera rolling, capturing all of the audio. There was something in the speaker, a noise like someone whispering.

Devin turned it up. "She's talking to herself."

Treha repeated over and over, "She's not my mother. She's not my mother."

Miriam imagined Treha with her eyes closed, typing on her lap. She didn't look at Devin. She couldn't. She put her head in her hands and listened to Treha's voice.

A couple minutes passed before Janice returned and plopped something heavy down. "These was all the pictures we took of you. This is you coming home. Here's the little swing we got you. This was before we knew you were the way you were, of course. That's Bill—he's your daddy or your stepdaddy or whatever you call somebody who adopts you and gives you their name.

"That's you in your pink outfit. You never liked anything pretty or frilly; you'd just cry and cry. And eat—you couldn't get enough to eat. I swear you came out looking fat as a pumpkin. Which is why we called you that. When you turned two—here's one about that time; see how big you were? And see that shirt?

If I didn't put that shirt on you, you'd take off every stitch of clothes and walk around naked. I swear you were a pill."

"Why did you name me Treha?"

"Oh yeah, I'm getting to that. The adoption was a special arrangement. It was legal, mind you, but we didn't go through some government agency or anything like that. This reverend at a church nearby, he's the one who heard about your mama. Knew some doctor who set the whole thing up. Something happened with your mama—he couldn't tell us what it was, but part of the agreement was we wouldn't ask.

"We both wanted a baby real bad. I can see now I kinda thought it would hold the two of us together, but we got you and it backfired. My plumbing never worked right to begin with. I had a surgery when I was younger and things got messed up, so we knew we'd never have a child the normal way. So the reverend came and told us about this special deal. He had heard about us from somebody in his church who knew my sister, something like that. Convoluted as all get-out. He called it a God thing, but in the end you turned out to be the baby from hell."

It was all Miriam could do not to run to the house right then and chew the woman out. But she knew she couldn't. This was Treha's life, her questions.

"Anyway, the agreement was we would take you and raise you in a Christian home. We did everything we could to bring you up right. We kept our end of the bargain. And we had to promise we'd never tell nobody how we came to get you or come looking for the mother. When we walked away from the hospital that day, you were ours and there was no turning back.

"Well, the only things we took from that hospital was a bottle of formula, your little blanket—which one of the dogs chewed up—and a letter from your mother." Rustling and shuffling. "I meant to send it with you when we gave you over to the county, but it was a pretty stressful time." More rustling and shuffling. "Well, maybe I didn't keep it after all."

Miriam closed her eyes. *Please, God, this girl has nothing to her name. Please give her this one shred of her past, this one piece of hope.*

Janice must have dumped the pictures out.

"What did it look like?" Treha said.

"It was just a white envelope with your name on the front of it."

"Did you ever read it?"

"Yeah, I think so. But I don't remember what it said. That was what I was going to tell you. The mother wanted two things: a Christian home and that we give you the name Treha."

Devin shook his head. "One for two isn't bad."

"Shh," Miriam said, holding up a hand.

"You could have our last name, but your first name had to be Treha," the woman continued. "She wrote it out, how to say it and all. I have no earthly idea what she was thinking or if she meant to write something else and misspelled it, but as I said, we lived up to our side of the bargain."

"Did she know who you were?" Treha said.

"No, it was anonymous on both sides. We didn't know her and she didn't know us."

There was a pause in the conversation and glass clinked again. Finally Treha said, "Could you have put the letter in some other place?"

"No, if it's not here, I don't know where it would be. Bill wouldn't have taken it with him when he cleared out. But you can have any of those pictures you want. I'll get you a poke to put them in."

A bag rattled and they heard the sound of photos being dropped in one by one. Miriam thought it was the saddest, loneliest sound she had ever heard.

"Thank you," Treha said.

The front door opened and Treha walked out alone, followed by the two dogs yipping and barking. She carried a small lunch bag. Devin recorded her walk to the car.

She opened the door and set the bag on the seat beside her. "Did you hear what she said?"

"Yes."

"She's not my real mother."

"I'm happy for you and sad at the same time," Miriam said. "It seems the questions we ask lead to more questions."

"I wanted to see the letter."

"I know. I can't believe she lost it."

Devin put a hand on the girl's shoulder. "You were great in there. Amazing."

"Do you want her to sign a paper?" Treha said.

"Let's wait on that," Devin said.

Miriam started the car and was pulling away when the front door opened and the woman rushed out, waving. Miriam got out and navigated the dogs to get to Janice, who stood wheezing on the porch, a cigarette smell hanging heavy in the air.

"You must be Miriam."

"Yes."

"I ought to punch you for lying. I don't know how you found me, but you should have told me you were bringing her here. I could have prepared."

"I didn't lie. We're just looking for answers."

"This is the only other answer I have," Janice said. "Give this to her. It's a letter from her mother. I had it in the strongbox. I remembered I put it in there. Kept it for her all these years."

She said it as if she deserved a medal or some kind of payment for her trouble.

Miriam took the faded envelope and glared at the woman. "What's the name of the pastor who helped you adopt Treha?"

"Pastor? He's been dead for years. Turnquist or something like that. Swedish man."

"Do you know the church where he pastored?"

"You're driving down a dead-end street. I suggest you turn around and try not to waste your time."

Miriam walked back to the car and handed the envelope to Treha. She put it in the paper bag and they drove away.

Streams from Desert Gardens
scene 27

Handheld shot walking toward front door of Desert Gardens, Devin walking slightly in front of camera.

Jump-cut to door opening, security guard waving a hand.

Tight shot of Jillian Millstone in doorway.

> . . . and I'm afraid you'll have to leave the premises.

> DEVIN (OFF CAMERA): **We had an agreement with Mrs. Howard and the residents of this facility. . . .**

> **Did anyone sign a formal release? Can you answer that?**

> VOC: **We're not here to hurt anyone. We're not trying to cause trouble.**

> **This is an invasion of privacy. You have no legal right to come on this property and take video footage. Mr. Davis, please escort them away.**

Tight shot of inside door, where several residents have gathered, including Elsie.

> DEVIN (OFF CAMERA): **Ms. Millstone, please give us a chance to tell people what's happened to Treha. What we've learned about her.**

You're upsetting our residents. This is your final warning. I will call the police if you don't leave the property immediately.

Buck Davis moves into shot, holds out his hands, and smiles at the camera.

Please, Mr. Hillis, let's just move on back to your car, sir.

Fade out.

CHAPTER 39

ELSIE PRATT's blood pressure rose and her heart rate accelerated as she pushed her walker past the reception area of Desert Gardens down the long hallway. She was dressed in the floral-print blouse Harold had bought for her birthday the year before he passed. She'd worn it on two occasions, her birthday celebration that year and their wedding anniversary, both times wearing it to please him. She wasn't fond of floral prints and the material was so thin she felt naked. It made her sweat just looking at it. After Harold moved on to glory, she couldn't put it on; it brought back too many memories and she'd go into a tailspin seeing it, so she shoved it in the back of the closet.

Putting the blouse on now gave her hope, made her think he was watching, somehow. Made her feel warm inside and that he would be proud of how she had carried on without him, proud of what she was about to do.

The usual gaggle of residents, those who were ambulatory and had at least half of their hearing, were gathered in the dayroom with the glass etching rising magnificently behind them. Around the outer edges of the wall was a bench of sorts, like a geriatric shelf. Some sat on chairs, others on the shelf, which seemed appropriate to her. When she walked through the door, the men who could stand did so and someone actually applauded, starting a wave of response. Applause from the elderly was always muted but twice as appreciated, and she smiled and tried to get them to stop, but she couldn't let go of her walker until she reached the fireplace at the front. By then the noise had fluttered to a single clap.

Buck Davis, who had come at her behest, was out of his uniform for the first time Elsie could remember. He wore jeans and a nice buttoned shirt that was freshly pressed. Black shoes. He handed her a wireless microphone and her voice sounded much too loud in the room as she began.

"I asked Buck to come down here today on his day off, so if you're going to clap for anybody, it ought to be him."

Another wave of applause. Buck flashed a white smile and stepped back to lean against the fireplace.

"He's the one taking the biggest risk today because this is his livelihood. He's worked here . . . How long has it been, Buck?"

"Thirty years," the man said, nodding and smiling.

"Well, we thank you for what you've done for us over the years."

"My pleasure," he said softly.

Elsie gathered her thoughts and looked at the faces around the room. "You all know that I'm a Christian. I don't keep that a secret from anybody. And I believe the Bible talks about obeying the authorities God has instituted—the government, even bad bosses who are over us need to be honored. So I've struggled with this. I'm not a pushy person by nature. I've been a good girl, a nice lady. But there comes a time when you have to speak up. And today is the day."

More scattered applause around the room and then a murmur rose from the back. Elsie saw the movement through the window, the imposing figure of Jillian Millstone, distorted by the tree etching and the ironic words by Emerson. Elsie was beating a new path and hoping to leave a trail.

"I lean on the Lord for strength every day," Elsie continued. "And I lean on him for direction. Proverbs 3:5 and 6. 'Trust in the Lord with all your heart and lean not on your own understanding; in all your ways submit to him, and he will make your paths straight.' I have done that at every turn over the past weeks, and there has been what I call a holy discontent in my heart. The straw that broke the camel's back, so to speak, was when Treha was let go."

"For helping Ardeth!" someone shouted.

"That's right. She didn't do a thing but help us and talk to us."

There were nods around the room and a positive response, except for those in the back who saw Ms. Millstone opening the door. Elsie could feel the air in the room shift, a low-pressure system changing things. She looked away, pretending not to see Millstone, and forged ahead.

"Now the Bible talks about how to settle disagreements. This is for two Christians who have a dispute. You're supposed to go to that person you have a disagreement with and have a talk. And if you can't resolve things and they won't listen, you take two people with you and you talk, and hopefully that person will listen—"

"Elsie, what's the meaning of this?" Ms. Millstone said from the back of the room.

Those who were seated in chairs turned or craned their necks and gave an audible gasp. Followed by the murmurs of the aged, much louder than whispers because of their hearing problems.

"There she is."

"I knew this would happen."

"Elsie's in trouble now."

Millstone walked forward. "Mr. Davis, did you set up the sound system?"

"I turned it on, yes, ma'am. Miss Elsie asked if I would help her."

Millstone set her jaw and turned to Elsie as if saying she would deal with Buck later.

"Don't you blame him," Elsie said. "He came down here on his day off because I asked him to give me a ride after this meeting. If you want to get mad at anybody, get mad at me." She spoke to the crowd again. "Now as I was saying, I went to Ms. Millstone and laid out my case. And when she wouldn't listen, a few of us got together and wheeled our way to her office—"

"That's quite enough, Elsie." Millstone turned to the gathering. "This is an unscheduled and unapproved meeting. We're adjourned now. You can all go back to your rooms. Go on."

A few struggled to stand. They were stopped short by a lone voice near the window.

"Stay where you are," Hemingway said, his hair kinked on one side and his beard white as the snows of Kilimanjaro. "Since when did we give up our rights as citizens to congregate?"

"That's right," another said behind Millstone.

"Since when do we have to ask your permission to talk to each other? To get together for a meeting?" Hemingway continued.

"Your rights are not absolute," Millstone said. "The rules are here for the good of all. It's why we have traffic lights. This meeting is adjourned. Mr. Davis, help me clear the room."

Buck kept his arms crossed.

"Mr. Davis?"

"This is his day off," Elsie said.

Millstone's jaw flexed and she stared daggers at the man.

"Ask not for whom the bell tolls; it tolls for thee," Hemingway said.

Elsie saw her chance and started speaking in the microphone again. "I've asked all of you here today in an effort to—"

"I said that will be quite enough," Millstone snapped, reaching for the microphone.

Elsie pulled it out of reach. "It's not nearly enough," she said. "I don't think you've heard a word we've said since you arrived. You treat us like sheep, herding us from one place to another, and expect us to thank you for it. Well, we're not going to be treated that way any longer."

"It's true," Henry, half of the Lovebirds, said. He was clutching Ruth's hand and she was patting his with the other, both looking up from their wheelchairs. "When Mrs. Howard was here, she treated us—"

"Mrs. Howard is not here," Millstone interrupted. "And she's not coming back. I know that change is difficult for people like you. But I was given this job and I'm going to do it to the best of my ability. Now if you have a grievance, I'm willing to talk in a civilized manner. But this meeting is unauthorized." She held out a hand. "Give it to me."

Elsie set her jaw. "You can have it when I'm finished."

Millstone looked at Buck. "Shut off the sound system."

Buck lowered his head and turned toward the equipment. All he had to do was flick the power switch. But he hesitated and caught Elsie's eye.

"It's okay, Buck. We understand. You do what you need to do, but what I have to say won't go unheard because you turn off the power to a microphone."

Buck folded his arms and nodded.

"If I have to call security to clear this room, I will. I'm doing this for your own good."

There was an awkward silence and no one moved. Then Hemingway cleared his throat. "Who are we, Ms. Millstone?" His voice was gravelly and razor-like.

"What?" Millstone said, her brow furrowed.

"You just said that change is difficult for 'people like you.' I would like to know what type of people we are."

"I wasn't making any value judgment; I was just stating that any kind of change is difficult for the elderly—it's difficult for all of us."

Hemingway walked slowly through the room, the tie around his robe dragging behind him. His leather slippers scuffed the wood flooring until he stood before Millstone. He really did look like Ernest Hemingway in this light.

He took out a sheet of paper and unfolded it. "I wrote something this morning. It might be appropriate now."

"I don't think we need to hear your rambling verse—"

"Let him read it," the Opera Singer said.

Hemingway turned and nodded a thank-you, holding the page a little farther away as his eyes adjusted. "'I know what it's like to live in fear. And I know what it's like to live with love. Not many men have the courage to drink deeply from both. I wait for the morning sun each day, wondering if this might be my last sunrise. And when the evening sun reaches the Catalinas, I make a choice to fear what the night will bring or to embrace it and pull it to my bosom like a lover. All our stories, if you follow them long enough, end at a graveyard. This is no secret. What happens between here and that sixteen-legged walk is what matters, and to keep that from you would be an abrogation of my sacred duty.'"

He folded the page and looked at Millstone. "I will tell you who we are. I will tell you what sort of people are before you. We are brave and fearful human beings set adrift on a skiff in an unending sea filled with predators and prey. And the sun beats down on us and leathers our skin. Everyone here, every face, every beating heart has a story behind it you will never know. Because to you, we are simply 'those people,' a class unto ourselves. You feed us and house us and protect us from everything out there, until you finally decide to protect us from everything in here." He pointed to his chest. "You protect us from ourselves. You try to take our dignity. And this is your miscalculation. Because there are some things a person cannot take. No matter how hard you try, you cannot take our dignity if we will not offer it to you. And today, I believe we are saying we will keep this, this one thing. Though it's all we have left, we will not let you take it from us."

Elsie saw something in Hemingway's eyes, some spark of knowledge, a recognition that he was no longer running with the bulls, that he was fully here. And she loved him for it. She clapped and others followed. Millstone stood her ground but seemed to shrink before them.

"That was beautiful," Ruth said, patting Henry's hand.

Elsie spoke into the microphone. "I have a meeting set up today with the head of the board of directors of this place. I am going to deliver the petition that many of you have signed, and if you didn't sign it and you want to, it's here." She pulled folded pieces of paper from her purse. "The first few sheets are for residents and the rest are for family members and people who care—"

Millstone grabbed the microphone quickly and the speakers clanged loudly above them. Elsie was surprised but not shaken. She raised her head and her voice.

"If you haven't signed, come on up here and do it before I leave."

Millstone raised the microphone to her lips. "That's quite enough. Go back to your rooms. The party's over."

"You got that right—the party is over," someone said in the back.

"I can take you treating me as less than a real person," the Opera Singer said with perfect diction. "I can live with your edict of quiet times when there can be no singing in our rooms. But when you treat workers like Treha as chattel, those who are under you will rise up."

"We're the ones who pay your salary," someone said.

There was a general chorus of "That's right" around the room.

Millstone tried to appear in control, but she was outnumbered. When she turned back to Elsie, she wagged a finger in the old woman's face. "You will lose privileges."

Elsie's head shook—from age or fear or her own will, she didn't know. "You're not king around here anymore, sister. In their infinite wisdom the board decided it was time for a change. They can certainly change their minds again, and I'm going to see that they hear about your decisions." She pulled out another sheet of paper. "I have a list I'm going to read them, starting with the cleaning out of Jim Crenshaw's room after he was taken to the hospital."

"I have the full support of the board," Millstone said.

"I doubt that'll be true after today." Elsie stepped closer and the woman retreated a step. "Do you know how long I've been here? And do you have any idea how many people have come here because of what I have said about this place? This was an oasis, the best place on earth to grow old. But in a short time, you've taken the life away. I don't wish evil on you; I pray God will bless you. But I pray he'll bless you right out the front door."

Buck Davis moved toward Ms. Millstone. "Come on, ma'am. Let these folks have their meeting. It means a lot to them."

Millstone's eyes shifted from Hemingway to Elsie and the others. She handed the microphone to Buck, turned, and walked out.

CHAPTER 40

MIRIAM SAT with Treha in a conference room at Tucson Medical Center. They were meeting Dr. Melinda Graco, head of the department of neuropsychiatry at the University of Arizona, who was the lead doctor on the team that had studied Treha's test results. Treha stared at shelves filled with medical journals and reference books. She wore blue-green scrubs and swayed beside the mahogany table.

"Can we see Dr. Crenshaw after we get through here?" Treha said. She wore a blank look, but there was something different about her, Miriam thought. Or perhaps there was something different in the way she saw the girl now. In the hope she had moving forward. That colored everything.

"I'd like that," Miriam said. Though the thought pained her because she knew Crenshaw's condition had actually worsened. "You haven't told me what was in the letter your mother gave you. You've read it by now."

Treha's eyes wandered and her fingers typed. "No. I haven't."

"Why not?"

A shrug.

"Don't you want to know what she wrote?"

Treha looked down. "I'm afraid."

"Afraid of what?"

"That she won't be what I have thought she would be. That maybe she is sick like me. That she didn't want me because . . . I'm like this. And a thousand other things."

"Treha, I don't think there was any way for her to know." Miriam put a hand on her shoulder. "Do you want me to read it for you?"

Treha shook her head. "If I can listen to what a doctor says about me, I can read what my mother wrote."

Miriam smiled as the doctor entered, followed by two others. She wondered if they were integral to the analysis or if they just wanted to see the anomaly that was Treha.

Dr. Graco shook Miriam's hand and reached out to Treha, who seemed unable to look at the woman. The doctor had salt-and-pepper hair cut to frame just enough of her face to see she had struggled with acne early on. She was professional but with a circumspect smile.

"I've been reading the news about the settlement, Treha. What an adventure. You must be very proud of what you've accomplished."

"I didn't accomplish anything. I was just living."

"Yes, but Phutura is going to pay those people who were injured. And it looks like Mr. Hollingsworth will be punished." She leaned closer. "How do you feel about that? Being responsible for bringing him to justice?"

Treha turned her head slightly and answered toward the wall. "I don't think I had much to do with it. Devin and Jonah took the video. And Mrs. Howard helped."

Dr. Graco smiled at Miriam and scooted closer to the table, raising a stack of papers and bringing out bifocals. "Treha, I wanted to share some of the results from your tests. There are a few that take longer to process, but the blood work and some of the neurological testing, the imaging we've done, give us an idea of where to go from here."

Treha looked at the woman. "Is it good news?"

"Well, let's see what you think. You were exposed to a drug very early on that damaged your brain. When a child, in utero, encounters such a toxic load of psychotropic drugs, there are consequences. The central nervous system, the liver and its metabolic enzymes—these are not fully developed, so the fetus is affected. That is what happened to you.

"To put it mildly, your brain was subjected to a tsunami at a vulnerable point in your development. A hurricane of chemicals and stimulation. It's a miracle you survived. That you've been able to function with this much impairment is a testament to your heart, your will. You are a very strong young woman, Treha."

Dr. Graco looked at her pages, then took off the glasses and placed them on the table. "The good news is, I think we can help you."

"Help me what?"

"Progress. Move further toward becoming connected with the world around you."

"Heal," Miriam said.

"I don't like the term," Dr. Graco said. "This is not like a surgery on a damaged rotator cuff. The brain is different. Your mental processes are heightened in some areas—like your cognitive ability with words and letters—and in other areas your abilities have been lessened or dulled or are nonexistent. The question is whether we can, through various treatment methods, stimulate the impaired parts of the brain and retrain it to make you function properly. Do you understand what I'm saying?"

Treha nodded. "What does treatment mean? Does that mean taking other drugs?"

"With the toxic hit you've taken, I wouldn't suggest it. There are other ways, if you're open to them, to repair that part of the brain. I won't lie to you. It will require commitment. It will be a lot of work, a lot of rehabilitation. And there's no guarantee—"

"How long?" Treha said, interrupting.

"I don't look at it in terms of time. You can get in a trap that way. But I understand why you would want to know. I think we could see true progress in a year. Perhaps two. The real evaluation will be in five years. But what progress means is different from individual to individual. Some who have neurological impairment respond quickly. For others it takes longer. Some don't respond at all. And with your history, that is a possibility."

She inched a little closer. "Treha, with what you've been through, you have to understand that this may be the best your brain can get. But my experience is that if you are committed, you'll look back and compare your brain function and see improvement."

Miriam studied the girl, who seemed to go away, inside herself, computing something, perhaps running the words around and jumbling them in her mind.

"What do you think, Treha?" the doctor said. "Do you want to give it a try?"

She looked up. "Who will pay for this?"

Dr. Graco folded her hands. "Phutura has agreed to cover all of your treatment. It's in their best interest from a public-relations standpoint to do so. And speaking on behalf of the team—the endocrinology specialist and the others who will work with you—it would be an honor to help."

Miriam leaned close. "What about you, Treha? We've been

talking about tests and rehabilitation and work. But you don't have to change for us to love you."

"I know that."

"Good. So the only question is, what do you want?"

Like a river meeting another tributary, something happened in the girl. Miriam sensed the change and watched her eyes fill until one single tear spilled over the edge and ran down her cheek. Treha let it run all the way to her neck before she spoke.

"Can you stop my eyes?"

Dr. Graco's eyes filled in return. "There's no harm in trying."

And at the edge of Treha's lips, microscopic as it was, there seemed to be a turn, cracks in the cheek, the hint of something coming. Something grand.

After the meeting, Miriam and Treha took the elevator and walked to Dr. Crenshaw's room. The girl seemed encouraged by the meeting with Dr. Graco, but who could read Treha's mind?

"What are you thinking?" Miriam said.

"If changes happen, if I get better, maybe I won't be able to reach people. Maybe I don't need to change. But I want to."

"Maybe trying to get better will help you gain something rather than losing."

"I wish I could know what would happen."

Miriam took a deep breath. "I think whatever it is, it will be good, my dear. And I want to be there to see it." She paused at the door. "Would you like to go in alone?"

"No. I'd like you to come."

Dr. Crenshaw's heart monitor beeped evenly, but the old man's mouth was open and there was a patch of blood on the white stubble surrounding it. His lips were chapped and his skin pale.

"He doesn't look like himself," Treha said.

"He's nearing the end of the road, Treha."

She looked at him, then back at Miriam, a frightened animal. "Why didn't he tell me? He could have explained all of this at Desert Gardens. Why he searched for me. He could have told me about my mother. He could have explained everything."

Miriam put an arm around her. "I don't know, Treha. Perhaps he felt guilty about what you went through. And as he came to know you, he must have been torn. He wanted you to have a normal life."

"My life will never be normal."

"I know. But you've been able to ask the question. I think that's a breakthrough."

Treha turned back to the old man in the bed.

"Talk to him, Treha. Tell him what you're thinking. Tell him what you want to say."

She looked at Miriam as if just then comprehending, making the connection between her gift and the unreachable man in the bed.

Treha pulled a chair close to his bed and began massaging his arm and neck, speaking his name softly. Miriam moved behind her and listened.

"Dr. Crenshaw, it's Treha. I miss your word games. I miss your voice. And I know that you brought me to Desert Gardens. I know what you were trying to tell me. Now I have something to say to you.

"You gave medicine to my mother. And it hurt me. I know you feel bad about this. You feel responsible for me. We found Mr. Davidson and he told us everything. And now I'm going to get help."

She leaned closer and Miriam thought she heard the girl's voice crack a little. "So now I want you to wake up for me. I want to thank you. I want you to give me another riddle. You liked that so much, and so did I."

Miriam watched the rhythm of the man's breathing. She thought she noticed the beeping of the heart monitor increase slightly. His blood pressure rose as well and there was a slight fluttering of eyelids. But she couldn't tell if he was reacting to Treha's words.

The girl was leaning over him now. "I want to tell you something important, Dr. Crenshaw. Listen carefully. I forgive you. I need you to know that. Can you hear me? I want you to wake up now and tell me about my mother. Please wake up."

She continued massaging, her hands moving in time with the heartbeats. Then she leaned over again.

"If you can't do that, I understand. You look so peaceful. You have waited for me, haven't you? I'm here. I'm right here."

Miriam did a double take at the man's face. From his left eye, a single tear was running down his cheek.

"If you need to leave, if you need to let go, you can. I'm all right. Mrs. Howard is here and she is all right. And Elsie and Hemingway and the others will be all right. No one wants you to suffer. We are grateful to you. We love you, Dr. Crenshaw."

Treha sat back and the man's breathing suddenly became more shallow. It wasn't instantaneous, but soon the blood pressure level dropped and the heart rate slowed. It was as if he were letting go of life as slowly as a child will release a balloon and watch it rise into the air. As Miriam watched, he slipped from them and the monitor sounded continuously. The line flattened and nurses arrived and stood behind the girl who continued stroking the man's weathered hand.

CHAPTER 41

THE CALL CAME the next day, midmorning, as Miriam was finishing her cup of coffee. She had her Bible open, reading in the book of John, marveling at the simple truths she encountered and the questions sprouting like mustard seeds in her soul.

The ring startled her, as did the voice on the other end. It was the chairman of the board of Desert Gardens. They had made a decision regarding the director position. She listened, wondering why he was telling her this.

"Miriam, the feeling on the board was unanimous," the man said. "We'd like you to come back in the interim, to fill this position and help us transition."

"What happened with Millstone?" she said. "I mean, Ms. Millstone."

"It wasn't as good of a fit as we thought."

She wanted to tell him, *"I told you so."* But she bit her tongue. The man's voice was pleading and a little pathetic.

Instead, she said, "The last thing the residents need is a revolving door with that position."

"I understand, and you need to know we all feel terrible. We made an error in judgment. We'd like you to come back."

"For a week, a month? How long?"

"For as long as you want. You set the agenda as far as the next transition. If it's a year, two years, five—whatever you think is what we'll go with, Miriam. We trust you."

"I'll need to think about this," she said. "I've made plans. Charlie and I have made plans." That wasn't completely the truth, but the chairman said he understood.

"Take as long as you need to decide. A few days? A week? Ms. Millstone is gone effective immediately. She's gathering her things. Perhaps if you went over there to calm the residents, no matter what you decide. I know you care about them."

After Miriam hung up, she stared at her reflection in the black coffee. She hadn't wanted retirement, hadn't desired leaving Desert Gardens. She had been forced out. The opportunity to return should have sent her clicking her heels. She should have said yes right away. But something held her back.

Charlie walked into the room and poured coffee. "Who was that?"

She told him.

"What did he want?"

She held the mug with both hands and something inside her trembled. Maybe it was fear. Maybe it was the questions that came from the pages in front of her.

"Charlie, how would you feel if I went back to work at Desert Gardens?"

"You don't need my permission. You can do what you want."

"I know that. Thank you." It took everything in her to say that. And then a Herculean effort overcame the resentment and pain and disillusionment of life with her husband and she said, "I really want to know what you think."

"If they've tossed Millstone out on her keister, which is what they should have done to begin with, it makes sense. You put your heart and soul into that place. The people love you. You love them. It's a no-brainer. The only question is whether you want to keep working or not. You don't have to."

"Thank you for that," she said. And was surprised to find that she really meant it. "But what about you and me?"

He sat and cradled his mug with wrinkled hands. "What do you mean?"

She wanted to say they had an opportunity to grow together. To do more than just exist. She wanted to tell him so much. But she couldn't. Not yet. It was too soon. She'd have to ease into it.

So instead of saying any of that, she said, "I mean lunch. Would you like me to make you a sandwich?"

He pulled his head back like she had just spoken a new language. "Well, sure. Yeah, I'd like that."

Miriam met Elsie and Buck at the front of the building and both of them beamed. The mood inside was one of muted celebration.

"You should have seen Miss Elsie stand up to her," Buck said. "You would have been so proud."

"It wasn't anything," Elsie said, waving him off. "He's the one who took the chance. This fellow here is the real deal, putting his career on the line."

"Is she still here?" Miriam said.

"Everything's about loaded up on the truck out there," Buck said. "I've been helping the movers a little to keep things rolling."

"Did you hear we had a prospective resident come through yesterday?" Elsie said. "Name's Davidson."

Miriam smiled. "I was hoping he would take my advice and join us."

"Us?" Buck said. "Does that mean you're coming back?"

"Where else would I go? I belong here. Just don't tell the board. I have a couple of staff positions I'd like to create. One that will bring back a previous employee and another to make room for a single mother I've met. Plus, I'm holding out for repavement of the parking lot."

The two laughed as Miriam walked toward the office, waving at several of the old faces. It felt like coming home. It felt like coming alive. How strange to feel so vibrant in such a place.

Millstone was exiting the office with a box under one arm and a picture under the other. The one about *Excellence*. When she saw Miriam, she stopped and cocked her head. "I suppose you've come back to tell me how right you were. To rub it in."

Miriam shook her head. "Not at all. I'm sorry this didn't work out for you. I really am. You are a gifted administrator."

"Gifted? That's not how the board described it."

"I hope you find something that's a better fit."

"Like a prison? Is that what you're thinking?" Millstone walked past her, then turned. "To show I'm not a complete washout as a human being, there's something for you on the desk. I'm not an evil person, you know."

"I never thought you were. I'm sorry it had to . . . I'm sorry."

"Good-bye, Mrs. Howard."

Miriam entered the empty room, the carpet and paint still fresh from the previous tenant. On the empty desk was a single manila folder. And on the top was written *Treha*.

She picked it up and held it like it was some lost manuscript, a family heirloom that had washed up on the shore of her life. She sat and opened to the first page. Notes scribbled by Dr. Crenshaw. Observations about Treha and her abilities to solve word puzzles. Riddles of his own heart, almost like a medical diary, explaining her condition and what the drug had done, the devastation, but also the gift.

I don't think Treha's ability to connect with people who have retreated from life comes as a side effect of the medication, her injury. I don't know where it comes from, to be honest, other than God. But perhaps the truth lies somewhere between the injury and the longing of the human heart for connection. For love.

Miriam found medical records for Treha in the back, photocopies of hospital forms blacked out in certain sections. She would give all of these to Treha's medical team.

She went through the file from front to back three times before she closed it. There was nothing on the medical forms or in Dr. Crenshaw's notes about the name of the mother. Nothing about why Treha had been placed for adoption. Nothing about the circumstances surrounding the birth. They had answered so many questions about the girl, but this one piece of the puzzle had fallen out of the box.

Perhaps the letter from Treha's mother would give them something to work with. Or they might never find the woman. They might never know.

Miriam stood and tucked the folder under her arm. That would be okay. If this was as much as they discovered, that would be okay. It would have to be enough.

CHAPTER 42

TREHA SAT in her apartment with the lights off, listening to the traffic and eating to the bottom of a white Chinese food carton. Mrs. Howard had helped her clean up a little when she dropped her off and they had gone to the grocery store and then picked up Chinese from a restaurant around the corner. Mrs. Howard had ordered extra for Charlie.

The time spent at Mrs. Howard's house had given Treha a taste of what a family was like, something missing from those years in foster homes. Something she had blocked out or forgotten altogether. The doctor said there was a reason she couldn't remember certain things and a reason why her mind worked so well at others. Relationships, living and existing with other people, would always be a challenge. But life was more meaningful with a challenge.

There was talk from Mrs. Howard of Treha moving in with her. Treha could stay as long as she liked or permanently. Charlie was fine with it. He'd actually said it was a good idea, that he wanted Treha there with them. They had the extra room, Mrs. Howard and Treha could ride to work each morning, it would be easier to get to her rehab appointments, and it would bring life to their humdrum evenings. He also said if they played Scrabble, Treha would have to play blindfolded.

One day she might be able to get her own car. She couldn't imagine the freedom that might bring.

Treha's lease was up at the end of the month. Everything fit together, hand in glove.

But something felt off-kilter. Maybe it was the feeling of dependence that was growing between her and Mrs. Howard. She was taking the place of the mother Treha never had. So what was wrong with that? Or perhaps it was that Treha was losing her life, losing what she had scratched and clawed to bring together, which wasn't much, but at least it was hers.

Treha finally decided it was fear. What if Miriam, as she asked Treha to call her now, rejected her? What if she abandoned Treha like her mother had? What if Charlie got tired of watching her eyes? What if there was something sinister behind all of this and they were using Treha? She knew that wasn't true, but this was how her mind worked, how it went over the puzzles and questions. And this was where Treha knew she had to choose. She could choose fear and live alone with the consequences, or she could place her trust and faith in someone else and, with that, move toward others and away from isolation.

She put the carton in the empty trash bag and walked outside to stand by the railing, listening to the noise, the cars passing, families huddled in their apartments and homes, the music and laughter and shouting and arguing while television screens lit the faces of children. She drank it in.

Du'Relle and his mother had gone back to North Carolina for the funeral. Vivian Hansen from James 127 House had stopped by and delivered some supplies and a book to them, and Treha had told the woman the developments in her life.

But there was no one to hang around her apartment and pester her. No one to say bad words and have her correct him. Miriam said as soon as Du'Relle's mother came back, she was going to offer her a job at Desert Gardens. She might be able to move to a nicer place. Treha hoped it would happen.

She retreated to her room and opened the book she was reading. The stories seemed to get into her bloodstream and show her what the world was supposed to look like, supposed to feel like. They were her guide and guise. She lived in them as much as they lived in her.

She lay there with the overhead light on, that harsh bulb staring down as she tried to focus on the words, unable to concentrate because of the envelope on the shelf. She had put it at the end of the row, wedged between the edge of the shelf and a worn copy of *Little Women*. There was something about having the letter there, the physical presence of it, that gave her hope. At any point she could open it. But if she read the entire letter in one sitting, the mystery would be over. The voice of her mother would come through, and maybe she wouldn't like the things she said.

There, on the shelf, it was like her mother was asleep. Just an envelope with her name on it.

Treha closed the book, walked across the room, took the envelope from the shelf and held it, studying the formation of the letters of her name. Perhaps there was nothing inside. Perhaps her mother had written a nasty note saying she never wanted children in the first place and good riddance. Perhaps it wasn't from her mother at all but from some state agency telling her where to apply for assistance. Or it was a trick by Janice.

Treha examined the paper, just a plain, white envelope with the flap tucked inside. But in the center of the flap was a slight tear, as if the note had been sealed with her mother's own mouth—a lick on the underside. A quick kiss that had been broken by Janice opening and reading and then forgetting.

Her mother had touched this envelope. She had held it in her hands. Had no doubt thought about this moment when Treha would open it and read the words, decipher the lines and try to read between them.

She could tell from the way her name was written on the front that the handwriting would be elegant, unlike her own. But would she sign her name? Would she give an old address or phone number or some location where Treha could find her? Surely there would be a clue to her identity.

Treha opened the flap and pulled out two sheets of paper. The words flowed, letters rolling and gliding across the page like a dancer on a smooth floor. She took in the whole page with a glance, then the next, trying not to focus on any sentence or word, standing back from her mother to gain some perspective before she drew close.

She held the pages to her nose and smelled the smoke from Janice's house. There was also a musty, dusty smell. But somewhere in the fibers, somewhere in the deep recesses of that long-ago-written page, she caught a faint scent of perfume. Sweet and tangy and full of life.

Treha closed her eyes, took a deep breath as though it were a prayer, and opened them.

My dearest Treha,

I don't know when you will read this letter. I don't know when your mother will give it to you, but I'm praying you will be ready to read it. I imagine your head is full of questions about yourself, about the family you've grown up in, and about me.

You are my heart. You are everything good in the world. And my heart breaks in writing this because I will not know you. Your first steps, your first words. I won't get to hold you or take pictures or see you off to school and cry over you.

I have given you only two things, your life and your name. And now I give you one more gift, though I'm unable to peer into the crystal ball and know how old you are or anticipate all your questions. Words are such simple things, but they are the best. So I will give you these words.

First, an explanation of your name. An anagram is a word that you make using the letters of another. I wrote at the beginning that you are my heart. So I took those letters, I took my heart, and I fashioned "Treha" from them. I don't know any other person in the world who has this name. And one day, I believe I will look in a newspaper at a famous young woman who has just won the Nobel Prize for some great discovery, and I will see your name. But you don't have to accomplish anything great in order for me to be proud, because you are part of me, part of my heart. And I pray you feel my love through these markings of my soul.

Treha, remember this: your mother, the person who has raised you and provided for you and loved you—honor her. Honor them. My only request for you other than your name was that you be brought up in a home that would care for you with the love of God at the center.

Now I must ask you, if there is some bitterness in your heart about me, to forgive the choice I made. I didn't

*want to give you up. I wanted to hold you and keep you.
I wanted us to make a life of our own, but that wasn't
possible. Do not be angry at God for this. He is a loving
Father and I pray you will come to know him more and
more as you grow older. He is not the author of evil or
abandonment. He is good and loving and gentle and kind.*

*But the world is not, Treha. The world is cold and
cruel and crushes what is good. The world will rip your
heart from you. Perhaps you know this. I pray you will
not have to learn the hard way as I did.*

*I made a tragic, terrible mistake. I trusted someone
with my heart. This was a good thing, to trust and reach
out for love from another human being, but that other
person was not trustworthy. My heart was broken and a
series of events happened that I deeply regret. I went into
a fog so thick that I couldn't see. I thought I would never
come through.*

*But know this, my daughter. All the bad, all the
heartache and pain—I would go through it again and a
thousand times more because the end of it all was you. The
end of it all was something good and lovely and true. You
were not a mistake. You were the morning sunrise after
the dark night of my soul. You were the stone rolled from
the tomb.*

*I gave you life. Your name. And now I give you these
words: I love you. You are loved, Treha, though you may
not feel that from me and you may have many questions.
For your own good, I have stepped away from you, but I
will pray for you every waking moment, and every night
before I go to sleep, I will speak your name. If God allows
it, one day I hope you will run into my arms and I will*

hold you and speak these words. And ask you to forgive
me if I've caused you pain.

Until then, you are forever in my heart.

With all my love,
Your mother

Treha put the second page behind the first and read the letter again all the way through, running the word *heart* through the grid in her mind. With all the puzzles she had solved, all the word jumbles, she had never considered her own name as a jumble, but now it made sense. She read the letter from beginning to end five times and then neatly folded the pages and placed them back in the envelope and held it to her chest.

"I have a mother," Treha said aloud. She spoke it into the room so the light could hear, and her books and the bed and the walls. "I have a mother."

As she closed her eyes and drifted off, the woman came to her, sun-drenched and smiling, a billowing dress. And as Treha dreamed, she whispered, "Mother. Mother."

CHAPTER 43

DEVIN GOT to the chapel at Desert Gardens early and found Jonah getting the screen ready. They adjusted the color and brightness so that the faces on-screen were vibrant with the lights out. People began to arrive a half hour early, shuffling through, saying hello and greeting the two as if they were long-lost grandchildren.

Chaplain Calhoun arrived and went through the order of service. Devin asked if the video could be played at the end and the man was happy with that. Dr. Crenshaw's son and daughter-in-law arrived with two children and sat uncomfortably in the front.

Miriam Howard hugged Devin and Jonah warmly. "I'm so glad you could make it to his memorial."

Jonah gave Devin a look. "She doesn't know?"

"We have a little surprise prepared for you," Devin said.

Miriam raised an eyebrow. "And how is the documentary coming? I don't want to miss the world premiere."

"We're closer than we've ever been. We're trying to finish in time to get it to a film festival, so fingers crossed and all that. Trying to get it there by the day of the deadline."

"Sounds like a horror film, doesn't it?" Jonah said. "*Day of the Deadline*."

"It felt like a horror film going to that lady's house again," Devin said. "You know, Janice."

"You got her to sign the release form?"

Devin nodded. "It took a little coaxing and a couple of Ben Franklins, but I got her signature so we can use her voice. It's the most gripping moment, when Treha discovers she's not her real mother. Other than the voice-over of her mother's letter at the end."

"Did Devin tell you we got Meryl Streep to read it?" Jonah said.

"Really?" Miriam said.

"No, my mother read it. But she sounds kind of like Meryl Streep."

Elsie wheeled past, accompanied by Treha, and the two took seats near the front.

"She's looking good," Devin said, nodding at Treha.

"The rehab work she's doing is intense. She's exhausted at the end of the day. But I can already see a difference."

"How much better do you think she'll get?" Devin said. "Do the doctors say?"

"We're taking it a day at a time," Miriam said. "She's content, which is a gift. But she's willing to work hard to move forward. I have hopes that . . ."

"That what?"

"Maybe someday she can go to school. Put that intellect to work. But at the same time I'd hate to lose her."

Devin crossed his arms and studied Treha.

"What are you thinking?" Miriam said.

"I thought when we first started shooting that this place

would hold the story. And then I thought showing Treha's gift was the story. Now I think there was something bigger going on all along."

"Like what?" she said.

"Like she was the one being awakened. It was making Treha come out that was the point."

"And she still changed us. She really did."

Chaplain Calhoun stood at the front and welcomed them to the memorial service for Dr. Crenshaw. Devin surveyed the crowd as the chaplain spoke. He had come to know these people through their memories, their intertwining lives, but now he was seeing them differently. There was something deeper than just their stories, something more they had shared. But what?

The minister began with a reading of the Twenty-third Psalm and Devin felt the verses wash over him. The green pastures, the valley of the shadow of death, and dwelling in the house of the Lord forever. The man then read the words of Jesus, who, Chaplain Calhoun said, was the Good Shepherd.

"'I am the resurrection and the life. Anyone who believes in me will live, even after dying. Everyone who lives in me and believes in me will never ever die. Do you believe this?'"

Devin recalled the words from the Garrity funeral. In the face of death, terrible loss, there was life. This was irony. And beauty.

They sang two songs and the Opera Singer performed a solo. Miriam Howard stood with hands full of tissues and gave a tribute. The chaplain read more Scripture and gave a brief sermon about the care of the Shepherd, the comfort of the Shepherd, and the compassion of the Shepherd. Devin looked at the Lovebirds and wondered how long it would be until one of them was in this same room bidding farewell to the other. He shook that off but still wished he had the camera for one more shot of them. That was the trouble with a documentary: there was always more to the story. More to observe.

"We have something special for you to end with today," Chaplain Calhoun said after he had given the mostly silent congregants time to remember. "You know Devin and Jonah have become a fixture around here. And they have a presentation they'd like to make. Devin?"

The man invited him to the front with a wave and Devin stood. He hadn't prepared anything; he only had the video. But something drew him forward as Jonah smiled.

Devin rubbed his hands nervously. "Dr. Crenshaw was one of the first people we interviewed when we came here. And as we put the film together, we went back and unearthed some things I think you'll appreciate."

He smiled at Treha. "Our stories intertwine in ways we can't know when we first hear them. And maybe the point of all this is that we'd do well to listen. I hope you enjoy this tribute."

The lights went out and the screen was dark when the music began to swell, a plaintive piano tune. Then Dr. Crenshaw's name and dates of birth and death faded in and out as his voice-over began.

"My name is Jim Crenshaw. And if it's stories you want, I have a lot to tell. I've delivered babies in the dead of night. I once delivered a calf for a farmer who got me out of bed at three in the morning because he said if I could birth boys and girls, I could certainly birth his Guernsey."

Close-up of Dr. Crenshaw. The lines in his face. The age in his eyes. The camera told so much of the story, but the words were the avenue to the heart.

"The things I remember . . . ," Crenshaw continued, looking

past the camera, connecting them with the memories as he spoke. "I remember the trembling legs of mothers exhausted from labor. The first sign of the crown of the child's head. And the tears and anguish and the encouragement, telling them one more push. Just once more. Then the baby in my hands, slippery and wet. They talk about catching babies—it really is that way. I never fumbled one, but I came close."

A few people chuckled and white-haired heads nodded. Elsie wiped at the tears on her face.

"I've never forgotten putting the child on the mother's chest. No matter how long she had been struggling, no matter what that mother had been through, there were always tears of joy. This is the moment I remember most. A mother looking into a child's face for the first time. All that weight gain and swollen ankles and food cravings had been worth it for this moment, this connection between mother and child."

The music faded and Crenshaw's voice was all there was because it was all they needed. Just his voice and the movement of his hands when he spoke and the light on his face.

"I have accomplished a few good things in my life. And I've done some things in my past that I'm not proud of. I used to think I could never rid myself of those things. That whatever you have done is like a saddle put on you, or one you put on yourself, that is cinched tightly around you and then this becomes who you are. It marks you. Impossible to release. But now I know that's not true. A dear friend helped me understand it."

Devin looked at Elsie and saw her shaking in her seat, Treha with an arm around her.

"When you accept the love of God, the forgiveness he offers, it's like he takes that saddle off you and frees you up to run and gives you a new life. Then death transforms from something you hate to talk about or think about into the final stage of your final birth."

He waved a hand and gave a wry smile. "I don't know why I'm talking about this; you'll probably never use this rambling. But it's true. I no longer fear death. And when these people around here read my obituary, I want them to know it's just the beginning. The umbilical cord has been severed and I am looking into the face of the One who created me. So don't weep for me when that time comes. I'll be starting a journey I've waited for all my life."

The video faded to black and the music returned, covering the sounds of sniffling and soft sobs in the room. And suddenly there was another face, eyes moving, no emotion. Devin had shot the interview in Treha's apartment a few days after the death of Dr. Crenshaw.

"I miss my friend," she said, trying to look at the camera, her fingers typing. "Because Dr. Crenshaw was my friend. He gave me riddles and we played word games. And he made me feel like I was a real person. Not someone with a problem. Or someone to fix. Just someone to love."

Treha looked beyond the camera as if to ask if that was okay. If what she said was what they were looking for. And then she continued.

"I used to say I don't know what it's like to have a father or a mother. Because I never had them. But I can't say that anymore."

Fade to black.

Epilogue

S<small>HE SLIPPED</small> into the Avant Garde, a fine-arts theater that served wine and beer in plastic cups and whose seats were just as worn as those at the Second Run across the street, the cheap theater where you could see films that were coming out on DVD the next week. She stayed close to the wall and kept her head down as she walked up the stairs, glancing once at the sparse faces trained on the screen. Mostly middle-aged and wealthy. People hungry for art but only enough to assuage their guilt over watching too much television.

She held the sticky railing and ascended to the last row, where she sat, watching dust particles rise through the flickering light. A trailer was playing, a Focus Features film with children, it seemed. The same ages as most of her students. Girls in skin-tight jeans and boys in baggy pants. Hair hanging down in faces and mumbled lines with lips barely parted. This said something about the next generation, but she wasn't sure what.

She didn't go to the theater much. It wasn't that she didn't appreciate good cinema—she did. Immensely. But she preferred not hearing the crunch of popcorn and conversation about work or the latest video game controller or some elderly person with bad hearing asking what the character had just said. She preferred to watch alone in the comfort of her own home, with the sound as loud or as soft as she wanted. To lose herself in the setting and characters and story without the ravages of other people to pull her from the experience.

Something had drawn her to this documentary. Colleagues had raved about its humanity and beauty. And because it was crafted by a couple of amateurs, a David-versus-Goliath effort, two young men with a camera and a dream, these stories of individuals at the end of their lives became even more compelling.

But this was not what drew her to the theater. No, it was the girl she had heard about, had read about in the reviews. This strange, blurry-faced creature. A force of nature. With a name they had never heard before.

But she had.

She settled into the creaking chair and realized she was trembling, literally shaking with anticipation. Suddenly she was in the delivery room, and the sweat and pain came back to her. The shaking legs and sheer exhaustion like she had never felt before and the loneliness of it all. The gritted teeth and the promise that she would not scream, would not cry, would not give in to the pain. She would manage this, simply push through and push on, but her death grip on the bed railing had given way to surrender. Wails. Screams. Tears coming from some subterranean ocean she didn't know existed inside her.

Then like a sunrise it began, bringing her back. Images on the screen. Words and music and voices. Magic. Every wrinkle, every musical punctuation of the film, every choice of camera angle that pieced together the disparate lives of the actors on the stage engrossed her. And the pauses. The moments when the old people would stop and lose their train of thought, like a dog pulling away from its owner on a walk, the leash only a few feet ahead but moving farther and faster until you knew the dog would either run away forever or have to turn of its own accord.

Finally she heard the girl's name spoken and held her breath as she appeared, shot from behind. The dark hair. The small, pudgy build. A gentleness to her with the old people. Though she couldn't see the girl's face, she imagined it. Sweet and inviting and kind.

As the film progressed, the story became less about the elderly and more about the girl, the questions her life brought to the surface for everyone around her. She felt her chest rise and fall with each labored breath, wondering, hoping, inwardly cheering for the girl. Wanting to shout, wanting to reach out to the screen or jump inside and look her full in the face, with no blurring, no hiding of the truth. No hiding her abnormality. No hiding the broken places.

In one shot, the director filmed her eyes, shifting, moving, involuntarily taking in life. She saw herself in those eyes. And him. And she wanted to run, her heart nearly beating out of her chest.

The film took the audience back and forth between the elderly and those who had been injured by a pharmaceutical company, then returned to the girl, connecting their lives, their stories. And then, in a setting that should have held no cinematic suspense, shot from inside an automobile looking at a ramshackle house, they had captured audio of the conversation taking place inside.

When the girl whispered to herself, "She's not my mother,"

it was the end. She couldn't take it any longer, couldn't stay in that seat in that theater.

She rushed down the stairs and out the front, clutching her purse to her chest like a newborn.

"She's not my mother" echoed in her head and through her very being as she ran toward her car and fumbled with the fob to unlock it, holding back the dam. And she fell in, literally fell into the car.

"Treha," she whispered and managed to close the door before the racking sobs surfaced.

Acknowledgments

THIS BOOK was a labor of love because of how closely the story parallels some of our personal journey as a family and the big questions raised by Treha's life and condition. "If this is as good as it gets . . ." is a question we continue to ask, and this book is part of the processing of the answer. Thanks to Andrea for encouragement throughout and for sharing the journey, and to my children, who continue to amaze me.

Special thanks to my Tyndale family for allowing me to dive into Treha's story. To Sarah Mason, Stephanie Broene, Shaina Turner, and especially to Karen Watson for helping rescue Treha from a lesser fate. This story is much better because of your input and direction and I'm grateful.

About the Author

CHRIS FABRY is a 1982 graduate of the W. Page Pitt School of Journalism at Marshall University and a native of West Virginia. He is heard on Moody Radio's *Chris Fabry Live!*, *Love Worth Finding*, and *Building Relationships with Dr. Gary Chapman*. He and his wife, Andrea, are the parents of nine children. Chris has published more than seventy books for adults and children. His novel *Dogwood* won a Christy Award in 2009. In 2011 *Almost Heaven* won a Christy Award and the ECPA Christian Book Award for fiction.

You can visit his website at www.chrisfabry.com.

Discussion Questions

1. *Every Waking Moment* begins with a vivid scene between Treha and her mother—a scene we later learn Treha has "borrowed." Why do you think she takes other people's stories as her own? Have you ever been tempted to change your story or to live vicariously through the stories of others?

2. When characters first encounter Treha, they're often uncomfortable or even disturbed. What was your impression of Treha early in the story? Did your perspective change as you got to know her?

3. Devin frequently runs into tension between following his creative vision and trying to make a living. Do you identify more with Devin in his artistic idealism or with those like Charlie, Jeffrey Whitman at the bank, and even Jonah who encourage him to think more realistically? Can a balance be struck between creativity and practicality?

4. How did you react to Treha's gift for calling people back to awareness and mental clarity? Do you think such

awakenings are possible? Miriam tells Treha, "I think what you offer is safety. . . . You listen. You validate." What does this story suggest about the value of listening? Are there aspects of Treha's gift you could apply?

5. Miriam approaches her retirement with sadness and anxiety about this new chapter in her life. Have you ever had to face a change that wasn't your choice? How do you respond to new phases in your life? With dread? Fear? Excitement?

6. Why do you think Dr. Crenshaw searched for Treha? Do you agree with the way he approached helping her? What eventually changed his mind about telling her the truth? If Devin could have had one more interview, what do you think Dr. Crenshaw would have said?

7. Early in the story, Miriam expresses her regret that she and Charlie never had children. How do you think this influences her desire to help Treha? Does Miriam find what she's looking for in their relationship?

8. Do you think Treha was right to stand her ground against the three men in the Laundromat? Why wasn't she afraid of them? If you were a bystander in that scene, what would you have done?

9. Elsie says that "[God] lets us go through deeper waters so that we cling to him; that's the whole point of having faith. If we could handle everything, there would be no reason for us to need God." Do you agree or disagree? Has there been a time in your own life when it felt as though God was giving you more than you could handle? If so, what was the result?

10. What was your reaction to Miriam's attitude about Charlie and their marriage? At one point, she confesses that "it is hard to see the good in a person when all you can see is what isn't there." Have you experienced this yourself?

11. In the search for Treha's story, we meet people like Vivian Hansen and Kara Praytor, who each played a brief role in Treha's past but continued to care and pray for her even once she was gone from their lives. Looking back, can you think of similar people God placed along your path? Or are there people from your past you still wonder about and pray for, even if they're long out of your life?

12. Devin believes that "a good film draws you in because it feels like life." Do you agree? Would Devin's documentary appeal to you? Why or why not?

13. When Du'Relle tells Miriam about his father's death, she wonders, "Was it enough to listen? Was there a response required?" What do you think is the answer to those questions? If you've been in a situation similar to Du'Relle and his mother, what acts of kindness did you find to be particularly helpful?

14. What did you think of Treha's decision to confront Ezra Hollingsworth, the Phutura vice president? Was justice served in the Phutura case? If not, what do you think would've been a better outcome?

15. We don't know much about Jillian Millstone before she came to Desert Gardens. What life events do you think might have precipitated her arrival and caused

her to manage things the way she did? Were any of her criticisms of Miriam's management valid? What do you imagine Millstone went on to do after leaving?

16. This story shows several perspectives on how the elderly are treated in today's society. How do you feel about facilities like Desert Gardens? Do you think Devin's vision to preserve the stories of previous generations is an important one? How else could society better value the elderly?

17. By the end of the story we learn the truth about Treha's biological mother. If for some reason you had to give a child up, what requests would you make of his or her adoptive parents? Would you want to sever contact forever or be open to the possibility of meeting your child sometime in the future? Why?

18. Both Treha and Miriam contemplate whether they're content with their lives as they are or if they want something more. What does each woman ultimately decide? How do you see other characters in *Every Waking Moment* asking similar questions? Look back at Chaplain Calhoun's description of contentment on pages 80–81. Can you look at your own life and say, "If this is as good as it gets, I'm okay with that"? Do you see this as giving up on life or embracing it?

also by
CHRIS FABRY

DOGWOOD

Small towns have long memories, and the people of Dogwood will never forgive Will Hatfield for what happened. So why is he coming back?

JUNE BUG

June Bug believed everything her daddy told her until she saw her picture on a missing children poster.

Christy Award finalist

ALMOST HEAVEN

Some say Billy Allman has a heart of gold; others say he's odd. Sometimes the most surprising people change the world.

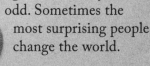

NOT IN THE HEART

When time is running out, how far will a father go to save the life of his son?

Christy Award finalist

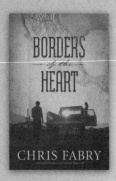

BORDERS OF THE HEART

When J. D. Jessup rescues a wounded woman, he unleashes a chain of events he never imagined.

Christy Award finalist

TYNDALE
FICTION

www.tyndalefiction.com

Reading group guides available in each book or at
www.bookclubhub.net.